"A tale of two sisters separated by the pursuit ui ....
an engaging and engrossing tribute to the power of revisiting the
past and asking for forgiveness. Enchanting, full of period details
and pluck, you'll find yourself on a seductive journey through Old
Hollywood, ambition, and a young woman's desire to start over. I
missed these characters long after the book ended."

BROOKE LEA FOSTER
bestselling author of *All the Summers in Between*

"A master storyteller, Jessica Ilse has woven a spellbinding tale full of
charm, wit, and nostalgia that takes the reader from Halifax in the
1930s to Hollywood at the tail end of the Golden Age. It's impossible
not to fall in love with the inimitable and delightful Majestic Sisters—
both the novel, and the dynamic duo themselves, who spring to
glorious life from every page.
This is a sparkling debut."

AMY JONES
bestselling author of *Pebble & Dove*

"*The Majestic Sisters* explores fame, fortune, and the sticky bonds
of sisterhood with authenticity and cinematic flair. A dazzling story
about ambition and duty, love and loss, and how the dreams that
take us away are often the same dreams that bring us home. A debut
worthy of its own marquee."

ALI BRYAN
award-winning author of *The Figgs* and *Coq*

"In glorious technicolour, an adoring homage to the sumptuous
movie palaces of a bygone era, classic films of the silver screen, and
Halifax on the brink of war. A novel masterfully alive with history—
the allure of fame, the bonds of family, and the balm of forgiveness—
a dazzling debut!"

STEPHENS GERARD MALONE
author of *Jumbo*

"A tender, passionate, heartbreaking tale of what it takes to follow
a dream. *The Majestic Sisters* pulls back the curtain on a pre-war
Halifax that sparkles with glitz and glamour."

LOUISE MICHALOS
author of *Marilla Before Anne*

Vagrant Press is an imprint of
Nimbus Publishing Limited
3660 Strawberry Hill St, Halifax, NS, B3K 5A9
(902) 455-4286 nimbus.ca

Nimbus Publishing is based in Kjipuktuk, Mi'kma'ki, the traditional territory of the Mi'kmaq People.

Printed and bound in Canada

This story is a work of fiction. Names, characters, incidents, and places, including organizations and institutions, either are the product of the author's imagination or are used fictitiously.

Editor: Whitney Moran
Cover design: Jenn Embree
Typesetting: Rudi Tusek
Cover image: *The Dolly Sisters, Rosie and Jenny Dolly*, ca. 1927, Ziegfeld Follies NB1706

Title: The Majestic Sisters / Jessica Ilse.
Names: Ilse, Jessica, author.
Identifiers: Canadiana (print) 20240395344 | Canadiana (ebook) 20240396626 | ISBN 9781774713433
   (softcover) | ISBN 9781774713440 (EPUB)
Subjects: LCGFT: Historical fiction. | LCGFT: Novels.
Classification: LCC PS8617.L74 M35 2024 | DDC C813/.6—dc23

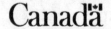  

Nimbus Publishing acknowledges the financial support for its publishing activities from the Government of Canada, the Canada Council for the Arts, and from the Province of Nova Scotia. We are pleased to work in partnership with the Province of Nova Scotia to develop and promote our creative industries for the benefit of all Nova Scotians.

The Majestic Sisters

Jessica Ilse

Vagrant PRESS

For Gramp Leon, who, if he were here,
would have probably said, "You wrote a book, eh?
On what, paper?" and then laughed
that delightful laugh.

How I wish you could hold this book.
How I wish I could hold your hand.

JI

Prologue

Saturday, January 1, 2000

W e were stars standing in tall shadows every night at the Majestic Theatre. We were The Majestic Sisters. The toasts of the town. Bonafide stars. Halifax's own dancing dames.

Back in the day—the '30s, understand—when everyone would put on their glad rags for the newest picture from Clark Gable or Shirley Temple, or who have you, and line up around the block to get into the most opulent movie palace in all of Halifax, my sister and I would wait in the wings for our cue.

If you were around then, you'd remember our faces and our gams. Majestic Melly—that's me—and Majestic Missy—that's my sister. Dancers, singers, actresses, comediennes...we did it all, performing prologue cabarets ahead of every movie showing for three years. Until one day in 1939 changed everything.

I've been approached countless times by countless publishers over the years to pen my memoirs, and each and every time, I've turned them down. But I am nothing if not a stickler for the truth. It's finally time to tell my own story, in my own words.

I have it on good authority that if you read the forthcoming *unauthorized* biography, *Mediocre Melly*, you will come away with an incomplete portrait of my life. Not only is it filled with inaccuracies and

1

egregious libel, it also implies that I ruined both the Majestic Theatre and my relationship with my sister. I have withstood countless lies bruited about me over the years, but to suggest I have been nothing but a ruinous presence is something I will not abide.

So I've decided it's finally time you hear from Majestic Melly herself. I am the hero of this story, but I'm also, in parts, the villain. You will read about hijinks that sound too preposterous to be true, but I assure you, it all happened. You will read about the pettiest sisterly bunfights. There are great loves and bitter feuds, loving remembrances to the late Old Man Prestel, and one too many pot-shots at Langdon Hawkes—but if you've heard one, you've heard them all.

For decades it was MGM's job to sell a version of me that the public would lap up, but the studio system's long gone and now it's finally my turn to introduce myself:

I'm Melanie "Melly" Calvert.

Oscar-winning actress (times two).

Singer.

Dancer.

Hostess of the largest Canada Day barbecue in Palm Springs.

Frequent co-star to Langdon Hawkes, failed crooner, failed husband.

The Pink Lady.

Sister to Missy Davis, The Blue Lady.

I can't promise sunshine and roses, or a happily ever after. All I can promise is the truth. Besides, what have I to lose except a guest stint on *Touched by an Angel*?

Melly Calvert

Act One

"Audiences always sound like they're glad to see me,
and I'm damned glad to see them."

Claudette Colbert

SHALL WE DANCE
Starring Ginger Rogers and Fred Astaire

FRIDAY, MAY 21, 1937

"**D** orothy Dix says that finding a husband is like finding a gold mine."

That's a Missy Davis original—sorry, we're a little early for married names, aren't we? She's still a Calvert at this point. Missy was forever consulting Dorothy Dix and Beatrice Fairfax—you know, those agony aunt figures—for pithy maxims to collect, and the husband-turned-gold-mine line was her latest ace. She held fast to the idea that life would be magnificent once she found herself a husband, and took to whispering this advice into my ear every chance she got, rather turning me off to the idea of any beau at all.

"I'd rather have the gold mine," I replied. And that was a Melly Calvert original. I barely had time to sleep in those days let alone hand out my dance card.

"You're off the cob sometimes, you know that?"

"Only sometimes?"

"Always," she said, pushing herself away from the mirror, satisfied that her eyes had been perfectly outlined in kohl. It was her trademark. Whenever she appeared in editorial cartoons, those arctic blue eyes would be circled darker than the X that marked the spot on a treasure map. My caricature always had large, smirking lips tinted with dark lipstick.

We were inseparable, though polar opposites. I was a feisty, raven-haired spitfire, and Missy, with her sleek blonde tresses, was about as prim and proper as you could get this side of the House of Windsor. But when you put us together on a stage—whether it was the storied stage of the Majestic Theatre, the hardwood floors at Miss Margaret's School of Dance, or the parquet flooring in Mother and Daddy's great room—we became a duo that audiences adored.

We were the Calvert Sisters before we were ever The Majestic Sisters. The only children of stuffy academics who read ancient tomes and espoused modern values—Mother often claimed she was a suffragette, though I've found no record of this in her papers—and who indulged our artistic whims, even if they always dreamt we'd outgrow them and settle down. They'd made it out of the Great Depression relatively unscathed, and because there was always food on the table and money for our hobbies, I never asked how.

Luckily, there was talent that motivated our hobbies. Legend has it that at the tender age of three, I waddled over to the Victrola, put on "Pretty Kitty Kelly" and changed the lyrics to "Pretty Missy Melly." Then I grabbed my baby sister, pulled her to her feet, and danced an approximation of the bunny hug. Mother was charmed by the movements and the witty lyricism, and immediately enrolled me in Miss Margaret's School of Dance. And where trouble goes, angels follow, so Missy was enrolled a year later.

Bunny hugs gave way to ballet, which later gave way to more modern movements like tap, jazz, and even the Charleston (which we taught ourselves while Miss Margaret was otherwise occupied), and soon we were among her most prized pupils. Sure, it was an honour to be trained at any one of the many dance studios in Halifax, but there was a certain prestige attached to undertaking Miss Margaret's tutelage.

Maybe I was a ham in the beginning but there was genuine talent underneath, Miss Margaret told my parents so. That feeling of knowing you can make people laugh and smile with a song, a dance, or a joke... it's a thrill I've chased my whole life. I wanted to be the best dancer in Halifax, the best singer (though my musical films would, admittedly, be few and far between), the best actress. I spent my early years rising to the top through hard work and determination. Missy was always in my shadow and always seemed to excel, though where there was effortlessness with my movements, if you looked close enough, you could see the labour involved with hers. She was great, but she could've been extraordinary if she'd only tried.

"There's no career in this, Melly," she'd remind me every so often on the short walk home from the dance studio.

"There is if you want it badly enough," I'd tell her.

But she was right. It was all supposed to be a whim; some childhood fun, something to look back on and laugh about when we had families of our own. But whether my sister wanted to admit it or not, we *thrived* under that limelight. When you had the Calverts, and the Williamses on Mother's side, lapping up our every move at family events; when Miss Margaret said we were two of the most impressive dancers she'd ever seen and that if we applied ourselves there could be a future in all of this...well, how could you even think of giving it up? It seemed more and more that showbiz, as close as you could get to it in shantytown Halifax, was our calling.

WHEN MISS MARGARET needed two new birdies for her prologue dances in early 1935, Missy and I were at the top of her list. After all, we'd been training with her since childhood; I was in my final year of high school and Missy just a year behind. This is what we'd been working towards: the first steps towards stardom.

Because in addition to running her own dance studio on Jubilee Road since time immemorial, Miss Margaret had a lucrative side business choreographing prologue routines ahead of all the weekend flicks at the Majestic Theatre downtown. She had been a stalwart of the Majestic since Mary Pickford left Biograph Pictures (a long, *long* time ago) and, in an era of change, successfully navigated the transition to talkies by staying the same: having her best dancers perform fifteen-minute pre-show routines based on fairy tales and classic literature. My first official stage credit, if you must know, was as a scarlet pimpernel in a prologue ahead of the 1935 film adaptation. You'd think there would be nerves, it being my first time in front of a paying audience, but it felt as natural as breathing. I was uniform in a cluster of dancers, but I knew it was only a matter of time before I'd seek a spotlight of my own. That applause was too addictive to pass up.

Miss Margaret's Silent Birds were completely devoid of individuality. There were firm rules on looks, demeanor, and personality, and even stricter rules for choreography. Sometimes even now, if my feet aren't in the correct position, I feel her dour figure slinking behind me, sinking her talons into my spine to straighten me up. I can hear her counting our steps under her breath. Urging us to smile those demonic stage smiles and open our eyes as wide as we could.

Ultimately though, it was worth it to play by her rules—for a while—because it meant we got to perform every evening at the Majestic Theatre. To you, it might just be a movie palace. But to me, it was the cradle of my career; where happily ever afters occurred not just on the screen but backstage as well. None of what came afterwards could have happened without it.

⌒◦ℓℓ◦⌒

HOW TO DESCRIBE the Majestic Theatre? Well, it wasn't simply the finest theatre in Halifax; it was the finest theatre on the east coast. Picture it: in the middle of all the hubbub of downtown Halifax—and granted, there wasn't a lot of hubbub in those days, back when all the buildings were drab shades of brown or grey, and sometimes an east wind would blow the stench of the Imperial Oil refinery into your face—a magnificently opulent Egyptian Revival theatre.

A place where Fred and Ginger cut a handsome rug three times a night at the height of the Depression. A place where Myrna Loy and William Powell traded witty one-liners over martinis shaken to waltz time. It was a magical place, and Old Man Prestel's savvy kept people lining up down the street no matter what the time of day, whether it was for a prestige picture or one of those blasted Torchy Blane follies. The

Majestic always got first-run movies from the Big Five studios: MGM—my later home—Paramount, 20th Century Fox, Warner Bros., and RKO. If you wanted to see it first, you saw it at the Majestic, full stop.

If you wanted to see other fare—and who am I to judge you but a two-time Oscar winner—you'd have to trek outside the downtown core to get your fix. Movies from the Little Three studios—United Artists, Columbia Pictures, and Universal Studios—were the toast of the Oxford on Quinpool Road. The Garrick and the Empire were movie houses I'd never want to be caught inside, not least because they played the lowest of the low Poverty Row pictures—those one-reel serials, or the campy Westerns starring actors you'd never heard of and would never hear of again, unless they were as lucky as Lang, and hitched their wagons to brighter stars.

I can count on one hand the number of times I ever saw a picture anywhere else. Why bother when the Majestic was a citadel with the biggest stars on the biggest screen in town? The Majestic Theatre was my first love. I used to blow my allowance there every week—it's how I managed to see my favourite film, *It Happened One Night*, twice every night the summer before I turned seventeen. My father wanted to punish me for staying out after curfew, but when he found out where I'd been, he simply laughed it off.

The Majestic had opened in 1900, and when Eugene Prestel inherited the theatre, he bought into the Egyptian Revival trend of the '20s and revamped it accordingly. Everything, and I mean everything, was replaced. The building's exterior became a sandstone dream, like a pyramid shooting up out of the middle of the street. Inside, the walls were covered with stucco terracotta tiles painted beautiful shades of aquamarine and sand to mimic the building's exterior. The lobby floor was covered in mosaic tiles that showcased various forms of Egyptian art: pottery, painting, hieroglyphics. You could spend an hour there alone, studying all the pieces.

As movie-goers made their way from the lobby to the theatre proper, they passed giant sarcophagi and pharaohs and Anubis himself, after which they came to a set of stairs and had their choice between the lower promenade and the mezzanine.

Just off the mezzanine was a short hallway that led to the smoking room, open to both sexes, and home to one of my favourite features: a fireplace with a sign on its mantel that read *Take Turns, No Burns!* The seats were cushioned and comfortable—a good place to pass the time if the feature didn't do it for you. Beyond that was the ladies' powder room and washroom, painted an elegant gold, which Missy and I sometimes ducked into between gigs to freshen up.

Inside the theatre itself, the walls were decorated with palm trees, palm leaves, and golden lotus blossoms, the seats plush and covered with royal blue fabric and the carpets thick, thick, thick in a darker shade of blue. There was seating at three levels: floor, mezzanine, and balcony. For my money, I loved parking myself in one of the loge seats. It's how I watched all the best Cary Grant films. In our heyday, we'd had special signs—mine painted pink, Missy's blue—that read *Reserved for Majestic Melly* and *Reserved for Majestic Missy*; I made good use of mine. You could fall asleep in those seats, as was the case with many a midnight show.

The job of rousing those sleepy patrons fell to the tireless ushers. They all wore blue pillbox hats and jackets with black pants, trusty heavy-duty flashlights always at the ready. And given that the Majestic could hold a cool twenty-five hundred people or so, it wasn't an easy job. But they always had the best stories: who'd yelped in fright, who'd cried into their handkerchiefs, which jokes landed, which fell flat. If there was a fella with a bouquet, they'd park him at the concessions and tell you how to find him afterwards; and if a newspaperman was there scooping for a story about one of us, they could sniff him out and inevitably drag him backstage for an interview.

I knew the Majestic like the back of my hand, and I knew that whatever the future held for me, it would begin in that building. In my wildest dreams, I let myself believe I could be on that screen starring in side-splitting comedies and tearful melodramas; reciting lines that fans would repeat over and over; one day winning an Oscar. I just needed to take the first step towards stardom.

But before I spoil the ending, let me tell you how we became The Majestic Sisters.

BIRDS WILL ALWAYS FLY the nest sooner or later, and by the spring of 1937, Missy and I had been Silent Birds for two years, and we were tired of the routines. So was the audience, who, more often than not, would remain in the smoking rooms or the powder rooms until the picture began because we were rotating the same three ballets over and over and over. Not to mention the worn and patched-over costumes. Miss Margaret was out of gas and someone had to tell Old Man Prestel. I decided the task would fall to me, and I've never been afraid of a challenge. Mother and Daddy had started asking why we were sticking with the troupe if we complained so much, and I knew this was my chance to take what I wanted. I never had the chance to apologize to Miss Margaret for what happened next. But I didn't try all that hard either.

"Where are you going?" Missy hissed, following me offstage. We'd been rehearsing for that evening's premiere of *Shall We Dance* with a routine based on *The Tempest* that I couldn't bring myself to perform for one more second.

"Where do you think I'm going?" I said, not waiting for her to catch up.

"We only get a ten-minute break."

"Missy, these routines have gone sour. If I have to dance this one more time, I'm going to lose my mind!" We came to a stop outside the powder room. The smattering of light from the sign above the door caught the sequins on Missy's leotard. She looked like a star, and she could be one if she dared to be brave.

"Melly, it's not a bad gig," she said. "It keeps us occupied."

"I bet you could pull a random gal from the audience, put her in the troupe, and she could dance better than half the other Silent Birds. We're better than this! You see that, right?"

"Of course," she mused. "But it's not like we'll be doing this *forever*."

I took a breath. "Okay, so what would you rather be doing instead? You want Daddy to fix you up with one of his students?"

"I'm sure it'll come to that if I don't meet someone first," she said. "Melly, we make spending money. This is a hobby."

"It doesn't have to be a hobby. It could be our *career*."

"What are you saying?"

"Imagine you and me onstage—" I started.

"We *are* onstage."

"—let me finish. You and me, *just* the two of us, up on that stage. We've got the talent. We've got the looks. We could be stars. The Majestic Sisters. Whaddaya say?"

"Majestic Sisters, eh?" She took a moment to truly think about it. "Majestic Missy and Majestic Melly."

My face lit up as I imagined our names in lights. "Yes! And it doesn't have to be just a stage gig," I said. "We could turn ourselves into Halifax's biggest It Girls. We could make headlines. I can work on the routines, I can hone my acting skills, and you could be the social butterfly flitting about at events in your spare time."

Missy put her hands on her hips. "Well, I'd want to help choreograph routines, too."

I blinked. We'd have to collaborate. "Of course. And who knows, you might even meet someone outside the Dalhousie English department."

She got a faraway look in her eye just then, almost as though she could see her future husband. She had no idea what awaited her.

"Maybe he teaches at Saint Mary's," I teased.

She laughed. "Daddy would disown me!"

"Let's do this," I said. I held out my hand for her to shake. "Together."

She took it easily. "Together."

"Let's fly the nest."

She snickered. "Lead the way, then."

Before we knew it, we were standing in front of Old Man Prestel's office; it was hidden just off the lobby because he loved to watch the crowds stroll in. (He still raved about the audiences for *Cleopatra* in 1934.) Now, here's the thing: when I screwed up the courage to open the door, knocking as I stepped inside, I laid eyes upon him and knew for a fact he had no clue who I was. That didn't stop me.

"Mr. Prestel, I think we need to do something about the prologues."

He'd been studying a pile of papers on his desk when I stormed in, but paused to examine me—and Missy behind me in the hallway. "How do you figure?"

It wasn't an outright dismissal, so I continued: "I don't mean to denigrate Miss Margaret's talents, but these dances? They've all been done before. We just did this one for the Jean Harlow flick, and the Joan Crawford flick, and the Joan Blondell flick—"

"And what do you suggest we do about this, Miss..."

"Calvert. Melly Calvert. I'm one of the Silent Birds, along with my sister."

"Silent Bird, eh? You squawk like a chickadee." He eyed the sequined leotard I was wearing. "And you dress like a peacock."

He looked out into the hallway, Missy still timidly hiding just out of sight. "Your sister seems to have the right idea." It was the last time he'd ever praise her over me. "Why don't you tell your peepless partner to step inside my office so we can discuss this further?"

Missy joined me in the room, the two of us standing shoulder to shoulder. I sucked in a breath, sent up a quick prayer, crossed all my fingers—and pitched The Majestic Sisters.

"Take a chance on me and Missy. We're the two best dancers in the entire company, and we have new ideas for scenes, choreography, costuming. It'll be a whole new show. It'll transform the prologues. We'll fill those seats for you every night!"

He didn't seem convinced, so I continued. "You remember the size of those crowds for King George's coronation newsreel a few weeks ago? When was the last time you saw an audience of that size for the prologues? They all straggle in and miss the overture. We're young and modern. We'll revitalize the show. All we need is for you to give us a shot, Mr. Prestel, and I promise we'll deliver you an audience fit for the king and queen every single show."

Old Man Prestel sized me up for a minute, then shifted his gaze over to my docile sibling who was standing as still as a statue, respecting her elders and maintaining that propriety she'd later become so famous for. (If I'd left it up to her, we'd still be Silent Birds.) I was so convinced we could handle the job, it didn't occur to me that he might say no. There's something to be said for flying headfirst towards a goal.

He decided then and there that he believed me, saw in me what I saw in myself. Because as soon as his eyes snapped back to me, he slammed his hand down on the desk, scattering receipts and paperwork all about, and called for one of the concessions stand operators to find Miss Margaret and bring her to his office without delay.

To the old bird's credit, when he threatened her with replacement she puffed up her chest and prepared to defend the nest. She might have thought loyalty would win out, counting on those long years of friendship she thought they shared, but when Old Man Prestel presented us as a full-blown act, a way to get rid of an inheritance he wanted to divest himself from, Miss Margaret glared at us, livid at the perfidy of the situation, said, "By all means," and vowed to return to her dance studio full-time. No other theatre wanted to hire her once the news spread, and so, for Miss Margaret, both the zenith and the nadir of her lengthy career took place at the Majestic. For the first time since 1913, there were no Silent Birds flitting about backstage.

While Missy and I were hard at work on new choreography, Old Man Prestel updated the marquee outside. The crowd began buzzing as, right under *FRED ASTAIRE* and *GINGER ROGERS*, a new line appeared: *MAJESTIC MELLY AND MAJESTIC MISSY: THE MAJESTIC SISTERS! ALL-NEW TONIGHT!*

We would only get fifteen minutes to sell ourselves to the crowd, and to Old Man Prestel, who would be watching from the loge seats—and who promised us a contract if all went well. Our confidence—and our nerves—was cushioned by our parents, who rushed headlong to the theatre with a trunk of dresses and dance shoes and promptly fell into the loge seats as we tossed together an introductory routine that would show off our gams and our smiles. Their shouts of approval—"Your smile is crystal clear from here, Missy dear!" and "Precise as always, Melly darling!"—rang throughout the auditorium in those final hours before the early evening showing began.

That introductory routine was a showcase, perfectly themed to *Shall We Dance*: we wanted to make a splash with the crowd and show them that those poised perfect swans were gone, and in their places, The Majestic Sisters. Our hair was teased and our makeup was bright—we were peacocks, not Silent Birds—and we'd just slipped into our costumes when we heard it: the cacophony of the audience. It was electrifying. It emboldened us.

"You ready?" Missy asked as the buzz grew louder.

I watched for the light bulb positioned just offstage to start flickering: our cue.

"I was born ready."

THE AUDIENCE *LOVED* US. The great thing about the theatre is that it attracts all sorts of audiences. For example, you might have a few sweethearts out on their first dates, girlfriends who always see these Fred and Ginger flicks in a gaggle, or, in our case, Bill Borrett from CHNS, who spotted a change on the marquee and found his latest scoop with the debut of The Majestic Sisters. A comment from Old Man Prestel after the show led to a radio hit the next morning, which led to a larger audience on Saturday evening—with more reporters in tow— which led to a full-scale publicity campaign the following week, and by the time we got over the Victoria Day long weekend, it was clear: the newspapers couldn't get enough of us. The movie-going experience was all the richer because of us, the *Star* wrote. The radio announcers loved our comedic timing and how we bounced jokes off each other. And that was just the first few nights!

After a weekend of sold-out shows from eleven o'clock in the morning until eleven o'clock at night, we were ushered into Old Man Prestel's office to sign an introductory six-month contract—fifteen dollars a week!—with an option to extend it to a year, if both parties were satisfied.

Mother and Daddy took us out for a late dinner at the Sea Grill to celebrate. Mother had pressed us, tried to talk us into at least taking a shorthand class in case our option wasn't renewed in December, but we wouldn't listen. If The Majestic Sisters didn't pan out, we would just move on to the next adventure, and it didn't include the pursuit of higher education. We had to forge our own paths.

OLD MAN PRESTEL launched a full-scale advertising campaign to market
The Majestic Sisters. He spent a magnificent sum to get us, and keep us,
on the front pages. Mother had the first article professionally framed
and hanging on the living room wall.

After a photo shoot, our images were papered onto the theatre
building: *Come for the frolicking, stay for the film!* Take that, Joan
Crawford! We were also papered onto the windows on either side of the
lobby doors in full colour, Missy leaning up against the ticket booth and
me gesturing for the patrons to *Open the doors and see what's buzzing!*

We took over the dressing room, left in such haphazard state
by Miss Margaret's hasty exit that it took an entire afternoon just to
straighten it out. Once it was styled to our taste, a photographer from
the *Halifax Mail* came to snap pictures for a spread. Everyone saw
the racks filled with dancing gear and stage costumes; trunks full of
makeup; movie magazines strewn across the table to provide us with
gossip fodder, makeup tips, and inspiration; and the genuine Tiffany
lamp from home we'd begged Mother for, purely for the ambience.
Soon, dress shops, beauticians, shoemakers, even grocers and hard-
ware stores were calling us up to offer free items in exchange for our
promotional prowess.

We modelled for Simpson's and attended store openings. We
helped launch community chest drives, sent kids to Rainbow Haven,
and taught underprivileged children to sing and dance. Missy thrived
at these kinds of events. It didn't shock me that once I was gone she
found her own spotlight. She wouldn't have lasted a year in Hollywood,
but she reigned over our hometown like a queen.

But back to me. You could hear me every weekday morning on
CHNS reading horoscopes or singing jingles for Farmers Dairy and the
Capitol Stores. I even had a newspaper column reviewing movies—it
only lasted a few months, until war was declared, and then it was onto
more serious fare.

The point is, we were *everywhere*.

We received invitations to every type of event imaginable and were in the newspapers almost constantly, front and centre in the "I Heard It Last Night" gossip column written by my dear friend, noted taleteller Raymond Swaine. Even after I'd long left town, they printed stories about us—*Is Majestic Missy Joining the War Effort?*—hoping that she'd return to the stage again (she did not return) or *Bring the Oscar Home, Majestic Melly!* after I won in 1944. The theatre had a party in my honour hoping to entice me to come home (I did not return).

Halifax had other stars over the years: there was Bunny Hobbs, the nightclub crooner who travelled across Canada supporting the war effort, and The Three Debs, another wartime musical act. But nobody would ever hold a candle to The Majestic Sisters.

For three years we ruled the city, and we didn't need a press agent to sell that to the public, we did it all ourselves. By the time we ended the act, we were the most fêted people in the city.

It's just a shame how it all turned out.

TAKE HER, SHE'S MINE
Starring Sandra Dee and James Stewart

THURSDAY, DECEMBER 19, 1963

The MGM mailroom workers knew to stack any letters from Halifax on top of the rest of my fan mail. That afternoon, just after lunch, when the mail boy brought the dispatches to the set of *The Kenmore Arms*—a flimsy melodrama whose sole redeeming quality was that it reunited Melly Calvert and Langdon Hawkes after an eighteen-year froideur, and whose plot closely resembled our previous picture together—I saw an envelope from Raymond Swaine, care of 34 Coburg Road, where he'd always lived and always *would* live, on top of the stack.

By then, Raymond was a recovering alcoholic who parlayed our friendship into a lucrative radio career with CHNS and a show syndicated across North America. I fed him Hollywood gossip—all above board, I didn't want to jeopardize my invitations on the dinner party circuit after all—and he fed me Halifax gossip in return. I'll let you decide who fared better in that trade-off. He'd been one of the first people to forgive me after I ran off, but only once I gifted him an all-expenses-paid trip to Los Angeles and a tour of the MGM commissary so that he could meet his screen idols. (He asked out Esther Williams and she turned him down flat.)

He always called with good news. He always wrote with bad news. I braced myself and slid my fingernail under the flap of the envelope

18

and sliced it neatly open, pulling out the letter and reading it quickly. Then, I did something I hadn't done since 1953 on the set of *Sirens Over Paris* (the circumstances of which I'll take to my grave): I walked off set. The director, some novice who'd cut his teeth on live television productions and who now had to prove his worth with a "women's picture" before he could direct the likes of Burt Lancaster or Rock Hudson in "films that matter" (his words), screamed at me with increasing loudness with every step I took. The disrespect women in Hollywood had to put up with. I could act circles around any of my male counterparts, but I couldn't get out of these "women's pictures" that had once propped up the box office but were now being pushed aside in favour of male-dominated films. I'd make sure this director never worked again.

MGM had approved of a publicity bullpen on set, this being the first Calvert/Hawkes film since our quickie marriage and even quicker divorce in 1945. We'd agreed to keep it civil in front of the muckrakers, and I'd just given them a primo scoop. I didn't betray any emotion. It wasn't a temper tantrum, like that poison-penned gossip columnist Louella Parsons claimed it to be. I'd been sitting next to Lang when I read the letter; the entire soundstage watched me walk off, ignoring him as he called after me. Contrary to what Cal York reported in his next gossip column, I wasn't "unleashing years of pent-up rage" by screaming my head off at Lang. Nobody knew why we'd agreed to a stalemate after all these years, and neither one of us was offering an explanation—and no, you're not getting one either. Not yet, anyway.

Lang had been on his best behaviour throughout the shoot. I guess when Frank Sinatra threatens to have you thrown off the top floor of the Sands if Melly calls with any complaints, you take it seriously. He always wanted to be friends with the Rat Pack, but then, Frank and Dino never could stand him. Still, he followed me to my dressing room after I stormed off, and I had to pretend I didn't hear him banging away at the door, booming in that crooner voice of his that he was going to break it down, *goddammit*, if I didn't open it right this minute.

Honestly, and the gossip rags accuse *me* of theatrics.

I read Raymond's letter one more time and felt my heart shattering as the words dissolved through my tears.

The gist: after trying and failing to find a successor, Old Man Prestel was closing down the Majestic Theatre on New Year's Eve and selling the building to whomever would take it off his hands. Even worse, rumour had it the Maritime Telegraph & Telephone Company wanted to raze it and erect a new central operations building.

For so many years, I'd successfully staved off feeling any particular way about my youth in Halifax. I wasn't Majestic Melly, and I hadn't been in a long time, but suddenly it was like I was backstage at the Majestic once more, Missy shoulder to shoulder with me in Bruyère knockoffs, waiting on the spiral staircase behind the screen for the crowd to settle for our prologue ahead of *I Met Him in Paris*.

Suddenly I felt like a fraud. Melly Calvert, vaunted star of stage and screen, was a façade after all. I could hide behind the laurels and the legions of friends and fans, but now I couldn't hide from the truth: there was a price I'd paid for fame. Missy. Everything I'd ever earned in my life—the Oscars, the cozy cottage in Palm Springs, the fan clubs around the world, charmingly named the Pink Ladies—had come at her expense.

I felt sick to my stomach and knew I deserved it. I'd always assumed that the Majestic would stand forever. After I became a star, the theatre became a sort of mecca for my fans, many of whom travel from across the continent to see it. Had they stopped coming? I always thought there would be time to go back. To make things right with Missy. Coward as I was, I always assumed it would happen when we were fragile old women with nothing left to do but forgive each other. But Raymond's letter had put the kibosh on all of it.

I knew from him that the VE-Day riots had resulted in significant damage to the exterior of the building a few decades ago; and with the rise of television ever since, fewer people were going to the movies. I thought of Old Man Prestel, who'd taken a chance on a mouthy dancer and her prim sister and turned them into stars. He gave us the moon and how had I repaid him? His legacy, Missy's legacy, *my* legacy was ending. Maybe, to a man who'd watched the film industry rise from a silent era to its modern, technicolour one, it wasn't enough anymore.

"Mel, you better open up," came Lang's muffled voice. All that huffing and puffing and he wasn't strong enough to blow the door down. And he'd have you believe he wouldn't look out of place in those sword-and-sandal epics.

I walked over to the door and flipped the lock, waiting for him to fall into my dressing room, which, by then, had been redecorated into a tasteful pale pink and teal pastiche. (When you win your Oscars for a set of films called *The Pink Dress* and *The Blue Dress*, it follows you around forever.)

"Congratulations," I said. "You just gave Hedda tomorrow's headline."

"Stuff Hedda Hopper," he said, waving me off. "What's in that letter?"

Wordlessly, I handed it to him and watched as those startling brown eyes scanned its contents. "All this over your theatre?"

I nodded.

"So buy it."

"Capital idea," I said, snatching the letter back from him. "Who's going to run it while I'm out here?"

"Mel, if you're making a movie with me, I know you haven't had many great offers lately. Why not go out with grace before you become a has-been?"

"You'd know all about that, wouldn't you?" I teased. His face reddened. This man was meant to be Bing's second coming, according to the trade papers, but his talent was overblown and now the likes of Elvis Presley and Troy Donahue were taking his place. The only way Lang made it out of trashy B movies—the last of which he'd made in 1960—was if my name was attached to the billing.

"It's *just* a theatre," he sniped, stung by the barb.

"*Just* a theatre? Lang, that's where I got my big break."

"You got your big break in Atlanta."

"You know what I mean. The Majestic means something to me."

"Please, you haven't been home since you got here. How can it mean that much to you?"

The question gave me pause. Even after a quarter of a century spent at the top of Hollywood, with a career anyone would sell their soul to have, I was treating Halifax like a spirit haunting me.

I hadn't gone back when Daddy, then Mother, passed away. I hadn't gone home when I won either of my Oscars, nor for the parties the Lieutenant Governor threw in my honour. I wasn't the first driver to speed down the newly named Majestic Street, which was unveiled on the tenth anniversary of The Majestic Sisters. I hadn't gone home when Missy had given birth to my nieces. Every time vacation came up, suddenly the Riviera was a must-see, or the gang was gathering in Jamaica, or Acapulco, or where have you.

"What are you hiding?" he asked. How could I begin to answer? He should have known better than anyone. I didn't answer. "You know, whatever you did all those years ago...it can't be that bad, can it? What, you didn't steal your sister's beau, did you?"

I rolled my eyes. "I had my own beau."

"Then what could have been so bad that you had to run from it all?"

"Lang," I sighed, "don't you ever get tired of asking?"

LIBELED LADY
Starring Jean Harlow and William Powell

FRIDAY, OCTOBER 29, 1937

W hat did I do that was so bad? Well kittens, I'm afraid I'm just not ready to admit it—to myself, most of all—but its roots were planted on the night the Majestic celebrated its thirty-seventh anniversary in October 1937.

By then we were a bona fide hit. That October alone, we'd modelled the latest fashions at Paulette's and earned ourselves a prime discount in perpetuity (which I still make use of through Raymond); won a tap-dancing contest at the Forum; and watched as famed tattoo artist Charlie Snow inked our likenesses upon the biceps of the hoi polloi. Daddy grudgingly admitted that he knew we'd "made it" when one of his prized students waltzed up to him after class, not to argue a grade or debate the finer points of "Ode on a Grecian Urn," but to show off his set of Melly and Missy tattoos. Didn't stop him from wishing we'd sooner—or later—find new careers, or husbands, for that matter.

But our biggest event that October was hosting our first jamboree at a Majestic Theatre anniversary show, one of the biggest nights of the year. Old Man Prestel slashed ticket prices, offered up free concessions, and swapped out whatever Famous Players sent him with a popular film of times gone by. Luckily for us, we could skip the routine we'd been doing for *The Prisoner of Zenda* and instead prepared a dazzling sketch for *Libeled Lady*.

The crowds started lining up around the block as the sun went down—no early shows that evening, just one show starting at ten thirty—and while they waited in line for our little theatre to open its doors, they were given another treat: watching limousines depositing the landed gentry to the Atlantic, a stunning turquoise tower perched on the waterfront that finally, after a year of construction, was opening that same night.

The *Halifax Mail* punctiliously reported on every aspect of the construction of the Atlantic Hotel, down to laughingly recounting how Edward Davis Junior, scion of the Davis Family, had practically begged his father on bended knee for the funds to purchase the old eyesore atrophying on the land he wanted. You have to understand that in such a small city, everything the Davises did made the news. When Bitsy Davis, Edward's fashionista mother, had lunch with a begrudging Amelia Earhart at The Halifax Club back in 1928, well, it inspired scores of aspiring aviatrixes to take up flying lessons, and scores of matrons to begin shopping at Mills Brothers, where Bitsy had purchased her luncheon dress. And now that the younger Davises were coming into their own, they were fresh meat for the pressmen downtown.

The story goes that Edward toddled right up to his father's corner table at The Halifax Club, where he lunched every weekday without fail, his knees knocking together though he had a solid business plan, and asked him for a loan to buy the derelict Carlyle Hotel—a building so old and abandoned that nobody could quite recall when it had closed.

I don't mean to imply that Edward Senior lent him the money. Oh no, he laughed until he was blue in the face, insisting that if his son was so adamant about checking into fool's paradise, he'd have to do it on his own dime. So instead, Edward Jr. went to Bitsy, who had her own income stream (the rumour was rum-running, but you didn't hear that from me), and topped off his trust fund with her help.

Building a hotel didn't seem like the kind of endeavour someone of Eddy's rank and station would undertake. He'd attended the best schools, graduated top of his class with a business degree, even did an extended tour of Europe before returning home to Halifax. We'd all expected him to settle into a corner office at L.F. Davis & Sons, the iron and metal import business his ancestors had set up in the early days of Halifax's settlement, but he had other ideas: he saw the corner lot at the intersection of Hollis and Salter Streets and fell in love with the idea of operating his own hotel with a perfect panoramic view of the Atlantic Ocean. In his mind's eye he saw a turquoise terracotta hotel; something to reflect the beauty of the ocean and to stand out from all the pallid concrete buildings downtown. At fifteen storeys tall, his hotel would be the tallest in the city. And the location! Only a stone's throw from the downtown shopping district in one direction and the Canadian National Railway station and ocean liner terminals in the other. It was perfectly positioned for those coming in and out of this bustling port city, and Eddy wanted to capitalize on it. The Great Depression had ended, and while Nova Scotia hadn't totally grown out of it, he thought that encouraging people to visit with such a luxurious place to stay could only stimulate the economy.

It took most of 1937 to build, but upon its opening, it was clear: this was no motor inn. And even though Eddy had struck a deal with CN to direct guests to the Atlantic, the hotel was built with the crème de la crème of society in mind, the people who could afford to hobnob with the Davises (think the Cunards, the Craigs, and the Killams).

And what better way for Eddy to show off his brand-new hotel—and show his father how wrong he'd been to doubt him—than by hosting an opening night soiree carefully planned by Bitsy? And here's the best part: guess who'd been invited?

"STICKING AROUND?" I asked Missy. It wasn't unheard of for The Majestic Sisters to stay for the show; we just had to tell William, our favourite usher, to save us a few seats in the loge area and we'd get VIP treatment.

"I'm beat, honestly," she replied, unbuckling her shoes. "I think I'll go home and go to bed." It wasn't a terrible idea, and without her, I didn't want to sit through *Libeled Lady*, so we quickly changed out of our costumes, and before we knew it, we were bidding goodnight to Charlie and Smokey at the concessions stand and walking out the door.

And there, waiting for us on the sidewalk, under a street lamp like a gangster in a Republic Pictures flick, was Raymond Swaine.

He could tell from our faces that we were beat, but if there's one thing Raymond hated, it was someone spoiling his fun.

"You're not cutting out on me, are you?" he asked, shuffling over to us. "Come on, I'm in my glad rags and everything."

Missy rolled her eyes—she tolerated Raymond at best and much preferred his younger sister, Amy—but couldn't help but smile at him after a fashion. The three of us had grown up together in the shadow of Dalhousie University, where our fathers taught. Missy and I had found the stage as our outlet, but Raymond was content to become the "man around town," best known for being the most-referred-to person in Halifax, both by name and anonymously, in the "I Heard It Last Night" gossip column published every day in the *Mail*. The very column he'd one day take over.

"You look fantastic, darling, but we're shot," I said.

He reached into his suit pocket and pulled out a square of turquoise cardstock. I recognized it: we'd left one on our dressing room vanity, but hadn't bothered to open it. We received so many invitations, understand, we couldn't possibly respond to all of them.

"Don't be all wet, we're going to that Atlantic Hotel shindig. With any luck, there's still champagne on ice."

"How'd *you* get an invite?" I asked.

Raymond, mock-aghast, replied, "I stole it from one Mr. and Mrs. Swaine, but don't tell them." I gave him a playful shove; he was always stealing invites from his parents. He laughed incredulously. "Now where do you think you're going?"

Missy had started taking quick steps backwards towards the tram stop across the street. One more step and she'd be on the Belt Line headed home. "I don't have your energy."

"Just come for an hour, then," he said, taking her hand and pulling her back to us. "You can be my fire extinguisher, make sure I behave."

"That's too tall of an order for me." She winked.

"That's why we keep inviting that sister of yours around with us. ʾe's the relief." Raymond winked back, sliding his arms around both of our shoulders and steering us towards the waterfront. He'd convinced us; but then, he always did.

⌒ℓℓ₂

THE CLOSER WE got to the Atlantic, the glitzier we felt. As we walked, Raymond recited all the names of the invitees he'd read in the paper, the who's who of the city had been invited that night. It looked like a movie premiere outside Grauman's Chinese Theatre, with the line of Wade Brothers taxicabs still dropping off stragglers and the blue spotlights flashing from the hotel roof.

And just inside the lobby, a dashing leading man by the name of Edward Davis, ready to be swept off his feet by one Majestic Missy.

How to describe my brother-in-law? Eddy, as I lovingly call him, has a smile to rival Cary Grant's. He's smart, charming, and terribly attractive—so totally different from his miser father and social-climbing mother (God rest their souls)—and with the Atlantic Hotel, he'd secured his legacy at the tender age of twenty-four. It's a shame Eddy never wanted to be an actor. The girls would've gone wild for him. But from the moment he met her, he's only ever had eyes for my darling little sister.

We were so late that Eddy had already shaken the hand of every single guest, the beaming smile frozen on his face. He'd made every type of chit-chat with every type of person, even the dinosaurs who swore up and down that they'd once been guests at the Carlyle. He'd recounted how he'd poached Chef Malcolm Stewart from the Lord Nelson Hotel and how he'd chosen every piece of décor, with his mother's help, naturally. He had no stories left to tell by the time we got there, but that was fine: once he saw her, Missy took his breath away.

I may have made our entrance sound more romantic than it actually was. To say that we'd hopped inside the chamber of the revolving door and gone around a few times like we were on a carousel may be a more accurate statement. Missy eventually slowed us down and hopped out, leaving me and Raymond trapped inside, and went up to greet the man of the hour.

27

"Don't mind them; Bill Lynch left them behind and they need to earn their keep somehow," she told him. Missy could be funny when she wanted to, but don't tell her I said that.

"I resent that statement," I said, halting the panel and hopping out behind her.

"And *I* resemble it." Raymond winked, then reached out to shake Eddy's hand. "Raymond Swaine, pleasure to meet you, and *these* ladies are the Majestic Sisters."

Eddy shook my hand but stared at Missy the whole time. He was a goner. "I've heard so much about you both," he said. "It's been a while since I went to the movies—"

"Surely you've been to see *them*!" Raymond cut in.

"Don't mind him, he gets a cut if he plugs us enough," I joked to Eddy.

"What this blabbermouth is trying to say," Missy said, "is that we're honoured to have been invited tonight and we thank you for your hospitality. Right, Raymond?"

He barely registered the comment, but nodded as he looked around the lobby. "Pretty nice place you've got here."

"I'm proud of it," Eddy agreed. "Care for a tour?"

How could we refuse! Our apologies to the slowpokes who came in after us, but Missy stole Eddy Davis away that night and never gave him back. I was witnessing a fairy tale unfolding. Eddy even called it one in their engagement interview a few years later. He said he'd remember every detail of meeting Missy for the rest of his life: how her icy blonde hair was pulled back into a chic chignon, and how the floral print dress hanging off her lithe frame reminded him of the summers he'd spent on the south shore wandering amidst the gardens at White Point. He was utterly, hopelessly captivated.

After Eddy showed us the finer points of the hotel, including its kitchen, its standard-size rooms, and its opulent suites—one got the impression he was making up things to show us so the tour wouldn't have to end—we all walked into the Coastal Ballroom, which boasted an unrivalled view of the Halifax Harbour, and headed straight to the champagne tower.

"I dare you to grab one from the bottom," I whispered to Raymond, plucking my own flute from the top like a well-behaved girl.

"I would, but I think that sister of yours would have me strung up if I tried," he whispered back, guzzling down the first glass.

"Spoilsport," I said, grabbing another glass and holding it out of his reach. Turning to Eddy, I asked, "So, you've been busy, eh?"

"It has been a lot of work, I won't argue," he replied to Missy. "It sounds like the two of you have been busy these past few months as well. Forgive me, Miss Calvert. Now that we're open, I'll have to make it up the hill for a movie or two."

"You're forgiven," I quipped, knowing he wasn't talking to me. "We'll save you the finest seats in the balcony. You and the whole family, if you'd like."

"I couldn't impose like that," he said.

"Oh, it's fine," Missy said. "Old Man Prestel always holds seats for us when we ask. We'd love to treat you."

"It must be hard work, running a hotel and everything," Raymond said, looking around the ballroom. I followed his gaze. A quick count and I'd spotted three aldermen, the police commissioner, the head of the fire department, and the owners of Simpson's, Purdy Motors, and Henry Birks and Sons. Not to mention several journalists with their pens and notepads primed for the scoop of a lifetime when they saw Eddy with The Majestic Sisters.

"I can't say I know just yet; we've only been operational for about twelve hours," he replied. He looked over at Missy again and noticed her empty glass. He deftly plucked it from her hand. "Miss Calvert, another?"

I quickly downed the last of my drink, feeling the bubbles tickle the back of my throat, and nodded, handing him my glass. "That would be wonderful." I had to laugh at the shock on his face before I let him off the hook. "Oh, Eddy, I'm just kidding. Fetch Missy another drink."

He winked at me. "I can hold two glasses at once, you know."

We had—or I should say Missy had—commandeered Eddy's attention for over an hour when the stately Bitsy Davis strode over and insisted that her son mingle with some of the other guests. She barely spared us a second glance before she departed back towards her gathering of aldermen's wives.

"She's right," Eddy sighed, placing yet another empty glass on a passing waiter's tray.

"Go out and offer them all a complimentary night's stay in the hotel. Why should the Wade Brothers get all that business," I teased.

"You know, that's not a bad idea."

"I work on commission," I said, draining another glass. I'd lost count by this point, but was handling myself admirably, I thought.

"I'll keep that in mind."

"Make the cheque payable to Melissa Calvert," I said. I turned to Missy, whispering in her ear, "Why don't you go with him, make sure all those playgirls behave."

"Capital idea," she whispered back, handing me her empty glass. Eddy, ever observant, offered his arm. "What'll you do?" Missy asked after she'd placed her hand around his arm. Raymond had long since abandoned us for a tray of canapés, so I was about to be stag at this shindig. No worries.

"I'm resourceful." I shrugged. "I might go see if any of these fine gentlemen have a flask they'd be willing to share with me."

"Don't do anything I wouldn't do."

"That's not a very long list," I called to her retreating back.

⌒ℓℓ⌒

OF COURSE, MISSY told me all about the rest of her evening with Eddy Davis once we got home. It didn't involve much hosting, if you ask me, but it did involve sneaking away to the rooftop terrace to stargaze and to point out the Majestic Theatre in case he, a lifelong citizen, didn't know how to find it. I didn't see her again at the hotel that night—I was escorted home by a Wade Brothers taxi at a more respectable hour.

It was the beginning of Halifax's greatest romance. Missy and Eddy never officially started seeing each other; they just sort of...fit together. Soulmates. The next morning, he named the hotel restaurant after their midnight sojourn: the Stargazers' Lounge.

"I think I'm in love," she gushed, slipping into my bedroom close to dawn. She quietly shut the door and slid to the floor in front of my bed.

"That quickly, eh?" I asked, shuffling over so she could crawl in next to me.

"I'm going to marry that man, mark my words." I didn't tell her that Raymond and I already had a bet going. Nor that I'd won. I'd never seen my sister smile like this before. Never over a man, certainly. Missy was gone from the moment she laid eyes on Eddy Davis. She'd found her gold mine.

"You'll have to let down the English department gently," I teased. A well-placed elbow nearly vaulted me off the bed, and then she yawned and leaned her head against my shoulder. "Are you just getting home?" I felt her nod.

"We were watching the stars and lost track of time. How did you get home?"

I leaned my head overtop of hers. "I owe it all to the Wade Brothers."

"You didn't leave with Raymond?"

"I had to pour Raymond into his own cab not long after you hot-footed away with Eddy. Parting is such sweet sorrow and all that, but you know how it is when you go out with him. Once he was gone, I decided to stay and mingle a bit longer, maybe see if you'd come back."

"Promise me you behaved," she mumbled, sleep tinging her words.

"Don't worry. I kept myself entertained."

That night, I'd met someone too. My number-one fan. But I wasn't ready to share my own secret just yet.

VICTORIA THE GREAT
Starring Anna Neagle

FRIDAY, DECEMBER 3, 1937

H eavy is the head that wears the crown and all that. I was sitting in the dressing room in full Victorian regalia when Missy popped in, red wig pushed high upon her head and a face caked with powder, giving her the appearance of a strawberry shortcake dusted with confectioners' sugar.

"I shudder to think what the dry-cleaning bill's going to be," she said, shuffling over to the vanity. Every step she took was punctuated by a powder cloud as she tried to maneuver into her seat.

"Let the costumers worry about it," I said, plaiting my hair and pinning it under the crown I was wearing. I'd ripped a page out of the encyclopedia at home—if Daddy ever caught me, he'd tan my hide—and was trying to emulate the braids in Queen Victoria's hair from her coronation portrait.

"I look dreadful," Missy said, glaring at her Tudor reflection in the mirror. "Truly horrid."

"Imagine," I said, "this passed as high fashion once upon a time. People paid money to look like that."

"The most powerful woman in the world looked like a Q-tip," she whined, pushing the red wig further back on her head, trying to expose more of her forehead like a true Elizabethan queen.

"You could've been my Prince Albert, you know," I teased.

"I'm a queen on my own," Missy declared.

The latest movie to play at the Majestic was *Victoria the Great*, and with all the hoopla that surrounded the abdication and crowning of a new king, we figured we'd treat this regal movie with a grander show than any we'd ever planned before.

Earlier that day, while the flunkies swapped out Marlene Dietrich's name for Anna Neagle's on the marquee, Missy and I enrobed ourselves in our regalia and paraded from the theatre to Government House to meet the illustrious Lieutenant Governor of Nova Scotia, who chuckled at our pompous costumes but dutifully posed between these two imposter queens "on behalf of" King George VI.

We were then invited to lunch with Premier Angus L. MacDonald, who posed with us in the Red Chamber at Province House. It was a room designated for real royalty. Portraits of past Canadian monarchs decorated the walls and two thrones sat perched upon a dais, waiting for royal usage should any monarch decide to drop in for dinner. A soft cough from one of the premier's aides quickly deterred any plans I might have had to sit myself upon one.

Our stunt did its job: by the time we'd made it back up the hill to the theatre, a mob of people were standing at the ticket window for that evening's premiere. The sight would become a weekly phenomenon, but these fans were among the first to flock to the theatre for us.

By then, we'd developed our own "Majestic" characters that the audience, and all of Halifax, really, accepted without question. Missy was the prim and proper sister and I was the wild and vibrant sister. Icy cool blonde and raven-haired vixen. Sweet and fiery. This and that. For Missy, that meant clean ballet moves and clear-as-a-bell singing; for me, it meant frenetic jazz steps and bosom-buddy jokes until Mort played us off.

⌒ℓℓ⌒

WE WATCHED FOR our cue, and when the light bulb in the wing flashed three times, we walked out—rather slowly under those layers of robes and regalia—and perched ourselves upon our wooden thrones, lent to us especially by the Theatre Arts Guild.

The curtain rose and we waited for the thunderous applause to die down before we began. Friday nights were always the most popular shows, you understand, so we had to ensure that everything was perfect.

When there was but a smattering of applause left, I began to speak with an affected English accent. "I'm glad you're here, you're not too late, to see *Victoria the Great*. A movie about a great regina, Victoria Alexandrina."

Missy piped in, "You've got it wrong, I must protest, for no queen was greater than Good Queen Bess."

The audience started to laugh. From my seat, I spotted Eddy, who now showed up for as many shows as he could sit through, watching his dame with those moony eyes from the box he rented from Old Man Prestel. How nauseatingly romantic.

"Who can argue that Gloriana is anything but top banana?" she continued, once the crowd's roar died down.

"I'd expect this kind of commentary from the nightmarish Queen Bloody Mary," I said.

"Could your quip be any ruder? We all know that I'm top Tudor."

"Go consult any historian, they'll tell you the best era was Victorian," I simpered.

"You shall regret your nonchalance, are you forgetting the Renaissance?"

"You can sit on that throne while you priss and preen, but we all know that I'm the better queen."

By then, the audience was goading us on and rooting for their favourite monarch; it was almost as though they'd bought tickets to a prizefight between Queen Victoria and Queen Elizabeth I, and the winner took the throne.

Before Missy could speak another word, Old Man Prestel came out onstage, dressed as a caricature of George V, to thunderous applause. It was the first time he'd ever joined us for a bit, and we could all plainly see that the audience loved the surprise of seeing the sprightly theatre owner in such fussy dress. It was so overwhelming, he couldn't even speak for a full minute or two. Finally, he held his hand up, a king commanding silence, and the crowd quieted. We gave him the final lines of this pantomime.

"Majesties: could it be we haven't found her yet, that England's greatest queen will be Lilibet?"

The curtains dropped as Missy and I whipped our heads towards each other, balking at the idea that there could ever be a rival upon our stage.

"Do you hear that?" I asked her. The crowd was cheering for us on the other side of that velvet.

"All that for us?" she beamed.

"They're not here for Anna Neagle, they're here for us!"

Maybe the dream of being famous *wasn't* unattainable. We were popular, certainly, but the audience was yelling my name. Missy's name. We were the queens of Halifax, and in that moment, it felt like the only way was up.

"That was fun, Chickadee," Old Man Prestel said, holding out a hand to help me stand. "I should join you girls more often."

"Majestic Mr. Prestel has a nice ring to it," Missy said, linking arms with me as we exited the stage. Our gowns were so heavy that the lights began to dim and the overture began to play—if we didn't scurry quickly, we'd be part of the movie as well! I knew then, with every part of my being, that I belonged on that stage. And still, I couldn't help but wonder what it would be like to be up on the big screen. The thought had crossed my mind every single time I'd watched a movie at the Majestic, but it was only then, onstage for *Victoria the Great*, that I really let myself think of it as a place I could one day belong. I started squirrelling away my money for the day I inevitably made good on my dreams—but you'll hear all about that later.

"I think I'll stick to managing this place," Old Man Prestel laughed. "Do you think the Theatre Guild will mind if I keep this costume?"

"Going to wear it every day?" Missy joked.

"It suits me, don't you think?" he said, fiddling with the coronet on his head.

Missy looked at me and winked. "I won't tell if you won't."

CHARADE

Starring Audrey Hepburn and Cary Grant

SUNDAY, DECEMBER 22, 1963

The publicity folks would have you believe that I spend a quiet Christmas at my home in Palm Springs, but here's the truth: I like to get a little rum-soaked at the Christmas Eve shindigs lighting up the star-filled town. I've won the eggnog-drinking contest eleven years in a row, after all. And then I spend Christmas Day by myself. I'll turn on the record player, listen to Bing and Frank and Perry croon about those white Christmases that we all used to know, and sit in the dark as I take in the bright multicoloured NOMA lights on my Christmas trees. Yes, that's trees, plural.

This year, however, I was packing up and shipping out on a private jet—supplied by Lang, who only glared at me when I asked how he'd found the money to pay for it—back to a theatre that needed me, a sister who wanted nothing to do with me, a bastion of a brother-in-law who practically ran our hometown, and two nieces I'd never met.

Double Jinx had cleared it with the top brass that they'd shoot around me and close down early for the holidays. Then he'd worked like the dickens to keep my flight path from the press. Lang promised to keep his mouth shut, too, and by the time anyone noticed I was gone, well...I was gone. Simple as that.

As I packed, I had nothing to do but think about my estranged sister. If Hedda'd ever gotten a whiff of the uncordiality between me and

Missy, no doubt she'd have magnified it—rented a house in Halifax for her little spies to follow the Davises around; put Raymond on the payroll; and made the feud between Olivia de Havilland and Joan Fontaine look like child's play.

I'd called Raymond on Thursday night and he promised to arrange everything once I landed. It was an offer as self-serving as it was advantageous: by picking me up at the airport and booking me in at the Atlantic under his name, he made sure he'd get the scoop. I would have been almost proud of him if the fear of what awaited me wasn't making my heart race.

"Your timing has always been spectacular," he chuckled. "Missy's Christmas party is Monday night."

I'd heard, over the years, of her total and complete transformation into Halifax's grand dame, and that the soirées she threw made Bitsy's look like childhood tea parties. It put a smile on my face.

"That's not why I'm coming home."

"Honey, you don't expect me to believe that, do you?"

He'd filled me in on what had been going on in Missy's life recently—her eldest, Bridget, had just married; her youngest, Leonore, had two years of university left; and the book sale she'd organized with the Women's Auxiliary of the Atlantic Symphony, her latest charitable venture, was a smashing success. "She was always meant to be a star," he'd said. "You just didn't like to share your spotlight."

I pretended his comment didn't sting, chuckled in all the right places, and listened as he further regaled me with the tedium of how he'd been stuck in line behind the whole Davis brood at the Fantasyland display at the Nova Scotia Lights & Power building the week before.

"Bridget going on and on about her honeymoon, the Blue Lady"— the derisive nickname a faction of people had given my sister when she married Eddy, viewing her as nothing more than a social climber only interested in his money and his hotel—"smiling like Princess Grace, Leonore rolling her eyes at the whole production, and Eddy himself arriving just in time for the flashbulb. Why that made the front page, I'll never understand."

But he did, on some level. Any crumb of news about one of The

Majestic Sisters would always make the front page—I've lost count of the number of times I've been in the papers back home. Old Man Prestel mails me a stack of fan mail and newspaper clippings every three months. It's always a hefty bag. They wouldn't forget me.

"But anyways..." he trailed off. "I bet your antics will make the front page easily."

"The only headline I want is *Majestic Sisters Save Majestic Theatre,*" I chided.

"Darling, don't act like you've gone soft now. Or am I remembering someone else who pulled on Robert Taylor's moustache and had to face Stanwyck's wrath the next morning?"

Mum's the word on that one. "I'm trying to behave this time," I said.

"Honey, you don't need a palm reader to know that this is going to be a total disaster, whether or not you save the Majestic."

"Don't sound so excited by that."

"Are you kidding? A Majestic Sisters confrontation? It's only been on my Christmas list since 1938!"

THAT CERTAIN WOMAN
Starring Bette Davis and Henry Fonda

FRIDAY, DECEMBER 17, 1937

I always believed I'd be famous someday. That was the one constant in my life. And when you're always looking for signs, you'll believe anything you see. That's how a palm reader gave me the confidence to believe that all this hard work would eventually pay off.

I was in our dressing room a week before Christmas, sitting around after a matinee of *That Certain Woman* and reading the newspaper, when I spotted an advertisement for Madame Ford, palm reader. She'd gained a bit of a following locally after she found a young boy who'd gone missing. She'd told the police to look for him in the Canadian Pacific, and they found the boy hiding in a boxcar down at the train station, bound for Vancouver and adventure. I figured if I'd managed to clap eyes on her advertisement, small as it was in that broadsheet, it was a sign. So I called her up and she agreed to see me that afternoon.

"I knew it was only a matter of time before I read a Majestic Sister," she said by way of greeting as I walked into her South End parlour room.

You know those turban-wearing fortune tellers you see at carnivals? That's what I was anticipating when I walked in to Madame Ford's home, but she was just a regular woman in a regular house in regular clothing asking to hold my hand. The whole set-up cheapened the production values, but I slid my right hand into hers and watched as she studied it this way and that until she'd seen enough of the grooves to make her predictions about the life and times of Melly Calvert.

She said I had water hands, which means I'm creative and prone to getting my feelings hurt, and that she was drawn to the mount of Mercury under my pinky finger. She said it suggested I was resourceful and had a strategic mind. Given that I'd soon uproot my life in absolute secrecy, I think Madame Ford had it right.

"You're going to live a long, healthy life," she said. "You see this?" She held my hand up, urging me to look at a line I couldn't see. I stared at the centre of my palm, hoping I was at least looking in the right direction. "Unbroken. Means you're going to have little in the way of tragedy in your life. And this curve? Means you're artistic. Though I think we knew that already, eh?"

Then she poked at my thumb. "The mount of Venus isn't as pronounced on you. Looks like you're only going to have one—maybe two—great love affairs in your life. You seem like the type to settle down, no matter that artistic temperament. Does that sound right so far?"

I nodded, not so much at the two great loves—I'd never been in love before and truthfully, I wasn't sure I had it in me the way Missy or Mother and Daddy did—but at the artistic temperament. I wanted fulfillment in other areas of my life, and I was grateful to Madame Ford for recognizing it so quickly.

She held my hand up to her face. "You've got a nice travel line. I see you going abroad and staying there. Soon, if I'm not mistaken." I thought of palm trees and the Hollywood sign. "I can feel the cool waters of the Pacific Ocean on my toes when I think about you," she said, and my hand jerked out of hers. "How old are you," she added, "if you don't mind my asking?"

"I just turned twenty," I replied. "Why?"

"Just checking your fate lines. Middle of the palm is where you'll be when you turn thirty-five."

"And where will I be then?"

"You'll be noteworthy, in every sense of the word."

SNOW WHITE AND THE SEVEN DWARFS

WEDNESDAY, MARCH 16, 1938

I t baffles me as to why I kept getting cast as royalty in our little bits when Missy was perfectly capable—her temperament was much better suited to a princess or a queen—but when *Snow White* came to town in early 1938, it wasn't our docile dancing debutante who was asked by the movie studio, RKO, to play her in the promotional pieces... they asked me instead.

THE LOBBY DOOR banged open and out popped Old Man Prestel's upper body. "There you are—what are you doing out here dressed like that?"

"I'm advertising," I said. It wasn't every day that you spotted a Majestic Sister standing on the sidewalk in a leopard print bodice and tutu. *Bringing Up Baby*, the screwiest screwball comedy of all time, was currently playing; I was just doing my part to help ticket sales. Old Man Prestel had already brought in a lion named Linger and his tamer to join us onstage that week—even though I'd given him much grief over the fact that 'Baby' was a leopard. He gave me more creative input after this, don't you worry.

He scoffed. "Chickadee, you're standing next to the Majestic Missy poster encouraging people inside, and there's a lion in the dressing room to help with all that. I think we can spare your services on this.

Get in here, I need to talk to you about the costuming budget."

I waved goodbye to Tracy, ever faithful at the ticket booth in all types of weather, and made my way inside. With March Break, all of the students were out of school and it was even busier than usual. The days were just beginning to lengthen, and it was an unseasonably warm afternoon, so I'd been taking full advantage of the great outdoors. We were midway through the week's run, with Linger the Lion stuffed in a dressing room roaring and growling as he and his tamer, Michael, waited for the prologue to begin, so could you blame me for wanting a bit of space?

"The costuming budget? Since when do we have a costuming budget?" I was suddenly on my pins. Missy and I had been paying for our costumes out of pocket, so if there was a budget he hadn't told me about...

"Not here, Chickadee," he said. Then he winked that charming grandfatherly wink of his, like he was about to pull a quarter out from behind my ear, and gestured for me to follow him back inside.

"If you insist, Boss," I said, following him through the lobby and into his hidden temple, my tap shoes clip-clapping against the wooden floor. I flung myself into the seat in front of his desk. "All right, you have me here. Let's talk about this costuming budget. I can assure you that we haven't spent a dime over fifteen dollars so far this year, and with that partnership with Paulette's for our evening gown needs, we should be able to stay within seventy-five dollars by the end of the year. I'm forecasting a surplus. If you even have a fixed clothing budget, which I doubt, because you run a movie theatre, not a playhouse."

Old Man Prestel fixed me with a stare. "Your mother finally convinced you to take business classes, eh?"

"No." I shuddered. "The bankers take their lunches at the Green Lantern and I like to eavesdrop." You never knew what detail might be important for developing your character work on the stage.

"I was lying about the costuming budget, Chickadee. It's still a secret, so I couldn't mention it to all and sundry on Barrington Street. But while you're still an actress, how about I give you some flashy work?" He slid a piece of paper across the desk to me.

I picked it up and skimmed it. "We're getting *Snow White and the Seven Dwarfs*?"

"RKO wants to do a big publicity push in all the major cities. We qualify, thanks to our box office returns."

"You mean thanks to The Majestic Sisters," I quipped. "How do I factor into this?"

"You're going to be my Snow White."

I laughed. "Beg pardon?"

"The studio has it all cooked up," he said. Then he explained how I would, at the behest of RKO, dress up as Snow White and visit all the kid-friendly spots in town to drum up interest in the movie. The studio had sent over a list of stops: the mayor's office, a princess lunch at the children's home, and toy shopping at Simpson's, where I'd hawk *Snow White* merchandise.

"Best part is that you get a copy of Snow White's dress—"

"Oh goodie," I interrupted, reading over the itinerary he'd produced.

"—and you get to take seven of our best ushers out with you as your dwarves."

"So *all* of them?" I joked. He looked at me over his glasses and silently slid another paper across the desk: a sketch of a real-life replica of Snow White's yellow and blue dress and instructions on how to mimic her bob. Behind her, seven large papier-mâché heads of the aforementioned dwarves illustrated the scale at which they'd swallow the scrawny ushers. "Why me, why not Missy? She's got the disposition for something like this."

He chuckled. "You want the truth or your ego boosted?"

"That depends."

"You're the better actress."

"Which one was that?"

He winked. "Plus, if I pick you, I don't have to splurge on a wig."

Who said blondes have more fun?

"WHAT'S THIS?" Missy sat up straighter in her chair the next morning at breakfast. We were sitting in the Stargazers' Lounge and she'd made it to the third page of the newspaper, where Old Man Prestel's advertisement, Snow White: *Walt Disney's first full-length feature film, Majestic Melly's first full-length solo performance!*, had been strategically placed to catch the eye.

I wanted to tell her the night before, but she'd zipped out of the Majestic before I could corner her and didn't return home until I was already in bed. I knew I'd get her with an invitation to have breakfast at the Atlantic—my treat—and of course, she'd woken up with the birds in case we got there early enough to catch a glimpse of Eddy before he went into back-to-back meetings.

I sighed. "It's what I wanted to talk to you about." This wouldn't be an easy conversation. Neither one of us had ever gone on that stage solo before, and in her eyes, I was stealing the limelight. "I didn't plan it this way, but—"

"You brought me *here*, of all places, to tell me that you're cutting me out of the act?!"

"I'm not cutting you out of the act, Missy. It's just for a few days."

She tried to argue and bargain, but for every parry, I had a dodge. Yes, she was still getting paid, she'd signed a contract; no, RKO didn't want the Evil Queen in the prologue lest it frighten the children; yes, we were The Majestic Sisters, but there had to be an exception to every rule, right?

"This is about the Majestic, not The Majestic Sisters," I said. "If it's what Old Man Prestel needs from us, then we need to do it."

Missy delicately set her fork down and smoothed her hand over the tablecloth. Nobody was going to know she was having a Missy fit if she disguised it like this. "That's a very convenient statement considering you're the only one who benefits here. Nobody else can take a step upon thine hallowed stage for one whole week?"

"Well, the seven dwarfs will be there. And if the film is popular enough, it'll be held over." Which was the wrong thing to say in the moment, but she needed to hear it all. If Missy weren't a perfect saint, she would have snorted her orange juice all over the table.

"So it's *not* just Majestic Melly up onstage, then. It's Majestic Melly and *seven* of her nearest and dearest...just not her sister. Her partner. For an indefinite period!" She looked furtively around the room and sunk a bit lower in her seat. "How can I show my face after this? What's Edward going to think!"

I startled. "Why does it matter what Eddy thinks? He's not your manager, he doesn't own a stake in the Majestic." I tried to keep my voice down, the dining room was full of course. "You're still his main squeeze whether you're on that stage or not, but all you can think about is him!"

"Of course it matters what Edward thinks, he's important to me," she hissed.

"And the Majestic is important to me, Missy," I hissed back.

"It's not the be-all, end-all, Melly," she chided. The familiar refrain: *you're taking this too seriously.* But Missy only ever seemed to take our careers seriously when it adversely affected her. "Someday we're going to hang up our dancing shoes forever, and you're going to wish you had someone to go home to."

"You know I don't want that," I said. "You know I'm working towards a legitimate acting career. And if you don't see a future in this, why are you so upset?"

"Because we're a duo," she said, like it was the simplest idea in the world. Her greatest mistake was thinking I felt that way too. "We do this together."

I let out a breath. "Not this, Missy. This isn't another silly prologue. This could be a stepping stone, if I want it to be. RKO *requested* me."

She surveyed me a moment, as if she were only just seeing me for the first time. Then she tossed her napkin on her plate and stood in a quick, elegant motion. "As long as you know who you're stepping on to get it."

⟡

WHEN I LEFT the house that Friday morning, Missy was waiting for me. She glanced up at me from her perch on the living room couch, looked me in the eye, and said, "Any applause you get today? It won't be for you. It'll be for Snow White. You can't get that kind of applause on your own."

Well, I wish I could've seen the look on my dear sister's face when me and those usher-cum-dwarves were greeted to an honest-to-goodness mob at the Armdale train station a few hours later. I'd never seen anything like it, and all of it for me! I'd already proven Missy wrong.

Bless RKO's hearts, they'd even sent over body language instructions for each of us to memorize. I had to hold my hands and arms "with elegance and grace," movements I'd practiced for *hours* in front of the bedroom mirror, and either smile or wink and gasp with "innocence and naivety," befitting the teenage princess. It was easy enough for the dwarfs: all they had to do was gesture grumpily, bashfully, sneezily—you get the idea—with their arms and keep mum.

Since we were closest to Simpson's, we stopped there first to shop in the toy department. The gracious owners had donated dozens of Snow White dolls and children's books for the lucky kiddies who happened to be shopping with their mothers that fateful day.

It looked like Christmastime at the department store, that's how busy it was. I sat in Toytown for about an hour, reading *Snow White* to the children and playing with them. Then once it was time to leave, I descended from the escalator with my seven little buddies lurching behind me into the parking lot, where a fleet of Oldsmobile convertible coupes were waiting for us, having been graciously donated by Halifax Motors for the day. In those cars, more gift bags for the orphans at the children's home. This charitable aspect was a fun side of fame I didn't experience too often in Halifax, but one I've focused on considerably since.

As a gift, Simpson's gave me my own doll, which sat upon my vanity at home until I left; a children's book, which I signed as *Snow White* and donated to the children's home later that day; and a set of buttercream fudge molds of the seven dwarves (the nuance on the Grumpy fudge's face!).

The princess party at the children's home was so much fun—even the ushers were in the spirit—and we spent far more than our allotted time playing with the kiddies, so much so that we almost missed the official welcoming ceremony at City Hall! Mayor Walter Mitchell would accord me and my usher friends the full privileges of the city—Majestic Melly was denied nowhere.

And as we walked up the street back to the Majestic, shop owners were standing outside gifting us with Snow White merchandise. I'd later wear my Snow White charm bracelet to the premieres of *Cinderella* and *Sleeping Beauty*, and rumour has it that Aurora's pink and blue gowns were inspired by my movies. My arms were full by the time we'd made it into the theatre, and I found Missy sitting at the vanity, gazing at her own reflection as though waiting for answers from a magic mirror.

There was an animus growing between us that wasn't helped when the box of costumes and dwarf heads arrived at the Majestic earlier in the week. Once it became a tangible fact that she wouldn't appear in the *Snow White* prologue, Missy's mood soured further. Eddy tried to placate her with a five-course meal and new jewellery, but now here I was, alone to face her wrath.

"What treasures did you get?" she said, as if speaking to herself in her mirror.

I gestured to the record from Birney's Music, the box of chocolates from Moirs, and the charm bracelet from Birks.

"How wonderful," she trilled, still refusing to look at me.

"Envious?" I asked.

"Of course not." She brushed her fingers against a stunning tennis bracelet gifted to her by her beloved to make up for the indignity of the week. Of course Eddy would pick an aquamarine gemstone—so complementary to those icy eyes.

We'd never fought like this before. This blow-up went beyond typical sisterly rivalry. It hung in the room, quiet but humming, working its way into our blood. Though we'd soon sweep it under the rug for the sake of public appearances, it was clear to us now that we were on different tracks, and we knew it. No hiding, no pretending. Missy wanted to be Mrs. Davis and all that entailed, and I wanted to be a star.

I stared at her through the mirror. "Green's not a good colour on you, Sissy."

CHARADE
Starring Audrey Hepburn and Cary Grant

MONDAY, DECEMBER 23, 1963

I 've stayed at the Plaza, the Carlton Hotel Cannes, and Claridge's, but nothing could compare to the lush beauty of the Atlantic Hotel. It was exactly the same as I remembered: a turquoise citadel gleaming against the waterfront. A crown jewel. Sure it was now a few storeys taller, its sign updated to a more modern style, but it retained every inch of its original opulence.

I'd arrived in Halifax mid-afternoon—Raymond had forgotten to factor in time zones—and was rushed off the tarmac before anyone could catch a glimpse of my face. Raymond dropped me off in front of the hotel with a "Save the fireworks for when I get there," and dashed off before I could thank him for the ride.

The perky young front desk clerk caught a glimpse of me under my red velvet hat and hadn't taken her eyes off me from the moment I'd wandered in the door. I doubted the couple attempting to rent a room from her would give her much of a tip. Around her, the hotel bustled with the festive frivolities of party planning. Thankfully Missy was nowhere to be seen while I waited, though I heard clatter in the Coastal Ballroom. Before I could wander over, it was my turn to be checked in.

"Welcome to the Atlantic Hotel, the Sapphire of the East Coast," the receptionist greeted. "Do you have a reservation?"

"It's under 'Raymond Swaine,'" I informed her. It didn't escape my notice that she'd already trailed her fingers down the list, stopping at the Cs.

"You've shaved since I last saw you, Mr. Swaine," she said, scanning the ledger again.

"Call it movie magic." There. Not an outright admission, but enough to give her something to tell her friends about later. I watched two men wheel an enormous, fully decorated balsam fir into the ballroom. They were quickly followed by another pair, and then another, until I imagined it looked like Point Pleasant Park in there.

"You're here for the party tonight?" she asked.

"Nice try."

She shrugged. "Worth a shot. Your reservation is through New Year's Day, Mr. Swaine. Just the one guest?" Her eyes darted behind me. I turned my head, expecting to come face to face with my sister, but only watched as a young blonde pranced into the ballroom.

"Unless Lang shows up."

Her eyes snapped back to me.

"That was a joke," I reassured her. She seemed to deflate. One of many who clearly believed that, sooner or later, Lang and I would rekindle our romance and remarry. One of many who'd be disappointed when that moment never came. She wrote in the ledger and then shifted the book over to me to sign in.

"Unfortunately, you'll have to sign under your legal name," she said.

"Fine, just don't sell it," I joked, picking up the turquoise fountain pen from its stand and scrawling *M. Calvert*.

"You're in the Imperial Suite," she said, sliding a set of keys across the desk and giving me an overview of the services and amenities provided at the hotel, like television sets in all the rooms, the open mic club in the basement, and the new rooftop restaurant. After she'd rung for a bellhop to take my luggage upstairs, she asked, "Is there anything else I can help you with?"

"Yes," I said, sliding the keys into my handbag. "Don't tell my sister or the *Mail* that I'm here and I'll make it worth your while at checkout."

The snow was falling in heavy flakes against the window as the bellhop opened the door to my room and ushered me inside. Of course, the windows of the Imperial Suite would offer up an unrestricted view of the Halifax Harbour, the lighthouse on Georges Island a beacon amidst the unrelenting snow. Say what you will about the Atlantean landscape, but someone once taught me to appreciate a street-side view when staying at hotels.

The bellhop kept glancing back at me, as though he knew he should recognize my face but simply couldn't place it. He made quick work of setting my luggage on the stand—and even quicker work of taking the handsome tip proffered—and left without asking who I was. No doubt the front desk clerk would fill him in once he returned to his post.

I waited about ten minutes before I, too, left the suite and headed back downstairs. No point in delaying the inevitable, right? The gilded elevator slowly carried me down to the lobby, and as soon as the doors opened, I came face to face with a young woman who looked so much like me it was uncanny.

Leonore Davis. My youngest niece.

LEONORE TOOK ONE look at me, at that face that so closely matched her own, and then jumped back as though the very sight of me terrified her.

"Does Mother know you're here?" Her voice barely carried above the jingle-jangle reverberating around us in the lobby.

I shook my head once. "Not yet."

"What room are you in? When did you get here? Who else knows you're here? *Why* are you here?" She fired question after question at me, not giving me a chance to respond at all. In response to my silence, she pressed the elevator button, and when the doors opened behind me, she shoved me back inside with a "Go back to your room and wait for my knock." Well, what choice did I have but to obey? Truthfully, I admired that bit of spunk. Missy hadn't raised a wallflower.

It felt like ages waiting for the knock to come, and when it finally did, it came with the muffled sound of two sisters arguing. It nearly brought tears to my eyes. I opened the door and found myself staring at a familiar sight: two sisters, both alike in dignity. One blonde, one brunette. Bridget and Leonore, dressed in their winter finery, obscenities spilling out of their mouths upon clapping their eyes on me.

"Kittens," I greeted. "I don't think we've met, officially. I'm your Aunt Melly."

The blonde, Bridget, guffawed. Then she clapped her hand over her mouth. Leonore elbowed her. "Play nice."

Bridget walked into the room, Leonore trailing behind her. "I'm sorry. It's just..." She paused. "I've only ever seen you on a big screen. You're quite tiny, actually."

"I manage," I said, holding out my hand once again. This time, she took it.

"I'm Bridget, but everyone calls me Birdie."

"Because she never stops chirping," Leonore quipped.

"I don't recall asking for audience participation." Birdie flopped onto the bed.

"And yet, here I am."

I watched them in amazement; I hadn't had a sparring partner like that in almost twenty-five years.

"And that must make you Leonore," I said, offering my hand to my other niece.

"It does," she said. "Call me Leonie."

"I call her Goldie," Birdie said.

Leonie rolled her eyes. "You never call me that."

"And why is that?" I asked over Leonie's protests. I knew the answer, but I couldn't help stirring the pot.

"Because she was born the same night you won an Oscar. Just save yourself the temper tantrum and never call her that in front of Mother. Trust me."

I chuckled. "We used to call those 'Missy fits' back in the day." My heart skipped when I heard them both laugh. "Though maybe we should keep that one to ourselves for now, hmm?"

"So, let's get to the point," Birdie said. "What brings you here?"

"What, I can't come home and spend Christmas with my family?" I asked.

"Family?" she scoffed. "That's a bit rich. You haven't spent Christmas with your family in years."

"Maybe I wanted a change in scenery this year. I haven't had a white Christmas in ages."

"She spends Christmas in Palm Springs every year," Leonie said to her sister. She sat down at the dinette. "There was a two-page spread about it in *Modern Screen* last year."

"You keep tabs on me?" I took the seat opposite her.

"Good lord, *no*. We have a subscription at work; I have to keep tabs for the movie page. Mother would have a fit if I brought that home. We didn't even know you were our aunt for the longest time."

I had to swallow down the lump in my throat. Is this how wide the gulf between my sister and I had grown? "Well, I'm here now. Ask me anything you want."

"Why now?" Leonie asked. "And tell the truth this time."

"I came to save the Majestic."

I remembered how it looked when the driver passed by the building less than an hour earlier, how it was in desperate need of a fresh coat of paint. It looked everything and nothing like I'd remembered it. It was already a relic, the Egyptian revival trend having long passed, and resembled the remnants of a crumbling empire. Back in the '30s, a neon marquee bore our names in flashing hot pink and neon blue: *Majestic Melly! Majestic Missy!* The current marquee looked heartbreaking in comparison: *CLOSING NEW YEAR'S EVE! SO LONG, THANKS FOR THE MEMORIES!*

"Why don't you spend your money on something *useful*," Leonie said. "You haven't seen the inside. The sound system was updated ahead of *The Ten Commandments*, and the screen gets repaired every now and then. There was a big hullabaloo a few years ago when they started showing VistaVision movies, but not much else has changed."

"Does the fireplace still have the carving above it?"

"*Take Turns, No Burns!*" Birdie smiled. "I always loved that sign."

"Has your mother ever—"

"No," Leonie interrupted. "Not once."

"They tried to get her over there for the rerelease of *Gone with the Wind* about five years ago," Birdie said. "She said no. I'm sure you can understand why she hates *that* movie."

The room went silent. "Well," I said, rallying myself, "this turned incredibly bleak. What do you say to some lunch? My treat."

They exchanged a look. "Mother will be expecting us to help her get everything organized for tonight."

"Of course," I said. "I can manage on my own, kittens. I've never been one for a chaperone."

"But we still have a little bit of time. We could run up to Palm's Lunch and get a sandwich," Leonie offered.

"That sounds delicious," I said, grabbing my handbag.

"It's not that long of a walk to the deli," Birdie said, sliding her hands into a stylish pair of sable mittens. "Nothing you can't handle, right Aunt Melly?"

"Kitten, you're talking to the woman who married Langdon Hawkes. I think I can manage a few blocks."

"It'll probably take longer to walk to Prince Street than it took you to marry and divorce him," Leonie countered. She wasn't wrong.

"Lead the way."

～ele～

I LET THE girls chauffeur me out of the hotel. Nobody stopped to question them, the Eloises of the Atlantic, but I knew there'd be gossip as soon as the public caught a glimpse of my face.

As we walked up the street and onto the main beltline of downtown Halifax, I couldn't help but peer back at the Majestic. Mid-afternoon and not a single person standing in line for *Charade*; they were standing in line to see the animatronic Christmas displays at Fantasyland. I made a note not to tell Audrey the next time I was in Switzerland. Instead, I pointed to its doors.

"There used to be lineups all the way down the street. Old Man Prestel used to send us out to entertain the people waiting sometimes."

"That only happens now when it's one of your movies," Leonie said. "Though there was a real hubbub when *Lawrence of Arabia* opened last year."

"Why do you know all this?" Birdie asked.

Leonie shrugged. "You hear a lot of things when you're compiling the movie listings."

"Leonie wants to be a journalist," Birdie stage-whispered. "But for now, she's confined to the movie section. The question is, did she get the job because of her father's last name or because of her movie-star aunt?" Leonie gave her sister a playful smack on the arm.

"I'd never doubt the cachet of the Davis name." I stared down the street at an invisible line of people waiting to get in to see *The Pink Dress* or *A Kind of Magic*. At the people who wouldn't get the chance to line up for *The Kenmore Arms*—or any other films, for that matter.

"If it needs repairs, I'll fund it." I looked up at the façade one last time.

"Are you going to buy the audience as well?" Leonie asked, turning her back on the theatre. I couldn't buy an audience, I thought. But I could figure out how to get it back.

WE HAD LONG abandoned our sandwiches and were now nursing our sodas, but the conversation flowed steadily from tales of Birdie's recent wedding—which I balked at, my niece was *far* too young to marry, but then I did the math, and realized that at twenty-three, she was older than Missy had been when she tied the knot. It seems my niece had married the up-and-coming, perfectly droll finance man Bill Wilson, who managed all purchases for special events at the Atlantic Hotel. Leonie's desire, meanwhile, to get her byline off the movie listings page and onto the front page at the *Herald*, consumed the nineteen-year-old's time. And in between, I sprinkled in tidbits of my Hollywood hijinks. I wanted them to know me as more than the remote figure on the big screen, to start thinking of me as a very real family member. Hopefully, one they'd eventually call Aunt Melly.

"She hosts dinner parties *all the time*, and brings in chefs from the best restaurants in California to cater them," I recalled of one of Joan Fontaine's legendary dinner parties. "The last one had an all-Russian menu, only pure Russian ingredients. The vodka was so strong I had to pay to replace her rosebushes once I'd sobered up. I had to make another picture with Lang just to afford it."

Birdie nodded knowingly, and smiled her mother's smile. "I've heard she and *her* sister don't get along either."

I smiled back. "They have their differences, sure, but they're both wonderful people. And I won't say a word against Liv. She's one of my oldest girlfriends. So, is there anything else you want to know?"

"How come you and Langdon Hawkes divorced?" Leonie asked.

I nearly did a spit take, laughing at her boldness. Then I swallowed my drink and gave it to her straight: "The only person Langdon Hawkes has ever been in love with is Langdon Hawkes. Six weeks was more than enough time to be in constant competition with his mirror."

Birdie laughed. "One of his songs was in the jukebox at the Atlantic. When Mother heard it, she ordered it removed."

"If it was 'Candlelight Serenade,' I can't say I blame her," I said.

"Maybe she's more of a Sinatra fan," Leonie said.

"Who isn't?" I winked. She winked back at me.

⁓⁓⁓

I LEARNED MORE about my nieces over that quick lunch than I had through any of my conversations over the past two decades with Raymond. The most I'd gotten out of him was that he thought Leonie was playing up her resemblance to me on purpose. He knew she'd been a cub reporter in high school and studied English only so she could one day be a journalist—competition, he'd scoffed, that he wasn't worried about. Leonie didn't strike him as a sob sister; he figured she'd rather camp out on Parliament Hill than underneath the Hollywood sign.

The scoop on Birdie was this: she was a headstrong young woman with strong principles and an even stronger sense of who she was and what she wanted to do with her life. She loved fashion. High fashion.

Couture. Leonie read the classics; Birdie read *Vogue* and *Harper's BAZAAR*. And more than simply admiring the work of fancy French designers, she loved the process of helping people choose what to wear.

In high school, she insisted on an after-school job—though she definitely didn't need the money—and began working in the junior ladies' section at Simpson's, learning everything she could about fits and patterns and how the department head decided on what to buy. She knew exactly what career she wanted. That experience, coupled with a two-year business degree and a summer course in fashion design at the Nova Scotia College of Art and Design, saw her graduate with a job at Mills Brothers as a fashion buyer, where she'd been for just over a year.

"Leonore's got nothing on her sister, though," Raymond had told me over the telephone, recounting Birdie's wedding. She'd gotten married at the end of November, and half the town had been expecting a stunt, but the big day went off without a hitch.

"Birdie suavely wore the Davis name like haute couture. I'm surprised she willingly gave it up. But at least she had her sister with her on her wedding day, eh?"

ON OUR WAY back to the hotel, those darling girls turned to me. "What can you tell us about Mother?" Birdie asked.

"She never talks about The Majestic Sisters," Leonie said. "She makes it seem like a dull period in her life, but that can't be true, can it?"

I smirked, remembering an evening long, long ago. I knew just what story to tell them.

"Kittens, has anyone ever told you about the time your mother came face to face with a lion?"

FIFTH AVENUE GIRL

Starring Ginger Rogers and Walter Connolly

SATURDAY, DECEMBER 9, 1939

O ne thing I want you to know is that I didn't walk into my fate unprepared. All those subscriptions—to *Photoplay*, to *Modern Screen*, to *Screenland*—kept me informed on Hollywood's ever-evolving tastes. Ever since my performance as Snow White, I'd been honing my craft. I bought books on how to be a dramatic actress and pored over them like a certain English professor studied his classics (and whose reaction to finding the scuffed-up 'Victoria, Queen of the United Kingdom' page from his encyclopedia would have surely won him an Oscar). Nothing about what happened next was by accident.

Every dime I'd made since my performance for RKO had been squirrelled away towards my escape fund, as I called it. Finally, in December 1939, it was time to put my plans into action: I was going to Atlanta, to the premiere of *Gone with the Wind*. I was going to get in front of the movers and shakers and waltz into a movie contract. Why go straight to Hollywood, when countless young women had tried and failed at just that? At least this way, I'd get a heck of a story out of it!

I now had over four hundred dollars to my name, and it would be a while—fingers crossed—before I'd starve with those kinds of savings. I was hopeful for immediate stardom, as every girl dreams of, but with my dance background, surely I could find a studio somewhere to teach while I made a name for myself. It wasn't an easy decision to step back from The Majestic Sisters, but it's one I don't regret, even though it cost me Missy.

⁂

I TOOK MY final curtain call on a busy Saturday night. The city was over-crowded, with the war on and Halifax becoming a strategic port, constantly sending soldiers and supplies overseas, but I'd never felt more alone. And still, despite the loneliness, I knew I was going to miss it. All of it. I wanted that night to stretch on forever. In fact, I arrived much earlier than usual—just after lunch—and threw Old Man Prestel off my tracks by telling him I'd been enchanted by the new Ginger Rogers flick and wanted to watch it without Missy nattering on in my ear about whatever last-minute wedding plans she'd dreamt up, or her latest article for brides-to-be in the *Mail*—yes, she and her dear Eddy were now engaged, to no one's surprise. Then I did it all over again for the mid-afternoon and suppertime showings. To this day, *Fifth Avenue Girl* remains one of my favourite movies simply for the memories it evokes.

That last routine? Instead of Fifth Avenue Girls, we were Barrington Street Girls, and we spent the entire act touting all the great businesses up and down the street, reminding everyone to do their Christmas shopping downtown, to spend their hard-earned money so that every penny could go back into the war chest, and to buy war bonds to support the boys overseas. And then...it was over.

"You've been a lovely audience," I crowed. "How about a hand for Majestic Missy?"

Missy smiled at me. She let the applause saturate the auditorium before she told the crowd to applaud me, too: "Majestic Melly never disappoints!"

I felt a twinge of guilt at that. Time would prove her wrong, but I pushed through the sadness. This was our last show together, and what a way to go out. She'd never been better than she'd been that evening.

I trailed Missy to the dressing room and took my time scrubbing off my stage makeup, changing back into my regular dress, and putting on my boots. Missy waited for me.

"Edward's treating me to a late supper at the hotel. Care to join?" she asked, hand on the doorknob.

"Nah, you go on ahead," I said, waving her off. "I'm tuckered."

"You sure?"

"Of course." I smiled, studying the way she looked in the doorway. Elegant and refined. She didn't need The Majestic Sisters any more than I did. She wouldn't want to continue on after marriage anyway, even if she wouldn't admit it out loud. I was just doing what neither of us had had the courage to do. "Tell Eddy I said hello."

She winked and then she was gone. I was well-acquainted with the length of the walk down to the Atlantic, so I sat in silence for a few minutes to ensure she was truly gone, then began cleaning out my half of the dressing room. Emptied the vanity of all my makeup and hair products. My hand lingered on a tube of Missy's orangey-red Tango lipstick, and I slipped it into my pocket: a memento. I tossed one of my near-empty 'Fire Red' lipstick tubes in after it, then threw the rest into the waste bin.

Took my costume jewellery out of our shared jewellery box. Plucked all of my postcards and ticket stubs and photographs off the vanity mirror; I had a photo album at home ready for these trinkets. Grabbed an unopened package of Snow White chocolates from Moirs, likely long past their expiration date. A turquoise matchbook from the Atlantic. Carefully placed a rose, dried and pressed, that had once bloomed in the Public Gardens into the pages of my well-worn copy of *Gone with the Wind*, its spine broken and its pages dog-eared, and stuffed it into my purse.

I tried to memorize the space: the throw rugs we'd bought at Simpson's because we thought they created an atmosphere. The wardrobe filled with the costumes we'd bought—the ones we'd made ourselves, and the ones we'd farmed out to dressmakers once our act began to grow.

Then, with one last glance around the dressing room where my career began, I placed the letters I'd written to Missy and Old Man Prestel against the mirror.

And then I shut off the light and left.

SUNDAY WAS QUIET. The theatre, as usual, was closed, and Missy and I stuck close to home, working on the seating plan for the reception—making sure there were at least three seats between Amy Swaine-Tully and Beatrice Fowler, Eddy's younger sister, don't ask why—and listening to the "Silver-Voiced Tenor" on CHNS.

In between all the theatrics of wedding planning—the splendour of which, as Missy and Eddy said, could only do good things for morale in those early days of an uncertain war—I'd taken a survey of our old Victorian home, wanting to remember every single detail of my life as it had been lived there: the order of the books in Mother's and Daddy's study; which cupboards held which items in the kitchen; how Missy's vanity was arranged and which photographs she kept on her night-stand; the 1939 Majestic Sisters calendar hanging on the wall in the entryway.

Only once I was satisfied that I could draw the floorplans of our house from memory did I cave and go to bed—the last time I would sleep in that creaky old bed with my grandmother's blanket draped over me—but then I couldn't stop tossing and turning. And when I realized sleep was futile, I lay in bed creating a list of everything I'd need to grab in the morning: passport, purse, suitcase, chequebook. I hadn't dared pack that afternoon, couldn't risk Missy finding me, but between Mother and Daddy and their morning classes and Missy no doubt off to breakfast with Eddy, I would have more than enough time to pack tomorrow for my one o'clock bus.

As the dawn light crept into the room, it hit me: if all went according to plan, just after lunch I'd be on a bus to New York City and, from there, Atlanta. I just needed to get to the bus terminal without Missy or my parents noticing.

See, I had the perfect ruse in place: I bought a ticket for a Wagner Tours bus to New York City under the guise of doing some last-minute Christmas shopping. There and back in just over forty-eight hours: more than enough time to be back for Missy's wedding, if anyone asked. And by the time the bus returned to the Lord Nelson terminal,

I'd be on a train to Atlanta. No forwarding address.

Before I could ruminate any further, my bedroom door flung open and Missy burst into my bedroom. "Have you seen my purple shift dress? I want to wear it to lunch with Edward."

"I haven't," I replied, stretching. Liar. It was buried in my sock drawer because it looked better on me anyway.

Undeterred, Missy walked over to the closet and started rooting through. "Well, it's not in my room and it's not in the laundry, so it must be here."

"You dig any deeper and you're going to find your wedding present—don't you want it to be a surprise?"

She straightened. "I hadn't thought of that. I'll rustle something out of one of my suitcases in the meantime." See, she and Eddy, naturally, would be moving into their own house as soon as they returned from their honeymoon (to Moncton, of all places, but then, where else do you honeymoon so close to Christmas and during wartime?), having found a darling house on Young Avenue to start their family.

"That's the sport," I said, stretching and getting out of bed. It was only eight o'clock. "Have you had breakfast?"

"Not yet."

"Whaddaya say, how's about I whip us up something quick and easy?"

"What's the occasion?" she asked, leaning against the doorframe.

"I just feel like cooking," I lied. I hated cooking. Never mastered anything with a skill level higher than scrambled eggs and bacon. Still, while I'll never host a dinner party of Joan Fontaine's calibre, I make do.

"You *never* feel like cooking. And Daddy will murder you if you waste all the eggs and butter. You know how expensive food is now."

"I know, I know," I said, crossing the room and heading down the hall to the kitchen. "But you're moving out next week and I'll be a lonely spinster living all alone with her parents, nobody to gossip with. Nobody to steal clothes or makeup from. Nobody my own age to play with. Just me and two old folks complaining about every sliver of light that escapes the blackout curtains."

"I told you already, we'll make up a room for you in the house," she promised. My stomach twisted. She'd already started decorating what she dubbed "The Melly Room"—outfitted in pinks and silks. Hopefully they'd be able to exchange it all for store credit.

"It won't be the same though, will it?" I asked. At this point, I wasn't sure if I was continuing the ruse or telling the truth. "I adore Eddy, you know that, but once you're married, you'll be his wife first, my sister second."

When had I become so sentimental? She hugged me before I could get too emotional. "Nothing's going to change, Melly. Just my address."

"And your last name," I reminded her.

"And my last name. Goodness, once I'm an official Davis, do you think his mother will let up?" Bitsy Davis, the great neutralizer. Nobody escaped her formidable gaze and forthright scrutiny. She'd sniped and griped about every detail of the wedding from the moment her darling eldest son had proposed, but nobody could figure out why she disliked Missy so. On paper, she and Missy should have been thick as thieves. Rumour has it she's the one who spread that nickname, The Blue Lady, but of course, she'd deny, deny, deny.

"Who cares." I shrugged. "You're going to say 'I do' at the end of the week. What's the worst she could do?"

Then I realized: it wasn't what Bitsy Davis could do in this final week of wedding preparations, it was what *I* could do.

⌒ℓℓ⌒

MISSY AND I were washing and drying the dishes side by side for the last time. Breakfast had dragged on so long, I only had two hours to get to the bus depot, and I still hadn't dressed or packed.

"I think I'll spend a lazy day around the house," I said, trying to nudge her towards the door.

"That sounds like fun," Missy said, wiping her hands with the dish towel. "I'd love to join you, but I have a busy afternoon ahead of me. Edward and I are meeting for lunch to go over house plans, then Amy and I are doing some last-minute shopping for my trousseau. You know how slow she is when she shops; I'll be lucky to make it to the theatre in time!" Time enough to read my note, I hoped. My heart thudded against my chest once more.

"Amy's an old pro at this point, though. She'll make sure you get everything you need!" She was already on her second husband.

I put the last of the dishes away and leaned against the counter. I looked my sister in the eyes, though it killed me to do it, and said, "You're going to be the picture-perfect bride, you know that?"

She blushed. "Oh stop."

"No, I'm being honest. I know I like to rib you about those Wedding Belle articles, but...you're really something special, Missy. I just wanted you to know that." Then I hugged her so tight, I could smell her perfume and the subtle hint of Halo shampoo long after I'd let go.

"The best part is that you'll be there with me, the whole time," she said. "In that va-va-voom red dress I still can't believe I let you buy."

My dress was a deep Christmas red, not unlike Bette Davis's in *Jezebel*. Amy, Beatrice, and our cousins Kitty and Laura would all be draped in pale pink to complement me. "Face it, darling. You can't stuff this"—I gestured to my body, clothed in pale pink cotton pajamas and a white housecoat, the absolute picture of elegance, I'm sure—"into pastels. It doesn't look right."

"You were meant to be bold!" She laughed. "Okay, I should go freshen up and get on my way."

I've never been great at goodbyes. The best moments don't require them. Despite how she would remember that morning, to me, it was heartbreakingly perfect. I was closing a chapter and Missy was starting a new one. We'd both, hopefully, get a happy ending threaded from this heartbreak. Why linger over how we got there?

Missy had already hopped aboard the Belt Line tram by the time I snapped out of it. I ran down to the bathroom, jumped in the bathtub for a record scrubbing, and then darted into the bedroom to get dressed. Once all that was done, I threw open the closet door and yanked out the suitcase from its place on the shelf.

In my haste, I knocked coats off their hangers and rushed to hang them again with shaking fingers. I sat the suitcase on my bed and started stuffing in everything I wanted to take with me. The stack of pre-folded clothes went in first, followed by a few pairs of shoes—plus my tap shoes, ballet slippers, and pointe shoes.

I wanted to leave plenty of room for trinkets, so after the hair brushes and makeup kit were packed, I slid a photo album into the pocket, and then stuffed in everything I'd taken from the Majestic next to it, then slammed the suitcase shut.

Once I was truly sure I had packed everything I'd need, I grabbed the suitcase off the bed and shut the door behind me. No need to look back. From the foyer, I called a Wade Brothers taxi—one last ride for old time's sake. They'd have to get Raymond home without me from now on, the poor dears. Speaking of Raymond, of course I didn't let him in on my plans. I wanted this kept secret, not broadcasted from the top of Citadel Hill!

While I waited, I pinned the navy hat to my head, checked my hair in the mirror, fingered my necklace chain, laced my boots, and put on my coat. Then I pulled two envelopes out of my handbag. The first was addressed to Mother and Daddy, which I placed on the kitchen table. I have to admit, I was less concerned with their opinions. They never understood how acting had totally and completely consumed me, so why bother explain? Besides, they always knew I'd be out of the house someday. This was just an unconventional way to do it. The other letter was addressed to Missy, which I placed on her pillow. I'd already left a brief letter for her at the theatre, but this one explained my feelings a little better, and I figured she'd read it last and know that I never meant to hurt her.

"I'll explain it all someday," I whispered into the empty room. The sound of the taxi's horn rang in the distance. Curtains on Coburg Road.

FIFTH AVENUE GIRL
Starring Ginger Rogers and Walter Connolly

MONDAY, DECEMBER 11, 1939

I'd made it down to the bus station with forty-five minutes to spare, so I doffed my suitcase in the baggage area and headed down to the American Newsstand to grab some magazines and a sandwich. Luckily for me, several movie magazines were available, so I snatched them all up. Seeing Clark Gable as Rhett Butler staring up at me from the cover of *Screenland* assured me I'd made the right decision.

Walking back, I wondered if I'd see anyone I knew. But then I figured they'd all be staying in town for the wedding—besides, there wasn't much anyone could do after we pulled out of the station. Just the same, I kept my head down so nobody could see my face as I picked a seat at the very back, away from everyone else—I didn't want any *It Happened One Night*-style adventures...not on this trip, anyway.

I was probably somewhere around Amherst, totally ensconced in *Photoplay* and the behind-the-scenes antics of Bette Davis and Errol Flynn on the set of *The Private Lives of Elizabeth and Essex*, when someone recognized me. As soon as she realized Majestic Melly was on the bus, she started auditioning for the role of Stock Best Friend.

"What a shock to see *you* here!" she said. She introduced herself as Geraldine. "I was thinking to myself, that looks like Melly Calvert, and here you are!"

"Here I am," I replied, trying in vain to get back to my magazine.

"Don't you have a show tonight?"

Of course I did. "Oh, Missy's more than capable of handling it on her own for one night," I said. We weren't the Dionne quintuplets; we were perfectly capable of performing solo from time to time. Still, I needed to ensure this girl would keep her big mouth shut. "Don't tell her when we get back, but I'm buying her a few last-minute house-warming gifts from New York City."

"Oh, how wonderful!" she gushed. "I'm so excited to see her wedding dress."

"It's one for the ages," I promised. Yards and yards of silk and satin and an even longer veil. This wasn't going to be some country bumpkin wedding; she might as well have been marrying the King of England for all the money Mother and Daddy had sunk into the dress. One has to wonder if they'd funnelled some of the money they had budgeted for my wedding into the pool, because the dress was far more elegant than anything a professor and a teacher's salaries could afford.

It seemed my minimal attention had given Geraldine carte blanche to talk my ear off. She had opinions on everything from fashion and flowers, to Christmas and how she'd never been on a bus trip before, to the war effort, to how she was always careful not to talk to strangers—but don't worry, she'd seen me onstage so many times she felt she knew me. Honestly, she didn't give me a chance to say much of anything, so I let her natter on until she tired herself out. That moment came in St. Stephen, New Brunswick. So awed was she at crossing the border into the United States she remained speechless for the rest of the trip.

Thank my lucky stars my travel partner got off the bus in Boston. For my sanity, anyway. I should've known that Geraldine, with that big mouth, would loosen those lips and sink a ship as soon as she got off the bus. Since it was the middle of the night by the time we pulled into the terminal, she couldn't head straight to the shopping district like she'd planned, oh no. She booked herself a room at the nearest hotel and then sent her mother—who lived a few blocks up the street from Mother and Daddy, it turned out—a telegram all about her escapades.

MOTHER— JUST SAW MAJESTIC MELLY ON BUS
TO NEW YORK CITY STOP HAVING A BALL SEE YOU
IN A FEW DAYS STOP

And of course, Mrs. Bowes, much like her daughter, couldn't keep a secret to save her life. She went straight to Mother and Daddy's door with the telegram just after dawn.

I do wish I could've spent more time in New York City, but I restricted myself to what I could see from the bus window: bustling and bright, even in the middle of the night. When we pulled into the terminal, I hotfooted it to Grand Central Station (imagine!) and booked the next train ticket for Atlanta.

OF COURSE RAYMOND got the scoop on how Missy found out—he always did. And lucky for me, he was one of the few people in Halifax still willing to talk to me after the events of December 1939, so he had no qualms about sharing every juicy detail.

According to Raymond, Missy was none the wiser when she hopped on the tram. She enjoyed a perfectly delicious lunch with her perfectly delicious fiancé, and she fussed over the house plans and furniture they'd ordered for the great room—did it clash with the curtains? Should they consider repainting? Perhaps an ecru instead of grey?— before she went out shopping with that busybody best friend of hers, Amy Swaine-Tully.

It was such a perfect afternoon, by Missy's estimation, that she was whistling as she walked into the theatre that evening. She paused for a chat with Tracy, as always, and nodded at Old Man Prestel as she walked by his office, and then made her way to the dressing room, where her life promptly "fell apart." Raymond's words, not mine.

Old Man Prestel claimed he'd never forget the piercing shriek that rang through the building (luckily the patrons in the auditorium figured it was part of the film). He ran to the dressing room, huffing and puffing, to find half of his star duo wailing on the floor, incoherent and inconsolable. He thought she was dying, truth be told, and Missy wouldn't answer him when he asked if she was all right, only pointed at the vanity, where my note to him was still taped to the mirror.

William, one of the ushers—or as I knew him, Bashful—rushed in to see what all the fuss was about. He told the other 'dwarfs' what he'd seen, and they told the kids at the candy counter, who went to tell Tracy, who went up to the projection booth to see if Mort knew anything, but he was, as usual, stuck in his own world and refused to speculate, so even she'd come to the dressing room—and you knew it was serious if Tracy was willing to put down her paperback to investigate.

Then someone had the bright idea to call Eddy, who, of course, rushed up the hill, never mind that he was hosting a hotel association meeting in the ballroom—he left in the middle of the keynote speech. That did wonders for the gossip mill. By the time he rushed into the dressing room, his future bride had moved to the couch, her audience watching her warily, waiting for the waterworks to start up again. There was talk of calling the police, the navy, the owner of the Chebucto Road Airport, the head of Canadian National Railways, but in the end, they only called Mother and Daddy. There was a war on, after all. My disappearance was only a 'family matter.' The note on the vanity proved there was no foul play.

But then Missy cancelled the show. William put a sign next to the candy counter: *There will be no Majestic Sisters show tonight. We apologize for the inconvenience. Please take this extra time to purchase war bonds to support our boys overseas.* The cub reporter assigned to the Majestic Sisters beat spotted it when he came in for the suppertime show, raced back to CHNS to broadcast the news, and caused a frenzy. We'd *never* totally cancelled the show before: if one was sick, the other went on.

Naturally, the city began to buzz about the reason why, and everyone put on their detective cloaks to examine the evidence. It couldn't be due to Missy, since she'd been seen shopping downtown that afternoon. And my voice had been on the radio that morning—a pre-recorded Red Cross advertisement—so it couldn't be due to me. It wasn't until

Geraldine's telegram arrived the next morning that the scandal began to grow.

Mother and Daddy had some initial goodwill left over for me, but it didn't last.

It's not that you did it, darling, it's how *you did it. We'll always love you and you'll always have a home with us,* they wrote just after Christmas.

But I never saw my parents again. The higher my star rose, the less they wanted to do with me. Then they stopped picking up the telephone, and my letters were returned unopened. They never cooperated with the press team at MGM, who'd reach out every time one of my movies came out, for a feel-good story to place in the fan rags. Journalists who'd hunt them down every so often to question them about raising a movie star were sent away without so much as a pull quote. Hedda called them up after every movie premiere; Sheilah Graham rang the hospital both times Missy gave birth. Eddy had calls screened at the Atlantic before they were patched through to him. My family had set up a wall around me, and eventually I gave up trying to penetrate it.

Eventually I stopped asking Raymond for updates and made up my own stories—how Daddy became department chair of the Faculty of Arts at Dalhousie; how Mother stopped teaching at Sacred Heart and began to volunteer at the library more often, and found her purpose in teaching children to read; how they'd sneak into the Majestic every time one of my movies premiered and quietly sit there with smiles on their faces, thinking to themselves, *That's our daughter and we're proud of her.*

Raymond said he only ever caught them at *Easy Does It*, my first film. To his knowledge, they never saw another. They both died before we ever got a chance to properly reconcile: Daddy first, in 1956; then Mother a few years later, in 1960.

Aside from my family, I felt most remorseful about my estrangement from Old Man Prestel. I'd flown the nest and hadn't had the guts to tell him to his face. Thankfully, I must have conveyed my feelings satisfactorily enough, because he did continue answering my letters, and would even forward me fan mail. In return, I'd send him notes and memorabilia that he could display whenever one of my movies premiered, but we never spoke on the phone, and he turned down a visit to California because he was so busy at the Majestic.

In his first letter to me, dated May 1940, Old Man Prestel thanked me for making that year's infamous Majestic Sisters wall calendar a bestseller. The year was nearly half over and he was on his twelfth reprint. Because after the photo of me sipping cocktails with Clark Gable made the front page of the *Mail-Star* on December 18, 1939, the first run sold out within a day.

FIFTH AVENUE GIRL
Starring Ginger Rogers and Walter Connolly

WEDNESDAY, DECEMBER 13, 1939

It hadn't occurred to me that maybe I wasn't the only person on the planet who'd thought of descending upon Atlanta for the premiere of *Gone with the Wind*. But when I hopped off the train at Peachtree Street, down the main line of that lush Georgia city, and saw the crowds sandwiched on the sidewalks, there was a fear in my stomach I hadn't felt in months.

Looking around, I became convinced that all the hotel rooms had to be booked and the movie tickets were sold out. Of course, I now realized, there *had* to be others like me, here for a taste of stardom, or a glimpse of Clark Gable or Vivien Leigh, enough of us that security would ensure we'd never get where we were going.

"Don't worry about it now," I muttered to myself. "You got here because you're supposed to be here. It'll work out." (A mantra I still repeat to myself like a prayer.)

I grabbed my suitcases, held the handles tight in my hands, and found the nearest porter.

"Where might I find a hotel room?"

He balked. "Lady, you think you're going to find a bed at this hour? This week?" Still, he pointed down the street. "It's long enough," he said, "that you can keep walking until you find something affordable."

I was still walking down Peachtree fifteen minutes later, and as I took in all the opulent buildings I wondered what the porter's definition of *affordable* was. As I fantasized about the inoffensive coffee and offensive cheese on toast I'd treated myself to mere hours ago, I came across a similarly inoffensive-looking motel with a vacancy sign in the window. I didn't take any chances; I stormed into the building as though I were fighting off a hoard of other roomless vacationers.

To my right: a small kitchenette with a few tables set up to create a dining room. To my left: the front desk, where a meek night clerk was focused intently on the crossword puzzle. As I made my way to the counter, he looked up at me, completely disinterested.

"Let me guess," he droned, "you're here for *Gone with the Wind*?"

"What gave it away?" I teased.

He grabbed a key off the wall. Room twelve. "Kitchen opens at six o'clock sharp. We lay out cereals, fruits, and muffins."

"What kind of muffins?" I asked, picking up the key from the counter. I slid him a couple bills; luckily for me, this wasn't the Atlantic. The hotel's one redeeming quality was the price.

"You'll have to ask the missus," he said, turning to write in his ledger.

I grabbed my suitcases and followed the tilt of his head until I was standing in front of the shabby door to the shabby room I'd booked for the night. The fatigue hit me then; the adrenaline that had carried me from Halifax to Boston to New York to here had run out. I opened the door. It brushed against the bed frame, the room so cramped I was practically standing in the middle of it while still in the hallway. I put the suitcase on the floor, dropped my weary body onto the bed, kicked the door shut, and was asleep before my head hit the pillow.

"ANN RUTHERFORD'S ARRIVING today," an elderly woman whispered as I walked into the kitchenette the next morning.

It wasn't six sharp or anywhere close to it, but free breakfast was still well underway.

"Who's she?" the man next to her asked, likely her husband, taking a bite out of what looked like a blueberry muffin.

"I think she plays one of Scarlett's sisters," the woman answered.

"Careen," I piped up, grabbing a muffin of indeterminate fruit from the basket.

"That's right," she said, smiling at me. "Pay attention," she said to the man, rapping her knuckles against the back of his hand. Definitely her husband.

I sat down at the empty table in front of the windows, Peachtree Street already bustling beyond them. Hollywood didn't often come knocking on Georgia's door, and it was clear from the hubbub this would be a premiere for the history books. Atlanta was doing a good job cleaning up and showing off. Up and down the street, wokers were wrapping lampposts in red, white, and blue. I watched as they fluffed each piece of fabric before moving on to the next post. Would Old Man Prestel decorate the Majestic for *Gone with the Wind*? He loved any chance to gussy up that theatre—maybe he'd erect his own Tara plantation in the middle of downtown Halifax.

After a quick bite, I walked up the street to Loew's Grand Theater, where the premiere would be held, to find a replica of Tara's façade covering the building. Above the theatre, an enormous billboard of Vivien Leigh and Clark Gable—as Scarlett O'Hara and Rhett Butler, locked in a passionate embrace—loomed over the entire city block.

I was there to buy a ticket—on the very offhand chance there were still tickets available. Imagine my despair when the ticket seller told me Friday night's premiere was sold out. And so were all screenings until Christmas Eve.

"You wanna see the movie, ma'am, you're going to have to check the want ads. Or get Clark Gable himself to escort you into the theatre," the ticket seller said, laughing at the scowl on my face, "'cause you ain't getting a ticket from me.'"

My charm has since worked on fickler men than Clark Gable, but a young Melly would have choked before daring to flirt with Carole Lombard's husband. So, I picked up a newspaper and checked the want ads. Sure enough, there were plenty of tickets for sale, so long as I wanted to pay up to fifty dollars for an orchestra seat. But of course

I did! This is what my scrimping was for. I rang up the number and bought the ticket. Everything was going according to plan.

Ann Rutherford descended upon Atlanta like a queen on campaign—from the same train station I'd departed from not even twelve hours before, no less—and headed straight to the Georgian Terrace hotel. It was the perfect location, directly across the street from Loew's. All the stars would be staying there. I imagined them making publicity appearances there before the movie and attending a post-premiere cocktail party afterwards. The only question was, how would I get inside on Friday night?

I was cramped in at the counter of a nondescript diner, packed like sardines with a group of young women, listening to the radio announcer describe with elation how the Eastern Air Lines flight carrying the film's stars had just landed at Candler Field on the outskirts of town: *"Pure pandemonium as the mayor of Atlanta makes his way to the platform to present bouquets to Miss Leigh and Miss de Havilland!"* he bellowed. *"Miss Leigh is wearing a wide-brimmed hat with a heavy fur coat. Behind her, Miss de Havilland is wearing a slightly smaller hat with a similarly heavy coat."*

"You just wait till Clark Gable lands tomorrow. He's so handsome," a teenage girl swooned next to me, knocking my elbow clear off the counter. She was lucky she didn't spill my coffee.

I TRIED TO ignore the date the next day—Friday; the night of the premiere. But also Missy's wedding day, and naturally, my first thought was of her, hoping she'd found a way to move past my absence and celebrate anyway. Any other bride might have postponed their wedding once their sister ran off, but not Missy Calvert. As I'd later discover, Missy made sure life went on without me and replaced me with Beatrice Fowler, her future sister-in-law, as maid of honour. Forbid anyone from mentioning me in the 'Vows' article Cecily Bernard wrote up in the *Mail-Star*.

I'd receive a scathing letter through the press department at MGM a few months later. According to Amy Swaine-Tully, Missy would never forgive me and, in fact, she'd been happier without me there. Who'd want such a hateful sister ruining the festivities, Amy wondered. I didn't dwell on anything that movie-of-the-week–looking busybody had to say.

That evening, outside the theatre, I joined the crowds and watched as Vivien Leigh arrived on Laurence Olivier's arm, draped in a heavy fur coat that concealed a gold lamé dress. Olivia de Havilland, dressed in black, also managed to cut a sleek figure on the red carpet. And you'd have thought the world was going to end if you based it on the shrieks and screams when the crowds caught a glimpse of the King of Hollywood, Clark Gable, live and in person.

Was I one of them? Well, darlings, of course I was! I'd been swooning over Clark Gable long before I'd been a Majestic Sister, and I'd swoon over him for the rest of my life. But golly, those crowds sounded like they were greeting the President of the United States! Not even King George VI and Queen Elizabeth had gotten that reaction when they visited Halifax that past summer.

Gable was all smiles as he walked arm in arm with Carole Lombard, who wore a blush satin cape dress. She was joie de vivre personified, happy to be on hubby's arm, and stoked the crowd's delight. I took note of their poses, the way they smiled, how they turned this way and that to ensure everyone in the crowd got a glimpse of them. Better I learned then, I figured, so I wouldn't need exhaustive red carpet training when I had my own movie contract.

But time was running out before the movie began, so I couldn't stargaze as long as I wanted to. The last thing I saw before I walked into the theatre was Margaret Mitchell, author of *Gone with the Wind*, standing in front of a sea of microphones, swallowed up by the blinding flashes from the hundreds of cameras directed at her.

I'd spent my entire professional career listening to the hum of anticipation before a film began; I knew what this evening meant, but this was the biggest movie of all time and nothing could quite prepare me for it. The mix of expensive floral perfumes and buttered popcorn floated in the air around this privileged bunch of spectators as the whispered conversations began: where were the stars? When would they join us? This was the night of nights and I wanted to remember *everything*. Soon enough, they all strolled in: Vivien and Olivia and Clark. Once they were settled, the lights dimmed, the curtains opened, and finally...the film began.

For nearly four hours, I sat riveted in my seat. I smirked at Scarlett O'Hara's scheming, swooned over Rhett Butler, and shed tears over Melly Wilkes's untimely death. I laughed and cried, and could hardly believe the movie was over, but with Rhett's pronouncement, "Frankly, my dear, I don't give a damn," and Scarlett's vow to follow him as the scene faded out, I couldn't help but join in the thunderous applause.

From the centre of the theatre, Vivien Leigh and Clark Gable waved to the crowd. Behind them, David O. Selznick, the film's embattled producer, looked relieved. His gamble of a film had paid off, and if Atlanta's reaction was anything to go on, the rest of the world would follow suit. We gave them a standing ovation that lasted long after the stars had left the theatre for the press party across the street.

Now, my real work began.

I rushed from my seat and found cover in a thicket of newspapermen—and to really sell it as we made our way inside, I pulled out my aqua Atlantic Hotel fountain pen and matching notepad, as though I were a sob sister primed to get a soundbite from Olivia de Havilland. I couldn't believe it worked! How'd you like that? If only the rest of the evening would go as smoothly...

I followed the reporters into the ballroom and couldn't believe my eyes: I was, at long last, in the midst of Hollywood royalty! The King of Hollywood was at the bar. Olivia de Havilland was chatting with someone over by the window. Vivien Leigh and Laurence Olivier were keeping to themselves, but she was happy to soak up the praise of every person who stopped by to congratulate her. If I wanted to be a star someday soon, I needed to figure out how to work myself into the conversation. I figured Clark Gable himself would be the easiest way to do it.

Only nobody would let me get close to the man. No matter how many times I jabbed my pen into the backs of the newspapermen around me, they wouldn't let me into their scrum. Honestly, I'd have a better shot at breaking into a bank, but this was the King of Hollywood, after all. He'd gamely answered question after question—full of quips for the movie mags and the morning rags—sipping at a waning whiskey, but now his glass was getting empty. Suddenly, I knew what I had to do: I had to make him a drink. If I could make him a drink, I could slide it in front of him and get his attention. He'd have to answer my questions then! How hard could it be to bartend?

I'd find out. Even the best laid last-minute plans have setbacks.

The Fiery Melly tipped, thanks to my shaking hands, and splashed all over Clark Gable's sleeve. Forget Hollywood's newest It Girl, I'd forever be the gal who ruined Clark Gable's tuxedo on the biggest night of his life.

He lifted his arm and reached for a napkin, while I attempted to sop up as much of the drink as I could. "I'm *so* sorry, Mr. Gable. That's not how I wanted this to happen."

"Oh yeah?" he asked. "How did you want this to go, then?"

I blew out a breath. All those times I wanted to swoon seeing him on a big screen and now here I was standing in front of him, gazing directly into those eyes? My knees were weak. But I couldn't waste this opportunity. "I wanted to offer you a Fiery Melly, tell you how much I admire you and your wife, and ask you for tips on how to make it in Hollywood."

"You could've ordered one from *that* side of the bar," the bartender grumbled behind me. "Seriously, kid, you can't be back here."

"It's fine," Gable intervened. "She's with me. You should try one of these, it dries deliciously."

"I don't take suggestions from dames who like to bluster."

"That's a fine way to talk to Clark Gable," I said.

I watched as Clark raised one of those famous eyebrows at the bartender, who'd been ready to serve another insult my way. Instead, he glared over at me and said, "You've got five minutes before I boot you outta here."

"Let's not waste time," Gable said, turning back to me. "Start with the most interesting thing you just said. What on Earth is a Fiery Melly?"

I couldn't tell him what the drink was (two parts rum, one part

Coke, a splash of grenadine and a dash of orange juice) without also telling him about The Majestic Sisters, so I tried to quell my nerves as I told him all about our escapades over the past three years. "I've done everything I can do back in Halifax," I said, nearly breathless, "now it's time to try it somewhere else."

"And that's Hollywood, eh?" he asked.

I nodded. "Got any advice?"

"Make yourself stand out," he said. "And don't pour any drinks on unsuspecting movie stars. They might not stick around long enough to find out who's behind the hooch."

"I'll keep that in mind."

He laughed, then looked me over. "You any good?"

I shrugged. "Good enough to share top billing with my sister, but she doesn't have the acting bug like I do."

He pulled a pen out of his pocket and wrote down a man's name on a cocktail napkin and slid it over to me. "Talent's fine, looks are better, but you'll need *another* gimmick to get you noticed. This should at least get you in the door."

I glanced down at it quickly: *Give her a chance. — Clark.*

"This'll work?" I asked, placing the napkin into my clutch.

He shrugged. "Might. Might not. Either way, it's a hell of a story."

"Who's telling stories?" a beautiful voice trilled from behind him. I looked up and came face to face with Hollywood's greatest comedienne, Carole Lombard. Her teasing smile was set in deep red lipstick.

"Story time's over, but this one—"

"Melly Calvert," I interrupted and held out my hand. I needed Carole Lombard to know my name. Her screwy persona was an inspiration to me when we did some of our daffier routines at the Majestic.

"—was about to pour us some Fiery Mellys. Two please, Miss Calvert," he said. Carole took the seat next to him, her honey curls bouncing around the collar of her gown.

"Is that what this is?" she asked, dragging her finger through a pool of alcohol I'd missed earlier.

And suddenly, the ice was broken and we were all talking like old friends. They even cleared a space for me between them, because the bartender made good on his eviction notice exactly five minutes later. That friendliness and familiarity truly helped me, because no sooner had I sat down than I heard the flashbulbs going off around us. I was too enthralled in the conversation to pay attention to anything else.

"They tried to get me to sneak in through the back of the theatre earlier. Something about security," Clark told me while he waited for the bartender to, reluctantly, pour him another Fiery Melly. "I told them, 'They begged me to come. The people want to see me. I don't want to go ducking in back doors.'"

"Of course you don't. It would be an insult to everyone who lined up out in the streets if they couldn't see you," Carole agreed. "And can you imagine the torrent of bad press if that had happened? Selznick would've had fun spinning that tale."

"Oh, the perils of royalty," I teased, sipping at the whiskey Clark had ordered for me. I've never developed a taste for it, but I was more than happy to oblige that evening. I didn't notice the camera's flash, but my face was wreathed in smiles all the same.

This was the shot that would grace the front page of Monday morning's newspaper back home. Because when you have two famous sisters, one marrying a prominent businessman and the other hobnobbing with stars at a Hollywood movie premiere, who do you put on the cover? The photo editors were stupefied when they spotted me on the Canadian Press photo desk, and, well, what with me missing and suddenly turning up, they ran with my picture instead: *Majestic Melly Calvert is* GONE WITH THE WIND *as she lands in Atlanta — FULL DETAILS, CONTINUED ON PAGE 3*. But in the top left-hand corner, relegated to one of the teaser headlines: *A Majestic Wedding hits the Atlantic — FULL DETAILS, SOCIETY SECTION, PAGE 9*.

I'd scooped her once again. Only this time I knew she'd never forgive me.

VOWS — SOCIETY NEWS

A Majestic Wedding for Halifax's Darling Daughter

By Cecily Bernard

December 18, 1939

*T*he most *"majestic"* wedding since Halifax's inception took place on Friday morning as *"Majestic Missy"* Calvert married fiancé and Atlantic Hotel owner Edward Davis Jr., at St. Paul's Anglican Church.

The bride—renowned as much for her stage work as for her volunteer work with the Canadian Red Cross and the Halifax Club of Business and Professional Women—wore a beautiful silk sheath wedding gown, her mother's veil anchored by a crown of roses in her flaxen hair.

"To see them together is to believe in soulmates," Amy Swaine-Tully, bridesmaid and long-time friend of the bride, told me a few days before the wedding. *"They've been in love from the moment they met."*

Their romance has covered ample column inches since their courtship began in October 1937, and reached a fever pitch upon their engagement last New Year's Eve. A December wedding date was always the plan for Missy, who said this is her favourite time of year because *"everyone is in bright spirits."*

Poinsettias dotted the pews, and candles lit up the altar behind the couple as they exchanged vows.

But despite the gaiety, one couldn't help but notice the absence of the bride's vivacious sister, *"Majestic Melly"* Calvert, who disappeared from this city just days ago. Despite a reported sighting in New York City, Melly has not made contact with her family. Both the Calverts and the Davises are keeping their silence about her disappearance, and The Halifax Mail understands that foul play is not suspected, nor have the police been instructed to investigate.

Melly had been set to star as her sister's maid of honour. One imagines that the startling scarlet evening gown worn by last-minute stand-in Beatrice Fowler (the groom's sister) would have looked amazing on her, though Mrs. Fowler was an admirable replacement.

Missy's bridal party was rounded out with Swaine-Tully and maternal cousins Katherine "Kitty" Williams and Laura Williams as bridesmaids. Edward's best man was his brother, James Davis; his groomsmen were brother Jonathan, and maternal cousins Albert and Arthur Wamboldt.

A glittering reception was hosted by the Atlantic Hotel, where guests feasted on lobster bisque and roasted garlic bread prepared in the Stargazers' Lounge. The five-tiered rose cake was baked and decorated by Alain Lefebvre, pastry chef at the Atlantic. The party carried on until well into the night, culminating with the newlyweds departing for their honeymoon in Moncton.

"We'll take a longer trip sometime in the future, but for now we're just eager to settle into married life and start our family," Missy said.

The couple has purchased a house on Halifax's affluent Young Avenue, and Mrs. Davis says she's looking forward to decorating it when they return.

Should you wish to congratulate the newlyweds, they encourage you to make a donation to the Canadian Red Cross or to buy war bonds in lieu of cards.

Congratulations to Mr. and Mrs. Edward Davis Jr.!

CHARADE
Starring Audrey Hepburn and Cary Grant

MONDAY, DECEMBER 23, 1963

"**I** can't believe I'm sitting on the biggest scoop this city's seen since... well, since you left the first time, and someone else is going to get to write the story," Leonie lamented as we stepped back onto the snowy sidewalk.

Birdie had already departed after my story about Linger, rushing back to the hotel to receive the delivery from Mills Brothers—official outfitter of the Davis women that evening.

"Darling, if you break this story, Raymond will send his goons after you."

She waved me off. "Nobody's afraid of Raymond Swaine anymore."

We strolled back to the hotel, quick friends and quicker confidants. She'd peppered me with questions about her mother the entire way back. And I still couldn't give her the answers she wanted.

"I wish I knew what to tell you, kitten. My first instinct was to rush back here when I heard about the theatre. I'd *love* to talk to your mother and explain everything, but there's a lot of hurt there that won't go away overnight."

"It still doesn't make sense to me," she said. "You just, what, decide you're leaving? The week of her wedding?"

"It wasn't a snap decision, trust me."

"Were you in love with Daddy?"

"No, kitten. I promise you that."

She squinted at me. "I'll figure it out eventually."

"Good luck. People have been trying to figure out what happened for twenty-five years and nobody's gotten it right yet."

We paused at the intersection just before the hotel. "Can't you give me a hint?"

I watched the stoplight. "Have you ever wanted something so badly you'd do anything to achieve it?"

She locked eyes with me and I watched as her hazel eyes welled with tears. "I'd do anything to see my byline in the newspaper."

I reached out and squeezed her arm. "Then you have to fight for it."

"I know it's silly," she said. "Aside from school papers and a piece here and there for the *Dalhousie Gazette*, I haven't written anything of substance. I compile the movie listings. Do you know how easy that is? They don't even really *need* me to do it. My job could be made perfectly redundant if the theatre owners simply called into the *Herald* office once a week and told the entertainment editor what movies are coming next."

"We all have to start somewhere. You think I got my big break right away? Kitten, I had Clark Gable vouching for me and it still took me months to book a gig."

"It just feels like I'm spinning my wheels. I have a few years left at school, but what's waiting for me? They're never going to let me write about politics or international relations. I'm going to languish on the society pages writing stories about Mother's friends."

"How about the crime beat? One of Amy Swaine-Tully's ex-husbands *must* have met a mysterious end," I muttered.

"You're not funny, Aunt Melly." My heart thumped out an Eleanor Powell–worthy tap routine at hearing her call me that for the first time.

"Well, darling, you just need to search for a story. A story that'll land you your big break."

"Like what?" she asked. And the defeated look on her face—one I recognized from staring back at my own face in the mirror in those early Hollywood days—made me open my mouth and say it.

"How often does a movie star show up to town?"

"It never happens," she said. "You're the only..." she trailed off, her eyes widening.

I nodded. "Interview me. I'm perfectly willing to help you out. Surely that'd land you the front page of the entertainment section at the very least." I hadn't willingly sat for an interview since Sinatra refused to do any advance press for our two films back in 1960. But for Leonie, I'd make an exception.

"Aunt Melly, it'd be front page news, period!"

"Well, what are you waiting for? Go pitch it!" Bless her, but she was the sweetest little thing, and I was prepared to be her most vocal cheerleader. "Just let me know when you want to sit down."

"You know, I might have to ask some probing questions. Questions like...what really made you leave all those years ago?"

I laughed. "Word to the wise: open with the easy questions. I eat reporters like you for lunch."

"Not this one." She smirked.

And then, straight out of one of those bucolic holiday films, it began to gently snow. It felt as magical as it always looked on screen: here I was, the plucky heroine returned home to her family just in time for Christmas. You could almost hear the orchestral swell of a cheerful carol begin to play in the distance. There'd been so much heartache the last time I was here. Who knew being back in Halifax would feel this good?

Leonie smiled, taking my hand. "Thank you for listening to me."

"I know what it feels like when all you want is to be heard. You find me anytime, kitten. I'm always here to listen."

She squeezed my hand. "Mother will kill me for this," she began, "but...do you want to come to the Christmas party as my guest?"

I pondered it for a minute, but then figured, why not? Perhaps a surprise attack would be the best way to approach Missy after all this time. Maybe the snow was a good omen. "Kitten, I'd be delighted."

I WAS IN the middle of doing my makeup—trying to avoid looking like Bette Davis in *Whatever Happened to Baby Jane?*—when a timid knock came at my door. "It's open," I hollered, and then there was Leonie in her darling deep red chiffon cocktail dress.

"Well, Sandra Dee has nothing on you," I said.

She blushed. "Just wait until you see Birdie. I think I got the castoffs."

"You look stunning and you know it. But enough about that." I turned back to the mirror. "How did you make out at the paper?"

She smiled. "Very well. Turns out that's the kind of story they're very keen on."

"Who'd've thunk it?"

"They'll put it on the front page next week, if we can arrange it in time."

"Let's get through this evening first, eh?"

I hated press interviews—and show me one great actress who doesn't—but for Leonie I'd do it. I'd sit down and froth at the mouth about being a movie star and The Majestic Sisters and how much I'd missed Halifax and how we needed to save the theatre; I wouldn't be short or rude or counting down the minutes to say "I think you have everything you need?" or "Oh Hedda, the way you go on...."

We were going over a few basic questions in the elevator, but once the doors opened to the lobby and we could see the bustling crowds in their finest outfits, Leonie clammed up. Nervous at the attention, or perhaps nervous to be standing next to me?

I hooked my arm around her waist and together we walked towards the enormous ballroom—its décor updated but still magnificently golden after all this time.

"Own it, darling. You're going to be a star soon enough. Savour this moment."

She shook her head. "No, Aunt Melly. All eyes will be on *you* once they realize who they're staring at."

As we walked into the ballroom, I removed my ice-blue cape and handed it to one of the concierges. My matching blue brocade evening gown featured a beautiful overskirt that flowed behind me—Yves Saint Laurent had done it again.

In every corner sat a gigantic Christmas tree decorated in a different colour scheme: red, gold, and silver; blues and purples. The walls were wreathed with garlands, and pillar candles were placed on every table to lend an intimate atmosphere to the cavernous ballroom. If not for the Christmas decor, it was almost like waltzing back into the '30s. The place was still as opulent as ever, and it was all thanks to Missy.

Speaking of my darling sister, she was currently chatting with the bandleader, Don Warner, while his swinging orchestra played jazzy Christmas carols behind them. They looked busy. No doubt Missy was going over the song selection to make sure all the standards would be included.

I decided to wait.

Leonie pointed out a group of women gathered around one of the tall tables, eggnog in their glasses. "Did you ever meet Daddy's siblings? That's Aunt Beatty, Uncle Philip, and their daughters. They're a few years older than me. And Uncle Jonathan and Aunt Sarah, and Uncle James and Aunt Joan. Their kids are probably running around here."

I'd met Eddy's siblings, of course. Beatrice was the only one who wasn't a total bore. "I think Poppy was still a newborn when we met your father. I don't remember Sylvie, I'm afraid."

"She's a real snob." Leonie rolled her eyes. "Don't worry about her. Poppy's nice, though a bit subdued since Nana Bitsy died last year. Nobody knew they were that close."

I remembered Bitsy Davis and her gimlet eye fondly. Whenever I saw her at the Atlantic or another fine-dining establishment—and never, under any circumstances, at the Majestic Theatre—she looked meticulous and vital. She couldn't have been that old, either.

Before we could go over and greet the Fowlers, Birdie and Bill made a beeline over to us. Oh, we'd spotted them holding court in the centre of the ballroom as soon as we walked in but had stayed away at Leonie's suggestion. "You don't want to approach Bill when he's in the middle of an oration," she'd said. "The man knows everyone and everything, and if he doesn't, just give him an hour and he's an expert."

"He sounds..." I searched for the word.

"Boring," Leonie said. From her tone, I knew there was no arguing with her. "He's the human equivalent of watching beige paint dry."

"So why did Birdie marry him?"

"I have a guess, but this isn't the appropriate venue for it...besides, I think he's the one who ended up with the catch."

"It's uncanny how much she reminds me of your mother."

"She's always been a miniature of Mama," Leonie whispered back. "But don't let her hear you say it."

A waiter walked by with a tray of champagne flutes just as Birdie and Bill arrived, and we took the opportunity to grab four glasses before he shuffled past us. "Cheers, kittens," I said, holding up my glass. We all clinked and drank to new familial relationships.

"Cheers, Aunt Melly," Birdie said. "You look amazing!"

"And a little out of place, if I'm being honest. It's so unexpected to see you here, Ms. Calvert," Bill said, leaning towards me like he was riveted to the spot, and to the conversation. Something he'd no doubt learned from Toastmasters or the like. He looked like his whole life had been leading to this moment, when Melly Calvert imparted some great wisdom on him.

"Nothing wrong with coming home every once in a while, is there?" I asked, reaching out to pinch his cheek. "Now, how did you come to work at the Atlantic?"

"I like crunching numbers and hosting big events. This place checked off both of those boxes, so I accepted the job. Plus, the future of Nova Scotia is tourism-based, and it only made sense to hop on the bandwagon before it got full."

"Smart," I said. Then, to Birdie, "And with you as a fashion buyer, why, you'll be the flag-wavers for the future of Halifax." She beamed at me.

"And our little journalist over here will be too busy uncovering scandals and stories to stay in one place too long," I said, throwing my arm around Leonie's shoulder. "I almost want to snatch her up as my publicist, but something tells me she'd say no."

She laughed. "I want to *break* the news, not make it."

"You want a scoop now? I have some gossip about Troy Donahue that'd curl your hair." I let her ruminate while I sipped my champagne.

"If Mama ever heard us gossiping like this, she'd have a fit," Leonie said.

"What your mother doesn't hear can't hurt you." I looked around the room and couldn't spot her. "I think I'd like to switch to eggnog now." I might not have been in Palm Springs, but I still wanted to raise a glass for posterity's sake. I excused myself and left the girls to chat with Bill.

I'd only just grabbed a glass when I felt a hand on my arm, clutching me like Joan Crawford with her Oscar. The fingers dug into my skin and turned me around.

I could never forget those frosty blue eyes. That gorgeous mane of silken hair. For there she was, my dear sister, staring at me like the evil queen in a fairy tale.

Majestic Missy Davis.

CHARADE
Starring Audrey Hepburn and Cary Grant

MONDAY, DECEMBER 23, 1963

I raised a glass to toast my sister. "Merry Christmas, darling."

I watched her eyes flit down to my dress and back up to my face, memorizing it for the lost relic it was.

"I thought the photographer must have been joking when he asked me to come pose with Majestic Melly, yet here you are," Missy said, with a perfectly serene smile. Ever cool and collected. If the crowd was expecting a showdown, by golly, Missy wasn't going to give it to them.

"I'm here to save the Majestic, but I wouldn't turn down a photo opportunity if it's going to help our cause," I said, taking a sip of my drink. Bad luck not to, after a toast.

"This doesn't look like a theatre to me," she said, ignoring the second half.

"I heard the bellboys talking about the party when I checked in this afternoon," I lied. I didn't want her to set her glare upon little Leonie. Who knew I'd develop such auntly feelings so quickly?

"You've been here since this afternoon?" Her painted smile was slipping.

I nodded. Polished off my drink in the time it took her to accept that I was truly here in front of her.

"Why didn't you come and find me?"

"I didn't want to bother you."

"So, you thought ambushing me in the middle of my party was a better idea?"

"An ambush? Who do I look like, General Pershing? Trust me, Missy, the last thing I want is for *this* to wind up on the front page." Or in Hedda's New Year's Eve round-up.

The room around us had gone quiet—no doubt waiting for the catfight they all figured would happen once we saw each other again. I wouldn't give them the satisfaction, not that there was any anger on my side. If Missy wanted to claw my eyes out...well, I had a killer insurance policy.

Suddenly Eddy was standing next to her. Golly, looking at him you wouldn't think any time had passed. Sure, there were faint laugh lines framing his eyes and mouth, but he was still just as handsome as he'd been the last time I saw him. He wrapped his arm around his wife's shoulders and asked, "Is everything okay here?" It didn't escape my notice that he'd yet to look at me. Eyes only for Missy, now and forever.

"I'm fine," Missy said, daintily patting his arm, "but ask your sister-in-law how she managed to sneak in this afternoon."

Only then did he glance over at me. The shock on his face at seeing me again...I'll never forget it. "Melly," he breathed, "what are...how did... what brings you to town?"

This man has hosted everyone from Queen Elizabeth II and the Duke of Edinburgh to the King of Norway, President and Mamie Eisenhower, the Chancellor of West Germany, and every single Canadian Prime Minister since William Lyon Mackenzie King, but around little ole me he was tongue-tied.

"You're looking well, Eddy dear," I said. "I'm in town to save the Majestic Theatre. The Atlantic looks *great*, by the way."

They shared a glance. "I'm in the Imperial Suite," I said. "The view is splendid."

Before we could carry on this bit of homecoming, Birdie and Leonie joined the congregation.

"Please hear her out, Mama. She means no harm," Leonie said.

"You've met?" Missy turned to her daughters as though they'd confessed to helping the Soviets.

"Yes, I saw her in the elevator earlier," Leonie confessed. "We snuck her out of the hotel to avoid a confrontation."

"Has she told you—"

"No, she refuses to talk about it."

"But she's forthcoming on all the Hollywood gossip," Birdie chimed in.

"Bridget," Eddy said in warning.

Missy stared at her. "I can assure you that I am not interested in the goings-on of *Hollywood celebrities.*" She hissed those last two words with an icy glare directed at me.

Birdie looked over at me and shrugged in apology. She was trying to cushion the blow, but how could she? There was too much hurt there to sweep under the rug.

"I'm not interested in making a scene," I promised. "I came to town to help save the theatre. Once your party's over, we should talk. I have a few ideas."

"*Now* you're interested in saving it?" Missy asked. "You had no problem running off all those years ago, leaving Old Man Prestel—and *me*—in the lurch, but now you want to swoop in and play heroine?"

"It's not like that," I said. "If you'll just let me—"

"No." She held up a hand. "Not here."

Missy started to walk away, and we all watched her turn back to face me before she got too far; she didn't want her voice to carry, though all eyes were on us: "Silly me, thinking you might *finally* be back for me. I never was that important to you, was I? Finish your drink and leave. And don't you *dare* talk about me to anyone on your way out."

Eddy followed her, and soon Birdie went off to find Bill. Leonie stayed with me and we turned to order two more glasses of eggnog, our moods decidedly un-festive.

～ele～

AN HOUR OR so later, I was still working on my drink, albeit with a larger audience surrounding me, and they all wanted one thing: Hollywood gossip. I wanted to talk about the Majestic.

"How long are you in town for, Melly?" someone asked. I think he was a restaurateur downtown. He'd mentioned catering Birdie's wedding breakfast.

"Through the new year at least," I replied. "I'm here to square away a few last-minute details with Old Man Prestel. A toast to his longevity!"

As the crowd roared around me, I couldn't help but wonder: did nobody care that his theatre was shutting down? How could they all stand around toasting me while neglecting the very place that made me?

"You know, we used to go to the Majestic at least once a week just to see you," said a man by the name of Dr. Chambers. I'd never seen him before in my life. "Never got the chance to meet you then, too scared to approach you, I guess, but look at me now!"

"Indeed!" I said, placing my empty glass on the counter. "You know, it's a shame that the theatre's closing—"

"So tell me, what's Kim Novak like?"

"I'd rather talk about the Majestic, if it's all the same to you."

"That old eyesore? Who needs it!"

It must have been telegraphed on my face that I wanted to slug him, because no sooner had the words escaped his mouth than Birdie flitted over to my side, ready to diffuse the tension.

"I'm going to steal my aunt, Dr. Chambers, if you don't mind." She hooked her arm around me like a vaudevillian stage manager hauling me off stage.

"Thanks, kitten. Sorry if I caused a scene."

"Are you kidding?" she shouted. "This is the liveliest shindig Mother's thrown in years!"

I wasn't so sure Missy would love that pronouncement.

We snuck over to the seats in front of the bay windows—no longer with that envious harbourfront view, sadly; why did we always have to tear down beautiful buildings or hide natural wonders behind concrete views?—with a plate of sweets we'd snagged from one of the chefs. I tore into those little confections like they were the script of a George Stevens picture.

"This dress is getting on my last nerve," Birdie said, fiddling with her heavy emerald skirt—which was, bless her, sewn with ostrich feathers. "It wasn't meant for sitting. And I swear, if one more feather goes rogue, Mother's going to have my head."

"Kitten, you look like you wandered off the set of *Top Hat*," I said, helping her with the dress. She flopped down next to me, anything but graceful, but I smiled just the same at her uncouth display.

"This is the last time I swipe something from a buying trip. What was I thinking?"

"That dress is perfectly glamorous," I said, offering her a piece of brie. "You're the only one in this room who could wear it and not look totally ridiculous."

"Well, it was the toast of Paris, they told me. Bill just about had a heart attack when he saw the price tag. I managed to calm him down a little bit when I told him about my discount, but not by much."

"You just have to train him. Fashion is a necessity, not a luxury."

"I'd die to see your closet." I'd love to show her my closet. The free designer pieces—hell, the free department store ready-to-wear pieces—would have her heart aflutter. And wait until I told her I'd kept every gown I'd ever worn to the Oscars—at this point, I had decades of relics in storage.

"Someday, my dear. I have two walk-in closets at my house in Palm Springs filled with clothes," I offered. "I redecorated the spare once Lang moved out."

"Why are you making another movie with him, Aunt Melly?" she asked. "He's a square now. And I thought you hated him."

"I do hate him. And he was a square then, too."

"So?"

"It's complicated. And I don't mean that in a way to suggest you might find yourself with a crooner uncle any time soon."

"Again, you mean?"

"Yes, again."

"Well, next time I wouldn't mind an Uncle Rock, if you catch my drift."

"You know, your mother and I used to do fashion shows for Mills Brothers." I was eager to change the subject, admiring her gown anew.

"Really?" I gathered from the wistful look on her face that Missy hadn't told her daughters much about her majestic past. "I wish I could've known her then, you know? There's a whole part of herself that she keeps locked up."

I squeezed Birdie's arm. "Your mother's always had trouble opening up. I hope I can help with that while I'm here." I caught a glimpse of Missy across the room, scowling in our direction. "Although probably not tonight, huh?"

Birdie looked over at her mother and sighed. "Whatever it is, it's in the past, right?"

I nodded. "On my life."

"Well, for all our sakes, I hope you get the chance to clear the air."

"Me too, kitten. Now, remind me where the powder room is?"

"Down the hall and to the left. If you pass the front desk, you've gone too far."

"Roger that," I said, grabbing my handbag.

I'd barely had time to pull up a seat and reapply my lipstick—I'd been wearing Revlon's Jungle Peach exclusively since it had been introduced earlier in the year—when the door crashed open and, in an uncharacteristic display of public emotion, Majestic Missy stood in the doorway.

Luckily, I was so skilled at applying makeup I didn't need the mirror. I didn't miss a beat as I turned my head to her. "Great party, Sissy."

"You've had your fun, but I'd appreciate it if you'd leave now." She held the door open as if she could usher me out of it.

"The party, the hotel, or the city?"

"All three, preferably. Go back to your California mansion and forget about us. If you're so concerned about the theatre, write Old Man Prestel a cheque and be done with it."

"California mansion?" I bristled. "Missy, do you even read the newspapers? I'm all alone in a three-bedroom cottage in Palm Springs. By all accounts, you're the one with the palatial home life."

Missy rolled her eyes. "You *are* something, you know? You waltz into my party uninvited, abscond with my daughters, and you still haven't apologized for anything. Although why I've been expecting it, I couldn't say. Why would *my* feelings matter?"

"I do apologize, Missy. I'm sorrier than I can say, but if you let me explain a few things first..." I'd rehearsed this moment thousands of times, but now that I was finally in the moment, I couldn't seem to get the words out.

Missy stormed out of the powder room and I followed her. Just outside the door, Birdie and Leonie hovered like vultures waiting to swoop in. Their father was down the hall, standing at the ballroom entrance like a bouncer, keeping the guests from stumbling upon the simmering Calvert Family drama. This was just what Raymond wanted, and goddammit, Eddy wasn't going to let him get it.

"Have you enjoyed meeting your *aunt*?" Missy stared at each child, piercing them with her glare. They stared at each other for the longest moment, and I wondered if they would toe the line or if they'd be brave enough to admit they actually liked me.

"Is she really that awful?" Leonie asked. "She's quite fascinating."

"That's right, Mama. We've had fun getting to know her. She wanted to come and you know as well as we do that every guest gets an invite," Birdie added. Two new members of the fan club.

"*You* invited her?" Missy rounded on them.

"You've raised good girls, Sissy. Don't take this out on them." I stood behind her now.

"I don't know why you think I'd ever want parenting advice from you, but I can assure you, I don't need it." She scoffed at me. "That you think you can come back home and fix everything is truly laughable, Melanie. You must be a *great* actress because you've certainly convinced everyone that you're the leading lady rushing in to save the poor, dumb townsfolk from themselves. You can't fool me though. I know you, and we both know that deep down, you ruin everything. Get out, now—before I call the police!"

"Mama, what did she do that was so awful?" Leonie asked, reaching for her mother.

"You're not interviewing me, Leonore," she said, shrugging her daughter off. "Keep your questions to yourself."

"Missy, *please*—" I tried, not wanting the girls to get in trouble. She was right. I was the bad influence, the black cloud who always seemed to darken the brightest room.

"Don't." She silenced me with a word.

"You're being unreasonable, Mama," Birdie said.

"*I'm* being unreasonable?" Missy rounded on her. "*I'm* being unreasonable, Bridget?"

"She just wants to save the Majestic," she implored. "What did she do that was so bad?"

We were building to a climax; everybody in the room could feel it. Could they push Majestic Missy, Ice Queen extraordinaire, into a reaction?

"Mama, what did—"

"You both know I ran away before your mother's wedding," I interrupted. They'd never let it go until they heard a version of the truth. Better to say it now and move on. "The truth is, I was jealous," I said. The truth is often the simplest explanation. It felt good to finally say that little bit, at least.

"You ran away because you were jealous?" Leonie asked, like she didn't believe me. She searched my face for the truth.

I shrugged. "Yes."

"Didn't want to become the spinster aunt?" Birdie offered.

"It wasn't that," Missy cut in. "She'd been jilted."

I blinked at her.

"I remember Benjamin, Melly," she sniped. The air vanished from my lungs.

"Who's Benjamin?" Leonie asked.

I paled. My tongue felt too heavy for my mouth. I couldn't form words.

"Benjamin was her secret boyfriend, even though we all *knew* he existed. Go on, tell them all about your number-one fan, Melly."

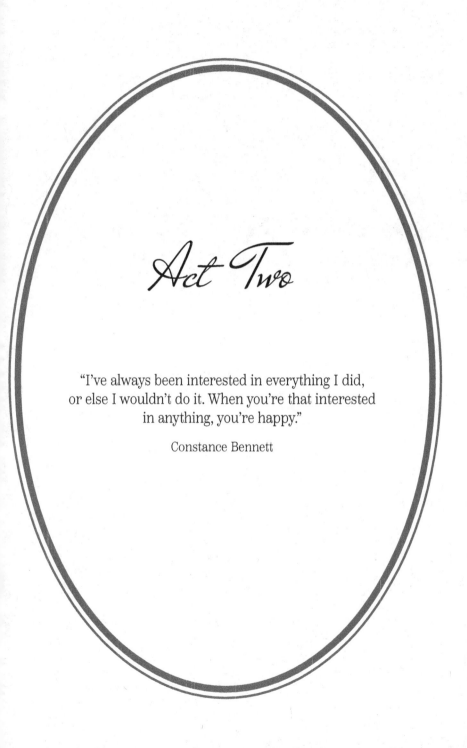

Act Two

"I've always been interested in everything I did,
or else I wouldn't do it. When you're that interested
in anything, you're happy."

Constance Bennett

LIBELED LADY
Starring Jean Harlow and William Powell

FRIDAY, OCTOBER 29, 1937

P ay attention to this next bit. It's not a story I tell often. Or at all, really.

So, I'm standing there, sipping at a glass of champagne, watching as Missy and Eddy slip away through the ballroom on their way to be sweet little hosts together though they've only just met, when Raymond, the big lug, sidles back up to me. He's played the flute one too many times for polite society and he's starting to cause a scene. Normally I'm all about causing a scene, but not in this case. There we were, surrounded by millionaires and movers and shakers—and maybe even a marquess or two—and Raymond's barely able to stand.

"Now I know you're not a high jumper, Raymond," I said, grabbing him by the lapels and hoisting him to me.

"You don't know what I am," he slurred. "If I want to be a high jumper, I'll be a high jumper. I'll be the best high jumper you've ever seen. Call up the Olympic Committee and tell 'em I'm on my way."

"If you say so. How about I pour you into a cab, darling?"

"How about you pour me another glass of bubbly?" he purred, leaning against me.

"How about the cab?" I asked again. "And you can show me how high you jump when we're in friendlier territory, hmm?"

"That sounds terrific," he muttered, draping his arm around my shoulder.

Now, I'm a strong lady, always have been thanks to those years of strength training at Miss Margaret's, but when Raymond Swaine throws his entire body weight onto your graceful little shoulders it's a cause for alarm. Mayday, we're going down! There was no way I was getting him out of the ballroom by myself, so I did a quick scan of the room, hoping to find that familiar icy-blonde chignon, but no luck. I'd later find out Missy had run up the flagpole, literally, and spent the rest of the night on the roof with Eddy dear, cuddled up closely—it being late October and all.

Just as I'd resigned myself to dragging Raymond out of the ballroom by the ankles and letting the gossip columnists have a field day, a saviour appeared: tall, handsome, a perfectly chiselled jaw, the deep brown eyes of screen star; and most importantly, he looked strong enough to lift Raymond into a fireman's carry and climb Citadel Hill if he chose to. And I quickly realized, those deep brown eyes were watching me.

"That's an interesting dance," he said, coming closer.

"It's called The Big Apple," I retorted, trying to keep Raymond from face planting. "Take this lug off my hands and I'll teach you the mechanics."

"I wouldn't want to cut in line, and besides, the song's not finished yet. You can't break that poor boy's heart."

"I'll break as many hearts as I want to," I said, pulling Raymond's arm back around my shoulder. It was hard work keeping him upright, but I wasn't about to lose face in front of this handsome stranger. "Forget it, who wants to dance with you anyway, you probably move like a cement mixer. Now, if you don't mind, I've got to deliver this fella to the Wade Brothers."

Remember what I said about dragging Raymond out by the ankles if I needed to? It seemed like the easiest way to get him out of there. I pushed his arm off my shoulder, ready for him to smack against the floor, but lucky for him, the stranger reached out and caught him first.

"He's going to have a sore neck tomorrow, flailing around like a marionette," I said, watching this Hercules catch Raymond around the waist without even a grunt.

"If the hangover doesn't do him in."

"Raymond can't hold his liquor," I said, admiring the man's strength in spite of myself.

"No, and you can't hold Raymond."

I rolled my eyes. "Would it be too much to ask you to carry him out to the lobby so I can fetch him a cab?"

He appraised me. "Depends. Are you leaving with him?"

"I wasn't planning on it. The Wade Brothers love Raymond. They take him home the long way and then his poor mother makes them haul him into the backyard so the neighbours won't see, even though *we're* the neighbours and we *always* check to see if he's sprouting the next morning. She always tips generously; if I'm with him, they won't get paid near as much. I'm only thinking of the cab driver, especially in this economy."

"How selfless," he said with a smirk. "In that case, I'd be delighted to help. How about you go grab us some champagne and I'll meet you back here in a few minutes. What's his address?"

"Just tell them it's Raymond Swaine. They'll know where to take him."

This Tarzan then hauled Raymond over his shoulder and walked out to the lobby with the Wade Brothers's latest jackpot. Burden lifted, I grabbed two glasses of champagne. I wanted to pay back the stranger for making me stand there like a wet sock before swooping in to help, so I walked all the way over to the other side of the ballroom, found an empty seat in front of the bay window, and stared out at the harbour while I waited, relatively hidden.

"I hear it's a better view in the daytime," he said a few moments later. "You know, when you can actually see the water."

"That a fact?" I asked, handing him his glass.

"So they say." He eased down next to me, held his glass up to mine, and we toasted Raymond.

"Can't say I've ever been a fan of the ocean," he said after taking a sip of champagne.

"You're in the wrong town then, pal."

"Maybe so," he agreed. "But the view's not entirely poor. I have to say I quite like it with you sitting there like a siren."

I tossed one of the turquoise chintz cushions at him. "You're a charmer."

"I've never had any complaints."

"Whatever works."

"Especially in this economy, as you said. So, who did you tag along with tonight?"

I raised an eyebrow. "You don't think I could get an invitation on my own?"

"Touché," he said. "Well, I'm here because the boss wanted to impress the country boy with a fancy night out."

"I'm guessing you lost him somewhere along the way?"

He chuckled. "He lost me, rather. Last time I saw him, he was practically dangling off the champagne tower like King Kong."

"I was wondering who that gorilla was earlier. I almost ended up like Fay Wray four champagnes ago."

His smile was utterly dazzling. I didn't want the conversation to end. "So, where do you and King Kong work, anyway?"

"The Bank of Nova Scotia. *The bank of choice for the Davis family dating back almost a century,*" he said, his voice deep like those radio announcers. "So naturally, we were invited."

"You handle their account?"

"I'm a loan officer," he corrected. "If the Davises ever need my services, it might trigger another depression."

"Perish the thought." I chuckled, looking around the opulent ballroom. I pointed at the turquoise-and-gold-tile flooring. "How much do you think it cost to decorate this place?"

"Well, I left my adding machine back at the office, but I'd have to assume—what with all the gold littered about—a couple hundred grand, at least. But it's not the décor that would've eaten up Mr. Davis's money. It's the turquoise outside."

"At least it's pretty to look at," I said. Well, it's true. And I've always liked pretty things. Day or night, the Atlantic Hotel was a beauty. On sunny days, when the sunlight hit that turquoise just so, it sang. And at night, lit up by the street lamps and the neon signs surrounding it, it danced.

"Sure, but pretty doesn't pay the bills."

"My bank account says otherwise," I teased. He reached over and clinked his champagne glass against mine. "Anyway, I'm sure Eddy Davis will land on his feet."

"That's almost a certainty," he agreed. "You know, you never did tell me what brings you here tonight."

I smirked. "The chance to cool my heels."

"Ah, yes. Perfect spot for it, too." He gestured to the orchestra, in the midst of another jazzy tune.

"You have no idea." I waited for him to put two and two together, to recognize me. But he had said he was a country boy...perhaps he was the only person in our fair province who'd never heard of me.

"So, since Raymond's now half seas over, does that mean you're here by yourself?" he asked.

"My sister's also around here somewhere. But, like you, I've been ditched."

"I think we make a good pair of wallflowers."

"We might be the only ones," I said, looking around at our company. It was nearing one o'clock and still the ballroom was full; the energy hadn't let up at all. Score another point for the Davises. "So, you're a loan officer? That sounds interesting."

"I enjoy crunching numbers. I just wish it wasn't so much telling farmers and fishermen we can't lend them money to repair their roofs or their boats while loaning out money to millionaires hand over fist."

"That doesn't sound so fun."

"The system isn't designed for the little man, but I've learned to play within it. Sometimes I can find the money to spare."

My heart melted a little just then. "I like that you care about the regular folks. Someone has to look out for them," I said.

"If I play my cards right, I could be the director of a big department by the time I'm thirty."

"In Halifax?"

"Truro," he corrected.

"Oh, I thought—"

"I've been floating back and forth between Truro and the main branch for the past few months. There's a shortage of qualified personnel, apparently. I'm in line for a promotion, or so they keep telling me. I don't want to get my hopes up until I see the paperwork."

"So banks aren't only interesting in the movies," I said, tossing back the last of my drink.

"You don't seem like the kind of lady who'd be interested in banking."

"I'm not," I admitted. But I'd taken his bait. I wanted to know what kind of image I presented to someone who clearly didn't know a thing about The Majestic Sisters. But more than that, I found myself surprised at how much I cared what this stranger thought of me.

"What kind of lady do I seem like?" I asked, wishing there was a bit more champagne left in my glass.

"I'm not sure yet," he said around a sip of bubbly. "But I'm quick; I'll figure it out."

I looked over his shoulder. Behind it, a mantel. Upon that mantel, a beehive clock—turn of the century, likely plucked from Bitsy Davis's own living room on Beaufort Avenue. "Thirty minutes ought to do it, I should think?"

"In that case, we should find somewhere quiet to chat. I find I make friends better when there isn't such a hubbub."

I didn't even want to imagine how much it cost to have The Carter James Orchestra perform, but they'd been playing a melange of jazz standards all evening and they'd been lively enough. "Before you drag me off to some secluded spot, don't you think you should tell me your name?"

"How foolish of me," he said, holding out a large hand. Do you believe in fate? I didn't think I did, but when I held his hand, it felt like I'd held it a million times before, like it fit perfectly in mine. There was a comfort to his touch, a familiarity. "Benjamin Trapper, pleased to make your acquaintance."

"Melanie Calvert," I said. "Everybody calls me Melly, though."

"A beautiful name. You look like a Melly; I could've guessed it. Someone full of fun and mystery." He winked. "Am I right?"

"I suppose you are." I smiled up at him. He hadn't let go of my hand. "You look like a Benjamin."

He shrugged. "Eh, you meet one Benjamin, you've met them all. But enough about me. Let's find somewhere quiet."

"I hear there's a terrace with a great view up there," I teased, nodding towards the elevator.

"Not private enough," he said, waving me off. "I bet there are dozens of men looking for a dish to take up there."

I pictured Missy and Eddy jockeying for a spot, a rooftop crowded with couples and Eddy pulling rank to get it to themselves.

"I believe the kitchen is on the other side of the lobby. If we stake it out, we'll get first crack at the potato puff balls. What do you say?" He stood and pulled me to my feet.

"Let's go," I said. I wanted to know everything about this man I'd only just met.

He guided me to a settee just outside the Neptune Dining Room— which, a mere twelve hours later, would be renamed in Missy's honour as the Stargazers' Lounge. "There's something about your face..." he trailed off, looking up at me. "I feel like I've seen you before. But that can't be true, I know I would remember you."

I didn't help. The novelty of not being immediately recognized as Majestic Melly was intoxicating. I decided to dance around the subject, see if he picked up any of my hints. "I teach dance," I offered. What? It was true, in a sense. I taught Missy new choreography all the time! "Just about every day."

"I'm a bit rusty in that regard," he said, looking me up and down.

"I offer lessons," I said.

"Private?" he asked. I wasn't one to blush, but I could feel my face redden. He smirked. "What styles do you teach?"

"I'm basically the Ginger Rogers of the East Coast," I said, clearing my throat. "You name it, I can dance it."

"Impressive," he said. "My mother signed me up for dancing lessons in high school. Any young man worth his salt needs to know the proper dances for when the Legion hosts a shindig, she said."

"And did you? Know the dances for the Legion?"

"Well, I'm not what you'd call 'the Fred Astaire of the East Coast,' but I think I hold my own."

I smiled. "Let me know if you ever want a refresher class. I'd be happy to teach you some fancy footwork."

He grinned at me, but before he could answer, the clock chimed twice. "Uh oh," he said. "Two in the morning. Is this the part where you turn back into a pumpkin?"

I smirked. "I didn't need a fairy godmother to get me here tonight."

He nodded solemnly. "Then this must be the part where *I* turn back into a pumpkin." He stood and offered me his hand. "Forgive me, Melly, but I've got to tie up a few loose ends at the office in the morning before heading back to Truro, and as much as I'd love to sit here talking until the sun comes up, I need my beauty sleep."

We walked back out into the lobby, where, unbelievably, a residual crowd stood chattering. Some were mobbing the front desk, booking rooms and keeping Eddy Davis's bills paid for at least another month, but was clear the celebrations were over. I craned my neck, looking around for Missy. She might have already taken off, and I wasn't about to sit around the lobby until dawn waiting to find out if I was right.

"Shall I call you a taxi?" Benjamin asked, drawing my attention back to him.

"Yes, please. I'll give the Wade Brothers one last commission tonight. How about you? Did you book a room here?"

He scoffed. "I know you're being polite, but I couldn't afford to stay here. I have a long-term rental up the street at the Queen Hotel."

One of the older, yet somehow still booming hotels in the city. Nothing extraordinary about it, but over time it had simply become part of the fabric of Halifax. Perhaps the most interesting thing about it was the barbershop just past the lobby, which was one of the best in the city, according to Daddy. Places like the Queen Hotel would stay open forever, unchanged, untouched, ready and steady.

"With a nice view of the ocean?" I teased.

He chuckled. "Believe it or not, some of us like the view of concrete buildings and busy city streets."

"You don't find it hard to sleep with all that light outside your window?"

"I barely notice it anymore."

"Well, whatever works, I guess." I held out my hand as the taxi pulled up. "Thank you for a wonderful evening, Mr. Trapper."

"The pleasure's all mine, Miss Calvert. Next time we pass each other on the street, how's about we say hello, eh?"

"That works for me," I said, sliding into the backseat.

"Until then, Melly," he said, ducking down and leaning into the backseat with me, his face next to mine.

"I'll be seeing ya," I said, kissing his cheek.

I watched as the man who, only hours ago, had been a stranger, straightened and backed away from the cab, a dazed smile on his face.

And you thought I'd had no fun that night.

THE BRIDE WORE RED
Starring Joan Crawford and Franchot Tone

SATURDAY, NOVEMBER 13, 1937

Like I said earlier: we were busy, Eddy was busy, the Christmas season was fast approaching, and now we needed to give the gift of The Majestic Sisters to the good people of Halifax for Christmas.

I have to give the old man credit: The Majestic Sisters wall calendar was one of Prestel's more inspired ideas. I bought the new edition every December—though I technically *stole* a copy of the 1940 edition before I left town—and delighted at seeing my and Missy's picture-perfect faces posing in increasingly glamorous settings.

On this unseasonably sunny November day, we'd spent a fun afternoon posing for the 1938 calendar. To make it equitable, we shared January and December, but alternated every other month with whimsical portraits—the birth month shoots for Missy in October and me in November were my favourites. We only had a few hours to shoot the whole thing before we were needed back at the Majestic for the evening shows, and we'd already been interrupted by an overly flirtatious camera assistant (me) and an overzealous flower delivery (Missy).

Back down on the street, amidst the bustle of a Saturday afternoon on Barrington Street, we turned to each other. "He was nice," was all Missy said about the cameraman's assistant. "You should've flirted back; you might've gotten lunch out of it."

I snorted. "Him? Don't insult me."

"Don't come crying April *showers* to me when you wind up an old spinster." When I didn't laugh, she continued. "So what, nobody's caught your eye?" She stared at me.

"Mind your own business, Melissa," I warned. Her icy blue eyes narrowed as I issued a new threat: "Or those roses will be mulch by the time you get home." She glared at me, but thankfully dropped the subject and then invited me to lunch with Eddy. I shrugged at the suggestion. They were still moony-eyed and weren't much fun to be around; he'd had a large bouquet of flowers delivered to her that morning simply because he *missed her*. "I'll pass, but thank you. I suppose I could always start my Christmas shopping early."

She chuckled. "Yes, better early than on Christmas Eve."

"My dear sister, you know nothing inspires me to pick out heartfelt gifts like the panic of leaving it to the last minute."

She smiled at me, then looked over my shoulder. "Well, try to behave, hmm?"

"I'm always on my best behaviour," I promised.

"Somehow I doubt that, Miss Calvert," a voice boomed behind me.

I'd recognize that voice anywhere. I turned to see that laughing smile aimed at me. "*Majestic Melly*, as I live and breathe," Benjamin said, taking my hand. "I'm a big fan of yours."

I laughed at the spectacle. Missy, naturally, was hooked. "Well, since your fan club decided to meet, I'm going to head out," she said, winking at me when I turned to her. "Make sure she behaves," she warned Benjamin. "She has claws."

"Remember what I said about those flowers," I sang, smirking as her fingers tightened around the vase.

"Would you like help carrying those?" Benjamin offered.

"Very gentlemanly of you to offer, but I'm only headed a block away, and besides, I don't want to intrude on whatever *this* is." Missy pointed between the two of us, smirking. "My sister so rarely goes out with anyone but Raymond Swaine."

He tutted, mock-frowning at me. "You poor thing."

"This gentleman gets it," Missy snickered. "You should keep this one around, Melly. I like him already."

"Goodbye, Missy." I glared. She saluted us both and turned to walk down the street. Benjamin and I watched her strut through the crosswalk, and once she was a block away, he turned back to me.

"It's pretty late for lunch, so how about dessert?" he asked, offering me his arm. "And then I'll tell you how I figured out your secret."

"Suits me."

THE GREEN LANTERN was relatively busy on Saturday afternoons, but worth the wait. Benjamin nodded at one of the booths, silently asking if I'd like to slip into one of the cushy green seats near the back, but I shook my head. Why go to the soda fountain at all if you weren't going to sit at the counter and chat with the soda jerk while you ate? It's a principle I still live by, though the long-suffering soda jerk is an all but extinct species.

"You don't want to preserve your anonymity, *Majestic Melly*?" he asked, emphasizing my stage name. He grabbed my hand and helped me hop onto the stool.

"Whatever for?" I asked. "I'm not Greta Garbo, I don't *vant* to be alone."

He smirked and watched as heads began to turn. The place was stuffed to the gills, and Majestic Melly always caused a commotion. I figured we wouldn't get through our meal without at least a few women clamouring for autographs—which suited me fine, I never turned away fans.

"So, how did you discover my big secret?" I asked.

"Oh, let's see," he mused. "It couldn't have been that I started calling dance studios and got on the horn with one Miss Margaret who bandied about words like 'floozy' and 'birds' and 'Majestic Theatre' and said to never mention the name 'Melly' ever again before she hung up on me."

"She holds a grudge, it seems." Sore loser.

"So then I put my detective hat on and figured you had something to do with the Majestic, and after a couple of nights of research, here we are. Do you have a fan club I can join?"

"Not yet, but maybe someday when I'm a famous Hollywood star. You can be the first member, if you play your cards right."

"I'll take you up on that offer." He smirked, reaching for a menu. "I can't remember the last time I stopped in here for an ice cream. I'm always rushing back to Truro; or if I have a lunch meeting, it's always at the Lohnes Café."

"Well, I'm glad you've invited me to help you wade back into the green waters," I said. I plucked the menu out of his hand and slipped it back behind the napkin dispenser. "But you don't need that. Here, watch." I whistled at Fred, the soda jerk, the sound piercing above the cacophony of the restaurant, and waved him over as soon as he shifted his eyes in our direction.

"What'll you have, Melly?" Fred asked, bracing himself for my order.

"Give me a Georges Island Special, please. Stretched."

He sighed, leaning against the counter. "I keep telling you, Melly, nobody knows what you're ordering when you use that slang."

"Nonsense." I waved him off. "Aren't you fellas always coming up with funny lingo for ice cream?"

"You watch too many movies," he said, poised with his notepad and pen. "So tell me, what's in a Georges Island Special."

"Chocolate soda with a scoop of vanilla ice cream and a cherry on top, and pistachios sprinkled all over." The hoi polloi would be calling it a Georges Island Special before the day was out.

"Uh huh," he said, grabbing a soda glass.

"And give my friend here a Dionne Special while you're at it."

"Melly—" Benjamin began to interrupt, but I held up a hand. "Don't worry, this one's a real thing." He gave the soda jerk that look men give each other when they think the womenfolk are putting them on.

Fred reluctantly nodded at him. "She's telling the truth, unfortunately."

"What's a Dionne Special?" Benjamin asked. "Named after those babies?"

I was pleased he was playing along. "It's five scoops of vanilla ice cream with cherries and sprinkles on top."

"The *normal* customers call it a Super Sundae," Fred muttered.

"Fred, be a sport. I'm trying to impress this one."

Benjamin reached for my hand under the counter and laced our fingers together. "You don't have to try so hard."

⁓⧫⁓

BENJAMIN NUDGED MY sundae glass with his spoon. "So? How does Georges Island taste?"

It was wonderful, of course, and I'd finished it with gusto. Had my eyes on his sundae as well, but figured I'd better be polite. He followed my eyes and laughed, nudging his dish towards me. I was over the moon that we could have such an intimate moment in such a thick crowd. But of course, we'd soon have to take steps to guard our privacy. In the meantime, I basked in the joy of being out in the open with Benjamin.

"You can't go wrong with Green Lantern ice cream," I said, licking my spoon. "You hear that, Fred?"

"Whassat?" he asked, elbow deep in a tub of vanilla ice cream.

"Your desserts are Majestic Melly approved."

He smirked. "I'll let the boss know. Do I get to put that endorsement in the window?"

"If you want," I said.

"How do you do that?" Benjamin asked.

"Do what?"

"You just *know* everyone. Everything."

"Darling," I said, "Majestic Melly gets invited everywhere. It's my job to know everything that happens in Halifax. Better for business, too, since I'm going to be famous someday."

He nodded. "You've got a head start on a fan club, then. The girls who ordered after us asked for the same thing as you."

I smiled. "They're dears. I don't mind it, if that's what you're asking. Missy laps it up, too. She's just quieter about it than I am."

"Your poor parents."

"Oh hush, we were absolute dolls."

"I bet." He smiled, gently sliding his dessert back in front of himself and taking a bite. "At least there was only the two of you. I have six brothers and we all grew up in one small farmhouse outside of Truro."

"What was it like?" I'd never been farther than the train station there, and hadn't even gotten off the train, if I'm telling the truth. Everything seemed flat and stretched on for miles the farther you got outside of Halifax.

"Lacklustre," he said. "It's incorporated, but far more rural than the city. Had to tend the chickens, that was my job. I used to feed them before and after school, and pick their eggs."

"That sounds fun," I said. It didn't sound fun, not really. I thanked God I was a city mouse.

"Fun until they get attitudes." He rubbed at his arm, some phantom memory tinting his words. "They got out once. All forty of them. I still have nightmares where I'm trying to find that last little bugger."

"And? Did you?"

"Not for a week. You know where I finally found her?" I shook my head. "The attic. I noticed a loose feather in the floorboards, ran upstairs, and sure enough, there she was, nestled in amongst the winter clothes."

"The poor thing."

"The tasty thing," he corrected. "Once I was done with her, Mama made up a nice chicken soup that lasted a week."

"And to think, the most exciting part of my childhood was hopping on the tram unattended and ending up lost in Simpson's," I said, trailing a finger through the melted vanilla ice cream pooled at the bottom of his dish. Before he could stop me, I leaned in and traced that finger down his cheek. He sputtered. I laughed. Fred laughed. We all lived happily ever after. I pushed away my dish so he couldn't retaliate. No siree, I was not wearing pistachios in my hair this close to showtime.

"You think you might not be a very good chicken farmer, then? I mean, if they kept getting out and all," I said.

"My parents begged me *not* to go into the family business. I was awful at it. Always got the easy jobs. My oldest brother runs it now that Pop's getting on, but I help on weekends, when I can."

"And you stay away from the chickens?"

"Yes, smarty pants, I stay away from the chickens." My, but that smile was magnetic.

"So why do you keep running back and forth between here and Truro? Surely there must be banking jobs here, if you're that *invested*. Ha, get it?"

"Very funny. But that's just the thing, I'm not that invested. Not yet, anyway. I want to work with investments and stocks, but there isn't a permanent opening here yet. But I'm good with numbers, and I'm proving my mettle going back and forth. They've already told me that when a director's job opens up, it's mine. I just have to be patient."

I couldn't help but notice how, whenever the bank came up, his brows furrowed a bit above those chestnut eyes. He took his job seriously, even as he sat here joking around with me over two bowls of melted ice cream.

I smiled. "I've never been good at patience. I quit my last gig and set up The Majestic Sisters within an hour. Can't stand having idle hands." That heavy hand covered my own, almost as though he was ensuring I'd stay.

"You don't seem like the type to sit still."

I never had been, but I wanted to sit and talk to him for hours. For the first time since I became Majestic Melly, there was somewhere I wanted to be even more than the theatre.

I wrapped my fingers around his. "I'm not."

I knew someone might see us, but in that moment I just didn't care. Everything I wanted was right here. He reached a finger out to stroke my left cheek before cupping my face in his large hand. I looked up into those warm brown eyes.

I blushed. "You're awful charming."

"It comes easily with you, I find." His expression changed, more charged than it had been seconds earlier. "You asked me the night we met what type of lady you seem like. I didn't have an answer then, but

I think I have an answer now. You're passionate and vivacious. You're warm and friendly. You have impossible dreams but they don't seem impossible when you're talking about them. I think you could conquer the world, Melly. Truly."

Well, what do you say to that! Nobody had ever noticed me the way Benjamin did. Certainly none of the Howards and Bobs I went on dates with in school would *ever* think to string those sentences together. And even the fans who fawned over me night after night had no idea who the real Melly was.

Is this how it felt to be lovesick? Despite the busyness of the soda parlour, I couldn't help but press a kiss to his cheek—the last time we'd ever be so cavalier in public—and quietly thank him.

But then I caught a glimpse of the clock—nearing five. "Oh shoot, is that the time?"

He looked behind me. "You in a rush, Cinderella?"

"I'm due at the theatre in an hour and I need a good square meal before I can go out and dance." I made to get up and rush out to catch a tram home, but Benjamin held out a hand to stop me.

"Well, luckily for us this place serves fine meals as well. You want to grab a booth?"

The devil! He'd magicked one date into two and I couldn't blame him. This might have been the first time I wished there wasn't a crowd over at the Majestic waiting for me. But in the meantime, we could make the most of this double-date.

He helped me down from the stool, and as I led him to the very last booth in the back, I shouted over my shoulder, "Hey Fred! Whip us up a couple of Waterfront Specials and tack it onto the bill, would ya?"

DOUBLE WEDDING
Starring Myrna Loy and William Powell

MONDAY, DECEMBER 20, 1937

"Would you believe me if I told you that I haven't bought a single present yet?" I asked as I slid into one of the wooden benches on the so-called Banana Fleet—a Birney No. 5 tram car—that would take me and Benjamin out to Simpson's so we could do my holiday shopping.

"I mean, not even a Christmas cracker or an orange for anyone's stocking," I added. "And don't even get me started on Missy's Christmas list. She asked for a pair of skis so she and Eddy can head up to Wentworth. Imagine Missy skiing for a minute, please, and tell me that's not the most ridiculous image you've ever conjured in your life."

Missy and I had been busy all of December. There hadn't been time to shop. First, there was the premiere of *Victoria the Great* and a food drive at the Majestic in early December. Then the next weekend was the Goodfellows Dance at the Atlantic Hotel. Missy and Eddy had roped me into agreeing to dance with anyone who made a twenty-dollar donation. After much discussion about wanting to keep our relationship private—we didn't want to let Halifax gawk at our romance the way they were lapping up the other Majestic lovebirds—Benjamin showed up but donated his money for a dance with the Simpson's perfume counter girl instead. Then Uncle Mel, the owner of Mills Brothers, invited us to appear on his Christmas radio show over the third weekend in December. We raised over a grand for young people in need while drumming up business for the theatre. A win for all involved.

But it meant I was completely unprepared for the holidays, and with my days dwindling, I confessed to Benjamin that the only way I'd be able to put anything under the tree would be to go first thing on a weekday morning before my dance card filled up. I wasn't fishing for him to offer to go along with me; it was an added bonus.

"That's why I'm here," he said, sliding in next to me. "I've written down the names of everyone you need to buy for, and we're not leaving until you've crossed them all off your list."

"You're a saint," I praised, laying my head against the window, pretending it was his shoulder, and losing myself to a few moments of light sleep until the tram pulled up to the entrance at my favourite department store—Bullocks Wilshire, eat your heart out.

It was getting harder and harder to hide that I was totally and completely over the moon for Benjamin. He had an uncanny ability to make me laugh in one moment and swoon the next. Frequent lunches at out-of-the-way diners; the knowledge that he was hiding out somewhere in the middle of the theatre watching us dance at the Majestic; arranging to meet him on the busy sidewalks too crowded to stop and talk—a wink and a smile had to be enough for us.

So much secrecy, but I truly felt, for the first time, that I had something to lose. I'd never been myself the way I was with Benjamin, and I wasn't willing to share him yet. I didn't want to lose myself, or have him absorbed into the Majestic Melly persona...I didn't want to be my sister. We knew our families. We'd have been wed, bed, and sent out to pasture to raise a passel of little Trappers before we knew it. And while I caught myself dreaming of that kind of life here and there, it wasn't what either of us wanted. Not yet.

CHRISTMAS AT SIMPSON'S was truly a sight to behold, and part of the reason I wanted to get there bright and early was to listen to the staff singing Christmas carols at the bottom of the escalators. Plus, there were at least ten fully decorated Christmas trees outside where the trams pulled up. I never could pass up a Christmas tree.

"Look up," Benjamin whispered. I noticed the mistletoe hanging above his head and stepped up on tiptoe.

"Cash or cheque?" I asked, tilting my head back.

"Cash," he said, quickly pressing his lips to mine. Hopefully no candid cameramen were lurking around waiting for a snap.

I didn't end up buying Missy a pair of skis—Eddy saved my bank account, bless him—but I did find a few "frou-frou" gifts, just as the Simpson's ad had promised. "She's always complaining about how cold the house is," I told the cashier as she wrapped the pale blue satin bed jacket and matching slippers. "This should keep her warm."

For Mother and Daddy, easy: in a pique of board game hysteria, they'd tossed their backgammon board onto the front lawn. I was positive they would be happy unwrapping a new one on Christmas morning (and they were—until it landed in a snow bank on Boxing Day).

For Eddy, I took Missy's advice. Apparently Eddy loved to cook, or at least own the latest gadgets. I bought him a set of carving knives and a steamer saucepan, whatever that was.

Old Man Prestel, predictable: a set of tartan neckties (which he wore with pride for weeks).

"You don't have to buy anything?" I asked Benjamin over lunch at the soda fountain.

"Oh, I finished all my shopping weeks ago," he said. "But we're both so busy; I just wanted a reason to spend time with you."

I swooned. "So, what did you get me for Christmas?"

"No way, not telling." He leaned back in his chair. "That'd spoil the whole business."

"What if I guess?"

"You'll never guess it, Sweets." I'd earned this nickname since our sojourn at the Green Lantern, which had evolved into a tradition of sampling every dessert in town.

"I might," I warned him. "But I can be patient, I suppose. Now, tell me what you want for Christmas."

"As long as I'm with you, that's all I need, Sweets."

"That's charming and all," I said, "but you're not being helpful here."

"I like fishing, reading, and jazz music—does that help?"

"It's a start," I muttered, trying to remember if I'd seen anything worthwhile in the music section.

"Whatever you get me, I'm sure I'll love it."

A FEW NIGHTS later, we were entangled in Benjamin's hotel room, dancing to the Christmas carols playing over the radio, enjoying a precious few stolen moments before he drove back to Truro to spend the holidays with his family. We'd been moping and kissing and whispering sweet nothings into each other's ears all evening, but time was running out. I pulled back.

"Okay, enough sadness. We're supposed to be festive. Let's exchange gifts."

"Oh goodie," he said, letting himself fall backwards into the wingback chair and pulling me onto his lap. "I finally get to find out what you bought me."

"I hope you'll like it," I wavered, looking over at the box I'd hastily dropped onto his bed when I'd first come in the room.

"I told you, Sweets, what we have between us is good enough for me. Anything else is a bonus."

I crossed the room quickly, picked up his present, and tossed it into his lap with a hasty "Merry Christmas."

He ran his fingers over the package, trying to figure out what was inside.

"Here's a wild thought: how about you open it rather than try to feel it through your hands?" I've always been impatient about opening presents, sue me.

"Ooh, I hadn't thought of that. Excellent call," he quipped, ripping the paper. "Colwell?" He unwrapped the box to reveal a handsome sable cashmere sweater. He held it up, admiring it.

"I saw it on one of the mannequins and thought you'd look handsome in it."

"I'm assuming the mannequin was stiff competition?"

I laughed. "You are infinitely more handsome."

He hauled the sweater on over his shirt, then stood and modelled it for me. "How do I look?"

"Like a mannequin."

He rolled his eyes. "You know, it's Christmastime. You have to behave if you want presents. Bad girls get coal."

"I think you're making that up. Santa delivers gifts to all of us girls regardless of our behaviour. Only naughty boys get coal."

"You city folk tell the story wrong," he said, moving to set the package aside, but I stopped him.

"There's something else in there."

He felt along the bottom of the box and pulled out a thin, flat package that, once unwrapped, revealed a Majestic Sisters wall calendar. He whistled. "Just what I've always wanted."

He flipped to the back to see the small photo panes that previewed each month's photograph. "Every other month? I'll count down the days."

I bit my lip. "It's already opened, but you're not allowed to hang it until the new year. Bad luck." I didn't tell him about the handwritten messages inside—all lovey-dovey and prose more purple than I'd ever written in my life. Some surprises are good surprises, after all. If only I'd been brave enough to tell him those things that night.

Benjamin produced a slim package from his suitcase, wrapped in shiny red paper. "Now, you're sure you've been a good girl?" he asked, dangling the gift in front of me.

Finally, he placed the package in my outstretched hand, and held his breath as I opened it. Nestled inside the case was a delicate gold chain with an "M" charm dangling from it.

"I saw it at Kay's and thought of you," he whispered, carefully fastening it around my neck. "Now you can carry me with you everywhere."

It was the best Christmas present I'd ever received, and that's counting the custom dollhouse my parents gave me when I was six. I found myself without words. I touched the charm and it was as if I could feel his love for me radiating from it.

"Only the best for my girl," he whispered.

MERRILY WE LIVE
Starring Constance Bennett and Brian Aherne

TUESDAY, APRIL 19, 1938

My least favourite part of working at the Majestic Theatre happened every spring without fail. This was when the DeBoth Homemakers' School would sweep into town for a weeklong series of lectures presented under the watchful eyes of a homemaking expert from the United States. Old Man Prestel was only too happy to capitalize on the housewife demographic, so he enthusiastically rented out the Majestic at a discount in return for a share of ticket sales. And it was the hottest ticket in town.

The homemakers ate it up. Not just for the opportunity to learn the best techniques in man-fetching, housewifery, and husband-keeping, but for the overstuffed prize baskets—graciously donated packages of Morse's tea, Lux soap, Robin Hood flour, and other sundry items wrapped up with a neat little bow—and the Eaton's fashion show at every intermission.

Naturally, Old Man Prestel insisted on having The Majestic Sisters represented in some way, and to our amazement, Miss Dala Grant, she of the DeBoth Homemakers' School, was all for the extra pairs of hands. Little did she know what she was getting herself into. We'd demonstrate how easy it was to make the recipes, show off the cutting-edge appliances, and do a little song-and-dance while the Eaton's models made their rounds, but we'd do it with our expected flair.

Missy, to no one's shock, excelled immediately at home economics. She made it look like easy work. I, on the other hand, needed all the help I could get.

"I'm going to teach you everything except how to wind a clock and put out the cat," Miss Grant said that first morning, setting the tone straight away.

"Those were the two things I desperately needed to learn," I said, untying my apron. "Oh well, there's always next year." I tossed it onto her makeshift countertop and began to exit stage left when Missy ran up behind me and yanked me back to the kitchen, stage-whispering the whole time.

"Melly, darling, you don't have a cat *or* a clock. Get back here and pay attention!"

We could hear the women in the audience laughing at the bit. The movie screen had been lifted, all the props behind it pushed to the wings, and in their place stood a fully functioning kitchen, dining room, and living room set for Miss Grant to perform her magic tricks.

Miss Grant's matronly stare fixated upon us as she unpacked more of her wares. The woman wielded a twenty-four-pound bag of Robin Hood flour as though it were a feather duster, and she did it all without breaking her stare.

That first day I learned everything there is to know about Robin Hood flour. Miss Grant spent an hour or two just lecturing on the various ways to use it before showing us any practical demonstrations (which ended with me coated in flour), and at the end of the day, one lucky housewife dragged away a heavy flour bag of her own.

I'll tell you why I hated those homemaking demonstrations: it reinforced a principle that I loathed. Chiefly, that a woman was only as good a housewife as the "homemaking expert" deemed her.

What's more, Miss Grant always took over the theatre, and it was frustrating to have to disassemble her workspace every evening. Not an inch of the stage was spared in her desire to replicate an entire house, though, I think—Halifax usually being polite society and all—Old Man Prestel must've drawn the line at featuring a bathroom.

"I think we ought to keep this staging up permanently," I told Missy that night ahead of *Merrily We Live*. "We could live here. You'll have to excuse us," I added to the audience, "Missy and I are learning how to be the *best* little homemakers this week."

"Tell the crowd what you learned today, Melly."

"I learned I'm going to need all the help I can get!" I ribbed. The strategically placed smear of flour on my left cheek added to the illusion, and the audience began to laugh.

"You weren't *that* bad," Missy chided. "I was standing right next to you."

"Missy, darling, no matter how long you put me in the oven, I'll still come out a ham."

IF THERE'S ONE thing I've always known for certain, it's this: I, Melly Calvert, have never once dreamt of having children or a husband. And let me tell ya, it's not an easy thing to admit to your parents, progressive though they claim to be.

The idea of her daughters helping out the DeBoth Homemakers' School got Mother's brain working, and as we were sitting down for breakfast the next morning, she ambushed me, so to speak. I'd been in the midst of describing how to make a pineapple tomato sherbet—we truly ate some *awful* things before modern refrigeration—when Mother interrupted.

"So, Melly," she said, buttering a piece of toast with more care and attention than was necessary. "Do you think you might like to settle down someday?"

I scoffed. "I'm only twenty, Mother. I have plenty of time to settle down."

"You're the only girl in your class who isn't married yet." She took a well-timed bite of toast.

"Didn't you march with the suffragettes?"

Now she chewed longer than was necessary. "The suffragettes aren't going to help you pay the bills when your father and I are gone."

"I'll pay my own bills," I said, taking a bite of my own.

Mother and Daddy exchanged a look over the rims of their coffee mugs, and it didn't escape my notice. "Are you two kicking me out? Dying? Why the sudden interest in Mr. Majestic Melly?"

"I have a senior student this semester who has a particular way with words," Daddy said. "You want me to introduce you?"

I balked. "No, Daddy. Trust me. I'm fine."

"We just want you to be looked after," Mother said. "You're not getting any younger."

I rolled my eyes. "Times have changed since Austen, Mother." I'd no intention of telling her about my own Mr. Darcy.

She sighed and took my father's hand over top of the table. "Sometimes I wish Missy was more like you, Melly, but more often than not, I find myself wishing you'd take after *her*. You need to start considering what happens *after* The Majestic Sisters. There's going to come a day when she won't want to be Majestic Missy anymore, and then where will you be?"

"Alone and without prospects, if your lack of faith in me is this severe." I chuckled, though it wasn't funny at all. "I'm sure there'll be another spotlight waiting for me once Missy wants to settle down."

"That spotlight can't shine down on you forever," she chided. I should've made her bet on it then and there.

"Mother, I promise. When I'm ready to settle down, I will let you know. Let Missy walk around with Cupid's arrow stuck in her back. I'm in no rush."

"Well, I want grandkids," she said. "From both of you. Just remember that."

"I'll give you two of each someday if you promise to end this conversation now," I said, fingers crossed behind my back.

⌒◟◞⌒

"SO, WHAT DID you learn today at school, Sweets?" Benjamin asked, stuffing a forkful of mashed potatoes into his mouth.

We were enjoying a late supper at the Cornflower Automat following the show that evening. I hadn't had a bite to eat since mid-afternoon, when we'd been fed slices of American beauty cake. (Don't ask. I'm still not entirely sure what Miss Grant put in it, but I swear I was missing a lipstick after that demonstration.)

"How to season your coffee, darling." I wiped at my lips. "Would you like me to demonstrate?"

He pushed his mug towards me. "By all means."

I walked up to the counter and leaned over, whispering my unusual request to the waitress. She handed it over wordlessly, and I sauntered back to our booth. I opened the tin and tipped it over Benjamin's still-sizzling coffee, laughing at the look on his face.

"Now, dear, it's just a simple stir to blend in those flavours, and once that's done, you'll swear you never had coffee so good." I pushed the mug back towards him. "Try it."

He eyed me hesitantly. "Are you sure this isn't a prank? You're not getting back at me for St. Patrick's Day, are you?"

He'd been out of town for April Fools' Day; otherwise, he'd said, he would've pranked me then. Instead, he had all seventeen suggested flowers for a proper St. Patrick's Day bouquet—lily of the valley, potted violets, carnations, hyacinths, narcissi, tulips, irises, roses, lilies, orchids, daffodils, sweet peas, snapdragons, sweetheart roses, shamrocks, green carnations, and cypripediums—bundled up by The Flower Shop and sent over to the Majestic with a card that read, as Missy had so joyously orated, *From your sweetheart*—" and at this part, Missy gasped, until she got to the sender's name: Reddy Kilowatt. The cartoon mascot of Nova Scotia Light & Power.

"Water under the bridge," I murmured. "Try the coffee, dear."

He picked up the mug and took a tentative drink, the expression on his face sliding from satisfied to sickened as the coffee went down his throat. "That's awful."

"Oh no, darling, it's supposed to be the *best* and newest way to drink coffee. Miss Grant says 'a pinch of mustard brings out the volume of goodness,' and when has Miss Grant ever been wrong?"

"Okay, you've made your point," he said, pushing the mug away and gesturing for the waitress to bring a fresh one. When she did, he handed her the mustard tin and offered her a handsome tip to hide it from me.

"You don't know what you're missing," I chided.

"Oh, is this how Majestic Melly drinks her coffee from now on?"

"Goodness no," I chuckled. "Miss Grant practically poured the coffee straight down my throat onstage this morning. She's lucky it didn't come straight back up all over that pristine ivory apron!"

"Tell me, do they teach you ladies anything practical at these sessions? How to balance a chequebook or how to patch a tire until you can get to a motor station?"

Well, this was refreshing. Could this mean he didn't want a fussy hausfrau someday soon?

I shrugged. "They assume the husband's around to do all that."

"They only teach you cooking and cleaning?" At my nod, he continued. "So what would you do if the doorknob fell off your front door?"

"Move houses, clearly." I shot him a sardonic smile. "*I* know where the tools are. I bet I could figure out how to use about half of them if I needed to."

"Those homemaker schools set women up to be too dependent. Yoked to their men, unable to do anything for themselves with any lasting impact," he grumbled.

"That's important to you?" I asked. How had we made it this far without a conversation like this coming up?

"Of course it's important to me, Sweets. I don't want you to ever have to rely on anyone to get by, not even me."

I bowed my head and shot him a look through my lashes. "I wouldn't mind relying on you."

He shook his head. "We're going to walk through life in the same direction, Melly, hand in hand. You're never going to have to follow me."

I smiled. "So you don't care about how a lunch table and a supper table should have different colour schemes to keep the husband and children intrigued?"

He balked. "Of course not! Please tell me you don't."

"Of course not!"

He looked at me over the top of his coffee mug, then carefully set it back on the table. "No wife of mine's going to set the table in a different colour scheme every meal or move houses because she can't fix a door." My heart fluttered. "She's going to know how to change the light bulbs *and* the oil in the car. And she definitely will not be adding mustard to my morning coffee, because that was the worst thing I've ever tasted in my life."

"Wait until you try my American beauty cake recipe."

"I'll feed it to the fishes, and then you'll have to explain why the catch is so low this season."

"But you'll *grow* to love it."

"I love *you* enough already," Benjamin declared. "And if that old maid won't teach you practicalities, I'll do it myself," he said. I linked our pinky fingers together on the tabletop.

"I love you for wanting to take care of me like that," I murmured. Everyone assumed that I was happy to be independent and carefree, but there was something so reassuring about basking in the warmth of his love.

"Do you ever think about marriage?" he asked. I looked up at him and noted the way he was trying to gauge my reaction without looking me in the eyes. How to tell him I'd marry him in a minute if he asked but that I didn't want him to ask just yet?

"Of course, with the right man."

"Of course," he repeated. "It's not an institution you waltz into with just anyone."

"Exactly. I want a husband who values my knowledge and independence and who encourages me to push boundaries."

"Naturally."

"Naturally," I repeated. "Of course, I'm only twenty. There's still plenty of time to get married. Is it really so awful to wait a few years?"

He shook his head. "Of course not. You'd have to make sure you're happy with where you're living, too."

"I like Halifax quite well," I hedged, looking up at him.

"Of course," he said, nodding. "There's plenty of time for me to get settled in Halifax, too. If you're willing to wait, that is."

"I'd be willing to wait," I whispered. He lifted my hand and kissed the back of it, as if sealing the conversation with a promise.

"I suppose it's time I told you then...the farm's having a poor spring," he said, rushing out the tale of the crops that wouldn't grow and the chickens that laid dud eggs earlier that month, as if trying to cover that he'd been waiting for me to admit I'd wait for him.

"That's awful," I said, covering his hand with mine. "Hopefully your family can turn it around."

"That's the thing," he said. "I'm probably going to be spending more time in Truro over the next month, just to help out when I can."

"Of course," I agreed. "If you can help, you should do it."

"It means passing up a promotion at the main office, though," he hesitated. "I hope you can understand that I haven't—"

I held up a hand to stop him. "Benjamin, darling, it's okay. You have to help your family and this is the best way to do it. There will be other promotions and more opportunities to see each other once the farm's back at its best."

He still looked unsure, so I stood up and crossed over to his side of the booth and slid in next to him. "I promise, on everything I hold dear, that I'm telling you the truth right now. You take care of your family and the farm, and I'll still be here waiting for you to come back."

He kissed me full on the lips. In that moment, I couldn't care a whit if every newspaperman in the city saw.

***

MISS GRANT'S HOMEMAKER'S sessions thankfully ended the next day. I'd been up earlier than normal, having an early breakfast with Benjamin at the Queen Hotel before giving him a kiss and sending him off to Truro for the next couple of weeks, and so was exhausted by the time Miss Grant tried to stuff a spoonful of flamingo pudding—a concoction that was pinker than any food has a right to be—into my mouth. It landed on my shirt instead, which the audience loved. I didn't; I'd paid a mint for that emerald green blouse at Paulette's.

"Don't fret dear, this flows nicely into my next lesson: how to get stains out of coloured clothing in the washing machine!" Miss Grant said, leading me over to the laundry room set-up on stage right. Missy appeared with a fresh shirt. "Luckily for you we just had that Eaton's fashion show, eh?"

"How kind of you, darling." I smiled through gritted teeth. Of course Missy excelled at this stuff. I didn't care about any of it, but I did care that she was getting all the attention. I only liked being the clown on *my* terms.

"Think nothing of it, Snow White." She smiled back, equally as frigid.

MOVE OVER, DARLING
Starring Doris Day and James Garner

TUESDAY, DECEMBER 24, 1963

I 'm not often willing to admit when I've been licked, but when I woke up on Christmas Eve day, I had to admit it: I was licked.

After Missy's revelation about Benjamin, I couldn't bring myself to argue with her further. And Birdie and Leonie had quickly sidled back over to their mother—not that I can blame them—with nary a second glance back at me. I hadn't been forthcoming with further details on who Benjamin was, nor the nature of our relationship, so naturally they fell back into the fold.

Not wanting to be a zoo exhibit on display, I went straight upstairs to my suite and packed my bags. I was out of the Atlantic and checked into the Lord Nelson Hotel within the hour.

How to explain who Benjamin Trapper truly was? That was my qualm. We'd kept our relationship relatively quiet compared to the inferno that was Missy and Eddy's courtship. I suppose it didn't make much sense, but our love had been fierce enough for me to protect it. I was used to being Majestic Melly, and having my every move followed and glowingly written up in the papers. The one thing I didn't want was to make a mockery of Benjamin or what we had together. It felt like the only *real* thing I'd ever had; the one part of my life I didn't want to shine a spotlight on.

Truthfully, a part of me was also trying to avoid the circus that followed Missy and Eddy around. As their courtship continued on throughout 1938, press interest in their every move grew to a fever pitch—to the point that there was an engagement countdown in the *Mail* and street corner gambling on the odds of Eddy proposing on any given day (Christmas Eve 1938 was the odds-on favourite, though he managed to award some second-place betters a small fortune when he finally popped the question on New Year's Eve).

This hadn't been the point of my trip. I hadn't wanted to get into the thick of my relationship with Benjamin. I just wanted to save the theatre and see if Missy would pitch in. But mostly, I'd wanted to see my sister. I wanted us to be friends again.

I should've known better. Maybe it was the nostalgia that blinded me to the truth. Missy wanted nothing to do with me, no matter how many times I apologized. No matter how long I grovelled.

⌒ℓℓ℈

RAYMOND MUST'VE HAD me tailed to the Lord Nelson, because there were already several messages for me at the front desk inviting me to lunch or out on the town for the night. He'd inherited his family home, so it would be like old time's sake, he said. Only this time, his impassive father, who'd barely spoken to us, wouldn't be around to jangle jingle bells up the stairs to spook us into behaving lest Santa find us.

I'd agreed, wanting to get him off the telephone, and asked him to meet me at the Cornflower for lunch. It was one of the only old haunts of mine still standing, and if my ghosts were being uncovered, I might as well sit amongst their spirits.

I'd asked the front desk clerk to call me a cab, and as we slowly wound down the snow-covered streets, I couldn't help but narrate the drive, like those busybodies who cart tourists through Beverly Hills pointing out all the celebrity homes.

"And if you look on your right, you'll find Kara's Luncheonette. That's a new one for me. It used to be the Havana Tavern. I think I lost my shoes there once," I told the cab driver. He had no choice but to listen to me. "In fact, I had to be piggybacked home. If you ask Raymond Swaine, I believe he'll corroborate the story."

We turned onto Morris Street. "The Cornflower Automat, truly a relic of a bygone era, ladies and gentlemen. Their pies were delicious once upon a time. Are they still delicious?" I waited for the cabbie to answer, but I somehow managed to grab a ride from the only person in this city who didn't want to talk my ear off. "Who knows? Will Melly find out? She hopes to." I left only a small tip; his conversational skills needed work.

The door clanged open and the waitress on duty barely lifted her head. "Sit anywhere, hon, it's just you."

Not quite the reception I was used to, but anonymity could be nice once in a while. I walked over to my favourite booth and tossed the fur coat into the empty seat. I tried not to think of who would've normally occupied the seat opposite me, and then I slid—no, unfurled, like a snake—back into the booth. I listened as the crackling static of the radio played faint Christmas carols, and it depressed me to compare what I heard on the tinny radio to the full jazz orchestra I'd heard at the Atlantic the night before.

"Coffee? It's terrible, but it gets the job done," the waitress asked when she finally came over.

"I remember," I sighed, quickly ordering a cup. Benjamin always ordered it, and it was always scalding. I fought the urge to ask for the mustard.

"What can I get you, hon?"

I ordered an eggnog for Raymond and waited for him to show up. He arrived just as the waitress slid the glass across the table, gliding into the booth across from me with a vainglorious smile pasted onto his face. "Some party, eh?" he crooned, watching me with those pawky eyes.

"I'll say. I suppose you heard everything?"

"Enough to fill in the blanks." Of course he had. "There's a rumour going around that King Eddy issued a decree to his staff this morning." He paused for effect as he sipped his eggnog.

I took the bait. "Oh?"

"Yes, I've heard that you're likely to receive an official letter declaring you *persona non grata* at the Atlantic Hotel and all of its subsidiary properties, and that if you are caught on any Davis-owned premises you will be arrested and charged with criminal trespassing. A lot of hooey, but then, I'm not a lawyer."

The hurt I'd caused all those years ago had, it seemed, hardened into cement. This whole trip had been pointless. "I'll add it to my pile of Christmas cards when I get home."

"Frame it between Martin's and Lewis's." He winked, but the smile slowly faded from his face. "Melly, don't panic when I tell you this. Nobody overheard the family spat, so your secret is safe, but...I know about Benjamin. I always have."

I jumped. "What? And you never said anything about it?"

He nodded, sheepishly taking another drink of eggnog.

"Why?"

He looked at me over the rim of his glass. "Dear, don't you wonder why *every* innocent glance and hand brush was reported about Missy and Eddy, but all those times you and Benjamin were caught canoodling in this very automat stayed out of the papers?"

This automat. All those dates. All those times I thought we'd been so clever. All because this flibbertigibbet was my friend and valued my privacy over the scoop.

I blinked. "You mean..."

"Now, if you'd been dating a bootlegger, forget it. I would've announced it hourly on the radio. After I'd arranged a nice trade with the man, naturally."

I chuckled, despite myself. If only Raymond knew the whole story.

"Your secret is safe with me, Melly," he assured me.

With lunch over, I paid the bill—of course I did—and bid adieu to Raymond. While it was clear my grand plan to involve Missy had failed, I couldn't put it off any longer. It was time, finally, to pay a visit to Old Man Prestel and the Majestic Theatre.

BLUEBEARD'S EIGHTH WIFE
Starring Claudette Colbert and Gary Cooper

FRIDAY, MAY 6, 1938

The other theatres in town weren't short on gimmicks to entice audiences to their sticky-floored premises, but when the Garrick Theatre brought in bona fide Broadway topliners for a week-long revue show titled, appropriately, Broadway After Dark, it was our first true competition.

The Garrick, let's be clear, was never *anything* to write home about. Half the time respectable audiences wouldn't be caught dead inside it. Though it was nestled up on a bustling corner of Sackville Street, it wasn't a place I'd want to be caught patronizing.

And yet, somehow, the Garrick scrounged up a team of Broadway "stars" that included Tommy Stockley, a singer who'd grown up in Halifax but quickly hot-footed it to Boston; and a comedic duo who bantered so well, the audience roared through the entire segment (according to the review Old Man Prestel scoffed at in the *Halifax Mail*). There was also Rankin and Norman, a husband-and-wife team of tap dancers; Peggy DeCourcy, an interpretive acrobatic dancer; heaps of chorus girls and an in-house band. All for the low, low price of thirty-five cents a ticket.

Sure, they had all that, but we had the dark side of the moon—and by that, I mean Claudette Colbert's elusive right profile—and two Majestic Sisters. Still, the Broadway After Dark revue was enough to inspire some curiosity, and, naturally, the first evening at the Garrick was crowded to the rafters. People like the new and exotic, after all.

I don't want to give the impression we were performing to an empty auditorium; Missy and I were still very much in demand in those days. In an attempt to put our differences behind us after the *Snow White* fracas, we'd spent the week crafting a delightful routine to premiere for *Bluebeard's Eighth Wife*, a loveable farce involving Claudette Colbert and Gary Cooper, and we'd even rounded up a team of our own to accomplish it. We didn't need those starving vaudeville impresarios at *our* theatre to get a laugh; we could manage all on our own.

What we had were six other girls, three blondes and three brunettes, plucked from the barre at the Atlantic Dance Academy, since Miss Margaret refused to let her pupils perform with us. We dressed them all identically to match Missy and me, and then did an eight-person song-and-dance routine that featured tap, interpretive acrobatic dancing, not-too-shabby singing, and a hint of comedy. Honestly, it was just like seeing Broadway After Dark; I still don't understand the fuss over it. It was timed to go over by a few minutes, just long enough for Old Man Prestel to make his way onstage to yell at us.

"What are you girls doing?" he shouted, stomping out from stage left. "Mort's going nuts in the booth! The movie was supposed to start three minutes ago!"

"Sorry, Mr. Prestel," one of the fake Mellys said.

A fake Missy checked her watch. "We weren't paying attention to the time."

"Well," he said, rubbing his head, "I suppose that's all right. There's a first time for everything."

"Gee, thanks, Mr. Prestel," another fake Melly said, walking over to him and lacing an arm through his. "We won't let it happen again."

"Wait until Edward hears about our goof!" another fake Missy chuckled, which earned some laughs—especially, it should be noted, from the front row, where Eddy was watching the whole bit. The fake Melly she'd been paired with simply rolled her eyes. Atta girl.

The final pair of phoney Majestic Sisters did an exaggerated tap-shuffle off the stage, walking ahead of Old Man Prestel while Missy and

I stayed behind, watching it all play out. We sat on the edge of the stage and let the audience laugh at Old Man Prestel's obliviousness. Missy, bless her comedic timing, pulled out a file and began conspicuously buffing her nails.

Mort stuck his head out of the projection booth window—utterly terrifying the people seated directly below him—and yelled to us, "Aren't you girls through? Can I roll the film yet?"

"Nah," I yelled back. "Claudette Colbert can wait!"

"What's the holdup?" he yelled.

"Cool your jets!" Missy hollered. "The bit's not over!"

I looked over at Old Man Prestel, catching his eye and winking.

He sauntered back over to us. "Do I want to know how much this bit's going to cost me?"

I shrugged. "Take it out of Missy's pay and we'll call it even."

"What're you, some kind of cookie pusher?" she said, elbowing me.

"No, but I've got a tab at D'Aillard's that I need to pay down. You can afford to have your paycheque docked." Harsh, perhaps, but true. The audience certainly chuckled at it.

Before Missy could get a shot in, Mort stuck his head out of the booth once more to yell at us: "Okay ladies, can we get moving again, please?"

"You know what, Mort? Fine. We'll get off your stage; give us *just* a minute. Heaven forbid," I said, slowly getting up from my spot at the edge of the stage. "Ladies and gents, you're in for a treat tonight, *Bluebeard's Eighth Wife*. I'm Majestic Melly and this is my sister, hopefully soon to be Edward's *First* Wife, and we hope you enjoy the show!"

The look on Missy's face! The audience roared with laughter as I yanked her off stage with me and the lights dimmed.

She wheeled around, barely in the wings, her foot slipping on the spiral step. "What did you say all that for?!"

"What—the truth? I'm not in the mood for one of your Missy fits. Let me by."

"Never use me or Edward at the expense of a laugh *ever* again, Melanie. Don't be as cheap as that shot was." She followed me into the dressing room. "And find your own dinner date, because you are hereby *uninvited* from the Stargazers' Lounge."

Missy ignored me as she began the painstaking process of removing all those caked-on layers of makeup.

"Fine by me, I was going to sneak into Broadway After Dark anyway." The thought of walking into the Garrick—of walking out with sticky shoes and who knew what ailments—grossed me out, but I'd be lying if I said I wasn't curious.

At this, she met my eyes in the mirror. "You? Going to the Garrick? I'll believe it when I see it."

"Why don't you tag along. You might just learn something from a *real* performer."

The hairbrush thudded against the wall near my head, and I left without a backward glance.

DO THEY LET anyone on Broadway? I wondered, watching the tired husband-and-wife shuffle across the stage. Rankin and Norman had nothing on me and Missy. Still, I always loved being in the audience; it was like peeking into another world. I was so busy plotting out my Broadway debut—I bet I could've made "Anything Goes" my signature song if given the chance; I certainly played the Ramona Davies recording enough around the house—that I didn't notice the gent sidle into the seat next to me. When he elbowed my arm from the armrest, I made to give him a wooling—until I realized who he was.

Benjamin.

"Don't worry, your secret's safe with me," he whispered, offering me his popcorn. I waved it off. I didn't want to know what was coating the floors, and I definitely didn't want to know what was coating the popcorn. Besides, I had more pressing matters to attend to.

"What are you doing here?" I whispered back.

"I think it's pretty obvious, Sweets," he said. "I'm watching the show."

I shook my head. "No, what are you doing in Halifax? You told me you'd likely be another week or two back home."

At this he shrugged, and whispered something about turning the farm around and the bank tossing money at him to return to work in Halifax for a couple of weeks.

"Fine way to tell your gal." I slid further into my seat.

"I'm telling you now." That smile. A follow spot always poised to find my heart. "I was going to surprise you at the Majestic, but then you stormed out like a woman on a mission, so I figured it'd be more fun to follow you and surprise you at your destination."

"We're paying to watch the show, not this scene," an older man's voice behind me muttered.

"Yeah, pipe down!" hissed a high-pitched female voice, presumably his date.

I aimed an errant handful of popcorn over my shoulder, but we did start whispering softer. "So what are you doing here, Sweets?"

"I'm planning out how to become a star," I whispered.

"You're already a star, but I agree. It's time the rest of the world sees it, too."

I looked up into those twinkling eyes. Benjamin never tried to dull my shine. I loved that about him. "You really think?"

"I'll be the first member of your fan club when you strike it big," he vowed.

THE ADVENTURES OF ROBIN HOOD
Starring Olivia de Havilland and Errol Flynn

WEDNESDAY, JUNE 15, 1938

T hanks to the ever-present media pack, by which I mean the *Mail*'s intrepid "Candid Camera" lad who liked to sneak up on people while they were out and about to grab their photos for the next day's newspaper, my secret romance was exposed.

Benjamin and I were snapped leaving the Riviera Tea Room on Spring Garden Road. It was newly June, you know, when it's always sunny and you've got that sense of hope that summer will be endless blue skies? We'd eaten a quick lunch before he had to get back to the bank when the photographer loomed up with his Voigtländer and caught me smoothing down the collar of Benjamin's coat, a Cheshire Cat grin on my face. Of course, Benjamin looked as handsome as ever, smiling down at me.

That moment was printed in the June 15th edition of the *Mail-Star*—front page and everything. It wasn't long before Missy came skipping into the dressing room with the issue in her hand.

"What's this?" she asked, tossing the newspaper onto the table in front of me, spilling my cold cream in the process. I picked up the paper and read:

> *Who's the gent with Majestic Melly? We're not sure, but we snapped him in the nick of time! We bet he'll be front and*

centre at the Majestic all week watching our own 'Maid Melly'
introduce The Adventures of Robin Hood. *If he wants a sou-*
venir of this moment—and we want his name in exchange—
we'll have to hope he comes in to pick up his 4 × 6 enlargement
at the Classified Ads counter!

"Oh," I said. "Him. You can read. It says right there: he's a *gent*."
I'd already sat through an inquisition at the breakfast table, I was in no
mood to sit here and listen to Missy natter on.

"Don't play coy with me," Missy huffed. "Is he your new beau?"

This was exactly why I'd kept him a secret. Missy would want to
sit around gossiping and braiding our hair, talking about our beaus,
forgetting everything else we were working on. She'd be *insufferable* if
she knew the full story, and selfishly, I just wanted to keep Benjamin to
myself a little while longer, so I shrugged.

"What's his name?"

"Well, if the newspaper doesn't even know, how do you expect *me*
to know?"

I was waiting for her to remember she'd spoken to this same *gent*
on the sidewalk last fall when we'd posed for the Majestic Sisters calendar. That she'd seen him sitting near the front of the house most nights,
or that she'd noticed him hanging around the lobby—so stiff and formal
next to the sphinxes he could've passed for one—waiting for me, but it
never came. For once, Missy's self-centredness was coming in handy.

Instead, she dropped it—reluctantly, I think—and said, "Well, at
least he's handsome. You know, in a Ray Milland sort of way." And that
was that. Until later that fall, when she met him officially for the first
time.

Oh, and before you ask: of course Benjamin never went to pick
up the photo. Neither of us wanted to fan the flames, so we decided to
pretend as though nothing had happened. If we gave no reaction, we
figured nobody else would.

But just because Benjamin didn't want to pick up the photo didn't
mean I didn't want it for myself. I waltzed right in to the classifieds

desk, demanded the photo, refused to give them Benjamin's name—I might have let slip that he was so embarrassed by the attention he'd gotten he might never show his face in public again—and left with my newly printed picture in a custom frame at no extra cost.

WHITEOAKS
Starring Ethel Barrymore

MONDAY, SEPTEMBER 12, 1938

"**E**thel Barrymore...in *my* dressing room?" I shrieked.

"*Our* dressing room," Missy corrected. I ignored her.

"I believe that's what I said, Chickadee." Old Man Prestel chuckled. We'd known Ethel Barrymore was coming with a stock company to mount a production of *Whiteoaks*, a pompous play in which she'd be headlining as the affable matriarch, but what we hadn't anticipated was that she was going to move into our turf.

Nor that she would be right behind Old Man Prestel.

She entered the room chuckling, taking in the site of The Majestic Sisters in glorious repose, and thanked us for the use of the space while she was here.

I was too starstruck, too tongue-tied to say anything to her except a garbled "the pleasure is all ours" before I was out of there like a lightning bolt.

"I would've thought you'd attach yourself to her like a second shadow," Old Man Prestel told me once he'd joined me in the hallway backstage. "For all you go on about wanting to be a big star someday, you just wasted a plum opportunity."

I WAS STILL kicking myself at home later that evening. We were enjoying a quick dinner before the four of us made our way back to the Majestic for *Whiteoaks*'s premiere.

"Edward will meet us there," Missy assured us. "We'll have five seats together in the loges." Her gaze cut across the table to me, daring me to acknowledge Benjamin, who kept popping up these last few months. She'd spotted him at the concession stand during the Radio Queen pageant in July, and coupled with the 'Candid Camera' fiasco, she was biding her time for another appearance. I kept my lips zipped. She didn't need to know that Benajmin would be seated somewhere in the lower auditorium, perfectly hidden from her view. Our secret romance would continue another night, at least.

"It's so exciting," Mother gushed. "Ethel Barrymore. Can you stand it?"

"I can't," I said. "I clammed up when we met her earlier, too. I have so many questions for her and now I'll never get the chance."

"Questions?" Missy asked. She looked over at Daddy, who was silently eating his green beans. "What questions could you possibly have for Ethel Barrymore?"

"How she hones her craft. How she memorizes her scripts. Decides on character details. Staging. Costuming. Projecting. If I'm going to be a star, I'll need—"

Daddy's hand suddenly slammed down onto the table. "You need to stop talking like you're Mary Pickford, Melanie." Typical Daddy, to name an actress who hadn't been in demand in over a decade. "What you do need is to start thinking rationally about your future v-᠎ going to bother Ethel Barrymore. You're goin- and then you're going to figure ou encyclopedia set. Oh yes, I couldn't job the other day."

They'd never understand. I sat t᠎ Kept up the silence all the way to the formance—which was splendid, by the through the foyer, as they all zigged left, hall to the dressing room.

I could hear her inside bustling around, and I knocked quietly, waiting for her to invite me into my own dressing room.

"Oh hello, dear," she said. Ethel had a radiant smile and a propellent disposition. "Did you enjoy the play?"

"I did," I replied, joining this matron of the stage at the vanity. I had a lot to learn, and I wanted to know everything. "I didn't get to introduce myself earlier—"

"Oh trust me," she chuckled. "I've heard a lot about you from Mr. Prestel. Said you want to be an actress and that you actually have what it takes to pull it off."

My heart swelled in gratitude to Old Man Prestel. "I just want five minutes of your time. I want to learn from you."

We didn't become best friends, then or ever, and I'm not sure she'd remember having met me if pressed, but she gave me pointers on how to be a better stage actress—tips I've employed in my career ever since. It also inspired me to consider more carefully all of my professional jobs. No longer did I only participate in department store fashion shows and store openings; I started recording radio dramas at the CHNS station up the street and even auditioned for a play with the Theatre Arts Guild, though they ultimately chose not to cast me in *Candida* (their loss, I figured).

And by my side through it all, Benjamin. He was enough support, he assured me. "Don't listen to your family, they don't know how radiant you are on the stage. I see it, Old Man Prestel sees it, and you *know* you have it in you. Be brave, Melly. Be bold. It'll all be yours someday."

THE SISTERS
Starring Bette Davis and Errol Flynn

MONDAY, NOVEMBER 14, 1938

"You know they call this the Persian Room?" Benjamin asked, skeptically glancing at the wallpaper and wingback chairs lining the small parlour at the Queen Hotel.

"It's to make it sound more exotic, I think," I replied, walking into the room. "I could've sworn Polynesian was all the rage these days, but what do I know? Say, how's about you grab one of those palm fronds and fan me whilst I lie on the chaise lounge?" A girl never outgrows the Cleopatra fantasy, I'm afraid.

"As tempting as that sounds, Sweets, I don't want a palm tree billed to my room. Heaven only knows what they cost to import." He pulled at one of the leaves, watching as the branch bowed with the tension then snapped back into place like a rubber band.

"Romance is dead," I sniffled, dropping into one of the elegant chairs with my hand thrown across my forehead like Gloria Swanson.

"Romance didn't pay for my gas all summer," he countered, sliding into the chair next to me and picking up the newspaper.

"But it has been keeping you in such high spirits," I reminded him.

"The Cameo for dinner tonight?" he asked, changing the subject.

"Oh, so you have money to spend on steak dinners but not on palm trees? Got it." I winked.

"You know, you're not as funny as your sister," he replied.

"Why you—"

"And we're not getting the steak. It's all-you-can-eat lobster. We're going to clean out their tanks."

"That sounds like a challenge I'm ready to accept." I felt my stomach rumble at the thought. "The show will likely be done around eleven. Is that too late?"

"For seafood? Never. For me? I'll have to ask Mrs. Crandall for a wake-up call."

"Oh, you poor baby," I simpered. "You know, you could always tag along and sleep in the loge seats. They're almost as comfy as a bed."

"Speaking from experience?"

"Let's just say it wasn't my idea to sit through *The Good Earth*, and we'll leave it at that. Anyway, I'll meet you outside the theatre when we're done. The crowd should be big tonight," I said. "It's a Bette Davis movie."

"Who's she? Is she any good?" His favourite game was pretending not to know who my idols were.

"*Is she any good?* She's only one of the best! Imagine that."

"And the routine?"

"A ballet Missy choreographed...about sisters."

He laughed. "An inspired choice."

I shrugged. "She gets testy if I don't let her put together the routine every once in a while." My feet still hurt from the bruising choreography she'd dreamt up.

"Poor Sweets," he said. I smacked his chest and then grabbed my purse. Before I could get up off the settee, he took my hand and kissed it. "See you soon."

꩜

"YOU'RE LATE," MISSY taunted when I breezed into the dressing room a few minutes later, having detoured to the candy counter for a chocolate bar to ward off the hunger.

"You found a good use for that watch Eddy bought you, I see." I tossed my handbag onto the couch and sat beside her at the vanity to start putting on my stage makeup.

"When the great *Melanie Calvert* strolls in late after chewing my head off for the same crime, I can't help but take notice."

"Don't worry, I wouldn't miss your skills review for anything."

"What does *that* mean?"

"This whole routine? It feels less like an act and more of a test to pass before I can progress to pointe. The applause was pretty sparse last night, in case you hadn't noticed."

"Well maybe if you weren't so distracted—" she started.

"You're a fine one to lecture me on being distracted, Melissa."

"Well then, Snow White, next week you can come up with the routine again, something befitting your talent." She stood abruptly and stalked over to the wardrobe.

"Of that I have no doubt."

⌒ℓℓᵹ

"BIG CROWD TONIGHT," I said after our final show of the evening, stumbling into my seat, my fingers already unbraiding my hair. I began pulling out the errant bobby pins that had been scratching my scalp all night.

"Big applause, too," Missy teased. I didn't bother to correct her. She was smiling, like she always was by the end of the night: it meant she was *that much closer* to seeing Eddy. "I think the ladies wanted a glimpse of Errol Flynn."

"Some of us bought tickets to see The Majestic Sisters," came a voice from the hallway. Missy rushed to the door and threw it open. Eddy was on the other side, bouquet of roses in his outstretched arms. By my estimation, the man was singlehandedly keeping The Flower Shop in business.

"You shouldn't have!" she gushed. This was already a familiar song-and-dance. He'd show up at our dressing room door with a bouquet of roses, she'd tell him he shouldn't have, she'd take them anyway, then tell anyone who would listen about how sweet her beau was, and all about her collection of dried flowers she couldn't stand to get rid of.

"And yet every week, you take them," I teased. "What'd you think of the show, Eddy?"

He nodded. Bless him, he never tried to wade into the technical terms; he just gave blanket approval to anything Missy ever did onstage. Every routine, even if it was lousy—the routine for *Romance in the Dark* springs to mind—was golden in his eyes, and the only elements he ever commented on were costuming. Namely, how gorgeous Missy looked in whichever colour we were wearing ("You looked great, too, Mel!" he'd always tack on at the end), or how beautiful her hair was.

"I have flowers for my second-favourite Majestic Sister, too," he said, producing a bouquet of orange blossoms from the ether.

"It's nice to know I did so well in polling," I said, watching as Missy plucked a flower from my bouquet and added it to hers. I took the bouquet from Eddy and gave him a quick kiss on the cheek. "Oh, you shouldn't have. Was there two-for-one deal on or something?"

"What, a guy can't celebrate the city's most famous sisters?" He winked.

"I do have some good news," Eddy said, after Missy and I had changed back into our regular clothes. We walked out to the lobby in a cluster, my thoughts on the lobster and Benjamin, who'd be waiting for me outside the theatre.

"Well, don't leave us in suspense," Missy said, stopping by the Anubis statue. "What's the good news?"

"The head of Eaton's has chosen the Atlantic for their company Christmas dinner and dance," he gushed. "That's nearly eight hundred guests."

Missy shrieked, jumping into his arms. "Oh, Edward! I'm so proud of you."

"Eddy, that's wonderful," I said, clapping his shoulder.

He'd been talking about expanding the hotel, adding a few extra floors to keep up with the demands and I knew this bash was the icing on the cake.

"I think we should celebrate," he said. "Let me treat you both to some champagne and dessert at the hotel."

I was just about to beg off, but Old Man Prestel came strolling down the hall, a man on a mission. "Chickadee," his voice boomed in the near-empty corridor, "you've got a visitor here. Says he's a big fan. Wanna meet him?"

I lifted an eyebrow. It would be so perfectly Benjamin to pull this kind of prank on me, but before I could make an excuse and meet him without an audience, Missy had to open her big mouth: "An elusive member of the Melly Calvert Fan Club? You've finally got a quorum to meet!" And of course I couldn't let an insult like that slide, so I quipped, "One more than you."

Old Man Prestel gestured for the gentleman down the hall to come closer, and soon, a tall fool whose profile I'd recognize anywhere stood with us.

"Miss Calvert?" Benjamin asked.

"Which one?" Missy teased.

"The other one." He winked at her.

"That's me. How can I help you, young man?" I said, holding out my hand like I was Queen Victoria.

"I'm Benjamin Trapper," he said, enveloping my hand in his. "I'm a big fan."

"I've seen you somewhere before," Missy said, staring at him. "You wouldn't, by chance, have been dining with a certain Majestic Sister of mine earlier this summer? Say, at the Riviera Tea Room?"

I rolled my eyes. "Okay, Mata Hari, give it a rest. Yes, this is my beau from 'Candid Camera.'"

"I knew it!" she squealed. "You thought you could keep him a secret, but I always find out." Then she walked up to him and grabbed his hand. "Benjamin, you say? I'm Missy, and it's such a pleasure to *finally* meet you."

"And you," he replied, a perfect gentleman. "I've heard so much about you."

"Have you, now?" she sang, rounding on me.

I lifted an eyebrow at him. "He probably reads Raymond's column," I said. "Don't get ahead of yourself."

Missy pouted but remained undeterred. "Want to join us? We're heading down to the hotel."

"We have plans—" I started to say, but Benjamin covertly finished my thought for me, "—but I'm sure it's nothing we can't rearrange," he added.

I wasn't backing down. I had no desire to give in to the prosecutorial line of questioning that would come of dinner with my sister. "Benjamin and I had plans for all-you-can-eat lobster at the Cameo, though," I said, squeezing his arm. "So as much as dessert and champagne would hit the spot, darling, I'm afraid we'll have to beg off."

"Unless you care to join us?" Benjamin piped up. I looked up at him, expecting a playful grin, but the placid smile on his face told me it was a genuine offer.

The lovebirds shared a look, and then Eddy said, "If you're sure?"

The longer I spent arguing with Benjamin meant less time to spend with him, so I caved, reluctantly. "Why not?" I said. "The more the merrier."

"Shall we head up?" Missy asked. At Eddy's nod, they linked arms and hailed a cab. "We'll meet you there. Don't take too long!"

I waited until they were gone to round on him. "So much for a quiet meal!"

"I thought it was high time I met your dear sister and the esteemed Eddy Davis," he said, with the solemnity of a funeral orator. "I hope you aren't too upset with me."

"You'll regret this before you crack the first lobster tail, mark my words," I promised.

"Maybe so," he conceded. "But she means a lot to you, and I want to know who you know and love who you love." Well, how could I refuse when he put it like that? He offered me his arm. "Shall we?"

I took his arm and said, "It's all I'll hear about for the rest of time. 'When are you going to see Benjamin again?' and 'That Benjamin sure is swell, eh Melly?'"

He was ignoring me. "Now tell me, how much is dinner going to set me back?"

"Good luck fighting Eddy for the bill." I guffawed. "He'll find *any* excuse to toss his wealth around. Missy's probably telling him to pay for your meal and move you to the Atlantic so they can spy on you better."

"No can do, Sweets," Benjamin said, once we were out on the sidewalk. "I'm a faithful patron of the Queen Hotel. Plus, they aren't too picky about my having visitors." He gave me a wink.

⌒ℓℓ₂

MISSY AND I were accustomed to shutting down the Cameo Soda Grill whenever we held court there. Their seafood was always top-notch, and the atmosphere inside the elegant restaurant was always jovial. As Benjamin and I entered, we scanned the room for my sister and Eddy. Of course, they were seated at a private table off to the side of the dining room. They'd be able to see anyone who entered, hovering over them in their forest green chairs like royals on their thrones.

"Over here!" Missy yelled, giggling as she sipped from the green concoction in her hand.

"We see you," I yelled over the din of late-night revellers enjoying their root beer floats at the soda counter by the window.

"About time you got here," Missy said, once we were all seated.

She pushed two Fiery Mellys towards us and gestured to the shrimp cocktails at the centre of the table. "I was about to eat these for you, but you showed up in the nick of time."

"You're a dear," I said, clinking my glass against Benjamin's. "How nice of you to abstain for our guest."

"I make no promises when that dessert cart goes by again," Missy teased, watching the waiter push the cart filled with pies, cake slices, and chocolates around the room.

"Mmm." Benjamin licked his lips and held up my signature drink. "This is delicious."

"I told you." I took a sip of my own.

"So, Benjamin," Missy started. "How long have you known the fair Melanie Calvert?"

"You're the fair one, *Melissa*," I interjected. She knew how much I hated to be referred to by my full name. I could only conclude that she was trying to goad me in front of Benjamin to make up for all the times I'd teased her in Eddy's presence.

"I swear, they get along," Eddy promised. "They just don't know how to show it sometimes."

Benjamin laughed. "I have a big family; I know all about it," he said. "To answer your question, Miss Calvert, I had the great fortune of running into her at party once upon a time, and she's had me hooked ever since."

"Once upon a time, eh? You know she stole the role of Snow White from me once—"

"So, Missy, what did you get up to today?" I interjected.

"Oh, the same thing I do every day." She waved me off. "I'm boring. Let's talk about you some more, Benjamin."

As I'd expected, Missy peppered him with questions, barely giving him a chance to breathe, but he sailed through them all.

"You want to ask him which novels he read in eighth-grade English next, Missy?" I muttered. Then she kicked me under the table. "Ouch! Are you practicing the can-can under there?"

"Are you okay, Sweets?" Benjamin asked, peeking under the table-cloth at my leg.

"I'm fine," I promised. "She has a twitch."

"I do not, *Sweets*," Missy retorted. My cheeks reddened.

"A minor one. It's why she doesn't tap dance anymore. She can't control it."

"Shall we go to the powder room?" Missy asked. "Your witchy undertones are starting to show."

She yanked me from my seat before I could protest, and then shoved me into the ladies' room and dropped onto a settee, examining her lipstick.

"What is wrong with you?" I asked, rubbing my leg.

"*Me*? What's wrong with *you*? He's a catch! Why have you been hiding him?" she hissed.

"I haven't been hiding him, you goon."

"I recognize him, you know. From last year, on the sidewalk. I thought he was just another fan accosting you, but you spoke like you already knew each other. Then he shows up in that 'Candid Camera' feature and that radio pageant... How long have you two been sneaking around?"

I shrugged. "It's nothing serious, Missy. Just two people having some fun."

She eyed me. "It doesn't look like nothing serious. He looks at you like you hung the moon."

"I did hang the moon," I reminded her. "Remember the routine for *My Lucky Star*?" I caught Missy rolling her eyes at me as I slipped back out of the ladies' room.

⌒ₑₗₑ⌒

"IT MUST BE close to midnight," Benjamin mused. "If not dawn."

"I've aged a century in this seat," I mumbled, too much lobster and one too many Fiery Mellys burning a hole in my stomach.

"They're comfortable seats, at least."

"Not as comfy as the seats in the Stargazers' Lounge," Missy babbled. "We're eating there next time. The chairs were custom made by a woodworker in the Annapolis Valley. The rest of the hotel is Art Deco-inspired, but these chairs are pure Sheraton-style."

"She pretends she knows what 'Sheraton' means," I stage whispered to Benjamin. "Eddy took a photo of the dining room at the Hôtel Ritz to the woodworker and told him to make chairs that looked like that."

"He did not!" Missy hissed. "His mother picked out the chairs! She said the reeded edges on the legs would complement the straight lines of the architecture and décor!"

"Bitsy Davis strikes once more," I said. "A toast to Bitsy!"

Eddy rolled his eyes and removed the napkin from his lap and placed it on his plate. "Ladies, I think it's about time to call it a night."

"I agree," Benjamin said, following suit. "I need to be up early for work."

"Are you okay to get back to your hotel?" Eddy asked. "I can put you up tonight, no charge."

"Don't look a gift horse in the mouth," I whispered. "I've been trying to get a free night's stay since that joint opened. Take the offer."

Eddy chuckled. "All you've had to do is ask."

"It's the principle," I muttered.

Benjamin laughed, then nodded at Edward. "That would be nice, actually. I haven't had a chance to stay there yet."

Eddy nodded. "Don't worry about it. What's the point of owning your own hotel if you can't offer your friends perks?"

"Friends!" I squeezed his hand. "You've made a new friend, Benjamin!"

Eddy shook his head. "How about you, Melly. Shall I get you a room key as well?"

I paused, as if taking stock of my body, trying to figure out if I'd make it all the way back to Coburg Road. "Who am I to refuse?"

"Separate rooms," Missy teased. "My Edward runs a proper establishment." I stared at her and watched as her cheeks flushed crimson. She tossed her napkin on the table and stood up, waiting for Eddy.

"Do you have everything?" Benjamin asked, holding his arm out behind me, guiding me towards the door. "Purse, hat, coat?"

"Yes, Dad," I teased. "I have everything but a kiss goodnight."

"I'll save that for later, if you don't mind."

⌒ℓℯ⌒

EDDY SPARED NO expense in putting me and Benjamin up for the night. Two of the most opulent rooms on the top floor were waiting for us—down the hall from his and Missy's rooms, naturally, and we were treated to their moonlight sonata as they kept kissing each other good night. Eddy apparently stayed at the hotel more often than not these days, not finding the Davis compound on Beaufort Avenue good for much.

I looked up at the handsome man whose fingers were trailing down my spine. "I'll just be down there." I pointed at my room.

"It's good that you're nearby. Safety and all," Benjamin said.

We kissed until the elevator doors opened and the ruckus of the late-evening crowd, likely returning from Buckingham Tavern, drowned out our silence.

"That was close," he whispered, kissing me again.

"I should go in," I said, between kisses. "I can hear the telephone ringing. Missy probably wants a rundown."

"I'll give you something real good to tell her," he said, wrapping me into a tighter embrace. I lost myself to his kisses for long minutes, before pulling away again.

"Thank you for talking me into this. It felt nice to finally share you with Missy."

"It wasn't so bad, was it?"

"No, it wasn't. Wake me up for breakfast?" I asked, taking a few steps backwards towards my room.

Benjamin perked up at the mention of breakfast.

"The eggs benedict is my favourite. Plus, it's one of the most expensive items on the breakfast menu. Don't worry, Eddy will comp it."

"Expensive and on someone else's dime is my favourite meal."

"Maybe we can order room service. Escape Missy's watchful eye."

Benjamin laughed. "You're ridiculous."

"You're handsome. I love you."

"I love you too, Sweets."

VIVACIOUS LADY
Starring Ginger Rogers and James Stewart

SATURDAY, DECEMBER 31, 1938

A s Majestic Sisters, our New Year's Eve dance cards were always full. Not at the hottest parties, mind you, but at midnight showings. Much like his anniversary stunts, Old Man Prestel would pick a special movie to play as midnight struck. To close out 1938, he allowed Missy and me the honour of choosing the film, and we picked one of our favourites: *Vivacious Lady* starring Ginger Rogers.

"It describes me perfectly," I told Old Man Prestel in the meeting.

"No, it describes *me* perfectly," Missy interjected.

Old Man Prestel put his head in his hands and then rushed off to find the reel.

The flowers arrived while Missy was onstage for the early evening show, when the theatre was full of people who had actual midnight plans, y'know? The arrangement was, once again, so large it brushed against the doorframe as the delivery man walked into the lobby. Old Man Prestel had simply laughed when he signed for the order, then walked it back to our dressing room.

When Missy came back after the routine and saw the overflowing roses and carnations, she squealed. She picked up the card:

I'm sitting in the back row all by my lonesome,
looking for someone to ring in the new year with.
Care to keep me company? – E

I've never seen someone hotfoot it the way Missy hotfooted it from the dressing room. "Be back for the nine o'clock show!" I called behind her. You could always count on her to scurry to Eddy's side whenever he called. It was getting tiresome.

⌒⟋⟍⌒

"I NEED TO cut out early tonight, sis," Missy said, as we were preparing for the midnight show.

The little sneak thought if she sprang the news on me at the last minute I'd be fine with it. We were due to go on a bit early for the midnight show—Old Man Prestel wanted us on the stage to count down the new year, and then curtains up.

"We're here until midnight," I said, re-applying my eyeliner. "*We're* the ones ringing in the new year; whaddaya mean you're cutting out early?" How could she even think of leaving the Majestic in the lurch?

She had the goofiest smile on her face. "I need to meet Edward for a *secret rendezvous.*"

"It's not much of a secret if you blabber about it," I said, tossing my mascara down on the vanity.

"You'd know *all* about secrets, wouldn't you?" she sneered. "Besides, it's not like you're singularly focused on the Majestic anymore either. I don't know why you're giving me such grief," she huffed, dropping down beside me to touch up her lipstick.

"The difference between us is I know how to keep one. You don't know the first thing about secrets. First you're telling me, then next thing you know, you're telling the sweetest-looking German spy all about what's going on at the Navy yard."

"I have no idea what's going on at the Navy yard."

"No, but you might know something tangentially that sinks a ship or two."

"Melly, we're not even at war."

"With the way everyone's tiptoeing around each other, it's only a matter of time."

"Well, thank you for this geopolitical chatter. Now, can we get back to what matters? Me cutting out early?"

"Missy, Old Man Prestel has been promoting this show all month: Ring in the New Year with the Majestic *Sisters*. Plural. Though I'd have no problem taking the limelight all for my own, I think some customers may be upset that they paid to party with both of us and only the fun one showed up."

"You're no fun," she said, sulking in front of the mirror.

"Of course I'm fun. But if it'll make you get ready quicker, you can be the fun one tonight, okay? Now, show me that winning smile. Make sure you flash it bright enough for Eddy in the balcony."

"I wish you wouldn't tease him so."

I met her eyes in the mirror. "How do you mean?"

"Teasing him about the hotel," she said, but then she got on a roll. "Acting like the overprotective chaperone whenever we go out, all three of us."

"Well, someone's gotta look after you, and since Raymond's too often out on the roof to take on the job, it falls to me to make sure he's treating you right."

"Of course he's treating me right, he's my—"

"He's your soulmate, *I know, I know*. It's *terribly* sweet." I mimed throwing up, just to see the look on her face.

"I hope you find a love like this someday," she said, picking up her powder brush to touch up her stage makeup. "I want to spend forever with him."

I met her eyes in the mirror. "I can guarantee that he wants that, too."

I know what you're thinking: here's another perfect opportunity to tell your sister all about how much Benjamin means to you. She'd let you gush about his face, his smile, how utterly, utterly perfect he was; and she'd laugh the whole time that the career-driven Majestic Melly had *finally* found her majestic match. She hadn't seen him since our lobster binge at the Cameo, but the busyness of Christmas kept her from asking. Besides, I knew what Eddy had planned; I was in on it. We'd spent an afternoon at Birks earlier this month picking out the perfect ring for Missy—the handsome tip Eddy left behind kept the news out of the papers, thankfully. There was a twinge of sadness when I thought about Missy's impending engagement. It's one thing to lose your sister, but with the additional knowledge that she's moving towards a life you don't envision for yourself? Still, I'd smile through the heartache. The last thing I wanted to do was take the attention off of her. That evening, at least.

I'll spare you the full details of the act that night but, suffice it to say it remained unchanged throughout every performance except for one minute detail for the midnight show.

Vivacious Lady, in case you haven't seen it, is a romantic comedy starring Ginger Rogers and Jimmy Stewart as a couple who get married and try to hide it from his parents. Can you figure out what happened next?

Well, there I was, standing onstage in front of all of Halifax, a few pharaoh statues, and the entire staff of the Majestic Theatre, ready for my little bit about this important piece of jewellery I was holding—an engagement ring, naturally—when I made a very theatrical gesture and, oopsy-daisy, there goes the handcuff, sis, let me just grab it and we'll continue. I could feel Missy's eyeroll, the penetrating stare, the telegraphed thoughts—*are you trying to make me late? Did you dip into the champagne a little early?* Old Man Prestel had offered us each a flute before we went on, but being dedicated performers, we'd turned him down. Why get fizzy around the edges and celebrate early when the real fun began at midnight? I poked around on the stage floor looking for the ring.

"Excuse me, ma'am, but I believe I have something that belongs to you," a man said, stepping into view, dark blond hair illuminated by the stage lights. Eddy Davis, as he lived and breathed, a guest on The Majestic Sisters' stage. He'd better enjoy it; it was enough to have to share the spotlight with Missy.

He held up the ring—honestly, it might as well have come from a

Crackerjack box, as tacky as it looked. "It's not mine," I said, gesturing to Missy behind me. "It's hers."

Intrigued now, Missy came over to stand with us. "What's going on?"

"He has your ring," I said.

"This isn't in the bit," she mumbled under her breath, stage smile painted to her face. Cool Missy Calvert never betrayed a hint of worry.

"Play along, darling," I whispered back. "I thought you wanted to be the fun one?"

Eddy winked at her, then stepped around me. He stopped right in front of sweet Missy, light blush on her face, and held up the ring again. "Is this yours?"

"It's not mine," she said, confused. No one had told her about this gag, and the poor thing was still acting like it was my ring.

"It's not yours, eh?" Eddy brushed his fingers against his inimitably square chin, deep in thought. He handed the cheap ring to me, and I slipped it onto my pinky finger—I kept that ring, in fact. It's in my jewellery box in Palm Springs.

Then, as if the universe's mysteries had suddenly revealed themselves to him, Eddy snapped his fingers and reached into his pocket. "Say, my darling, maybe this one's yours."

Then, kittens, well, he did the most romantic thing. He fished a blue velvet Birks box out of his pocket, dropped to one knee right there on the stage, and opened it to reveal the largest diamond solitaire engagement ring I'd ever seen.

Wallis Simpson, eat your heart out.

Missy gasped. "Is this really happening?"

The audience laughed. "I think he's about as serious as one gets," I teased.

"What are you thinking?" she asked Eddy.

"I won't speak for him, but I think Missy Calvert's about to become Missy Davis," I continued. "Unless you say no."

"Bite your tongue!" she admonished.

"Bite yours," I retorted. "Let him speak; he's been rehearsing all afternoon!"

Eddy winked at me then. It was still funny to view him as the kind of pal you'd plan these kinds of surprises with, but then, he was about to become my brother-in-law, after all. "You look," he breathed, "amazing."

Suddenly, the curtain directly in front of the screen lifted, and the screen behind us flickered on. Mort, the projectionist, bless him, had put on a newsreel that had been shot from the sidewalk across from the Atlantic Hotel.

"I remember the first time I ever saw your beautiful face," Eddy said. "It stopped me in my tracks. I'd never seen such perfection."

"Ed—" Missy tried to interject.

"The best night of my life happened just over a year ago," he pressed on. "My hotel opens, and I meet the love of my life. A man couldn't ask for anything better."

The scene on the screen changed to a view from the terrace itself, framed by the cityscape of downtown Halifax in the background. In the distance, you could see the Majestic Theatre marquee. The lights dimmed slightly, and several ushers rushed onstage to fill the area with candles.

"I brought you up there that night to show you the constellations, but I had no idea the brightest star was standing right in front of me. You pointed up at the sky, at some cluster of stars, and you asked me—"

"Which constellation is that?" Missy finished.

"And I said, 'I haven't the foggiest, but it pales in comparison to you.' The smile you gave me...everything in my life suddenly seemed to fall into place. There she is, I thought. The woman I want to spend my life with. Missy—Melissa. I don't know all the constellations' names. All I know is I want to spend the rest of my life with you at my side. My North Star, my guiding light. The brightest star I know. I want to see everything and do everything with you, if you'll let me."

Missy was sobbing at this point. I glanced out into the audience. Mother and Daddy were sitting in the front row; behind them, every member of our extended family that could be called together on such short notice. All misty-eyed and smiling. It was rare for the whole gang to get together these days, as spread out and sparse as our family tree was, but this was the biggest occasion in our family's history. Missy was about to become a member of Halifax's very own royal family! Also in the crowd, perched on their thrones in the loge seats, the Davises.

"I want to call that star Mrs. Missy Davis, if you'll let me. Missy, will you marry me?"

She threw herself into his arms, like she couldn't wait a second longer to embrace him. "Yes! Yes! Of course!"

The audience behind us roared its applause as Eddy placed the ring on Missy's finger and jumped to his feet, hugging her like a lifeline. "Thank you!" he whispered into her hair, pulling her in for a kiss. They hugged and kissed for a while, and then, remembering where they were, they jumped apart. Missy turned to me and threw herself into my outstretched arms.

"I'm engaged!" she shrieked, holding out her left hand for me to check out the rock.

"You're going to be in traction lugging that diamond around," I teased, admiring the ring. I pulled her back to me. "Congratulations!" I whispered into her ear.

We stuck around long enough to ring in the new year, the three of us onstage with Old Man Prestel, and then scuttled down to the Atlantic and danced and celebrated until dawn. I called Benjamin just after midnight to wish him well—he was back in Truro with the family, naturally—and told him the plan had gone off without a hitch. He told me to pass along his best wishes and to give Missy a kiss from him.

TO SAY THE society pages blew up would be a grand understatement. Missy's engagement was front-page news the next day—and all the attention went directly to her head.

I'd never seen such mania—and wouldn't again, until Prince Rainier proposed to dear ole Grace and whisked her off to Monaco. And just like Grace, as soon as Missy became engaged, the questions started: Will she keep working? Will she quit her popular act to run the

Davis household? What does Majestic Melly say? (*She* was all smiles, of course, the supportive sister; no matter that her younger sister beat her to the altar—even the papers knew I was too wild to be matrimonial at that point in my life.)

The *Mail* thought it would be a swell idea to give Missy a column in the society pages to talk about wedding planning, as if she had the faintest hint of an idea of what she was doing. It turned into the biggest advertisement package the paper could offer.

"The Wedding Belle" became her new moniker, and one of the paper's biggest features. If Majestic Missy talked about the flowers she wanted for her bouquet, suddenly a pageful of florists were advertising their stores. If she mentioned wanting a chignon for her wedding hairstyle, suddenly all the hairstylists were advertising their expertise. Bright red lipstick on her beautiful visage? Several beauticians knew how to pick her perfect shade! And on and on it went.

Her trousseau was sponsored by Simpson's, Mills Brothers, and Paulette's. Her flowers came free of charge from The Flower Shop. Jewellery gifted from Henry Birks and Sons. MacAskill's offered to do the wedding portraiture and custom framing. The restaurants—good gravy, the restaurants!—fell over themselves to offer up their food for the reception, but like good little girls and boys, Missy and Edward chose the Stargazers' Lounge. The venue: St. Paul's Church in the heart of downtown—the more people lining the streets to catch a glimpse of Missy Davis, the better. The reception venue: the Coastal Ballroom, naturally.

It got to the point where if I even saw the words "Wedding Belle" in that ridiculous scripty font in the newspaper, I'd skip ahead. She even lured me into the fracas, detailing how we'd gone shopping for the maid of honour's dress (we went to every dress shop, for the publicity, and settled on a crimson dress from Paulette's) and how sweet of a sister I was to help her out. I'm sure she regretted those words later.

I loved her, good heavens how I loved her, and I loved what love—true love—had done for Missy, but once she got engaged she was insufferable to be around. This was still the era of big society weddings, though it would end up a little more subdued, what with the war on. But the big day was now set in stone: they'd marry on December 15, in the year of our Lord 1939.

They were a beautiful couple. Deserved every happy return. They truly were soulmates who would spend every wonderful moment of their lives together in a beautiful daze. They'd travel the world; they'd have adventure after adventure. They'd brighten their homestead with beautiful daughters and watch them fall in love and marry and grow their own families.

It was almost beautiful enough to make me want it for myself.

Almost.

THE COWBOY AND THE LADY
Starring Merle Oberon and Gary Cooper

FRIDAY, JANUARY 13, 1939

By the time David O. Selznick was ready to announce he'd finally found his Scarlett O'Hara, I was just about at my wits' end. It was exhausting, scanning the newspapers every morning to see if there'd been an official announcement. Old issues of *Photoplay* piled up on my nightstand as I earmarked the pages with any gossip about *Gone with the Wind* I could find.

It felt like every actress in Hollywood—and indeed, any woman who passed by an MGM executive who bore a resemblance to the spirited Scarlett O'Hara—was given a screen test and a chance at the biggest role in movieland's history, and the tabloids loved reporting on each and every one of them.

"Bette Davis wanted the part," I told Benjamin one night at the Cornflower. "But she'd never get it, so the Warner Brothers made their own *Gone with the Wind* especially for her: *Jezebel.* They reaped the benefits at the box office and now she gets to tell anyone who'll listen that she turned down the role of a lifetime. Imagine."

Bless him, my darling indulged my incessant chatter. By the time Selznick had finally cast Vivien Leigh, Benjamin probably knew more about the production than most Hollywood insiders.

"I thought you said Paulette Goddard was going to play Scarlett," he said, wiping his mouth with his napkin.

"Well, that's the newest rumour. Who knows, it'll probably be Merle Oberon or Katharine Hepburn for all we know, and this has just been a ruse to drum up public support for them."

"You know, you keep talking about this book, I'm going to have to read it one of these days," he said, picking up his knife and slicing into his meatloaf.

"You've never read *Gone with the Wind*?!" I balked. How had this never come up? He shook his head.

"I've only been talking about it since we met. You never once thought to tell me you've never read the book that will soon be the biggest film of all time?"

"I was going to get around to it, eventually," he replied.

"Eventually? When?" I asked, knowing full well he never had any intention of reading it.

"Well, I think I get the general idea because you never stop talking about it." He shrugged. "They fall in love even though they hate each other; they spend the next ten-odd years doing the same song and dance until she realizes that she loved him all along, but he leaves her anyways. The end. Is that it?"

"Yes, that's *it*. But there's so much more! So much nuance. And then there's Melly Hamilton. Honestly, Benjamin."

"I bet she'd be my favourite character." He winked.

"Don't try to placate me," I warned. "I'm nothing like that melo-dramatic little limpet."

"Aren't you?"

"I'd never let anyone walk all over me the way she lets Scarlett and Ashley. You mark my words."

"Duly noted. And if it will please you, I'll borrow this great tome from the library once I get around to acquiring a library card. How's that? Does that please you?"

"It's a start. But don't wait until the last second to read it."

He chuckled. "This is rich, coming from someone who normally doesn't read anything that's not serialized in the newspaper."

"*Gone with the Wind* is the only book I've ever willingly read," I cut in. "And you'll read it whether you want to or not. I'll make sure of it."

And that's how Benjamin came to own his very own, brand-new copy of *Gone with the Wind*. I'd bought it specially for him at The Book Room in between matinees and signed the bookplate, *"Tomorrow is another day" but you should not wait until then to begin reading this masterpiece. With love, Sweets.*

I didn't bother with gift-wrapping—he didn't deserve it—and instead volleyed it at his head outside the theatre later that evening in lieu of a polite and proper greeting. Good thing he caught it, too. If it had landed in the snowbank, I would've made him dig it out and dry it over the radiator in his hotel room.

"Good evening to you, too," he said, flipping it around and reading the cover. "Is this the one about life in the Chinese village, and the film starred Luise Rainer for some reason?"

I rolled my eyes. He could be such a ham. "Exactly. Start reading it soon, I want to be able to talk about the movie with you and not have you gawk at me like I'm speaking an alien language."

He chuckled. "I don't gawk, I admire. But I'll try my best." He flipped through the pages quickly. "How *long* is this?"

"If I read it in a matter of weeks, surely you can, too."

"Well," he said, tucking it under his arm. "Hopefully you'll forgive me if I start reading it later? We have a reservation at the New York Café and I'm starving."

"I need to know you'll actually read it! Cross your heart and kiss your elbow."

"As God is my witness." He kissed my hand. "I shall put it on my nightstand, fair lady, and chip away at it every night."

───◦ℓℓ◦───

WHEN I WOKE up that Saturday morning, Daddy was already at the kitchen table eating his breakfast and poring over the morning edition. I pulled out the seat next to him, gave him a quick kiss on the cheek, and sipped a glass of orange juice as I waited for Mother to finish cooking the bacon and eggs.

"Morning, darling," Mother droned over her shoulder. "Richard, show her the newspaper."

Daddy, no doubt nestled somewhere between the hockey scores and prognostications about the upcoming racing season at Sackville Downs, quickly picked up the front pages and presented them to me like a bill in need of royal assent. "Front page, third column."

I scanned the front page and found what he was referencing, and there it was: *Scarlett is cast at last.*

"Oh my goodness!" I gasped. "Vivien Leigh? A *British* actress?"

"Hopefully she can do a Southern accent," Daddy muttered.

I recognized her name. She'd been in a few pictures, but nothing major. Mostly British productions with bigger co-stars, like Rex Harrison and Lionel Barrymore. Just another tiny-waisted brunette, and at the end of the day, that's all that was necessary for Scarlett O'Hara.

"Hopefully," I agreed, reading the rest of the article.

"Who's playing Rhett Butler again?"

"Daddy, surely you didn't forget that Clark Gable's playing him!"

"Oh yes, I remember now. It's been a few days since you mentioned it," he said, winking over his coffee mug.

"Very funny," I said with a smirk. "I hope this means filming is going to begin soon. I'm going to go mad before the movie comes out."

"Better start planning the routine now," Mother said, bringing over three warm plates fresh from the stove. She joined us at the table.

"Better start fighting Missy for the main role is what you mean," I teased. "Speaking of my darling little sister, where is she?"

"Having breakfast with her fiancé," Daddy said around a mouthful of bacon. They sure did love that word! I clocked the smile on Mother's face and was once again left wondering about her views on equal rights. Why was she so zealous about her daughters marrying and giving her grandchildren? She'd marched for the vote!

"As one does," I said. "I'm sure he has breakfast all prepared à deux atop the hotel and they're ensconced in their private terrace, gazing out over the city."

"Maybe soon you'll meet a man like Edward." Mother sighed dreamily. "You know, those brothers of his are around your age."

They were perfect bores. "I don't understand why you can't accept that I'm happy with my life the way it is."

"I just want what's best for you," Mother said. "We both do. We worry about you."

"I keep telling you that you don't have to worry about me," I said, pushing the scrambled eggs around my plate with my fork. "I don't understand you at all, Mother. You were a suffragette, but you want me to be yoked to a husband?"

"I don't want you to be chained down, Melanie," she said, smoothing the tablecloth, "I just want to know you're taken care of. A husband could do that."

"I don't want to live Missy's life, Mother."

She balked. "You don't have to live—"

"Then why do you keep pressing me on this?" I stared into her eyes, striking in their similarity to mine, and hoped to find an inkling of understanding. "Let me just be me."

She squeezed my hand and said nothing. This tepid truce wouldn't last, but in that moment, there was a shred of understanding. It would be enough to carry me through those final months in Halifax.

I stood from the table.

"Where are you going?" Daddy asked. "You didn't even finish your eggs."

"I'll grab something at Mr. Green's. I'm heading downtown."

⌒ℓℓ⌒

I WAS AT the Majestic early that afternoon, desperate to work the news about Scarlett O'Hara into the act that night.

The routine was a staid Western song-and-dance about cowboys—sometimes we went with literal interpretations, and *The Cowboy and The Lady* provided us a creative respite, at least—where we played up our personality traits.

I'd envisioned us bantering about Scarlett O'Hara and Melly Hamilton in a sort of who's-on-first–style, where Missy would tell me that Vivien Leigh had been announced as Scarlett and I'd reply *"Yes, but who's Melly?"* with some fine back and forth, like, *"You're Melly."*

"I'm Melly?" I'd reply.

"Yes, you're Melly."

"I'm not Melly."

"You have to be, I'm Missy."

The audience loved it, by the way. But trying to convince my newly engaged sister to drag her head out of the clouds almost ruined the gag. She was too lovestruck to pay attention to anything beyond the diamond sparkler on her ring finger. If you asked me, that engagement ring was almost a manacle; if the topic didn't revolve around weddings or marriage, it didn't interest her.

Minutes away from showtime and here we were, still going over the bit in our dressing room.

"I don't get it." Missy was paying more attention to her eyeliner than her script notes, meaning I'd had to explain it a few times already.

"What's not to get? It's your classic 'Who's on first,'" I said, dropping into the seat next to her. "You're just saying my name."

"Is the audience going to get it?"

"Not if you say it like that," I muttered.

"Like what?"

"Bored, uninterested. At least pretend that you care about *something* other than your engagement ring."

"Of course I care about other things, don't be ridiculous." She tossed the eyeliner back into her makeup kit, then spared another quick glance at her ring.

"Every time I look at you, you're gawking at that ring."

"You sound jealous."

"I sound fed up."

"Keep that up, you won't be my maid of honour."

"Keep it up, I won't go to the wedding at all," I threatened.

She looked at me then with her icy-cold stare, as if daring me. And that's when I realized I meant it.

MOVE OVER, DARLING
Starring Doris Day and James Garner

TUESDAY, DECEMBER 24, 1963

I remembered what Old Man Prestel had once said about the architectural beauty of the Majestic as I stared up at its timeworn visage: the Egyptian theatre craze had long since become passé, but he vowed he'd never modernize it. Represented an era, he'd told us back in the '30s. A golden age of cinema and a golden age of entertainment.

I bought a ticket to the new Doris Day picture that had just opened that day, and startled Tracy in the process. "It's just little ole me, Tracy, no need to get so excited," I said, slipping her a five-dollar bill. "Is he here?"

She nodded, eyes wide, a sad smile. "He spends night and day in that office crunching the numbers."

"Say no more." I held up a hand. "D'you think he'd mind if I popped in?"

Her eyes shone. "Melly, I think he's been waiting for you a long, long time."

OLD MAN PRESTEL'S office was in the same place it had always been. I knocked once, then opened it and popped my head in. I wasn't surprised to see it so cluttered—some things never change—but what did shock me was the walls behind him.

He'd built a veritable shrine to The Majestic Sisters.

Every wall calendar we'd ever printed hung in a row behind his desk, above them twin photos of me winning my Oscars. A telegram I'd sent him in 1940 telling him I'd booked my first film was framed next to a photo of me on the stage for our routine ahead of *Maid's Night Out*.

He'd kept up with me, even though I hadn't kept up with him. It broke my heart.

And much like the rest of the theatre, Old Man Prestel looked past his prime. But I could see that he was still the same gruff and stocky man I'd known way back when. When he clapped eyes on me, the warmest smile rose on his mouth as he took in a slightly older Majestic Melly standing right in front of him.

I cleared my throat. I hadn't expected to be so emotional. "I'm here to talk about the costuming budget, sir," I said by way of greeting.

"That right?" he said, pushing aside some papers to find his adding machine. "I don't have John Wayne's money, but I'm sure I could juggle a few things around to get you something from Mills."

Then he looked at my expertly designed green Givenchy coat and said, "Seems your taste has gotten more expensive since I last saw you."

He gestured for me to take one of the seats in front of his desk, though both were full of paperwork. I bundled up a bunch of invoices and neatly placed them on the floor, then stared up at him.

"What brings you to town, kid?"

"I can't come home for Christmas?" I teased.

"You haven't been home for..." He paused, as if unsure whether to mention my parents' deaths. "Don't spin me a story that you've gotten nostalgic in your old age."

"My *old age*?" I cut in. "I'm not even fifty years old and I'm still in demand out there!"

"Why don't you tell me why you're really here?" he said gently.

For as much as the loveable old grump truly cared about me, he'd never once lost himself to purple prose or flowery language. Always straight to the point with Old Man Prestel.

"I'm here to see the new Doris Day picture. I like her." Everybody liked her, she was one of Hollywood's biggest stars. But why weren't more people coming out to the Majestic?

"If Doris Day's returns were enough to keep this place open, I'd be in better straits," he said, motioning at the stacks of invoices next to me.

"Well...that's why I'm really here," I confessed. "I want to help you save this place."

He gave me a sad smile. "Who said I want to save it? Maybe I'm looking forward to retirement. Maybe I'm tired of running this place. I'm an old man."

I looked him over once again. He was right. He was an old man, but he was one of those men who'd always looked older than he was. His hair had gone pure white by the time he was forty; even I didn't know its original colour. He must've been in his seventies by now, but he'd always run this place with the vigour of a young man.

Maybe chasing that excellence had worn him down over the years.

"It used to be an event to go to the movies," he said. "Now I've got teenagers wanting the next Troy Donahue flick."

"They wanted me to play his mother once," I scoffed. Old Man Prestel raised his eyes in surprise like the good man he was. "Well, I'm here to help however I can."

"That's a sweet offer, Melly," he said, searching through the papers for one with the ticket returns on them. "Take a look at this. Historical, over the past decade."

I studied the numbers, but they weren't as dire as I'd expected. "I don't know much about the number side of things, but from what I know at MGM and the other studios I've worked with lately, these sales aren't anything troubling."

He eyed me. "You remember how the lines used to wrap around the block back when you were still performing here?"

"No," I teased. "I was usually inside getting ready."

"Smart-mouth." He laughed. "I guess I just find myself wishing for the good old days. Back when the movies had purpose. The stars were big. People planned their weekends around what picture they'd go see. Now it's an afterthought. And with the Paramount up the street..."

His heart wasn't in it anymore.

"Do you want to watch the movie with me?" I asked, grabbing my handbag.

"You bought a ticket?" I nodded, because of course I'd bought a ticket. "Tracy *actually* charged Majestic Melly for admission?"

"Tracy was a little starstruck, I think," I admitted. "I more or less slid the money at her and walked in. I doubt an usher would dare stop me."

"We have usherettes now," he said. "Got a strongly worded letter from a high school senior about how I was depriving her of her rights to earn some money and work in her favourite place. I figured why not. Keep up with the times."

"Another chickadee in the roost," I said. "I'd like to meet this girl."

He stared at me over his messy desk. "There was only one Chickadee. She flew the nest long ago."

I blinked away the tears and swallowed down the lump in my throat. "Well, she still sounds great."

"She'll faint when she sees you."

"You know, that might be nice. It's been a while since anyone fainted in my presence."

"You want me to grab your old reserved sign? I think I still have it somewhere in storage. Might need a new coat of paint. Doubt you can read it, but it's yours if you want it." He wheezed, pulling himself up from his chair and reaching for a cane. That was new.

"I'd love to have it. I'll hang it above my kitchen door in Palm Springs."

Prestel slowly showed me around the theatre. The whole place was a time capsule. Just as I remembered it, but with a veneer of age. Truly, nothing had changed, though the candy counter—replete with a sign that read *#2 in sales in Canada 1963!* hanging above the popcorn machines—boasted modern appliances and updated candy offerings. "You can't come all this way and not try the best popcorn in Canada," he said.

"Your sign says it's the *second-best* popcorn in Canada," I pointed out. He sighed, grabbed two bags, and we were off to meet this famous usherette.

MISS SHARON GOREHAM led us up to the loges with her mouth agape, the beam from the flashlight in her hand trembling along the blue-carpeted floor. I winked at her on our way to the seats, my arm hooked in Old Man Prestel's, as we walked at a slow pace to keep from winding him.

Once we were in our seats, Sharon returned to her post. Little did I know, she was calling her friends about whom she'd spotted at the Majestic, and they, in turn, were calling their friends, and soon telephone hour began. They were calling the radio stations, the television stations, and the newspapers to let them know who was at the Majestic Theatre.

But while the quiet was still humming around us up in the balcony, Old Man Prestel and I sat in contented silence.

I stared up at the ceiling, with its painted blue sky and clouds, imagining we were back in the heyday. "You know," I said, turning to him, "I've travelled the world and seen so many wonderful things. But nothing compares to this view."

He smiled that ole Prestel smile I knew so well. "It's always nice to fly back to the nest. It makes you appreciate how far you've flown."

"It's been too long." I let out a breath. "I'm sorry I never asked you about what was going on. All those letters back and forth and I was only focused on myself. I should've—"

"You're here now, Chickadee, and that's what matters."

My eyes welled up again. "I can't imagine Halifax without the Majestic," I whispered, taking his hand and squeezing it.

"Me neither," he said, squeezing back. "But it's getting too difficult to maintain, and I'm no spring chicken."

"*This* is Halifax to me," I whispered, leaning my head on his shoulder. "Everything I am is because of this theatre."

"Me too. It's been a gift," he agreed, pressing a kiss to my hair. "I enjoyed every second."

I smiled ruefully. He'd made up his mind. "I'm sure it was a thrilling adventure."

"It wouldn't have been without you and your sister."

I sighed. "You don't have anyone who wants to take over?"

"Nobody I'd trust." We were silent for a moment. "I know the telephone company wants to get their hands on this land."

I sat up and looked over at that warm, sad old man. "Oh, you can't! Don't let them raze this place, Eugene. It's too important."

If he was struck by me calling him by his real name for the first time, he didn't say so. Maybe he was finally seeing me as more than the prima donna who'd stormed into his office all those years ago. "I don't have the money to save this place." He sighed. "Or the vim and vigour to do it myself."

The lights dimmed and the curtain opened, and as the music began to play, with Doris Day's mellifluous singing, I whispered to him, "Give me until Boxing Day. I have an idea."

"Well..." he trailed off, then looked me in the eye. "I suppose a few more days won't hurt. What are you planning, Chickadee?"

"You'll see."

MOVE OVER, DARLING
Starring Doris Day and James Garner

TUESDAY, DECEMBER 24, 1963

I spent the rest of the afternoon practicing a masterful apology for Missy. One that would immediately convince her once and for all that she needed to help me save the Majestic Theatre.

That is, once I'd managed to slip out of the theatre itself, after that chatty usherette managed to cause a small riot on an already busy day downtown. Not only were the shoppers rushing home with their treasures, they were stopping along the way to gawk at a legitimate Hollywood star.

I smiled and demurred and avoided answering any probing questions, but who was I to resist heading over to the CBC's studios—which wasn't *all* that far out of the way from my hotel—to help Rube Hornstein with the Christmas weather forecast? As soon as I finished promising the kiddies that Santa would find all of their houses, I settled back in at the hotel and got to work.

First order of business: I called up Double Jinx. Charges reversed just to josh him.

"About time you called me, Mel," his gruff voice barked at me down the line.

"Oh, DJ, don't act so put out. You knew I'd call you back eventually."

"I'm just teasing, kid. Look, how soon before you're back? The producers are keen to wrap up this flick."

"The plan is unchanged, DJ. I'll be back after New Year's." I paused. "Well, that depends on how tomorrow goes, actually. I might be back sooner."

"I don't like the sound of that."

"It's nothing for you to worry about right now. Enough of the present, I need to start looking ahead. What have you got lined up for me next?"

He chuckled. "There's a drama with Paul Newman and Joanne Woodward—"

"It better not be as one of their mothers," I interrupted.

"It's not, don't worry. The other is a comedy with Lang."

I groaned. "Another one?"

"It was just a suggestion," Double Jinx soothed. "*His* suggestion, actually."

"He's got to pay off the private jet rental somehow."

"You don't *have* to do it."

"Let's see if we can get through *The Kenmore Arms* first," I said. Who knew if this truce between Lang and me would last.

Double Jinx milled through the rest of the offerings he'd been fielding for me, and the gossip he'd heard about town, before asking about my visit.

"So, how're things going there?"

"Not well at the moment...Missy and I had a blow-up last night. I'm banished and exiled, contemplating my next move."

"Well, I'm sure you'll figure it out." He didn't sound surprised. Or reassuring, for that matter.

"I'm trying," I said, looking around at the papers spread on the bed. "I may have a few questions for you. Just about the business side of things."

"Sure, sure," he said. "Just don't reverse the charges when you call back."

Next, I called Lang. I'd sent him a quick telegram upon arrival in Halifax but hadn't heard from him since. Of course, he had to gloat as soon as he heard my voice.

"You know, I'm thinking I might try to win that eggnog-drinking contest tonight. Frank's upping the prize bucket since you're not around to drink us all under the table."

"You never achieve anything professionally without it coming in my wake," I teased.

"It's a winning strategy, Mel," he said. "Why mess with perfection?"

After a few minutes of gossip, I finally told him all about Halifax and my visit so far. He let out a whistle when I told him my big plan. "Remember who gave you that idea, huh? You sure you're up for it?"

"The Majestic's worth it," I said. "And I'm certain this will work."

"Well, let me know if I can help you out. I'm always a phone call away."

I couldn't help but laugh. "I can't believe we're actually getting along. Imagine that. If only we could've while we were married, perhaps things would've turned out differently."

"Hey, don't give us too hard of a time. We would have driven each other nuts eventually. You got out just in time."

"I've still got the battle scars."

"Contrary to what you believe, Mel, I think that scar tissue existed long before I ever stepped foot on the lot."

I was silent.

"I asked you before you went, Mel," he started, when I let the silence hum between us, "and I'll ask you again. Don't you ever get tired of hiding?"

"I do," I whispered.

"Then what's stopping you from coming clean?"

"What if it's not a good enough reason?" I asked. For that was my fear. I'd endured the last twenty-five years without Missy's forgiveness, and I was afraid that when she finally learned the reason *why*, it simply wouldn't be enough.

"Look at everything you did to get away from the situation," he said softly. "You don't upend your entire life on a whim."

I sighed into the phone. I certainly seemed to have a knack for it.

"Call me back tomorrow and let me know how it goes, huh? And who knows, maybe I'll have a brand-new trophy to brag about as well."

"My money's on Lucy," I said. "I'll call you tomorrow night."

"Merry Christmas, Mel."

"Merry Christmas, Lang."

I released a breath and went to bed. The clock had finally run out. If I wanted to save the Majestic, I'd need to tell Missy everything. And soon. Every last little gory, terrible detail of what had happened with me, with Benjamin, with her and Eddy... She needed to hear me out: our entire relationship, and the future of The Majestic, hinged on it.

I didn't sleep a wink.

⌒◦ℓℓ◦⌒

ROUGHLY TWELVE HOURS later, I was out on my sister's gaily decorated veranda, telling Eddy that I meant no harm, I just wanted to apologize, when Missy stormed out to where we were standing.

"No, Edward, darling, it's okay. Let her in. Let's hear what the *great* Melly Calvert has to say for herself," Missy said, herding me into their perfectly decorated living room where, moments before, the Davises had been having themselves a merry little Christmas.

"I want us to save the Majestic Theatre," I said. "Like I *keep* telling you."

A decidedly unladylike laugh escaped Missy, and she clapped her hands together. "You want *us* to save the Majestic Theatre? That's rich. All these years I've been taking care of everything back here *by myself* while you're off galivanting around without a care in the world—just like you *always* used to do—and now, when your precious little movie theatre is closing, suddenly here you are, ready to save the day!"

I watched her, eyes widened.

"You win Oscars; I bury our parents alone. Tell me, Melly, have you even been to visit their graves yet? Did you even bother to read the obituaries? I know that *blowhard* calls you up and tells you *all* about us."

"They never loved me the way they loved you, Missy."

She gave a cruel laugh. "That's rich! When they gave you a roof over your head and indulged your every whim."

"That might be true, but they never stopped reminding me that I was just a frivolous little girl who wasn't doing it right. Not like you.

You had Eddy, you were guaranteed a husband and family, and there I was, dancing and singing and acting, and every time they thought I'd come to my senses and be more like you, I'd up and take a job with the Theatre Arts Guild, or the radio dramas, or rush to tell them all about this new idea I had for the act, and you know what they'd do? They'd shut me down every time. Be more like Missy. You're wasting your good years. Who's going to love you when you're older? We can't take care of you all your life."

She scoffed. "Oh please. Poor little Melly; her parents wanted her to be practical and all she ever did was break everyone's hearts."

I balked. "It was *nothing* like that, Missy."

"I'll bet you tell yourself that so you can sleep at night. But you're wasting your time here. There are some things you just can't fix," she said.

"Let me try. Let me explain everything."

"Explain? I'd rather have the apology. You know that you haven't once apologized to me?"

"I've been apologizing since the day I left." Missy had marked every letter *return to sender*. I'd kept a filing cabinet full of them.

"It's not good enough. It'll *never* be good enough." My sister turned her back on me. Walked over to the bay window.

"Missy—"

"You know," she said, wheeling around to face me, "you didn't walk into Old Man Prestel's office alone all those years ago. You act like you built this legacy singlehandedly, but I was there with you every step of the way. You didn't have to drag me kicking and screaming into anything, I willingly took every step."

I didn't have anything to say to that.

"We created The Majestic Sisters together. And you didn't hesitate to leave it all behind. Didn't hesitate to break my heart. For what? To go meet Clark Gable? In Atlanta of all places? If you'd waited another week, you could've hopped the train for Hollywood and met him then! Why was it so easy to run away from me? Why was it so easy to destroy the bond we had?"

She walked over to the imposing oak bookcase that spanned the entire west wall of the living room and pulled a navy-blue photo album from the top shelf: *December 15, 1939* was embossed in pale gold lettering across the spine.

"Here I am in my wedding dress," she said. "I'm not sure if you ever saw me all dolled up, or just at the fittings. I carried a bouquet of scarlet roses. Beatrice was my matron of honour after you left. She was the only one who fit in your dress, and she wore it better than you ever could have."

"Missy, please—"

"Edward looked so handsome in his suit. I'm sure to you he was nothing special, since you were too busy imbibing with *Clark Gable*, but those of us left behind thought he was the bee's knees."

I looked over at Eddy and he stared back, almost daring me to argue any of her points. This wasn't a new pain Missy was hinting at; it was over two decades worth of scar tissue built up and now freshly wounded once more.

"I was supposed to be feted, congratulated. I was supposed to be the centre of attention for once in my life. But you know what I heard instead? The murmurs in the church and at the reception: 'Where do you suppose Melly is?' 'Do you think she was in love with the groom?' That was a particular *joy* to overhear. Even the write-up in the newspaper was all about you."

"Did you ever stop to ask yourself why I left?" I finally asked.

"I know why you left," Missy hissed back.

I rolled my eyes. "Enlighten me."

"It's like you said last night: you were jealous. It's such a cliché, isn't it? The spinster sister, last to find love, watching her younger sister get the happily ever after she'll never have. I mean, you could have had that with Benjamin—until you ran him off, at least. What, did he not fit into your Hollywood plans?"

"You really believe I left because I was *jealous* of you? Of you and Edward?" Suddenly I was angry. "Oh Missy, you haven't changed one bit. So wrapped up in your own world and how everyone orbits around you."

"Well then, tell me, movie queen. It'd better be a good story, too—twenty-five years in the making."

I held my head up. Ready for my close-up. I struggled to make eye contact with her. But finally the words tumbled out: "I was a widow when I left Halifax."

Missy gasped, a sharp noise that pierced the living room. Nobody moved. "How could you possibly have been a widow? You and Benjamin had broken up before we got married."

"No, we didn't. I let you think that because it was easier than telling you the truth." I felt my throat tighten. "Benjamin died a few months before your wedding."

Missy was speechless. I watched her trying to figure out how my confession could possibly be true.

"What happened to him?" Eddy asked, tentatively stepping towards me.

"The Queen Hotel," I murmured.

"But," Eddy trailed off, waiting for me to finish his sentence.

"You remember what happened to the Queen Hotel, Eddy?"

He nodded, his head bowed in sorrow.

"Why would you keep all of this a secret?" Missy's voice was shrill and shaking.

I tried to smile but my lips were trembling. "I didn't want to steal your thunder. You were in full wedding mode, happier than I'd ever seen you. We were in love; a big wedding didn't matter to us. We just wanted to be married. We were going to reveal it all later."

"But you never got the chance," Missy whispered, her eyes shimmering with tears. "Melly, why didn't you tell me?"

"I wanted to," I whispered back. "So many times. But I couldn't find the words."

"Tell me now," she said, leading me to the couch. "Tell me the whole story. Tell the truth."

Act Three

"Only I know my life."

Ginger Rogers

PARIS HONEYMOON
Starring Shirley Ross and Bing Crosby

TUESDAY, FEBRUARY 7, 1939

I'm sorry that I kept the truth from you, kittens, but no word of that is a lie. Once upon a time, I'd been Mrs. Benjamin Trapper.

It was a short but joyous period of my life, one I've looked back on fondly in the years since. But let me tell you how we got there.

There'd been blizzard upon blizzard in Halifax throughout those first months of 1939. You'd dig yourself out of a mountain of packed snow and have to turn around and do it all over again the next day. It made seeing Benjamin spotty at best, because oftentimes he'd get stuck in Truro and would wait days for the roads to get plowed, or he'd have to leave the city early to get back to the Truro branch before another storm trapped him here.

That week, he'd gotten stuck in the city, and we were surreptitiously watching the late showing of *Paris Honeymoon* from the loge seats. Missy had gone off to write a "Wedding Belle" column in time for Thursday's newspaper. How odd that we'd swapped places! Here I was, canoodling with my beau at the Majestic; and her off working after hours.

"I could do that," Benjamin whispered, nodding at Bing Crosby's crooning face up on the screen. The whir of the projector behind us only added to the privacy.

"I think Bing's the only person on the planet who can do that,"

I whispered back. I hadn't even heard of Langdon Hawkes yet, but I stand by my statement.

"You saying you don't believe in me?" he asked, nudging my arm off the armrest.

"I'm saying I've heard you sing and you should stick to counting numbers." I slid my hand onto his knee and squeezed gently.

We stayed until the credits rolled and house lights came on, then walked out together hand in hand. It was late enough that the theatre was just about abandoned, and we were willing to risk being seen together. When we were bundled on the sidewalk, Benjamin stopped to look at the marquee. It never failed to impress him that my name was up in lights, especially alongside an actor like Bing Crosby. That week, above Bing's name: *THE MAJESTIC SISTERS: MAJESTIC MELLY & MAJESTIC MISSY! NIGHTLY PERFORMANCES!*

It used to be my go-to dinner party trick, when I was first starting out in Hollywood and in desperate need of friends: I'd tell the seasoned pros that my name had once appeared on the marquee at my hometown theatre above theirs. Clark always got a chuckle out of it. Imagine anyone receiving top billing over him.

"I like seeing my name up there. Makes me think Hollywood's not such a lofty dream after all," I said, taking Benjamin's arm and propelling him past the theatre.

"If anyone can do it, it's you, Sweets."

I pushed him into an alcove and fell into his arms. Who could resist such a sweet talker? "I'm glad you're stuck here with me."

"Me too, Sweets. I think things are *finally* moving in my direction on that front."

I kissed him once, twice, three times. He pulled back and looked at his watch. "Come on, I have a surprise for you."

"At this hour?" I asked, peeking at his wrist.

"Why not?"

"It's freezing out," I whispered, burrowing into his chest.

"It won't take long," he promised, tugging on my hand. "It's only a little walk down this way." The sidewalks were still covered with snow, the streets slushy and greasy as it packed into the grooves of the cobblestone. That's the twisted beauty of a Halifax winter, and one of the few things I haven't missed over the years.

"So, what's Missy doing tonight?" he asked. I looked up at his handsome profile, illuminated only by the street lights.

"Writing her latest column," I said. "But more than likely sitting over the typewriter dreaming about Eddy." Luckily, she had a ghost-writer to polish up her stories.

"What's this one about?"

"Wedding invitations and how to narrow down a guest list."

"How many people do you think get invited to a Davis shindig?"

"All of them."

He chuckled. "I'd bet they don't know *everybody* in Halifax."

"I think you'd lose that bet," I chided. "The people who *matter*, certainly. When I get married, I'm inviting a maximum of ten people—including me and the groom."

"Well, don't sound so romantic, Aunt Het," he teased, brushing into me. We ducked down a side street and headed towards the waterfront.

"Now I know you're not taking me for a moonlit stroll along the water," I said. "I have your number, King Triton. Where are we going?"

"Ah, but you'll find out soon enough," he promised, and soon we were standing in the middle of the financial district right in front of the Bank of Nova Scotia building.

"It's a little early to report to work, isn't it?" I looked up at him.

He winked down at me. "I wanted to show you something."

"The Davis family vault? Are you finally going to tell me how wealthy they really are?" He ignored me, pointing up at a window towards the top of the building.

"You see that?" he asked.

I tried, in vain, to follow the line from his finger, but when I lost sight of whatever particular window he was pointing at, I nodded instead. "What is it?"

"My permanent office," he said. "If you read tomorrow's"—he checked his watch—"well, this morning's edition of the *Mail*, you'll find a bulletin in the front pages: I'm the new Director of Small Business Loans here at the main branch."

I whirled around. "What does this mean?" I didn't want to hope, not until he spoke the words himself.

"It means, my dear Melly, that as of a week from now, I'll be permanently based in Halifax."

I threw myself into his arms. Finally, we'd be together in one place! We could start dating openly. We could tell people about us and build a life together.

He set me gingerly back onto my feet. "This is a wonderful surprise."

"Your sister's not the only one who'll be in the papers." He flashed me a hundred-watt smile. "I have one more surprise for you, if you'll indulge me?"

"I'd follow you anywhere, Mr. Small Business Loans."

"That's the spirit," he said, hailing a taxi. Once the driver pulled up to the curb and sloshed the wet snow onto our boots, Benjamin held open the door for me and whispered our destination to the driver. "You'll find out soon enough."

The cab pulled up just outside the gates of the Public Gardens. Hardly the speakeasy I'd imagined. But I should've known, since this was one of Benjamin's favourite places in Halifax—for as much as he hated the water and the ocean, he loved greenery. I loved to feed the ducks that made the Gardens their home, so Benjamin always made sure he had bread with him whenever we took walks through the grounds.

There wasn't any bread in his pockets this evening. But something else he hoped I'd love just the same.

Benjamin paid the driver and we walked towards the wrought iron gates at the street corner. They were lit by moonlight...and locked. "Are we breaking in?" I asked. "You should've planned this outing before sundown."

Benjamin gave me an impish grin. "I hope you're not averse to committing a bit of petty crime."

I smirked. "Luckily for you, I draw the line at mail fraud."

"Don't tell your sister, or that'll be the subject of next month's column."

We walked around the block until we came to an entrance shrouded in total darkness—no street lamps or peeping eyes to catch us. "I'll go over first to help you through," Benjamin said once we'd found the perfect spot.

He started to hoist his large body over the gates, wheezing as a bar dug into his stomach.

"You have no finesse...what happens if you get stuck?" I asked.

He took a deep breath, sucked in his stomach, and tried to force more of his upper body over the bars. "That's easy. If I get stuck, just leave me here."

"What, like some sort of scarecrow?" I hissed.

"I'd make a great scarecrow," he wheezed, teetering on the bars.

I rolled my eyes. "Not on my watch. If I push you, do you think that will help?"

Benjamin shook his head. "I think I'm stuck."

"What do you mean, you're stuck?!"

"Don't panic, Sweets."

"Don't tell me not to panic, you idiot! You're going to live and die stuck on this gate!"

"Probably only until the groundskeeper gets his hands on a ladder," Benjamin wheezed. "It's only a few hours until sunrise."

"You'll be frozen solid by then," I said, noting the gentle snowflakes that had begun to fall around us. "And the police will tell the grounds-keeper to leave you here as a warning!"

"I'll suffocate long before that happens."

"This is a disaster!" I looked around in despair, my every move frantic as I tried to hatch a plan to free this giant oaf. In the distance, I saw the glow from the Lord Nelson Hotel just down the street.

"What if I ring up Eddy and see if he can send someone to help us? He knows everybody!"

"You're not calling anyone, Sweets," Benjamin wheezed, trying to pull a little bit more of his body over the bars. "I didn't mean to cause a panic. It's just going to take some careful maneuvering to get myself free, that's all."

"You know, you *would* make an excellent scarecrow," I said, sizing him up. "Since you're obviously lacking in brains."

"You're not helping, *Dorothy*," Benjamin grunted.

I walked up to the bars; all those years of strength training meant I could vault myself over with relative ease and panache. Once inside, I walked over to Benjamin and grabbed his arm.

"When you quit the Majestic Sisters, you should join Ringling Brothers," he said. "I'd follow you, you know." He coughed, catching his breath. "We could live a happy life on the circus train."

"If you're implying I could be a circus freak, I will walk away, Benjamin Trapper." I hooked my hands under his armpits and tried easing him over the bar. I still felt the tug of resistance, so stepped back to look him over. His coat had bunched up at the waist and the pocket was stuck on one of the pointed finials, making it impossible to get over.

"It's your coat," I said. "That's what's trapping you. Let me..." I reached for his pocket to smooth it out.

"Melly, no—" He tried to stop me, but my hand was already inside. I pulled out a small ring box, the size and colour of the one I'd seen when Eddy proposed to Missy. And Benjamin could do nothing but watch as I ruined his final surprise.

In his haste to stop me, he gained that final bit of momentum and tilted over the bar. He landed headfirst into a snowbank next to me, and as soon as he'd righted himself, I held the box out to him.

"Sweets," he sighed. "I didn't mean for it to happen this way."

"How did you mean it to happen?"

Benjamin choked out a laugh. "Well, for starters, I thought we'd have no problem getting over the gate." This time I laughed in antici-pation. He kept talking. "I find my best laid plans never seem to work around you. You continually surprise and amaze me, and I love it."

He knelt in front of me. "I want you to surprise and amaze me for the rest of our lives. Marry me, Sweets."

I couldn't speak, floundering in the excitement of the moment. Tears flooded my eyes and trailed down my cheeks. I'm sure I looked like Bette Davis.

Truthfully, I never thought I was the kind of girl who'd marry; it never seemed to fit into any of my life plans. Benjamin happened to be a wonderful surprise—one I never saw coming, but one that I now couldn't picture my life without.

I was overcome. Couldn't speak except to vigorously nod my head and hold out my shaking hand for him to slide the ring into place. And what a sparkler! Nothing on the level of what Eddy Davis could afford, but our love wasn't like that. My engagement ring was a simple yellow gold band lined with pavé diamonds that glinted against the street light. It didn't matter which way I turned my hand, it was always sparkling. He'd planned it that way, he said. "Reminded me of a star, and that's what you're going to be someday, Melly. And I'm going to be right there with you."

I caught him off guard, launching myself at him, raining kisses on his face and giggle-crying. He matched me kiss for kiss.

"Melanie Trapper," I whispered.

Benjamin lifted me off my feet, swinging me around in the snow-bank. My feet brushed against the powdery snow, leaking into my boots. "*Mrs.* Melanie Trapper," he repeated.

"Wife of the Director of Small Business Loans at the Bank of Nova Scotia."

"Husband of the greatest actress in Halifax, and soon, Hollywood."

I shook my head. "I don't need Hollywood."

Benjamin tutted me. "Nonsense. We're going to Hollywood and you're going to show Bette Davis who's boss."

"Benjamin..."

"Until we get there, though, I wonder how the crowds will react to the Majestic Matrons."

I scoffed. "Please, as soon as Missy becomes a Davis, she's through with our act."

"Has she told you that?" he asked.

"No, but she doesn't have to. And speaking of sisters, we should keep this quiet for now," I told him. "Missy will absolutely throttle me if I upstage her at all this year."

He laughed, but I poked his chest. "I mean it! If the paper offers me a rival column for my own wedding planning, she'll throw a Missy fit unlike anything we've ever seen."

He led us down the left walkway as the path we were on forked. "That's fine, Sweets. I don't want her to throttle you so soon after I proposed."

"Missy's not getting married until December, though," I suddenly remembered. I stopped and turned to him. "That's a long time to keep a secret."

He nodded. "Too long."

I stared into his eyes. "What are you saying?"

He swallowed, his Adam's apple bobbing with his nerves. "In fact I don't want to wait at all. Melly, let's get married now. It's easy to get a license. We can get married by a judge. Keep it secret. Then, after your sister's wedding, after the newlywed glow has abated, we announce our news."

"You want to get married now and not tell anyone for over a year? What, we host a New Year's Day brunch and announce, 'Oh, by the way, I've been Melanie Trapper since February, but I'm terrified of my sister so I kept it secret?'"

He nodded, the snow falling from his hair with each clipped movement. Those brown eyes were calculating, trying to find the easiest way to get us out of this quagmire. "When you put it like that, it sounds quite unchivalrous."

"You know," I said, reaching a hand up to brush at the wet pieces of hair sticking to his cool brow. "We could just pretend we got engaged next Christmas. Only we'll know the truth."

"You're right," he agreed.

I smirked. "There's something to be said for all this secret-keeping, huh? We're old pros by now."

Benjamin smiled back at me, the private smile he saved just for me: those brown eyes crinkled and his lopsided grin and brilliant white teeth on display. "Well, Miss Calvert, I say we get hitched as soon as we can," he said, holding out his hand.

I took his hand without hesitation. "I can hardly wait."

He pulled me into his arms, pressing a gentle kiss to my lips. "I'll go to the courthouse in a few hours and file for a marriage license."

I smiled. "I'll find a dress."

He kissed me again, hands roaming at my waist, running up and down my spine. "Something beautiful."

"I have been to a wedding before, Scarecrow."

ZAZA
Starring Claudette Colbert and Herbert Marshall

WEDNESDAY, FEBRUARY 8, 1939

I t took all my effort to keep my mouth shut. Don't think I didn't want to hire a skywriter and announce it that way. That I didn't want to march my fiancé down Spring Garden Road with a full military parade. But sometimes secrets are worth keeping, and I wasn't going to share this one on my life.

'As soon as we can' turned into forty-eight hours, waiting for the marriage license to come through. Benjamin shared that nugget of information with me over a bleary-eyed lunch the next day.

"They're conspiring against us," I said in a moment of fatigue, grabbing the ketchup and nearly adding it to my coffee.

"Hold it, Sweets," Benjamin said, grabbing my arm at the last second. "I thought you said it was mustard that pairs well with coffee?" He took the ketchup bottle from my hand. "And it's standard procedure, I've been told. They have to comb our records to make sure we're not interrelated way back or committing some sort of fraud."

"Perish the thought."

"We'll be married as soon as we're approved."

I looked at the date on the newspaper spread out on the table. I'd bought it as a keepsake; he'd rifled through it to read the stocks. "Well, if we're going to wait, why not make it worth it. Let's get married on Valentine's Day."

He looked at me then, as if imagining me framed by winged Cupids in my wedding dress. A slow smile bloomed on his face. "Say, that's not a bad idea at all!"

"I have a good one every now and then."

"Then it's settled. Unless the Province of Nova Scotia deems us unsuitable for marriage, you'll be Mrs. Benjamin Trapper by the end of next week." He beamed as he slid the mustard over to me. "Now let's celebrate with a mug of mustard coffee."

"Nice try, but I'll pass. Are you coming to the show tonight?" We were dancing a cabaret routine to *Zaza*, a Claudette Colbert comedy where she plays a dancer who has an affair with a businessman. The irony wasn't lost on me.

"Sweets, I wouldn't miss it."

⌐ℓℓ⌐

SINCE NOTHING ABOUT our courtship or engagement—all seven days of it—had been traditional, we were happy to once again buck tradition on our wedding day. A week after his proposal in the park, Benjamin and I were preparing for our courthouse nuptials in the privacy of his hotel room. It was modest, but we'd managed to choreograph a pas de deux that enabled us to get ready together.

"You look handsome," I said, watching Benjamin comb his hair out of his eyes. He'd put on his best suit—had to send it out special, he said, because he wanted to look his best when he became "Mr. Majestic Melly"—and pinned an orange blossom, my favourite flower, onto his left lapel.

"You look stunning," he said, watching me in the mirror. "I can't believe I get to marry you today." He came up behind me and held me close, and we just looked the picture of happiness then, held in that mirror, like our whole lives were waiting for us.

It was finally our big day, the marriage license having been approved easily and the justice of the peace reserved—and paid off for his silence—and the only thing left to do was to tie the knot and yoke myself to Benjamin until death do us part.

My dress wasn't anything special. It wasn't even white because I couldn't risk the saleslady at Paulette's tipping off the papers. Instead, it was pale pink, and looked more like something you'd wear to dinner and dancing at the Atlantic Hotel. The first in a *long* line of pink dresses I'd wear—and the secret beginning of my Pink Lady nickname. Now you know the truth!

I'd also splurged on a bouquet of orange blossoms and crafted myself a crown to wear instead of the Calvert family veil—too risky to try and lift it out of Mother's closet without Missy sniffing around, and, truth be told, I didn't want someone else's traditions getting tangled into our covert ceremony. I curled my own hair and applied my own makeup; it was the total opposite of what Majestic Missy was planning, and it suited me just fine.

I'll spare you the details of the ceremony itself, since it was all by the books. I take thee and ye take me and all that jazz. Rings were exchanged and he may now kiss the bride and as soon as we were out of the courtroom, we doffed those rings into our pockets. Later that day I put both of them on a chain around my neck, so long it tucked into my decolletage and nobody could ask about them, another way to keep Benjamin close.

"I'm officially Mrs. Benjamin Trapper," I gushed. We were back on the street trying like mad not to let the whole world in on our little secret.

"My wife," he whispered, kissing my hand.

And then? Well, and then it was back to the Queen Hotel for a properly secret-in-plain-sight honeymoon. We slammed the door behind us, formally became husband and wife in the biblical sense, and then we returned, as far as everyone else was concerned, to our regular lives. I was back at the theatre as though nothing of note had taken place that day, and Missy was none the wiser.

TOPPER TAKES A TRIP
Starring Constance Bennett and Roland Young

WEDNESDAY, MARCH 1, 1939

I t was just my luck that, of all the quality pictures the Majestic Theatre had played so far in 1939, Eddy was oddly adamant about watching *Topper Takes a Trip* before it was replaced by *Gunga Din*. And so, instead of inventing some featherheaded excuse to bail out on yet another invitation to an après-dance meal at the Stargazers' Lounge, I watched as Missy flitted up to the loge seats like her heels were made of firecrackers for some canoodling with her fiancé.

Normally I would've liked to stay and watch Constance Bennett putter along the screen, but if Missy was going to stick around the theatre, it left me free to head out and meet my husband.

In the two weeks since Benjamin and I had been married, I'd kept an even lower profile than usual. I'd avoided Missy, lest she pepper me with wedding questions, as her mind so constantly wandered towards the subject. Benjamin would invariably hide in the phone booth outside the Cornflower, backlit by the blue neon sign, waiting for me.

"Reversing the charges, I hope?" I called out to him.

"Nah, just talking to the operator until you came along," he called back, stepping out onto the sidewalk.

"Was she a sterling conversationalist?"

He put an arm around my waist. "She couldn't hold a candle to you, Sweets."

"Excellent answer, darling husband," I said, grazing his cheek with my gloved hand.

"I think I'm getting the hang of it," he teased, steering me towards the automat's door.

"You don't even have to try."

<hr>

BENJAMIN WAS TIRED that evening. His eyes cast a shadow. You could feel the exhaustion pouring out of him. But he still smiled, still winked, still kissed my cheek, still insisted on carrying my tray over to our regular corner table as I filled him in on all the theatre gossip.

We'd trade off over coffee—that was his chance to tell me the bank gossip. He didn't have any that night. Hadn't paid much attention, he said. Spent most of the day holed up in his office, begging off with the excuse that he was studying financial documents, but truthfully, he'd been catnapping off and on as his schedule allowed.

"What're you so tired for?" I asked, spearing a piece of lemon meringue pie with my fork and sliding it into my mouth.

"Well, I've been plugging away at a little novel called *Gone with the Wind*—I haven't been able to put it down."

That perked me up. "Benjamin Trapper! You devil."

"Well, I knew it was important to you, and when someone you love loves something, you want to love it too."

"How far are you?"

"Scarlett's just been summoned to see Melly in Atlanta."

"Not far left to go, then." I smiled. "I can't wait to see it at the Majestic with you."

He winked. "I've got to finish it first, Sweets. There's still plenty of time."

"Only a couple more months!" I crowed. "If you're not finished by the time the movie comes out, I'm going to be very cross with you."

"Well," he said, smirking, "you'd better not distract me."

"I THINK YOU can do better than that, Benjamin Trapper," I said, pressing my lips to his. We were outside the Queen Hotel, hiding in the shadows.

He kissed me full on the mouth this time, and I rested my hands upon his broad shoulders. Time stood still when we were together.

"How's that?" he teased.

"Better."

The front desk was empty at this hour, making it easier to sneak me up to his room. We hadn't yet told anyone—and I mean *anyone*—that we were married. If Mrs. Crandall, the matron of the hotel, knew the truth, it'd be a special bulletin on CHNS within the hour. Better to keep it to ourselves as far as Benjamin's lodgings were concerned, though we had started looking at houses and lots for when he took up his bank manager post in April.

By then, we knew the routine well: Mrs. Crandall retired to her room just off the desk shortly after 7:00 P.M., and was only available until the next morning by ringing the bell on her desk loudly and incessantly. More often than not, you'd just steal your own towels and bedsheets from the linen closet rather than wait for her to answer.

"I can't stay late tonight, darling," I whispered, tiptoeing up the stairs. "Missy has a dress fitting early tomorrow morning, and Heaven forbid I miss it."

"That sounds like nice sisterly bonding."

"Enough talk about the Wedding Belle," I whispered. "I can already hear those two old hens clucking in my ears about how I'm going to die a spinster if I don't settle down soon."

"If only they knew." He kissed my cheek. "Well, let me show you just how cherished you are, dear *wife*, before I hand you over to the matrons."

I walked over to the window, greeted by a view of the radio repair shop and the French grocery across the street. The dim aqua lights of the Atlantic just down the street lit up the buildings along Hollis Street. You had to hand it to him, he was consistent: he positively hated staring out at the Halifax Harbour. "Trust me, Sweets, a view of the water ain't that impressive," he'd say every time I asked.

"Really?" I'd say, peeling apart the thin curtains and peeking out to the street below. "How could you tell from this spectacular view?"

"I happen to like staring at those old buildings," he retorted. "What's so great about the water anyways?"

"You're probably the only Nova Scotian I've ever met who hates the view."

"Bully for the view," he said. "I've got a better one right in front of me."

It always made me shake my head. "And besides, the view out of my window back in Truro is nothing but farmland. At least when I see the buildings here, I know I'm close to you. And soon, it'll be a permanent view."

"Oh, we're going to move into the Queen Hotel then?" I teased. "I was hoping for somewhere with a backyard, at least."

"What do you need a backyard for?"

"Maybe I'll take up gardening?"

"I can't picture you tending to a garden, Sweets."

"Stranger things have happened."

He looked around the room. "You know, if I had Eddy's money, I *would* move into the Queen Hotel. I'd buy it outright, kick everyone out and turn it into our palace."

"Trapper Palace," I said, walking back over to the bed and trailing my fingers along his collarbones.

"I'll start saving my money."

"I've got some money saved up, too. It was supposed to be my Hollywood fund, but this might be a better use for it. Besides, as lady of the house, I should contribute to its upkeep, don't you think?"

"Save it for California, we're going to need it," he said, kissing my cheek. "I'll collect your dowry later."

I smacked him on the chest as we fell into a tangle on the bed. "The only dowry you would've received from Mr. and Mrs. Calvert is a complete encyclopedia set with the entry on Queen Victoria missing and a bone China tea set passed down through the generations. That is, if my parents don't kill us both when they find out what we've done."

"They won't be that upset, will they?"

I sighed, nuzzling my face into his neck. "Daddy will appreciate the unconventionality of it all. Mother pretends she's old-fashioned but she's really quite modern. It's Missy we have to worry about."

Benjamin laughed. "My mother, too. She'll have a hissy fit. She has it in her mind that we're an upstanding family. Pillar of the Truro community and all that. Trappers can't marry just anybody, so she says."

"Good thing I'm a somebody then," I said, "and that you don't care what she thinks."

He pulled me in closer. "That you are, Sweets. Plus, I've still got younger brothers who're more than happy to cuddle up under her wing. My oldest brother and his wife have basically taken over the farm from my father, anyway. I don't need to secure the succession."

"We don't need anyone else," I whispered. "We're enough."

He clicked off the lamp, and with that, all talk ceased. There were just the noises of two lovers sharing their hearts and bodies.

⌒ℓℓ℩

IT WAS PROBABLY close to one o'clock when I got out of bed and started gathering my clothes. I sat on the edge and was rolling my stockings up when I felt Benjamin's hand grazing my back.

"You need to get some sleep," I admonished, turning around to face him. "You've got a long day tomorrow."

"Sometimes I look at you and wonder how I got so lucky."

I smiled. "You're a flatterer."

"I mean it. Eddy can brag all he wants about his hotel and his bride, but I'm the one who struck gold."

I crawled back up the bed and laid my head down on his pillow, my face so close to his. "I don't want to go."

"Don't," he said, kissing my nose and throwing his arm over me and snuggling close. "You're warm. It's late. You're sleepy."

"If I'm not ready to go to the bridal shop first thing in the morning, my sister will throw an absolute Missy fit."

"Then go," he said, lifting his arm off me and rolling backwards.

I caught him smirking at me. "You sure change your mind quickly."

"Why don't we meet for lunch, then? Surely, you'll be done by then."

"You make it sound so easy," I said, kissing his cheek. "And now I have a reason to leave. Thank you."

"I'm already counting the minutes," he whispered. "I love you."

"I love you, too."

FOR THE LONGEST time afterwards, I was struck by that final conversation. How casually we talked about weddings and dresses just so we wouldn't have to say goodbye. How if I'd known that was the last time I'd ever talk to my husband, I wouldn't have wasted it on something so frivolous. I would've just whispered *I love you I love you I love you* into his ear until dawn. Maybe I would have stayed, if I'd known that was the end. Maybe it would have been a worthy ending to my story, to have it written with him.

But instead, I waited until my husband's breathing slowed and he fell back asleep. I turned off the lamp, gathered my things, and tiptoed out of the room. Then I snuck out of the hotel and hailed a cab at the corner, went home, and fell into my own dreamless sleep.

THE SIRENS WOKE me up.

It was just after six in the morning, as fire truck after fire truck after fire truck sped downtown.

Daddy turned on the radio and we gathered around it that morning as the sirens wailed in the distance.

"This a special news bulletin on CHNS: Inferno in downtown Halifax! A powerful fire broke out in the early hours of the

morning at the Queen Hotel on Hollis Street. Firefighters are
still battling the flames. Citizens are urged to avoid the area.
We will have more details in the coming hours."

The evening edition of the *Mail* would call it the worst disaster since the Halifax Explosion.

The official commissioner's report, which I only managed to get my hands on years later, blamed negligence on the part of the hotel owner for not complying with the results of a fire inspection in 1936.

It was nothing short of a tragedy.

The entire Queen Hotel up in smoke and flames in less than twenty minutes. An inescapable inferno. Those who weren't on the first or second floors were trapped in their rooms, none of which were equipped with ladders or fire escapes. Those who did manage to escape the flames either jumped from their windows or took their chances racing through the fire and out the front door.

I spent much of the day in a fugue state, but Missy was ever present and ever peppy—a cool head in a storm. Needless to say, she cancelled her fitting, and instead spent most of the day on the phone with Eddy, who'd set up a command centre for firefighters and policemen in the Coastal Ballroom and was putting up displaced guests in the nicest rooms he had available, free of charge, the saint.

"He said it's a vicious scene down there. They're still battling the fire. Can't manage it. Jonathan was watching from the roof, and all he saw was smoke and flames. Every once in a while, he heard a thud and, well..."

Missy didn't need to finish that sentence; my mind was already concocting a thousand tragedies. I tried to imagine Benjamin making it out alive. He was resourceful; he could've fashioned a rope out of bedsheets and blankets. He could've shimmied down the drainpipe. He could've done a lot of things. He wasn't trapped. He wasn't dead. Not yet. Not until they found his body.

"Edward said they couldn't reach the top floor with their ladder. So many lives needlessly lost." Missy sighed.

"That's awful," Mother said as she poured more coffee for all of us. We were gathered in the living room, unsure of what else to do.

"I'm sure there'll be a commission into this. Public inquiries. A change to our fire laws, at the very least," Daddy said, gripping his mug.

"Does Edward know what caused it?" Mother asked.

"He hadn't heard. He was going to ask the fire chief when he had the chance. It's just an absolute disaster down here. Are you okay?" Missy asked, coming to sit by me on the couch. I'll give it to her, at least she'd noticed I was subdued. But what could I say? She stroked my hair, tucked it behind my ear. I tried not to break down at her gentle gestures, but I could feel the tears welling up in my eyes, and I knew I wouldn't be able to hold myself together much longer.

"I'm fine," I said, jumping up. "I just...I can't imagine the horror those guests experienced. Excuse me."

I rushed down the hall to my bedroom, but Missy was hot on my heels.

"Melly?" she tried again.

I shut the door in her face.

⁓⧫⁓

I'LL LEVEL WITH YOU: I don't remember the act that night, and if you made me swear to God we'd actually performed, I wouldn't be able to tell you with absolute certainty that we did. I do know, though, that I was downtown that night.

The smoke was still wafting from the direction of the Queen Hotel. The firefighters had been battling it all day. They were pulling bodies out of the rubble throughout the evening—it was a recovery mission, not a rescue.

"I'm going to go down to the Atlantic to see if I can help Edward. Did you want to come?" Missy asked me, guiding me down the sidewalk.

Of course I didn't. What help would I have been? It was taking everything in me not to climb into the rubble and search for Benjamin's body myself. But still I let her guide me. As we turned off Sackville

Street and inched closer and closer to the site of the once grand Queen Hotel, I could feel myself tensing.

"They'll probably be working well into the night," Missy said. "Edward's been such a great help to the rescue team. I'm sure this will weigh heavily on his mind for some time."

I bit back the words dying to come out of my mouth. Of course it would weigh heavily on Eddy's mind. Being that close to burning bodies and total ruin? There's a reason I was never able to star in one of those grim war flicks, where the soldiers come home ravaged and wrecked by battle, their faces melted, their limbs torn off. I couldn't fault my soon-to-be brother-in-law, no matter how badly I wanted to unleash my simmering anger.

We stepped into the lobby at the Atlantic, and when I saw the pile of newspapers on the front desk, I snatched one. There, on the front page, and just a few blocks away, was the Queen Hotel, ablaze in all its horror. And there, down the left-hand column, was a list of guests who'd been rescued and where they were convalescing—at the Victoria General Hospital, the Atlantic Hotel, the Carleton Hotel, the Lord Nelson, otherwise escaped and accounted for, or missing.

I prayed, for the first time in a long time, and I never truly stopped. *Please God*, I thought. *I beg of you. I'll do anything. I'll be whatever you ask, so long as his name isn't on the missing list. Please let him be alive, give him a chance. Give us a chance.*

I traced my finger down the list. My heart thumped heavily every time I saw a name I recognized. There was a caveat at the top: the register was locked in the safe, and firefighters had no idea how many people were truly inside the hotel when the fire broke out. It could be days before they retrieved it. The list could grow. I could tell, just by eyeballing it, that it was incomplete. Though not a crown jewel like the Atlantic, the Queen Hotel had a low vacancy rate. There had to be more people missing. Hopefully escaped. Hopefully too shocked to have given their names to anyone. Hopefully safe.

Finally, I reached the bottom of the page, the tail-end of the missing list. This was it. He wasn't on any of the accounted-for lists. My optimism evaporated.

There he was.

Benjamin Trapper, Truro, N.S. – Bank of Nova Scotia

The newspaper fell out of my hands.

Missing.

Suddenly, "missing" didn't sound as hopeful as I'd imagined.

I knew what missing meant.

It meant that life as I knew it was over.

I was not yet twenty-two, and already a widow.

And I couldn't tell anyone.

"Melly?" Missy reached for my elbow. Caught me. Guided me to the ground. Called for help. I remember her shrieking. Then Eddy was there. My body placed carefully onto a bed. A pillow placed under my head. A cold compress against my brow. Missy's angelic voice, clear as a bell, singing a lullaby until I fell asleep.

IT'S DIFFICULT TO talk about this time in my life, but as much as I try to forget, the memories remain. Benjamin's car was never claimed. It had been parked out in front of the hotel. CHNS reported on its status with relish every morning. We were all hoping for a miracle, of course. But it never came. His Mercury blue Plymouth Coupe, now covered in soot and ash and bent by fallen debris, was quietly towed away a few weeks later, and I never saw it again. It probably became scrap metal for the war effort.

People really gravitated to the few good-news stories. I remember hearing about a little girl who was bedridden, sick with influenza, yet refused to leave the flaming building without her doll. Luckily, she'd found it in the nick of time, and was lowered to the street from her bedroom window.

I remember watching as a casket was lowered from a fifth-floor window on the Hollis Street side. Was that Benjamin's room? I couldn't tell. Couldn't even remember where his room had been after looking at the carnage. Everything became a fog.

I remember as the list of survivors stagnated; the list of those recuperating in hospitals dwindled as they were summarily released; and the list of those bodies, charred and unidentifiable, were identified one by one thanks to dental records and forensic autopsies.

They never did positively identify Benjamin. He's only a memory now. And when the obituary was published, my name was left off it. I never even met his family.

And through it all, there was Eddy to save the day. Missy, the éminence grise behind him, urging him on. They shone through the ashes of the Queen Hotel fire. Eddy on the front page vowing to reform hotel safety regulations and Missy on page three as the Wedding Belle. Maybe it was for the best, because they were too distracted to notice their friend's name in the list of victims.

When they finally did remember to ask about Benjamin, weeks later, I fed them a line about how we'd broken up. The distance between us had been too great, I lied, and Missy bought it hook, line, and sinker. It was easier on my heart to pretend that I was a spinster, not a widow.

In all, we were married for seventeen wonderful days.

You've got to hand it to me: I never could stay married long.

BRIDAL SUITE
Starring Annabella and Robert Young

FRIDAY, MAY 26, 1939

E ddy had some big news that, by golly, he just couldn't wait to share with us. Or rather, with Missy. I just happened to be in the dressing room when he burst in, out of breath and delighted with whatever cable had just come from the Western Union. He collapsed in a chair, Missy fawning all over him, trying to calm him down.

"Take your time, Eddy; we have a couple hours before we have to be onstage," I said, twisting a lock of hair around the curling iron and trying not to burn my fingertips.

"It's—" he wheezed. "It's the biggest thing that's ever happened to the hotel. This'll...it'll...it's going to put us on the map. *Really* and *truly* make us world-famous."

"Spit it out!" Missy yelled. It was so uncharacteristic of her to have an outburst like that—I know I've waxed about her Missy fits but she'd certainly, not to my knowledge, never yelled at dear ole Eddy. In fact, it seemed to have left him dumbstruck.

"Missy," I chided, "give the man a chance to catch his breath. I'm sure whatever it is can wait."

Turns out it couldn't, because no sooner had I tried to diffuse the situation than Eddy was up again, trying to sputter out this breaking news. So instead, I turned back to the mirror and continued curling my hair.

"I just got a wire that we're hosting," he said. "That the Atlantic's going to...we're hosting a lunch for the King and Queen when they visit Halifax next month."

Missy squealed, jumping into his arms. "Darling, that's fantastic!"

"That's great news, Eddy," I said, turning in my seat. "I'm on the guest list, right?"

"Of course! I'm sure you and the Queen will get on like old friends."

⁓

I FIGURED, MUCH as I'd been doing all spring, I should continue with the charade that everything was fine. I could barely sleep, haunted by nightmares of Benjamin trapped in his hotel room and me on the other side of the door, unable to save him.

I had no clue how the insurance worked—if he'd even registered me as a beneficiary anywhere. Why bother, though, when we were two young and healthy individuals. Who'd ever think they'd need to protect themselves and their loved ones at our age?

Eddy had set up a hotel safety association, and he blathered on about reworking the system to prevent tragedies like this from ever happening again. I tried to drown out any conversations about the Queen Hotel, but, like a good little fiancée, Missy couldn't help but parrot back all of the major talking points over dinner each night.

I continued to hide the wedding rings on the chain around my neck, and at night when I saw them gleaming on my naked chest, only then would I cry. Silent and alone. Grief is a mountain, I've realized. I was trying to climb down in the easiest way I could.

⁓

MY HEART WASN'T in it at that point. I couldn't tell you the routine we'd done for *Bridal Suite*—likely something centred around Missy—but I do remember being back in the dressing room after the early evening show when Old Man Prestel popped his head in.

"Got a minute, Chickadee?"

"Of course. Anything for you, old man." I cleared a seat for him, tossing my costume onto the vanity counter and throwing an errant "You go on ahead" to Missy. She waved goodbye to Old Man Prestel and left.

"I got a call from the good men down at Government House," he said. "They want to show the King and Queen all the culture this place has to offer when they're in Halifax."

"Splendid idea," I said. "I hear they're starting at the Atlantic."

He shook his head. "No, Chickadee. They're starting *here*. They've requested your services in particular," he continued. "Special perform-ance just for Their Majesties and a couple hundred esteemed guests. No movie afterwards, just a showcase of how we entertain ourselves here."

I began to stand. "I should go catch Missy, she should hear this." But he stopped me with a firm hand on my arm.

"You're the one I trust to put this together. You can tell her later."

I smiled back at him. Or tried to, anyway. "I won't let you down."

"I know you won't." He paused, looking me over. "I've noticed you've been a little more reserved than usual these past couple of weeks. You don't have to confide in me, but I'm here if you want to talk."

Bless him, he'd always noticed more than my own family ever did. "I'm fine." I swallowed down the lump in my throat. "I've had a lot on my plate lately." No plays with the Theatre Guild in rehearsals, but I was busy with radio announcements—at least when Missy didn't have me helping out with the wedding.

"If you're sure," he said.

I had to be, even if I didn't want to be. The city was closing in on me. It no longer felt like a stage I wanted to stand on. I was trapped and I had to get out. Trapped at the Majestic, trapped as Missy's maid of honour, trapped without Benjamin Trapper to stand beside me.

"You can count on me," I lied.

⌐ℯℓℯ⌐

EDDY WAS THRILLED for us—performing for actual royalty was, natur-ally, the ne plus ultra, and what he loved most of all was the coalition

we'd built across company lines. The next few weeks were spent preparing the hotel for the luncheon, and no expense was spared. Missy
and I spent hours putting together a thirty-minute showcase of our
work, after which a film reel showing the other cultural hotspots of
Halifax would be presented for Their Majesties.

Why, one barely had time to sit down and think, it was so busy.
And it got busier for me. Missy's column was paying dividends to the
Mail, enough so they figured they should ask me to write one as well.
They offered me a movie column: "At the Movies with Majestic Melly."

While everyone was out sweeping up the sidewalks and adding a
fresh coat of spring paint to the storefronts along the city streets, I was
sitting at a typewriter trying to write my first column. I reviewed all the
films that played at the Majestic, beginning mid-June with *Invitation to
Happiness*.

It kept me busy, it kept Missy off of my back, and it kept me from
being alone with my thoughts: just what I needed at the time. I threw
myself into writing it—made good use of my 'Reserved for Majestic
Melly' sign every week. Not only did it occupy my time, it also helped
me hone my craft. I could learn from Irene Dunne how to convey emotion with just a shift of an eyebrow; study how Claudette Colbert's pos-
ture changed her line delivery; imitate how Ginger Rogers used her
physicality even while standing still.

The Lieutenant Governor's office sent a protocol officer to the
theatre to teach us how to curtsey and act appropriately in front of
royalty, but they needn't have bothered: we were graceful enough on
our own that we could've passed for ladies-in-waiting. The only worry
was getting to the hotel in time, and to be presentable at lunch.

All of the hotel rooms were booked solid; the trains were running double time to accommodate all the looky-loos. From outside the
Majestic, you could hear the crowd of over twenty thousand jostling for
prime space on the Garrison Grounds.

There were nerves, of course, and it was a relief to feel something
besides grief. Maybe there was a light at the end of this tunnel? Before
we knew it, Their Honours arrived and were seated and a thunderous
voice announced: *"The Majestic Sisters in performance for His Majesty*

King George the Sixth of Canada and Her Majesty Queen Elizabeth," and then suddenly the curtain came up. To this day, I haven't the foggiest what we did. Then, just as quickly, we were back in the dressing room scrubbing off our makeup and rushing to get to the hotel for lunch— those royals like to stick to their timetables, let me tell you.

"You haven't been yourself lately, Melly," Missy said, as we were fixing our makeup.

I turned to her. Finally, she'd seen me. Seen my hurt. Maybe I could finally open up to her.

"You know what you need?" she said, smacking her lips and admiring her lipstick. "A new beau. Why don't you let me set you up with one of Edward's brothers?"

The balloon burst. Moment ruined. For that short period of time, knowing that the King and Queen were out there watching me, I could forget everything that waited for me beyond the stage. Suddenly, I was angry. "I can't imagine a worse fate than stepping out with Jonathan Davis."

"What's wrong with Jonathan? He's just about to graduate from law school!" Missy cried, holding the door open once we'd made ourselves appropriate. "It was just a suggestion."

"I don't want your life, Missy," I mumbled under my breath.

IN NAME ONLY
Starring Carole Lombard and Cary Grant

THURSDAY, AUGUST 31, 1939

I once wrote Dorothy Dix—Missy's favourite agony aunt—a letter myself. Not for advice, but as a sarcastic thank you for nearly blowing my cover. Don't worry, it never ran.

Why, you ask? Well, when Missy opened the paper that morning on August 1939 and scanned the columns for Dorothy's latest wisdoms, she couldn't help but read it aloud to me over breakfast.

"Oh, listen to this, this is great advice," she said, smoothing down the page. "If a woman cannot be married openly and honestly and live in the sight of all people...they should put it off until they can do so."

"Missy, please, you're about to have the most lavish wedding this city's ever seen. What do you know about quiet marriages?" She wouldn't know the first thing about sneaking around in a hotel room, dressing yourself without an entourage, having your wedding breakfast consist of only coffee and mustard. I *loathed* her in that moment.

She shrugged. "It's not bad advice. Maybe I'll do my next column about hosting a large party for your nuptials."

She'd already extolled the benefits of large flowers, large menus, and a large dress, and she'd milked all of the city's biggest businesses into donating their time and goods to her wedding, but there seemed to be no end to the topics on which Missy was prepared to wax philosophical, whether or not she knew what she was talking about.

"Why bother? You're getting married in one of the city's biggest churches and you're having your reception at the Atlantic. Who else can boast that?"

"Nobody," she giggled.

"So...why give women false hope?"

She stared at me then. Stared into my soul and tried to find the pieces of me she could laser-focus on. "Jealous?"

"Of your follies?" I laughed in spite of my aching heart. "I hardly think so."

"You never know. If you're ever lucky enough to get married, maybe you'll want the big shindig, like me."

I ignored her, anger reddening my face as I brushed the crumbs of my toast back onto the plate. I walked out of the room before she could spike me with any more of her barbs.

⌒ℓℓ⌒

THE SUMMER HAD been busy, ever since the King and Queen visited. In so many ways, that performance felt like the pinnacle of my career in Halifax. How would we ever top it? Performing for the regular joes who came to the movies every night definitely lost its lustre after that.

Wedding preparations for the Calvert-Davis union continued at breakneck speed, but the city had not forgotten the tragic fire, and neither had I. In the background of all of our regular duties, like attending shop openings, welcoming cultural visitors, and both of our columns for the *Mail*, loomed the spectre of the Queen Hotel.

An investigation into the cause of the fire still hadn't officially launched, but the *Mail* made sure to pontificate that each passing day without an exploration into the city's fire laws was a day spent in disgrace.

Eddy's hotel-safety association continued on, setting policies that made him look good but would likely be unenforceable. And a special fund for the firemen who'd extinguished the flames had been established, its pot overflowing with donations from ordinary citizens and big businesses, to thank them for the impossible job.

And in addition to all of my regular jobs, I had another engage-ment on my calendar—one I refused to break, one I kept daily over the lunch hour. A visit to the Camp Hill Hospital, to visit the last survivor of the Queen Hotel fire still receiving medical treatment.

Nobody knew who he was, and he was much too short to have been Benjamin, so if you were anticipating a last-minute happy ending here, I'm sorry to disappoint: those really do only happen in the movies.

He was savagely burned by the flames. Unable to escape his room, he'd remained trapped under debris until firefighters managed to pull him out of his window to safety. In the chaos, nobody had claimed him. He'd done a stint on the front pages of the *Mail* for a few weeks, but to the best of the doctors' knowledge he was a John Doe without family, without identification, and without a hope of leaving the hospital alive.

Once I learned this unknown man was suffering alone in the hos-pital, I began to visit him. I tricked the press into believing I was merely acting as an agent of Eddy's newfangled association—he never argued the point when asked; he knew that no publicity was bad publicity—and they quickly left me alone.

John Doe never regained consciousness. Never spoke. Never seemed alert to the world around him. Just laid there covered in salves and bandages, burned beyond recognition, helpless and nameless.

I sat at his bedside and read *Gone with the Wind* to him, and when I passed the last scene Benjamin ever read—when Scarlett is sum-moned to sit by the dying Melly's beside—the waves of grief rolled over me once again. Benjamin would never finish the book, but John Doe would. Such injustice.

I allowed myself to hope that perhaps, in some other universe, Benjamin was reading it on his own and thinking of me.

THE WIZARD OF OZ
Starring Judy Garland and Frank Morgan

SATURDAY, OCTOBER 21, 1939

T he way I look at it is this: tragedy can define us, pin us down, force us into holes we'll never be able to climb out of. Or we can stare back at tragedy and say not me, not now, not today.

When Benjamin died, it felt like the world was closing in on me. Here I was, a newlywed, a young woman with a handsome husband and the rest of her life waiting for her. Dreams of stardom, dreams of motherhood, dreams of a life with Benjamin that I hadn't even had the chance to realize yet. But life rarely happens how you want it to. I couldn't breathe. I couldn't sleep. All I could think of was how was I going to live the rest of my life as a widow, suffocating with this terrible grief I could never share with Missy while I watched her have the happily ever after I'd never get?

Now that war had broken out, my despair seemed deeper than ever. Every day, the large print on the front page told us of the woes in Europe and the hardships back on the home front. The rising cost of food, the lack of rooms for the thousands who had descended upon Halifax seemingly overnight. You couldn't escape the war. If I wasn't there on the front page, it was on the radio, constantly. The *Halifax Mail* had set up a bulletin board outside its offices and regularly pinned updates to it. You couldn't even get to the front to read it, but that didn't stop crowds from growing, eager for the news.

I wasn't safe at home either. The windows covered in heavy black curtains so we'd be ready if an air attack ever came. Blocking out every bit of light was depressing. As were the practice drills, late at night, called at random by the Air Raid Precautions Committee. They'd cut the juice for a second, long enough for us to get the hint to cut all the lights, then they'd turn off the power outdoors.

Daddy would prowl the property in the pitch-black night, looking for any source of light escaping from Casa Calvert. If he found it, you'd hear about it—trust me. Then you'd have to fix it until he was satisfied, and God help you if you hadn't by the time they'd turned the street lights back on.

Old Man Prestel was ordered, along with all the business owners, to turn off his neon sign at dusk. We had to dim the exterior lights of the theatre and Eddy had to put up heavy blackout curtains in all the windows at the Atlantic. They weren't fooling; and when the military took over control, you risked a heavy fine if you didn't comply with the precautions.

The city was crowded but I was alone, and everywhere I looked, I was reminded of everything I'd lost.

I lost count of how many times I'd walked down to the carnage. Most of the time, I did so without even meaning to. I'd be walking down to the Atlantic but find myself in front of the Queen. Or I'd be in the area and zigzag my way down to Hollis Street on my way to run errands. Sometimes I'd lose my breath staring at the mangled wreckage, remembering how, only months ago, I'd stared out at the bustling city from Benjamin's window. Other times I'd walk past, my heartbeat a tattoo as I tried not to look up.

I was in the dressing room reading the newspaper after our special kids-only showing of *The Wizard of Oz* when I spotted an advertisement for Madame Ford, palm reader. I knew I was suffocating under the grief, but I didn't know how to make myself better. I wanted a sign. I needed a sign. Something to tell me, after seven long months, that I would get through this.

I called up Madame Ford—who said she'd been expecting me, naturally—and went to see her that afternoon. This time she simply looked at my palm and said, "You've had a tremendous loss."

When I nodded, she added, "That wound will never truly heal. But you will rise again."

"How can I hasten that rise?" I asked her.

"You must leave town," she said. And then she traced an escape route on the lines of my palm.

⌒ℓℓ⌒

I DIDN'T WANT to head straight back to the theatre, and I certainly didn't want to chance running into Missy and all of her tulle-filled wedding ideas, so I did something I hadn't done in months: I ducked inside the Cornflower and sat down in a booth. Our booth.

I pulled at the delicate chain around my neck and fingered the wedding bands we'd never truly worn as I focused on my breathing, then waited for the waitress to offer me a cup of coffee. I fleetingly wondered if she'd remember me. Remembered him? I wondered if she wondered where he was.

"Haven't seen you around here in a while, sweetheart," she said. Of course she recognized Majestic Melly. Yoked to that nickname for the rest of my life. She never asked about Benjamin. Maybe she'd seen his name on the presumed dead list and figured I wouldn't want to talk about him. "We just replenished the lemon meringue pie," she said, quietly pouring a steaming cup of coffee and sliding it to me. It tasted burnt.

"Just the coffee's fine, thanks." I fought the urge to ask for mustard. How could I go on putting mustard in my coffee without him?

I grabbed the newspaper, thinking it would occupy my mind. That if I focused on the newsprint I wouldn't be able to focus on the empty space across from me. Before I could even read the headlines, I felt a nudge at my hand, and looked over at the mustard tin the waitress had slid onto the table.

I willed my eyes not to tear up and focused on the newspaper. I hadn't read a paper in a while either, even though I was still writing my movie column and Missy was all over it. I was afraid of reading more bad news, afraid I couldn't handle it. To this day, unless I know it's good news, I can't bear to read a newspaper. I have to get the hair-and-makeup team at MGM to read it for me as I'm getting dolled up.

That afternoon, however, I read something that would change my life. And prove Madame Ford's prediction correct.

I always read the movie page, even though I knew what was on it. I loved looking at the advertisements. Loved reading the gossip. I learned some of my favourite tidbits there, true or not. Like how Joan Fontaine had been attacked by swans on a film set in 1937, or the numerous times Barbara Stanwyck was placed on suspension by RKO, or how Bette Davis had tried to negotiate a new contract for two films a year. But that day, underneath a sweet little write-up about *The Wizard of Oz*, was a still from *Gone with the Wind*. It had only just finished filming despite its mid-December release, and David O. Selznick was rushing through the editing process to have something to take to Atlanta for its world premiere.

The article didn't focus on any of the frou-frou stories we already knew: how Vivien Leigh had been plucked from relative obscurity in England and marched to Selznick by his own brother, who crowed, "I've found your Scarlett"; how Clark Gable hadn't wanted the role at all, and insisted to reporters that if he were to play a part, he'd want to play "Gone"; and how behind-the-scenes drama had plagued film-ing. It focused on the premiere in Atlanta in December and how this would surely be the biggest movie event of all time. Anyone who was *anyone* would be in Atlanta, the article said. Stars would be made that weekend.

A hand beating against the window pane startled me. "Melly!" they screamed. "It's Majestic Melly!" It was getting harder and harder to paste a phony smile to my face and wave like a sideshow performer happy to be gawked at. It hadn't been fun these past six months, pre-tending I still felt like Majestic Melly—bright, vivacious, always ready with a clever retort. I wanted to hide inside myself.

I gave a stiff wave and smile and then looked back down at the newspaper. *Stars will be made.* Madame Ford was right. No more waiting for that someday. My time was now. I had the talent and the drive and I could be a star, I just needed to go to Atlanta. I had enough money, now that I wasn't saving it to buy a house with Benjamin. I could splurge. I could live off of that money pile for months. If I could manage to meet Selznick. Hell, even an endorsement from Clark Gable would be enough for some Hollywood executives. And what better way to stand out than as the one unknown woman at a movie theatre full of Hollywood royalty at the premiere of the biggest movie of all time?

There wasn't anything keeping me in Halifax. Who could stop me? Once the thought took root, I saw how it would all play out and how this path would lead to certain stardom. I knew I couldn't wallow in grief, and I knew I couldn't stay and bask in Missy and Eddy's love. I had to find my own way out. Be my own hero. I knew I had to leave and I knew I had to do it alone.

And I knew they'd never understand.

THE WOMEN
Starring Norma Shearer and Joan Crawford

FRIDAY, NOVEMBER 10, 1939

By the time I flipped the Majestic Sisters calendar to November and my once-beaming face, the Queen Hotel—what little was left of it—was a warped bundle of concrete and steel in a vacant lot. I was getting wound up tighter the more time went on, and I'd taken to using creative routes to avoid walking past the twisted carnage.

The commission assembled to investigate the cause of the fire carried on, but it was clear the Queen Hotel's owners had no intention of taking blame for what happened. It filled me with rage, especially when my nameless friend at the Camp Hill Hospital quietly succumbed to his injuries, after months of pain.

And, in the midst of all this, Missy was full steam ahead with her wedding planning as though the universe hadn't shifted. As though there wasn't a war on. Nobody told her to stop planning such an extravagance, though. Seeing two of Halifax's finest citizens married, paraded through the streets, could only cheer people up in that first uncertain winter. By the time *The Women* premiered at the Majestic in mid-November, I was a powder keg primed to ignite.

THE ROUTINE WASN'T memorable; none of them were after Canada joined the war. We needed to play our part. I thought so, Missy thought so, Old Man Prestel thought so, and so did the government. The whimsy was gone. Every routine now had to feature some sort of patriotism, or a call to arms, advising the audience to do their part for the war effort. We'd both started volunteering for the Red Cross and organized drives at the theatre to support the troops.

Eddy was waiting for us backstage, ready to chat about this or that or offer his opinion on the wedding plans Missy had so carefully prepared. I usually retreated into my own mind so I wouldn't have to listen to them nattering on, but that evening, they forced me into their conversation.

"Melly!" my sister's voice pierced through my daydream.

"Hmm?"

"Are you even listening to me?"

"Yes," I said, tossing the jar of cold cream back onto the table. "You have my undivided attention, Missy. Please, tell me what's on your mind."

"Eddy got a call from J. A. Snow that you paid for the burial of that last Queen Hotel victim."

"What of it?" I asked, turning to face them fully. I'd specifically told Snow's funeral home to keep my involvement hush-hush.

"Before it gets out to the papers, would you mind...maybe letting Eddy compensate you so we can release a statement that the Halifax Hotel Association paid for it? It'd look good for the group if they were seen to be taking care of the victims that way."

I gawked at her. "Missy, I didn't do it for the publicity. I did it because nobody, least of all the Queen Hotel, was willing to pay for it. I didn't even want my name associated with it."

"I know. That's why it's perfect. You don't want the publicity or need it, really. But this could really kick some life into the association. Show people it's a serious enterprise."

"*Is* it a serious enterprise?"

"How do you mean?" Eddy piped up. Coward, letting Missy doing his dirty work.

"Where was this association years ago when you first opened the Atlantic? Why only now, in the face of a horrible tragedy, did you think to create a body to enforce regulations?"

"You think *I'm* doing this for the publicity?" He leaned forward in his seat.

"I certainly don't think your motives are entirely altruistic here," I said, leaning back in mine.

Eddy laughed awkwardly. "Melly, you don't realize how poorly kept some of the other hotels are. If I don't take charge, who will?"

"That's fair," I allowed. "But I'm not letting you reimburse me for those funeral expenses just to make yourself look good in the papers. I'm sorry. Now, if that's all, I'm going home."

"Are you going to sneak in and call a demolition company next?" Missy yelled. "Going to try and take that away from Edward, too?"

"What do you mean, demolition comp—"

"They're finally tearing down that eyesore," she continued. "Nobody else will foot the bill, so Edward's going to formally offer tomorrow morning."

"Eyesore," I whispered. "Missy, people died in that 'eyesore.' I'm sorry that you're too selfish to see that."

"You're the selfish one!" she thundered, hands on her hips. "Here she comes, ladies and gents, Saint Melly, here to do her good deeds by day and entertain you by night!"

I started, but just as quickly as the instinct to argue came, it went. I had no fight left in me.

FIRST THING MONDAY MORNING, Eddy announced in a special CHNS bulletin that he was personally paying for the Queen Hotel carnage to be demolished, and that he would hold the land in trust until a suitable business decided to take over the deed.

Missy nudged me as we listened from our parents' kitchen, gloating that he'd beaten me to paying for this one. I ignored her, and twenty minutes after Eddy hopped off the airwaves and Missy hopped on a tram to join him for breakfast, I spotted an advertisement for bus tickets to New York City in the newspaper. The route followed my fate line...just as Madame Ford had traced it a month ago.

GONE WITH THE WIND
Starring Vivien Leigh and Clark Gable

FRIDAY, FEBRUARY 16, 1940

Don't accuse me of being heartless because I never went back. There was no travel into Halifax for a while and nowhere to stay— the only way to get around was by train, and I certainly couldn't expect there to be a vacancy at the Calvert residence on Coburg Road if I showed up.

And the mail had been slowed down. My now-famous name was suspicious to the postmasters and my address was, too. In the war years, they needed to make sure I wasn't spilling secrets—loose lips sink ships, remember. And Halifax had a harbour full.

But more importantly, I was made to feel unwelcome...so why would I have wanted to go back? My parents returned every letter unopened, as did Missy and Edward. Amy Swaine-Tully sent me a decidedly acidic letter once the news of my first movie came over the wire, and it was made crystal clear to me that my presence wasn't needed or appreciated. So I stayed away.

That's not to say that those war years were boring, if you'll allow such a crass description. I made sure I kept up with the goings-on. Missy and Edward continued to reign over the city, showing their support for the war effort in unique ways. There were dinners for foreign dignitaries, like Princess Juliana of the Netherlands in 1940 and Crown Prince Olav and Crown Princess Märtha of Norway in early 1941. The

Norwegians cooed over baby Birdie, who still has the rattle they gifted her with. They hosted dinners and dances for soldiers and donated all the proceeds to the Red Cross. When a housing shortage reached crisis level, Eddy offered hotel rooms at reduced rates in order to keep as many people as possible off the streets.

Eddy never served himself, and, truthfully, I'm not sure if there was a medical condition that precluded his involvement on the front-lines—I'd never ask—but he did his part at home, and Missy played her part as well. They participated in those popular wartime radio shows organized by "Uncle Mel," the owner of Mills Brothers, and donated money to various causes, hosted galas in order to raise even more money for the war effort, and lent their names in any way they could if it meant supporting our boys overseas.

In short, it was easy for Missy to move on and forget about me. Forget about the act, in fact. She'd only been back to the Majestic Theatre once since she resigned: for the premiere of *Gone with the Wind* in February 1940, with the proceeds to benefit the Canadian Red Cross.

Amy wrote that when the invitation to the Halifax premiere of the film arrived, Missy had wanted to bin it, but ultimately decided against it because Old Man Prestel himself had personally addressed it to "Majestic Missy Davis" and had it delivered by towncar, and she couldn't bear to break that old man's heart the way I had.

Besides, the Lieutenant Governor would be there. And the Premier. The Mayor. The Chief Justice of Nova Scotia. The Davises couldn't snub such an important event, though Missy knew that's exactly what those vultures at the *Mail* were hoping for. Majestic Missy, they'd say, couldn't hack it. Heartbreak at sister's betrayal still looms large in heart: *Majestic Missy was last seen running from the Majestic Theatre, tears trailing down her rosy cheeks, back to her new home on Young Avenue. Majestic Missy is in hiding. Where's Majestic Melly when you need her? Majestic Melly would never shy away from a crowd, or an adoring public. We want Majestic Melly!*

And Missy would never give anyone that satisfaction, Amy wrote. She hid all of her pain and anger, left it simmering under the surface, but to the greater public, it simply looked like Mr. and Mrs. Edward

Davis were being fêted at the Halifax premiere of *Gone with the Wind* in an extension of a very joyful honeymoon. Hobnobbing with Halifax's movers and shakers at the biggest movie premiere of all time.

Then there was the news I only found out through Amy: the delicate emerald green dress, with its beaded appliques on the shoulder and waist, was disguising Baby Davis. It was a perfectly matronly dress, appropriate for a high roller's wife, and Missy wore the hell out of it.

The newsreels were set up outside the Majestic Theatre. Flash bulbs went off everywhere. A lineup extended down the street—it looked like it went even past the Canadian National Railways passenger office—of people who stood no chance of getting into the theatre that night.

The brick exterior of the Majestic Theatre had been transformed into the façade of Tara, Scarlett's family plantation. But instead of the billboard-size poster of Clark Gable and Vivien Leigh like they had at The Loews Grand Theater, all Old Man Prestel could manage was a few small posters in the upstairs windows.

Missy and Edward walked the red carpet—their photo on the front page of the entertainment section the next day, Amy included the article in the envelope—all smiles, but if you asked Missy what her favourite part of the movie was, she couldn't tell you. She hadn't paid a lick of attention. Eddy fared a little better, but this was never his kind of movie. So it was an easy decision when Missy got home after midnight and vowed that she'd never step foot in that theatre again.

A promise she's kept.

HIS GIRL FRIDAY
Starring Rosalind Russell and Cary Grant

FRIDAY, APRIL 12, 1940

I arrived in Hollywood just after Christmas 1939, with about one hundred dollars left in my purse and a suitcase stuffed with clothes, a programme from the *Gone with the Wind* Atlanta premiere, and Clark Gable's cocktail napkin. He'd instructed me to find some MGM executive named Nick right after New Year's and tell him the King had sent me. At this hastily arranged meeting, Nick was only too happy to sign me immediately to a contract.

That's the official story anyway. The one the press agents cooked up while I was out of the room. Now it's time for me to finally tell the real story of how I wound up in Hollywood.

In truth, that once-in-a-lifetime endorsement didn't do much at all. I still have that napkin, for all the good it did me, and I did go directly to Hollywood from Atlanta, but it took months of wishing and hoping and good ole-fashioned tenacity to get a studio contract.

⌐₳₤₴

"YOU WANT MY advice, kid? Lose the red lipstick and the bounce. You're not Ginger Rogers," the scout said, not even bothering to pause his retreat from the room.

Can you imagine? The gall. Especially now that I'm renowned for the red lipstick. (I'm not too sure what "the bounce" is, but if it's vivacity, I'll claim it too.)

Those first few months weren't at all what I'd expected when I'd daydreamed of Hollywood on the train. I'd followed Carole Lombard's advice to a tee: hotel near the studios, splurge on a nice dress, make myself noticeable outside the studio, visit all the hotspots in the hopes of being spotted, and if all else failed, send her a wire and she'd pull some strings. I did wire her in February, and the strength of her endorsement got me in front of a few more casting directors, but it never led to a screen role. It was always something: Ginger was the go-to dancer and comedienne; Olivia was the go-to good girl; Carole did comedy like no other; and I couldn't touch drama while Barbara Stanwyck lived and breathed... But it went beyond the talent; it was the looks: Rita was the redhead; Ginger was the blonde; there were more brunettes than you could shake a stick at. I couldn't ply them all with Fiery Mellys, like I'd done with Clark, and so I'd inevitably ended up back in the Central Casting lineup by March, fighting for scraps—like Counter Girl or Student Number Four—and trying not to burn through the rest of my money. The thought of having to return to Halifax, tail between my legs, fuelled me, but I was getting desperate. I was starving. I was exhausted. I was homesick. I was doubting my every action. I called home so many times—only to immediately lose my nerve and hang up—I'm sure the operator had my number blocked.

But eventually, things did turn around for me. It happened like this: I was walking outside the MGM Studios in early April. Just walking, understand, not trying anything funny. I was in a mood that day after being passed over for the plum role of Smoking Car Girl Number Two. I'd bought a cigarette case expressly for this purpose and they'd *still* passed me over in favour of some blonde dish. I'd turned on my heels and made my way back to the sidewalk, where I was positively fuming and waiting for the trolley to take me away from dreamland—I'd go home, punch my pillow, and prepare for the next day of standing outside the gates of MGM like a prize cattle waiting for a blue ribbon.

Only I didn't make it that far.

"You look like you're about to blow."

I whipped my head around. An older gentleman leaned against the lamppost. Grizzled, but harmless. Probably drunk. "Maybe I am, it's a free country."

"I like that," he said. "Fiery."

Something about the use of that word piqued my interest. No one had called me fiery since I'd left Halifax. Nobody'd given me the *chance* to be fiery. "There's a cocktail named after me back home. The Fiery Melly."

"You got a drinking problem? Cause if you're a boozer, tell me right now and I'll save my pitch for someone worth hearing it."

"No, but I could sure use a drink right now." I mopped my brow. What was this strange old man getting at?

"Where's home?"

"Halifax?"

"I thought I heard a British accent."

"What? No, Halifax, Nova Scotia."

"Never heard of it."

"Well, I'm about to put it on the map," I said, starting to walk away.

"How?" he asked. "You're walking away from the only building that'll make you a star." He nodded at the MGM gates behind me.

I stopped. Was it possible he worked inside those gates? "What would you know about it?"

"I know plenty. I bet I can make you a star in a month flat."

I crossed my arms with dramatic flair. "How so?"

"I represent starlets. You know Bernadette Marin?"

"No."

"That's because I don't represent her. Everyone I represent, you've heard of."

"My condolences to Bernadette, then," I said, joining him at the lamppost. I was officially intrigued. This man reminded me of a younger Old Man Prestel, though his hair had only just started to salt and pepper at his temples. He was lean, like he spent his days dashing from studio to studio, pausing only for lunch meetings at the Brown

Derby and supper meetings at the Cocoanut Grove. All the best stars had agents, and I'd need someone to advocate for me. I wasn't getting anywhere on my own.

"But you," he said, sizing me up. "You're interesting. I bet I could get you a movie deal."

"You bet?" I quirked an eyebrow. "I'm not wasting my time on a bet, pal. I want a sure thing."

"Sure things are what I'm known for."

"Well, if you're the miracle worker you say you are, work your magic on me. I've been turned away from every audition I've been on. I even had endorsements from Clark Gable and Carole Lombard, and nothing."

He chuckled. "You have the King of Hollywood and the Hoosier Tornado backing you and you still can't book a job? No offense, kid, but are you sure you can even act?"

I balked. "You still haven't named any of your clients, so it's a mutual road of mistrust, pal."

"Touché. Let's grab some lunch. I'll tell you all about my success stories, and you can tell me all about Halifax and your bucolic seaside existence."

"I thought you didn't know anything about Halifax."

"I know everything, kid. Sooner you realize that, the easier it'll be."

MY FAST-TALKING, BOGART-LOOKING lunch date was Don "Double Jinx" Johnson. Agent to the stars—and starlets. Noted for turning nobodies into ingenues. He snorted his milkshake when I told him my acting credits included Snow White, Dorothy Gale, and Queen Victoria.

"That's one hell of a summer stock company."

"It wasn't summer stock," I said. "I was a prologue dancer."

He'd been only too tickled by the story of Majestic Melly and was impressed by her versatility. And when I told him about the stunt I'd pulled in Atlanta, it seemed to settle something for him. "So you just showed up at the premiere party?"

"Why not?"

"You've got brass, kid. Real brass. So, what's the backstory?"

I froze. "Backstory?"

"All the greats have 'em." He picked up another French fry and dragged it through a heap of ketchup, then used it to emphasize his points. "Hard-drinking father left 'em, or maybe their mother had to take three jobs just to keep 'em in clothes. Stage parents? Tree fall on you?"

"Nope," I said, popping the word. "Idyllic childhood, loving parents, doting sister. You name it, I had it growing up."

He popped the fry into his mouth. "You expect me to spin sweetness into stardom?"

"Well, why not? It works for Myrna Loy."

"You know why Myrna's getting the roles she gets?" I shook my head. "Brass. Took her walking away from the roles she'd been handed in order to get the roles she wanted. You have that kinda gumption? Cause no offense, kid, but I don't get an overall feeling of sweetness when I look at you."

It unnerved me that he could read me so easily. I figured, why lie? He'd been honest with me so far. So I leaned in and shared my biggest secret with him: "I kinda ran away from home. The week of my sister's wedding."

He jolted back. "No shit?"

"No shit."

"Older or younger?"

"Younger. And you can't tell anyone. It's a secret."

"Ah, couldn't stand being the old maid, eh? Say, how old are you anyways?"

I was so sick of that assumption, but I swallowed my pride. "Just turned twenty-two."

"Ancient," he scoffed. "You'd make Mickey Rooney look like a kindergartener."

"He already looks like a kindergartener."

He laughed. "The more you talk, the more I like you."

"Well, I'm flattered."

"You should be. You know why they call me Double Jinx?"

I shook my head.

"I can't believe you haven't asked. You've really never heard of me?"

"I must have missed that *Photoplay* centre spread," I mused.

"Smart-mouth. They call me Double Jinx because when I'm busy booking one of my girls for a role, I've already got a second movie ready for her to sign onto. Okay, here's what we're gonna do. We're gonna get you a screen test. No more of those bullshit stand-outside-MGM-in-the-extras-line-waiting-to-be-called-upon pony shows you've been doing. An honest-to-Jesus screen test, directed by one of the studio directors, with a cameraman who knows how to get an interesting shot. One that Mayer sees. Where are you staying?"

I rattled off the address. "Bah," he said. "Take this"—he opened his wallet, produced a handful of crisp bills, and shoved them into my hand—"and book yourself a room at the Garden of Allah. Try to get yourself noticed amongst the crowd there, huh? I'll call you there in a day or two with more details. Got it?"

I nodded. "What if nothing comes of this? I can't pay back this kind of money right away."

"You're lucky I've got such great instincts, kid."

I hailed a cab back to the clapboard hotel I'd been staying in and within the hour, on Double Jinx's dime, had booked myself a room at the Garden of Allah on Sunset Boulevard, and waited for the phone call that would change my life.

⌒ℯℓℯ⌒

WHEN DOUBLE JINX came knocking a few afternoons later with details about my upcoming screen test, he threw himself onto the couch and pulled out a pen and notepad.

"Tell me what you're thinking for a stage name," he said, pen poised.

"I've got the perfect one. Didn't even need to write any down. Want to hear it?"

He eyed me warily, as though he could tell what the next words out of my mouth would be.

"Melly Calvert."

He sighed. "That doesn't fit with your look."

"What's my look?"

"Fiery. You know what Melly Calvert sounds like? The wholesome girl next door, the one the male lead spurns because Jean Harlow moved into the neighbourhood. *You* are not the girl next door. We're not going to give them the chance to see you as the second lead. You're going to be the star."

"*This* star's name is going to be Melly Calvert. I was born Melly Calvert and I'll die Melly Calvert." (I guess technically a lie, but then I'd never filed to have my name changed back in Halifax. So although I was, technically, Melanie Trapper, nobody could ever know it.)

He blew out a breath, then changed tack. "This is Hollywood, kid. Nobody uses their real name. You don't think Cary Grant's really Cary Grant, do you?"

"Katharine Hepburn kept her name," I countered. "And so did Irene Dunne, and Olivia de Havilland, and—"

"But not Joan Fontaine," he said. "Or June Allyson or Barbara Stanwyck. Not even your best buddy Carole uses her real name."

When I opened my mouth to argue once more—Ingrid Bergman, Ida Lupino, Constance Bennett—he held up his hand to stop me. "All right, all right," he said. "I figured you wouldn't want to take part in this exercise, so I took the liberty myself. How about one of these. Tell me when you hear a name you like."

He pulled a small notebook out of his jacket pocket and then started rattling off all the names his other clients had already rejected: Melody Lane. Holly Daye. Eleanor Loretta. Julia Dunne. Marina Howell. Gertrude Gallagher. April Morn. And finally, a new one, Melanie King, which he loved because he thought it was hilarious that I'd had a note pinned to my pocketbook that said "The King sent me" in Clark Gable's chicken scratch and still couldn't book a job.

"You like any of those? I've got a few more. Ivy Williams. Holly Tremaine—"

"Do you trot out that list every time you find a new starlet?" I asked.

"Yeah, I just cross out the names they take, see?" he held up the list. I could just make out Tiny Halpert, Helena Solomon, and Martha S—

"Does that say Martha Scott? You named Martha Scott?"

"I wish. It's Martha Snow. Now, just tell me what name you want."

"With all due respect, Double Jinx, I'm not changing my name."

He heaved a long, deep sigh. "What's your middle name?"

"Guinevere."

"No shit?"

"No shit. My parents met in English class."

"Melanie Guinevere Calvert. That's a mouthful." He chuckled.

I don't know why that particular comment, out of all the jibes he'd been taking at my name, my personality, and my upbringing, was the one that stung, but I was homesick and didn't want to hear a word against my parents.

"So's Double Jinx Johnson, but somehow your name isn't on trial."

The room fell silent, and I was worried my mouth had gotten me into trouble. It felt like eons before he spoke, but finally Double Jinx doubled over and began laughing so hard he was crying.

"Okay, I was on the fence before, but now you're not allowed to walk away without letting me represent you. You're a firecracker. You're going to be a star, kid. What do you say?"

"I can keep my name?"

"You can keep your name," he promised, reaching out his hand.

"Then you have a deal," I said, taking it.

"Good," he gave my hand a vigorous shake, "because I've got you a screen test for a new Robert Young comedy over at MGM. Play your cards right," he paused with a smirk, "you could get your own seven-year contract."

∽ℓℓ∾

YOU KNOW WELL by now that screen test went very well, and I received that seven-year contract. The test itself was a meticulous, rather drab process of standing this way and that, turning my head this way and that, smiling, frowning, crying, laughing, longing, until they had more footage of me emoting than I'd likely actually emoted the entire past year. But then there was a chemistry reading with Robert Young himself. Surely they wanted to analyze my line delivery—can't be wooden, or no amount of glamour can save you—but mostly they needed to see how I looked with the leading man, which meant kissing him over and over and over again, which I couldn't complain about.

The ink was still drying on my contract when I was shuffled into the makeup room and given a total makeover. My hair was blown out and lightened to a dark auburn to match the fiery personality, my makeup softened and sweetened—though the red lips remained—and I was stuffed into a tight emerald green evening gown for my first round of publicity shots. One of those shots—me smiling up at the camera, head titled slightly to the side, wide-eyed and optimistic—made its way to the *Mail*, courtesy of Double Jinx. *Majestic Melly Signs with MGM!* the caption read. *First film due this summer:* Easy Does It, *co-starring Robert Young. Start lining up at the Majestic Theatre now!*

Easy Does It. Such a simple movie, and honestly, it represented the entire process to a newbie like myself. The real joy, aside from it being my first film role, was meeting Robert—a darling man who deserves more credit, more roles, more accolades than he's given. I made my one and only television guest appearance on *Father Knows Best* simply because I adore Robert so. I played Geraldine O'Brien, a young dame who befriends an art forger (Robert) and helps him continue his ruse as his exhibit is about to be displayed in her grandfather's art gallery. Mayhem—but in the best possible way—all around, and the critics agreed. *Time* called it a "witty farce as good as any dreamt up by Frank Capra" and *The Hollywood Reporter* said I was a "fresh-faced ingenue straight off the MGM lot who just proved herself a worthy dame for any script directors throw her way." And when Old Man Prestel received the reel, he played it until the film split. It was his most successful showing—unless you factor in *Gone with the Wind*, which I decidedly do not.

Sure, I'd seen my name on the marquee dozens of times as Majestic Melly, but seeing my name as a bona fide actress was an experience unlike any other. It felt like the beginning of a whole new life. I'd worked *years* to get here, and I wasn't going to waste this opportunity.

AFTER *EASY DOES IT* came out, I drove around town to all of the theatres, taking pictures of the marquees bearing my name. It's one thing to have seen *MAJESTIC MELLY* on the marquee in Halifax; it's something else entirely to see *INTRODUCING MELLY CALVERT* plastered all over Hollywood. My heart pounded every time I caught a glimpse of it. Here I was, finally. Watch out, Hollywood!

And through it all, Benjamin. He was the only one who'd known about my dream, and how hard I worked to get myself here. He wouldn't want me to wallow in my grief. He became a treasured memory. A fond remembrance whose presence I felt every time I touched the gold band necklace. So I vowed to soak up every moment, live with gusto, so that when my time came, I'd have one hell of a life story to share with him.

The excitement surrounding the premiere only lasted a short while, and before I knew it, it was time to report back to the lot to make my second movie, again with Robert: *A Dime a Dozen*. This time, I played a Wall Street heiress who has to earn her trust fund back by marrying a suitable husband. She decides to date one beau each month for an entire year, but runs into complications with the gentleman in April, played so dreamily by my co-star. The returns on the film were fantastic, and I was quickly climbing my way to the top. I started a scrapbook of my life in Hollywood, imagining it one day full to the brim.

And now, ladies and gentlemen, is where one Langdon Hawkes enters the picture.

TWO DOORS DOWN
Starring Melly Calvert and Langdon Hawkes

MONDAY, OCTOBER 7, 1940

C ontrary to what the publicity suits at MGM have been only too happy to push since 1940, there was never *any* whiff of a romance between me and Langdon Hawkes when we first met. From the moment I first laid eyes on him it wasn't, as Hedda Hopper so saccharinely suggested, "a buffet of barely concealed lust and red-hot passion simmering between the striking comedienne and the soulful crooner"; it was barely concealed hatred and red-hot rage simmering beneath the surface.

You'd be hard-pressed to name a movie carrying Langdon's name above the title in the past five or so years, so let me get you all up to speed on his goings-on before we first made *Two Doors Down* in the fall of 1940. Langdon Martin Hawkes waltzed straight out of the local radio station in Toledo one evening in the late '30s and directly into a contract with Republic Pictures to become their cheap remake of Bing Crosby. Unfortunately for him, his voice wasn't as powerful and his acting wasn't as great, but his mug still sold records, so the studio kept his option while they tried to find his niche. He made his money in one-reel Poverty Row pictures until the day came that Republic wanted Melvyn Douglas for a movie, and the—uneven, in my opinion—trade-off was that he was loaned to MGM for my third film, the one that made me a household name.

Two Doors Down was a screwball-esque comedy in which Langdon and I played neighbours thrown together to plan a winter carnival to raise money for the local theatre. He got to show off his voice; I got to show off my dancing chops. It made both of us stars and guaranteed that, much to my chagrin, we'd be making pictures together for a very, *very* long time. And, of course, because in those days the studios acted as morality and publicity hounds, the suits at MGM began to push the idea of a romance between me and Langdon to all the papers. We were instructed to go on dates, attend movie premieres together, be spotted together at the beach or at the tennis court (though neither of us knew how to play), and, in general, do anything (on this side of the law) to get our photos in the papers and people buying tickets to our movies.

And oh, the things we did to get our photos in the papers. Dining at the Cocoanut Grove, where he'd call me "frigid" just as the camera-man popped up, to ensure I'd take a bad picture. Watching the show-girls at the Earl Carroll Theatre where he'd tell the other guests I used to be a showgirl in Halifax. I had fun pouring every soup on the menu at Musso and Frank into his lap, and telling Hedda that we couldn't eat at Ciro's because Langdon had broken the heart of every waitress on the staff and was forbidden to show his face there again.

"God *damn* you," he said when he read that one in the rags. "You know how much I love their Nova Scotian salmon dinners. Now I can't go back!"

I smirked. "Why don't you go to Nova Scotia and eat all the salmon you like?"

He scoffed. We were on the set of *Piece of Cake*—a treacly romance about rival chefs set in blusterously freezing Chicago (*She warms the oven AND his heart*, the poster said)—fighting in between takes on our makeshift restaurant soundstage. "You'd like me to disappear, wouldn't you? You can't make a film *without* me."

"You want to bet?" I asked. I placed an order from Ciro's for lunch shortly after we broke for the morning. Nova Scotia salmon. I took great delight in eating it in front of him, and the MGM press team had a photographer snap a picture of me that made the papers back home: *You can take the girl outta Nova Scotia but you can't take Nova Scotia outta the girl! Melly Calvert (pictured) is enjoying fresh Nova Scotian salmon on the set of her newest flick:* Piece of Cake*! See it this winter at the Majestic!*

I later heard Lang screaming in his trailer that I was a monster and he was "only supposed to be in *one* goddamn women's picture, not a goddamn *baker's dozen!*"

Can you blame him? He wanted the acting career of Bing Crosby and the singing career of Frank Sinatra. He wanted to be a top crooner comedian, like Dean Martin, but he wanted a sidekick like Jerry Lewis, not Melly Calvert. He wanted legions of screaming girls to follow him on the road. He wanted fan mail delivered by the sackful to his dressing room. He wanted his name in the paper—and it was; he just didn't want me attached to any of his success, because, rest assured, he thought he was the one carrying me in those days. Never mind the fact that I'd had top billing on two MGM comedies by then or that the papers talked ad nauseum about Clark Gable and Carole Lombard anointing me as the next big name in Hollywood (bless them both: their publicists never denied it).

These days, Langdon books the jobs Eddie Fisher can't anymore, but in those days, Langdon was an affable screen partner, though it was typically my name attached to any critical praise of our films. That being said, after *Piece of Cake*, I was ready for a break and was loaned out to Paramount for the aptly named *In the Nick of Time* with the charming Ray Milland.

I think my biggest regret is that Ginger Rogers agreed to make *The Major and the Minor* in 1941. If I had to be typecast with a certain role, it seemed to be vaguely Ginger-esque in that I could sing, dance, and switch between comedy and drama, but I wasn't as stately or angular as Katharine or Bette, so could never play a grand dame or a scion of society. My mug, Double Jinx said, made a man think he could conquer Everest at my side; it wasn't meant to make ladies weep at the Tuesday matinees. Fine by me! I was here to climb the mountain, and I'd scale it by whatever means necessary.

By this point in my career, I'd developed a fan base. My face was on the cover of magazines, and people all over the world were writing to MGM asking for my autographed photo. If I went out to dinner, I invariably ran into at least a dozen fans who wanted to talk my ear off. There was no romance for me beyond the studio-assigned dates with Lang—no one could ever hold a candle to Benjamin and I didn't see the point in pretending. I did keep the rings around my neck, though, and doted on that lost love by kissing them every night and whispering updates to Benjamin's smiling face in that 'Candid Camera' photo— the only picture we ever took together—that sat upon my nightstand. I knew he'd be proud of all the progress I'd made. Double Jinx fed a story to Louella Parsons that they were my grandparents' wedding rings, and how my grandmother had always been my biggest supporter and left these jewels to me. Since nobody back home was talking to me, nobody could contest the story.

And now I was morphing into Hollywood's newest It Girl. It was divine, and the only way to go was up!

THE PINK DRESS
Starring Melly Calvert and Ray Milland

FRIDAY, JULY 23, 1943

Ingrid can keep her Ilsa. Vivien can keep her Scarlett. Louise O'Dell in *The Pink Dress* was the role I was born to play.

Back in those days, you didn't get much of a say in your own projects—it was whatever the MGM brass wanted to throw you in, and you'd better not complain lest you risk suspension. And this was prior to the de Havilland law, so my presence was required for *Jazz Club Princess* and *Midnight in Monte Carlo*—forgettable musicals with Lang, but the director sweetened the deal by letting me keep copies of the costumes.

Double Jinx told me my next film was still being arranged—I'd likely have a choice between *The Heavenly Body, The Pink Dress,* and *The Miracle of Morgan's Creek*—but once I got my hands on the script for *The Pink Dress*, I lobbied L. B. myself. And, luckily for me, I'd get a change in co-star: Ray Milland was contracted to star opposite me as the dashing Detective Chester Sampson.

With an Oscar on my horizon, I'd finally be in a position to make my own contract demands, and I knew exactly what I wanted—aside from a raise, of course. I wanted to wave goodbye to the Melly-and-Lang collaboration. As I told Hedda during my Oscar campaigning, *The Pink Dress* wasn't a movie Langdon Hawkes would want to star in. He'd tell you he was too good for the script; everyone else would tell you that the script was too good for him.

As Louise O'Dell, heiress to an oil fortune, I got to gallivant for ninety minutes in an Edith Head–designed pink dress whilst being falsely accused of murder. That I got to flirt with Ray Milland, the detective assigned to the case, was an added bonus. Plus, the vibrant colours of Edith's costumes paired with Cedric Gibbons's engrossing art direction made it look frothy and magical. The Oscar campaigning began almost immediately after the picture had been announced.

Double Jinx, bless him, whispered into the ears of anyone who'd listen—all the studio heads and power players, the upper echelons of the acting community, and all the press agents and columnists—that this was Melly Calvert's Oscar to lose. That, after several years playing opposite "limp noodle" Langdon Hawkes, it was finally my time. That comedic acting was just as difficult as dramatic acting, and *The Pink Dress* was going to prove I was every bit as capable as Bette Davis or Greer Garson.

And by golly, it worked.

⁓⁓

"DID YOU HEAR that Langdon's going around telling people he *declined* an Oscar nomination this year?" I threw myself into my favourite arm-chair. "That Paul Lukas was simply too good in *Watch on the Rhine* and Langdon didn't want to diminish *his* chances? Can you believe that?!"

Double Jinx and I were in my dining room, conferring over our next steps now that I'd officially been nominated for the Oscar. I was virtually a shoe-in, but there was still Lang to contend with.

"Mel, we all know the truth about Langdon," he said in the soothing tone he did so well. "Besides, why are you so worried about him? You're the winner here. I'm setting up meetings with producers left and right. You're gonna be working steadily for the next three years at least!"

"It's a slap in the face is what it is," I said. "Langdon cruises by because he's got a perfectly plain face and an inoffensive voice, but let's not act like he's the second coming of Gary Cooper."

"Nobody thinks that, kid, trust me," Double Jinx promised. "You just sit tight and wait for the nominations to come out. And for God's sake, don't go buzzing around to Hedda about how much you hate him. Not *yet*, anyway."

"I'll try to bite my tongue," I promised.

"There's a good girl," he said, leaning back in his chair. "You know, rumour is they're going to pull the plug on his concert tour. Tickets aren't selling. Meanwhile, Sinatra's selling out every venue he books." A fact Sinatra took only a hint too much delight in pointing out to Lang.

⌐◦ℓℓ◦⌐

BECAUSE THE STUDIO system in those days churned out movies as fast as we could make them, I'd had the briefest of breaks before reporting for duty on the set of my next film, *The Flamingo Hotel*. Unfortunately for me, it meant teaming with Langdon once again, our fifth collaboration, just after my Oscar nomination for Best Actress was announced.

"I just had to wait for Bette Davis to take a year off," I joked to the reporters gathered in the commissary. She'd been nominated every year since 1939; that she—and Greer Garson—would get an Oscar nod was something you could set your watch to. This year, my competition included Joan Fontaine, Jean Arthur, Ingrid Bergman, and Greer Garson. All I had to do was avoid scandal and surely the Oscar would be mine.

If I walked onto the set expecting a thousand congratulations, I should've known better of my green-eyed leading man. We'd started the scene where Langdon's character checks in to my hotel, and I'd only managed to get out a few lines before he broke.

"Why're you being so stiff, Calvert?" he asked, slapping his hand down on the front desk.

"I'm not being stiff," I muttered. "I'm doing the scene as directed."

"You're not being very welcoming," Lang continued. "I wouldn't want to book a room at your hotel if this is the mug you're putting on."

"This is my *face*, lovingly made up by my personal *makeup artist*," I sighed. "Can we move on with the scene, please?"

And on and on all day long. Not a word of congratulations. Not a smile my way. His mood, already terrible when we'd started filming early that day, only got bleaker as we went along. I had my doubts that any of those scenes would be salvageable—they weren't—and by suppertime the director, Howard Burke, was so infuriated with Langdon's antics he called it quits mid-afternoon even though there were still several scenes we needed in the can by the end of day.

"We'll try again tomorrow," Howard said. "Be better tomorrow, Lang, hm?"

I kept my composure as I washed the day off my face and slipped back into my own clothes. I kept my composure as I made my way off the lot, but as I was stepping into the waiting car, I heard footsteps behind me and knew at once it was Langdon, ready for a showdown.

"I don't get it," he mused. "I really don't get it."

"I'm sure there's a lot you don't *get*, Langdon, but you'll have to be more specific in this case."

"We're supposed to be a pair, you and me. That's what they want. That's what everybody wants. We make movies together, we're seen around town together off-screen, everybody wins."

He sounded like Majestic Missy. Never wanted me to shine without her, and now I had Lang to contend with. "I'm afraid I don't get your point."

"We're *both* supposed to succeed. You get an Oscar nod for…what? That eyewash? Mel, all you did was traipse around in a pink dress for two hours. That's hardly award-worthy."

I lifted an eyebrow. "Maybe it was finally acting opposite a worthy scene partner that got me the nomination."

He guffawed, hands on hips. "I hardly think—"

"You hardly think what, Langdon? You've made your opinions on my talent quite clear. I know I can't sing like you can, and I'll never croon like Peggy or Dinah, but I hold my own. I can act circles around you, we both know it. You're jealous."

"I am *not*—"

"Aren't you? You're the only one who couldn't be bothered to congratulate me when everyone else today was practically spraying me with pink champagne."

"You've got it all wrong—"

"And if you think I don't know all about your little whisper campaign, you're mistaken."

He paled. For once, he had no comeback.

"That's right. I know all about how you're going to Hedda and Louella to tell them that you could've been nominated, too, for...what was it? *Shine Your Shoes*? You think that rinky-dink musical holds a candle to the performance Paul Lukas put on this year? You think you're anywhere near his level?"

He cleared his throat. "Now—"

"And you think I don't know that you tell every man on the lot that my skirts are so stiff because there's ice in my girdle?"

"Melly—"

"Don't you '*Melly*' me!" I shrieked. I didn't give a damn who was listening, let alone whether our set-to made the front page of the morning entertainment section—I needed to let this out.

"I've been on this lot a while longer than you have, Langdon, and I didn't have to jet-set from some broken-down Catskills resort back to Toledo where I was paid four dollars an hour to sing Crosby covers. I brought myself here, and I got my contract myself. I worked my way up the ladder, and then they tell me I'm getting a new co-star. You. And I'm supposed to fawn over you and your talent while you can't even grant me the same courtesy? You make comments about my figure, my hair, whether my lipstick is too bright. You pan all of the films I make without you and act like you're the sole star of the films we do make together, even though—and I've counted, so don't bother to correct me—my dialogue accounts for more screen time than yours."

Lang looked completely bewildered, like he'd let Pandora out of her box and wanted to shove her back in. But I was on a roll, and I wasn't stopping now.

"You position yourself as some sort of teen idol—like all the girls should come running to you—meanwhile you're out partying all night and struggling to fill arenas the next day. So just how hard *are* you working, Langdon? I know you had to cancel your shows at the Coliseum. I know you're not getting the radio play you'd like. I know it's eating at you that rumours of your draft dodging keep coming up, but whose fault is that? Colour blindness is easy enough to fake, I suppose, but considering how *loudly* you keep talking about the shade of my pink dresses, it won't be too long before someone in the War Office overhears and ships you over to the Pacific Theatre. Maybe *that's* the stage for your talent, because it's certainly *useless* here."

And now, the pièce de résistance: "And furthermore, *when* I win that Oscar, I'll have earned it. I poured myself into that role, and I worked my ass off for every single shot. You, meanwhile, made that tart musical with an actress whose name I've already forgotten."

Not even Mort could've made me leave the stage at that point. This was years of hostility bottled up and exploding. If only I had a Majestic audience watching me destroy him.

"I know after this you're working on another B-list film with a B-list starlet, probably borrowed from Poverty Row—which is where you belong, by the way—and I'll fill you in: *Ready, Set, Go* is going to bomb. You're not Paul Lukas. You'll *never* be Paul Lukas. You can't even be Bing Crosby, let alone an actor someone would pay money to see if my name wasn't next to his on the marquee."

His mouth was agape at this point. I was breathing the death rattle into our personal and professional relationship. "So perhaps, Lang, the next time you go off spouting untruths about me, you'll consider how terrible of a friend you truly are, and know that I want absolutely nothing to do with you."

I heard a cough from the driver, who'd been idling this whole time. I have to admit I'd forgotten him. So I decided to put Lang out of his misery.

"We have one last film together, Lang. This is it. You'd better stare closely at my face in all of those lovey-dovey scenes, because it'll be the last time you ever see it close up, unless you sit through any of the five movies I already have in pre-production."

I walked up to him, put my hand on his cheek, and glowered at those nebbish eyes, and said, "Good night, Lang. Sleep tight and try to remember your lines tomorrow, hm?"

Exit. Flourish.

DOUBLE JINX CALLED me that evening, wheezing from laughter, to tell me Lang's agent had called him up, wanting to reiterate that 'per my client's discussion with your client,' this would be Melly Calvert and Langdon Hawkes's last project together. He couldn't keep it together long enough to tell the agent that we agreed, and then simply hung up on him. Then he took me out to dinner to thank me for finally telling Lang where to stuff it.

We wrapped *The Flamingo Hotel* with an early checkout: due to the immense professionalism on the part of both leads, Howard Burke managed to get everything he needed to turn in a film. The critics were weepy about the halcyon days of the Calvert–Lang partnership in their reviews, but even they had to admit that this was "not one of the better films from this dynamic duo" and "largely carried by the vivacious Melly Calvert" with support by "Langdon Hawkes, who couldn't seem to figure out how to play his role." That review went over particularly well.

THE PINK DRESS
Starring Melly Calvert and Ray Milland

THURSDAY, MARCH 2, 1944

The Academy Awards are the pinnacle of the motion picture industry. Everybody wants to win an Oscar—including me.

I tried not to think about how *lonely* it was to sit here with my greatest dream nearly realized and have no one but my Hollywood friends there to fête me. Old Man Prestel had sent a congratulatory telegram; I sent him back *the* pink dress to display at the Majestic. But there were no messages from Missy and Eddy, nor Mother and Daddy. No comments from the newspapers or the industry rags.

I'd spend nights out in Hollywood but I'd go back to my two-bedroom apartment in Bel-Air—I hadn't yet been introduced to the wonders of Palm Springs—all alone. All of my Halifax relics were lovingly displayed, but to keep the wolves at bay, I had to spin stories so my estrangements wouldn't become front-page news.

And here's the thing: I had no regrets. How could I? I was *this close* to achieving my dream, and everything had worked out the way I'd always wanted it to. But sitting alone in that dark apartment, K45LA blaring in the background, all I could think of was my Oscar speech and how hollow it would feel to thank people who didn't want to be a part of my success.

This was the only wallowing I'd allowed myself, but it was obvious enough that Double Jinx decided to cook up a publicity scheme for Oscar night.

"You have no beau, your father's not answering the phone...I think we know who needs to escort you on Oscar night."

"You?" I asked, a twinge of hope shooting through me.

He chuckled. "No, kid. Lang."

I'm not sure how Lang's agent convinced him to do it, but you can see the photographic evidence for yourself. I think it was our best performance to date.

⌐ℓℓℯ⌐

FOR ME, THAT evening in March 1944 was both a celebration of the previous year in film and an exercise in trying not to collapse in on myself with grief. It had been five years, to the day, since I'd lost Benjamin. Five hard years of pulling myself out of that quagmire. I think he'd have been pleased at what I'd managed to achieve, knowing it was the memory of his love and pride that kept me going in the darkest times.

Casablanca would take home the big prize—though Bogie and Bergman both went home empty-handed. Paul Lukas, as everyone predicted, won Best Actor for *Watch on the Rhine*. Charles Coburn, that loveable old man, won in the supporting category, as did Katina Paxinou for *For Whom the Bell Tolls*. The ceremony lasted only thirty minutes, but it might as well have been twelve hours later when Greer Garson finally approached the microphone, bantered with Jack Benny for a minute or so, and then began to announce the nominees for Best Actress.

Greer had made waves a few years earlier when she'd won for *Mrs. Miniver* and nattered on in an endless speech, and she seemed to enjoy taking her time in announcing tonight as well. Despite myself, I reached out and grabbed Lang's hand. To my surprise, he squeezed back.

"Thank you," she said. "It is my pleasure to present the Academy Award for Best Actress to one of the following distinguished actresses. The nominees are: Jean Arthur, *The More the Merrier*. Melly Calvert, *The Pink Dress*. Ingrid Bergman, *For Whom the Bell Tolls*. Joan Fontaine, *The Constant Nymph*. Greer Garson, *Madame Curie*."

It's a courtesy that the previous year's winners are called back to present the next year's, but I couldn't help wondering if Greer knew before she stepped out onto the stage whether her own name was in the envelope or not.

Finally, she opened the envelope and announced clearly, and with great joy: "The Oscar goes to…Melly Calvert, *The Pink Dress!*"

In moments of sheer happiness, you can't always account for your reaction. That's why I reached over, grabbed Lang by his lapels, and planted a big ole kiss right on his lips. I don't know if the photographers got a picture of the smooch, but they certainly snapped a few of his awestruck face, lipstick kisses all over his cheeks, watching me and my frothy pink gown waltz up to Greer.

I grabbed her, hugged her close, whispered something into her ear I've long-since forgotten, and took my trophy.

"Thank you, thank you, thank you!" I gushed, hand at my throat— hand over the gold band, keeping him close. The audience applauded again. "What a moment. I'm tickled *pink* by this honour. You can't even imagine the thrill of holding this statue and knowing all of your dreams have come true."

I was thankful for the stage lights at that moment, as I looked out into the crowd and saw nothing but the glare of the spotlight reflected back on me. I was blinded, momentarily, by just how truly *alone* I was at the zenith of my career.

"I couldn't possibly name every person who helped me along the way, but without Double Jinx Johnson, Howard Burke, and Ray Milland, *The Pink Dress* wouldn't be a success. And without my parents, my sister, Missy, my brother-in-law, Eddy, and of course, Eugene Prestel, all of whom are back in Halifax—hopefully listening in—I wouldn't be the woman I am today. Thank you to everyone, both here and departed, for your support. I'm truly, truly thankful."

DOUBLE JINX SIDLED up to me at the champagne table during the after-party and whispered into my ear: "Telegram from Halifax."

"Really?" I smiled. "Who's it from?"

"Eugene Prestel," he said. There went the brief hope I'd felt, thinking it was Mother or Daddy, or even Missy.

"He says congratulations on your well-deserved win, and you're an aunt again. Missy had a little girl overnight; no name yet, but he'll wire you again when he learns it."

I squealed and gave Double Jinx a hug. "Oh, what wonderful news! Can you arrange to have flowers sent to Missy's house? Are carnations in season? I think we should send those." Double Jinx assured me they'd be sent as soon as the first florist opened the next morning in Halifax. Then his eyes shifted over to Lang, ensconced at my side. "Cooling off?"

"We're celebrating, Double Jinx," he said, lifting his glass. "Don't spoil the mood!"

⌒ellᵔ

THE CLOUT THAT comes with an Oscar win is immediately perceptible. I was given an instant raise at MGM, with a bonus for earning the studio another trophy. For weeks, the studio receptionists answered the phones with a *"Mell-o!"* in my honour, and suddenly, I got the pick of the litter for scripts. No more leftovers, no more being lent out to other studios—unless I wanted to work on one of their projects—and no more *"AND LANGDON HAWKES"* next to my name on the marquee.

I saved every newspaper I could get my hands on, including the *Los Angeles Times* article headlined *Melly's Sissy, Missy, Offers Her Congrats!*—which I'd told Double Jinx was likely more fiction than fact, or else someone was posing as my sister. I kept mum, naturally. I never heard a word directly from my sister, or her husband, or my parents. No thanks for the carnations, no *Congratulations, Aunt Melly*. It was another stab in the heart, but I'd been hurt far worse before. My heart would keep ticking along.

I got to stick my hands in cement at Grauman's Chinese Theatre, and to add a dose of pink to the ceremony, they swiped my dried prints with pink paint. Like I said, pink became my signature colour. Double Jinx once asked if I was worried about being shoehorned into pink dresses for the rest of my career. I quipped back, "How many pink dresses can there be?" I'd find out.

But the most surprising reaction to my Oscar win? Lang and I became friends. Honest-to-goodness friends. And when the MGM production team slyly hinted that *maybe* we should tie the knot and boost our profiles in 1945, he didn't have to try all that hard to convince me it could be good for business.

"You carry a torch, Mel," he'd said at The Mocambo the night studio fixer Eddie Mannix urged us to marry. "You don't have to carry a torch for me. Just let me be a candle, give you a little light."

We'd last forty-five days before that flame blew out.

TAKE HER, SHE'S MINE
Starring Sandra Dee and James Stewart

THURSDAY, DECEMBER 19, 1963

I f you'd asked anyone, they'd tell you I've led a perfectly charmed life. Once I won the first Oscar, it was smooth sailing...except for that quickie Reno divorce.

That line Lang fed me about being a candle to light my way? A line from his newest single, 'Candlelight Serenade' (which peaked at number six on the Hit Parade). I didn't talk to him for years after the divorce, and I never dated again either.

Instead, I threw myself into my work, starring in hits like *Saturn's Harvest*, *Let It Snow*, and *Twilight on the House of York*, which allowed me to test my range—in aquamusicals, holiday fare, and historical epics, respectively. Comedies were matched with melodramas like *When I Call You Again* (which should've earned me a second statuette), *In the Midnight Hour*, opposite James Cagney, and *Where the Wind Blows*.

But then *The Blue Dress* came along, a sequel of sorts, and one that I couldn't pass up. That Ray Milland returned to play my now-husband sweetened the deal. Perhaps the real honour was my seventh Oscar nomination—against Doris Day, Audrey *and* Katharine Hepburn, and Elizabeth Taylor, all actresses I admire a great deal.

On Oscar night, April 4, 1960, I arrived at the RKO Pantages Theatre *stag* in a shimmering ice blue evening gown by Balmain with a wish in my heart that playing Louise a second time would snag me my second Oscar. When Rock Hudson announced my name, kittens, I can't tell you how overjoyed I was! Though I think my stammering acceptance speech—much less eloquent the second time around—might have given some indication.

That second Oscar was followed up by popcorn fares and musical comedies with Frank Sinatra and Jack Lemmon; a career cemented into legend status; and the comfortable knowledge that whatever I did would spin gold.

But sitting alone in my Palm Springs cottage the night I found out the Majestic was closing, I looked around and realized I'd been all alone for all of it, with only Benjamin's memory hanging around my neck.

My eyes caught the trinkets dotting the living room, most from my Hollywood career, but there were pieces from Halifax hidden in there as well: a photograph of me and Missy with our *Heidi* braids in December 1937; a Majestic Sisters postcard Old Man Prestel had printed for *Having Wonderful Time* in July 1938; the programme for the Theatre Arts Guild's production of *Six Who Pass While the Lentils Boil* in November 1938 (I played the Milkmaid)...and then, hanging on my wall, frozen in arrested development, the doomed 1940 Majestic Sisters calendar.

The memories flooded over me, of all the good times Missy and I had together at the Majestic. Everything that came from being a Majestic Sister. I wouldn't have this blessed life without the Majestic. Without Missy.

And now that the Majestic was closing, it felt like a permanent ending.

If I didn't have the Majestic, what did I have?

If I didn't have Missy, what did I have?

I picked up the telephone and rang Double Jinx. He picked up on the first ring.

He sighed. "Say that again, kid?" He always sighed into the phone when I called.

"I'm going home, to Halifax," I repeated.

"You hoping for a Christmas miracle?" He knew bits and pieces of why I'd left all those years ago, but he didn't know the whole story.

Nobody did. How do you tell a story like mine? It's not something you shout down the party line.

"Something like that. I'm leaving as soon as I can."

"They want to film until Monday evening," he said. "This director has a lot riding on *The Kenmore Arms*."

"Him and Lang both," I muttered. "I want to leave tomorrow."

"Tomorrow?" he echoed. "Kid, is everything all right?"

"No," I said softly. "But it will be. I just need to get to Halifax."

He sighed into the phone again. "You figure out how you're getting home; I'll handle everything else."

The only thing left to do was plan out how I'd convince Missy to help me save the Majestic. How I could ever apologize enough for all the wrongs I'd committed. This had to be an eleven o'clock number unlike any other.

I had to make her understand.

I had to tell her the truth.

MOVE OVER, DARLING
Starring Doris Day and James Garner

WEDNESDAY, DECEMBER 25, 1963

We were a sobbing mess, I have to admit. A hugging, sobbing mess. I held on to Missy like a lifeline.

"I'm sorry," she wailed between tears. "I'm so sorry, Melly. I should've paid more attention to you back then."

"Don't be silly." I sniffled, stroking her back. "It's all my fault. I did everything spectacularly wrong back then and it cost me so dearly."

"No, I could tell that something was wrong. I knew you were feeling off, but I was so determined to have the picture-perfect wedding I ignored everything that didn't fit my vision." She squeezed me tighter.

"Missy, you were engaged. It was supposed to be the best time of your life, and I ruined it."

"You didn't ruin it," she said, pulling back. She reached over to the side table and offered me a tissue. "Well, in a fashion, you did." She gave a teary laugh. "I hated you for so long because of it. But if I'd known... if you'd told me what was going on, I would've understood. I could've helped you."

"I know....I just didn't know how to tell anyone what was going on."

"I should've asked."

"I wouldn't have known where to start."

"Why did you keep all of this a secret?" she asked, wide-eyed.

The million-dollar question.

"He was mine," I said simply. "He wasn't a part of this, and I didn't want to have to share him with the rest of the world as *Majestic Melly's beau*. Not until we were settled and your wedding was over."

"We would have understood," Missy said, reaching over and threading her fingers through her husband's. He sat behind her on the couch, letting her rest her weary body against his—true partnership, from the moment they met. It was enough to make a girl go green with envy.

"It was...so hard to talk to you back then," I admitted.

"I know. I just wish you would have tried," she whispered. "I wish *I* would have tried."

"We were always on different paths, but we let the gulf widen until we had nothing in common but the act."

"There have been so many days that I've cursed The Majestic Sisters," she said, wiping away a tear. "Everything I am today, and that's all most people care about when they meet me. *Do I miss it, do I miss you, don't I wish I'd followed you to Hollywood, why can't I be more like you...*"

"You were always your own woman."

"But everybody wanted me to be you."

"Everybody wanted me to be *you!*" I crowed. "Perfect Missy, with her perfect boyfriend and her perfect plan to have a perfect family, and her perfect house waiting for her on Young Avenue."

"If only we'd talked to each other. Truly. Just once."

I took her hand. "I've wanted to, so many times...I used to pick up the telephone, and my throat would close every time the operator asked me who to call. But then that pain lessened. I knew I'd made my choice and it got easier to live with it. To live with the grief of losing Benjamin, of losing you." I told her about how Raymond would fill me in on the minute details of her life. "You moved on. I moved on. I won Oscars, sure, but you hosted The Queen, for heaven's sake, Missy! It just...it seemed like buried history."

"Until?" she prompted.

"Until I found out about the Majestic closing, and all those memories came rushing back. I couldn't think about anything but coming back home and finally getting closure. Trying to save a place that meant so much to us."

"And I've treated you like a beast." Missy started to cry again, burying her face in her hands.

"Missy, no," I said, pulling her into my arms. "How were you supposed to react? I only ever meant to come home, figure out a way to save the theatre, and see you again. I never meant to crash the Christmas party, or summon ghosts."

I looked over at my nieces, sharing the loveseat and watching like we were zoo animals. "But then I met Birdie and Leonie, and I'm glad I did. They're amazing young women, Missy, you both did an excellent job with them."

"We are pretty proud of them," Eddy agreed.

"Ever since I landed, all I've thought about is the chance to get into your ear somehow, if you might be inclined to talk with me. But I guess I underestimated just how much I'd hurt you."

"I'm sorry. Melly, I—"

"Stop," I urged her. "We're not getting anywhere sitting here castigating ourselves. I forgive you."

She went quiet, and wouldn't look me in the eye. "I don't know if I'm ready to totally forgive you yet," she whispered. "But I also don't want to hold on to any of this anger any longer. I want to be friends...be true sisters with you again."

"I want that more than anything." I pulled her even closer and gave her twenty-five years' worth of hugs. "Can I make a request?"

"Anything," she promised.

"Show me your wedding album again?"

⁓ℓ℮⁓

MISSY HAD BEEN an impossibly beautiful bride, and I was thrilled to go through every photo with her. Of course, some of the memories were tinged with sadness and anger, and I let her say her piece every time those feelings came through again. Once we finished with the wedding album, she had Eddy rummage through the boxes in the attic until he found an album positively stuffed with photographs and other trinkets from our Majestic Sisters years. And for the first time ever, Majestic Missy regaled her daughters with tales of our infamous antics.

"Do you remember the first time we performed?" Missy asked me, pointing at a photograph of us standing under the *Shall We Dance* marquee together.

I smiled. "Of course I do. I was so nervous. I was worried our audition had been a fluke and we'd be laughed off stage."

"Me too," Missy said. "But I looked at you just before we went out, and you had the biggest smile on your face. It made me believe we could do anything."

"We *could* do anything, don't you remember?" I quipped, pointing at another photo of us jammed into a booth at the Cameo, surrounded by admirers. "That was a fun night. Not as fun as the night we had all-you-can-eat lobster, but a close second."

Missy laughed, and I reached out to take her hand. "We slipped away from each other, but I want to be a part of your life, and I want you and your family in mine. I can't walk away now; please don't ask me to."

Missy smiled. "You'll never have to worry about that again."

⌁

I COULD FEEL a dormant, hidden part of my heart healing as I watched my family enjoy a perfectly prepared Christmas dinner. I had pushed them away the first time. I wasn't going to make the same mistake again. I wanted to know this stately sister and brother-in-law of mine. I wanted to know these lionhearted nieces. I wanted to come home to roost at the Majestic.

The Majestic! I hadn't yet mentioned my plan to save the theatre before New Year's Eve—or that I'd promised Old Man Prestel a plan for how I'd do it by Boxing Day. I brought it up before the fruitcake was sliced; hopefully Missy was too full to fight this crazy idea of mine. I turned to her, felt a pang as I saw her smile a smile she had only for me, fragile though it was now, and said: "Let's buy the theatre."

She stopped chewing and swallowed. "You can't be serious."

"Hear me out! We host a fundraiser to help with the cost of repairing and updating the place. Everyone loves the movies, and the place only needs a little renovating so it can sparkle again. And we can help Old Man Prestel retire comfortably."

Leonie and Birdie squealed with excitement at my proposition, Eddy trying his best to calm them down.

"Are you joking? You and me, perform once more?" Missy asked.

"Think of where we'd be without him."

"Melly, I haven't danced since our last show together. Haven't sang either. I don't...I just don't know if I can get up in front of an audience and do that again."

"Oh, Sissy, where's your sense of wonder? You can still act. And tell jokes. I can do the dancing. Hell, I'll call up Ginger Rogers herself and get her out here tap dancing if we need it."

An unrestrained squeal from the girls.

"I don't know..." Missy said, motioning for them to calm themselves.

"Let's do this for Old Man Prestel. I'll call up Frank, Liv, Joan— Lang, if I must—and see if they'd be willing to help out. We'll split the costs. Surely you and Eddy have connections who can run the place if Old Man Prestel truly wants to retire?"

She hesitated. Birdie didn't. "What about Bill? He's got a head for numbers. He could run the place for Old Man Prestel. And we could hire creative people to run the advertising and marketing..."

I looked back at Missy, who was still silent as Birdie came up with the business plan. "Oh Missy, please don't say—"

"No, you're right," Missy interrupted. "Let's do it. I have a few friends I can call to donate money as well; it'll be their feel-good project for the year."

I could have sobbed in relief. She wasn't giving up on the Majestic. She wasn't giving up on her Majestic Sister. "I'm so happy to hear you say that. Thank you, Missy."

Missy laughed, reaching for my hand. I squeezed it tight. "Can you believe it? We're reuniting the Majestic Sisters for one last show...

hopefully it'll be like riding a bicycle."

"And you really think this will save the Majestic?" asked Leonie carefully.

"I do," I said. "And Leonie, you just landed yourself the first Majestic Sisters interview since 1939." She perked up after that. Reporters have been trying for decades to get us to talk again, and here was the story, wrapped up like the best Christmas gift we could have given her.

"And Birdie, we need you to help organize this extravaganza. Use your event-planning skills and make this the biggest spectacle this city's ever seen."

"Free rein?" she asked.

Missy and I looked at each other and nodded.

"We'll host an after-party at the Atlantic, too. Get the alcohol flowing and the purse strings loosened," Eddy said. "All the money will go towards renovating the theatre."

⌒⌒⌒

WE NOW-REUNITED MAJESTIC Sisters were celebrating Boxing Day in Old Man Prestel's office, staring across the table at the puzzled man who'd hightailed it down to the theatre—bless him—to listen to our pressing news.

"You girls want to *what*?" Old Man Prestel asked again, leaning back in his seat. Nice to know we still had the ability to shock him.

"We want to bring back the act," Missy said. "One-night-only. New Year's Eve. The last hurrah we never got."

"Am I missing something? You two hate each other," he said.

"We're working on it," I replied. "But this could be something big. And if you want to go out on a high note, let's make it one for the angels."

Old Man Prestel's eyes flicked back and forth between me and Missy, waiting for Red Skelton to pop out from behind the door yelling "Surprise!" For a long moment, he was stunned speechless. Then, as if a director had called *action!* from somewhere off stage, he jumped up.

"We need to get to work." Old Man Prestel shoved aside stacks of paper until he found a blank sheet to write down his to-do list. "We need posters, advertisements—we need to spread the word."

"New Year's Eve will be perfect," I said. "It can double as a party, and people are always so sentimental. Plus, it's not like we don't already know the songs and dances we used to do. We'd just need a little rehearsal time to get back in shape."

"I haven't worn eyeliner as thick as I did back in 1939 since...1939," Missy marvelled.

"You know, red lipstick never goes out of style, sis."

"My Chickadees," Old Man Prestel said. Missy perked up when she heard him refer to her by the nickname he'd always reserved for me alone. He shook his head and stood from the desk. "Still squawking after all these years."

"We're going to do it," Missy said. She looked him in the eyes. "We're going to save the Majestic."

"Save it?" he asked. "It's too late to save it, I've already made up my mind."

"Have you sold the building or the land?" I asked.

"No, not yet." He sat back down. "What are you girls saying?"

I took a deep breath. "We want to buy the Majestic from you."

"How's that?" he asked. "Say that one more time."

"We're going to put together a show, promote the hell out of it, and try our damnedest to save the Majestic," Missy said. "Because we want to buy it from you and run it ourselves."

He dropped his head into his hands and we sat in dewy-eyed silence until he composed himself. When he finally lifted his head, tears were running down his cheeks.

"I knew I struck gold all those years ago." He sniffed. "You girls were a once-in-a-lifetime-act, and I thought we'd had our ending, but this..."

"Is a chance to rewrite the story," I finished. "We're going to give ourselves the happy ending we all deserve."

"Let's do it," Missy agreed. "Together."

THE MAJESTIC SISTERS:
ONE NIGHT ONLY!
Majestic Melly and Majestic Missy

TUESDAY, DECEMBER 31, 1963

Walking back into our dressing room was like stepping back in time. We gave it a good dusting and cleared out all of the forgotten props and costumes from travelling stage shows and then turned to our vanities.

Missy and I gasped and clutched at each other when we saw the photographs and newspaper clippings still stuck under the mirror frames. I picked up a yellowed clipping from 1938: *'Every Day's a Holiday' at the Majestic Theatre thanks to Majestic Missy Calvert, pictured here ahead of last night's premiere of Mae West's newest feature. Who'd have thought tap dancing in a tutu would be as fun as it looked? Watch out, Miss West, Majestic Missy's coming for your box office crown!*

The picture next to it showed us posing in expensive evening gowns from Simpson's for the 1939 spring fashion show. You could see the slight tension around my eyes, and after Missy examined the photo, she said, "How didn't I notice. It was all over your face." I squeezed her hand and put the photo back on the vanity.

A tube of forgotten lipstick fell from the vanity and rolled to a stop at Birdie's feet.

"Va-va-voom, ladies," she'd said, sticking the tube into her handbag, and when we simply stared at her, she added, "What? It might be worth something someday..."

Leonie contacted her friends in the *Herald*'s advertising department. Eddy said he wanted a full-page ad as close to the front page as he could secure—and, it being Eddy Davis and all, they gave him the entire front page. As soon as the citizens of Halifax opened their newspapers that Friday and saw the massive *MAJESTIC SISTERS REUNITED: NEW YEAR'S EVE AT THE MAJESTIC THEATRE! REVELRY, REMEMBRANCES, AND REELS!* headline, well, the telephone started ringing and it didn't stop. Raymond gave us free plugs on his radio show—acting, of course, like he'd been right there in the room when we cooked up the idea—some things never change.

Our antics carried over to the Saturday paper, too, for Leonie's first published article—right there on the front page. We'd sat for a joint interview in the loge seats—dressed by Birdie, photographed by Ross Taylor, who, I'd learned, had graduated from snapping those "Candid Camera" features back in the '30s to becoming the most respected photojournalist in the Maritimes.

"You remember me?" I asked him. "You took a picture of me and my beau at the Riviera Tea Room and almost ruined my life!"

Missy rolled her eyes. "I see how you won two Oscars now..." Ross simply chuckled.

"Do you? You haven't even seen those movies. Suppose those were the two years the Academy got it wrong," I said, slinging my arm over the back of her chair.

She shook her head. "You were always talented enough to win *ten* Oscars; I trust the Academy on this one." I could feel my eyes welling up. For once she'd acknowledged my talent without admonishing me for choosing a different path. We were healing.

I was determined to keep Benjamin a secret from the public, so we came up with a reason why I'd flown the nest all those years ago. Blackmail and bribery were too Hollywood, so we went with something much simpler, and much more befitting my Hollywood persona: "It was Clark Gable! What was I supposed to do?" Missy smirked, but added, "I would've preferred she ran away for one of his films that *didn't* open on my wedding day, but it's water under the bridge."

Leonie, of course, was pleased as punch to see her name on

the front page of the *Herald*, and even more pleased when both the Canadian Press and the Associated Press picked up the story. Suddenly her byline was on the front pages of international newspapers from Helsinki to Mexico City.

Birdie, meanwhile, was spending my money like it would go out of style. With an unlimited budget—per my orders—and an edict to find the best clothes in town—though Missy's needed to be slightly more luxe, per *her* orders—our reunion would be one of the most fashionable occasions in Halifax history.

And through all the endless rehearsals and planning, Old Man Prestel sat in the front row watching as the two lively dames who brought much panache to his theatre once upon a time were once again reunited to work their magic.

⌕

I'D CALLED DOUBLE JINX a few days after Christmas to tell him my plans, like I promised. He'd been sending wire after wire asking where I was and then complaining about how expensive it was to wire me, and I could only listen to the man complain so many times. He laughed down the phone line when I told him I was buying the theatre. "Just call up the bank and have the money transferred over. I've wired you the details."

"You need anything else, kid? You want to buy a department store while we're at it?"

"No, but I do want you to give a verbal agreement for that Joanne Woodward picture. I don't care if I *am* playing her mother. I own a theatre now; I need the dough."

Then I called Lang, who, as it turned out, had lost the eggnog-drinking competition but had a fun time losing... He was still hungover and couldn't remember much of the holidays, except that he'd apparently left several increasingly incoherent messages at the front desk of the Lord Nelson, and to forgive him for whatever gibberish he'd made the clerk write down.

"I haven't been back since Christmas Eve, so you're absolved for the time being."

He was pleased to hear that Missy and I were reconciled, and, like Double Jinx, laughed when I told him I'd gone halfsies on the theatre. "You going to put my movies on heavy rotation?" he asked.

"Dear, I want to keep the theatre running, not shut it down, have you not been listening?"

He almost hung up then, but then I made him an offer. "If you can get on the next plane out here, Eddy's looking for entertainment at the hotel on New Year's Eve. And he's serving salm—" and then he really did hang up. He was in Halifax by Saturday evening.

And then I had the embarrassing task of introducing my ex-husband to my family. As Langdon shook Missy's hand he said, "The one and only."

And then it seemed like such a fruitless task to tiptoe around that secret—with the family, anyway—so I told him all about Benjamin and the real reason I'd left Halifax so long ago. He took his new status as Melly Calvert's second husband on the chin.

Later that evening, Eddy drove Langdon over to the Atlantic. "Give him the second-best room in the joint," I said before they left. He winked at me. I elected to stay at the Lord Nelson. I had a beautiful view of the Public Gardens, and now that I wasn't so burdened with my secret, it was nice to be so close to a place that made for one of my most memorable evenings.

———

I DON'T HAVE a head for figures—never did, if my near-starvation once I'd gotten to Hollywood all those years ago is anything to go by—so I'll spare you the details of the sale. According to Bill, everything was on the up-and-up, and that was enough for me to sign the paperwork. I was now part-owner of the Majestic Theatre.

It felt like a full-circle moment.

"If only Miss Margaret could see us now, eh?" Missy said, blowing on her freshly inked signature.

"I wonder how often she wished she'd clipped our wings when she'd had the chance."

We gave Bill the job of running the place, which he was only too happy to accept, once Eddy promised he could still work at the hotel on all major events. Bringing a theatre back from the brink would be a fun project, he said. Old Man Prestel agreed to stay on as day-to-day manager, though we'd start a hiring campaign in the New Year to bring in the additional help he'd need.

Missy and I would split creative duties, along with the girls, as they wished. I would help arrange out-of-the-box advertising ideas, since I had a line on most of the Hollywood talent whose names would be on our marquee. As Halifax's doyenne, Missy would ensure that everything that happened at the Majestic made the news, and that the movers and shakers were there to hobnob amongst the regular patrons. Birdie was only too happy to help build up a stock company and run the costuming, and Leonie used her journalistic skills to help with the marketing.

After four days of calling in favours with everyone from Ava Gardner to Zsa Zsa Gabor, Leonie dashing out press releases like a one-woman publicity department (which she was), Birdie calling in her fashionista colleagues to help accessorize our costumes, and Missy hauling out her Rolodex to make sure everyone—minus Raymond, as per Missy's request—was on the guest list, we were ready.

⌒ℓ⌒

ON NEW YEAR'S EVE, we were packed backstage in the dressing room preparing for our grand debut. Leonie was flitting back and forth from the lobby to the dressing room—a good hike on a slow day—to tell us whom she'd spotted.

This time it was Libbie Christensen, a famed local CBC reporter and the girl's journalistic idol. "She's out there interviewing Amy Swaine-Tully," she wheezed. Missy and I exchanged a look.

When we watched the broadcast later, we'd see Amy, tears glimmering in her eyes, standing against a sarcophagus, gushing to Libbie: "This is so exciting! I never thought we'd get them in the same city ever again, let alone agreeing to perform together. But it's for a wonderful cause, and I say good for them. Good for the city. We need the Majestic Theatre and we need The Majestic Sisters!"

Old Man Prestel stood at the candy counter, watching as Haligonians emptied their wallets for concessions and signed photos of The Majestic Sisters. Hell, even my Oscars were there—behind glass, naturally—personally delivered by Double Jinx himself when he arrived the afternoon before. "Can you reverse the charges of a private jet?" he'd asked, kissing my cheek after he checked in to his suite at the Atlantic.

I'd given DJ a tour of the city in between rehearsals, showed him all of my old haunts, told him all about Benjamin. He listened intensely, never saying a word until I was finished. "You mean to tell me this is the secret you've been walking around with all these years?" At my nod, he threw his arms up. "Well, why don't you have a dozen more Oscars with those acting skills? I mean, *my God*, kid!"

I stood at the base of the spiral staircase backstage now, dressed in my signature pink—a candy-coloured off-the-shoulder evening gown hastily purchased from Mills Brothers—and delighted to see it hadn't been renovated. "All right, kittens. You're about to see two legends in action. Try not to get too jealous," I said, winking at my nieces.

Birdie, who was sauntering slowly behind me, asked the age-old question: "Aren't you nervous?"

"Oh, I'm terrified. The audience might only be here to see us fail and fight."

"I'll smack you back here if you chicken out now, but we are not fighting onstage," Missy said, joining us. She was dressed in a shimmering white gown and chandelier earrings, no longer the girlish Majestic Missy who dreamt of a knight in shining armour. She had her knight; she had her princesses...she was contented in a way she couldn't have been in 1939. She was beautiful. A Majestic Missy for the modern age.

"Wow, Mama," Leonie gushed. "You look fantastic!"

"Don't act so surprised. Now, give us a kiss for good luck, and we'll see you when it's all over."

We stood in the wings as Old Man Prestel took the stage. This man had given us a chance, had given blanket approval to just about every idea we'd ever had, and was now trusting us with his life's work.

"Ladies and gentlemen, you're in for a treat tonight," Old Man Prestel said, over the din of the audience. "You've asked and wondered and hoped for decades that we'd bring back these two special dames, and tonight, as we ring in 1964, I'm pleased to present, in a special show to celebrate their purchase of the theatre"—the audience burst into thunderous applause at this—"The Majestic Sisters!"

There's a thrill in live performance I'd missed. I'm not one of those actresses who has to go to Broadway to satisfy her creative needs, but stepping out onto that stage once more...it felt like a homecoming in more ways than one.

Naturally, the audience was made up of our peers, those who remembered the glory days, and they roared their applause as we made our presence known.

"You're too kind!" I yelled, holding my hand to my heart. "Entirely too kind. Listen to it, Missy. It's just like the old days."

"I'm afraid my ballerina days are well behind me," Missy teased. "If you came hoping to see Majestic Missy's fouettés, you're leaving disappointed, folks."

"I'd try 'em, but I think I had one too many dirty martinis backstage," I countered, again to peals of laughter. "But it is good to be back." The audience cheered.

"I'm glad you're back," Missy said, walking over to me and wrapping an arm around my shoulder.

"Well, not according to the *Star*," I said.

"Melly, dear, everyone reads the *Herald* now. How long have you been gone, exactly?" she asked as the audience laughed.

"Long enough for the fame to go to my head. Did I tell you about the last time I went out to dinner with a fella? Said he loved Nova Scotian salmon the best, and I'm sitting there thinking to myself, 'Didn't I just run away from all of this?'" The audience chuckled. "Then I married him. Imagine, I ran all the way to Hollywood and still ended up with a Nova Scotian guy!"

"You've got a story for everything, haven't you?" she teased.

"Depends on the subject matter."

"Well, I'm glad you're back. Reminds me of a song I used to sing."

She gestured towards the band, and suddenly the theatre filled with the strains of the vaudeville standard "After You've Gone." Missy grinned at me as the music swelled, and just as she opened her mouth—

"Are you sure you're not too rusty on that account either?" I said, pressing my fingers to her lips. Missy threw her head back in laughter. "Besides, I've got a surprise for you, too. It's not a song though. It's a letter..." The audience oohed and ahhed as I pulled the envelope out of my brassiere. "Should I read it?" I asked the crowd. They hooted and hollered a string of yeses, begging me to open it already. "It's from a certain crooner—but not your ex-brother-in-law, don't worry—who's in the audience tonight, if you want to actually meet him. I'll just read it, although I do love the suspense. Ahem..."

It was a letter from Frank Sinatra—my former co-star and, I have on good authority, Missy's favourite singer—pledging $50,000 to help save the Majestic Theatre. "*Pinky, it's the least I can do for a friend as special as you, and for a dame as beautiful as your sister. Yours, Frank.*"

"Wait, wait, wait...'yours' as in *you*, or 'yours' as in *me*?" Missy asked, grabbing the letter out of my hands.

"Me," I chuckled. "But he did throw in a signed portrait I could be persuaded to part with."

"You didn't bring me any Christmas presents this year," she said.

"I thought my presence was a gift?" I countered, over the audience's laughter.

"We're making up for lost time, though, aren't we?"

"That's true. I'll place the portrait on your nightstand?"

"I'll have sweet dreams tonight!" Missy crowed. From the front row, Eddy stood and coughed, right on cue, which made the crowd roar once more.

And on it went for a glorious two-hour show, and the audience loved every second. Leonie and Birdie joined us onstage with telegrams from Olivia de Havilland, Ray Milland, Robert Young, Dean Martin, Audrey Hepburn, and even Lucille Ball, the fink, to brag that she'd finally won the eggnog-drinking contest. But mostly, it was Majestic Melly and Majestic Missy lapping up the spotlight, together, just as we were always meant to.

With the clock about to hit midnight, we called the Davises up to the stage, and I called Lang and Double Jinx, and Old Man Prestel joined us too, a bottle of pink champagne in his hands. Tracy, bless her, trailed behind him with a tray of champagne flutes and started pouring us all a drink.

Even Mort, for once out of the projection booth, joined us onstage. He was a man of few words, but Mort loved the Majestic just as much as we did. He'd even spend his final moments there. Just after starting the reel for *Rocky II* in 1979, he'd pass away in the booth, taken by a heart attack.

"Thank you for joining us this evening," Missy hollered over the boom of applause. "If you're not ready for the party to end, join us over at the Atlantic Hotel for a little reception."

"And keep those pocketbooks open!" I added. "We're so close to reaching our goal of saving the Majestic!"

"HE'S CLEARLY STILL smitten with you," Missy said, nodding across the Stargazers' Lounge to where Amy Swaine-Tully had cornered Lang in conversation.

"Says you," I teased, sipping my Fiery Melly.

Missy ordered another Sweet Missy (three parts champagne, two drops of chartreuse liqueur, a squeeze of lemon juice, and a blueberry to garnish) and looked over at me.

"Why'd you guys divorce, anyway?"

"Don't you mean, why'd we reconcile?" I shrugged. "Sometimes saying you're sorry goes a long way towards healing your pain."

Missy wrapped an arm around my shoulder and pulled me into a quick hug. "It does."

I rested my head on her shoulder, basking in that sisterly love I'd spent twenty-five years without, and let my eyes wander across the ballroom. I spotted Lang watching me, begging me with his eyes to free him from Amy's clutches, but I stayed put. "Maybe the ninth time's the charm," I told Missy, sipping my cocktail and waving at the duo.

We partied till dawn. And paid for it for days afterwards, but once Bill had all the cash counted at the theatre and the hotel, the results were in: we were a hit. Since our performance, crowds had been lining up around the block to see films at the Majestic—just like in the good ole days.

"Thank goodness, because I don't think I can do all that again," Missy said from the chaise in her living room.

"You were cutting a rug with Double Jinx, what are you talking about?" I teased.

I was scheduled back in Hollywood at the beginning of the week to finish *The Kenmore Arms,* and not that I'd been hiding myself, given the fact that half of Hollywood had sent telegrams to congratulate us on the theatre, but Double Jinx, who'd already flown back, wired that morning to tell us that Hedda had a 'scoop.'

"Which diva with the dresses of many colours rang in the New Year at home for the first time in decades? And we're hearing that wedding bells may again *be in her future with a certain charming crooner, provided the box office receipts on their latest film pay dividends,"* Missy read, looking over the cable sheet at my face.

I blinked back at her. "I wonder who gave her that scoop... Maybe we should have invited Raymond after all."

And I watched as those beautiful blue eyes started to dance; watched that elegant face break into the most gorgeous smile I'd ever seen; listened as that beautiful voice laughed at me. "You're off the cob sometimes."

I winked back. "Only sometimes?"

From the Desk of Melly Calvert

SATURDAY, JANUARY 1, 2000

I t's easy, with the benefit of hindsight, to look back and say that everything turned out the way it was supposed to.

I'd thought those years performing as The Majestic Sisters would be the most monumental of my life, but once Missy and I reconciled over Christmas 1963, it changed the trajectory of my life completely.

Lang and I went back to California to finish *The Kenmore Arms*—which Bosley Crowther dismissed as the worst movie in my oeuvre—and though we stayed comfortable friends for the rest of his life, Lang and I never rekindled that flame. Besides, he married Amy Swaine-Tully the next summer. And then divorced her the next spring. Amy always rang me up to boast that she stayed married to Lang longer than I did, but as I always told my ten-times-married fairweather friend, God rest her soul, "That's not a prize to brag about, dear."

My trips back to Halifax became much more frequent. With the benefit of two Oscars, I'd achieved a rare feat in Hollywood and didn't feel like I had much to prove...until Katharine Hepburn won her third Oscar in 1968. But try as I might, I just couldn't catch up to her, though I did eventually beat Bette Davis in total nominations.

Missy and I have been close and loving sisters ever since our reunion in 1963. In fact, once I largely retired from the movies, I bought our parents' old house on Coburg Road from Missy and Edward (you didn't think our parents would leave me an inheritance, did you?) and it's where I now live most of the time.

I thought about buying a house in the South End, but Missy and I do like to have our space, too. Living in my childhood home also meant I inherited Raymond as a neighbour, and now I watch as he pokes his liver-spotted head over the fence every morning, begging for the latest gossip. Some things never change.

My sister and Eddy, now retired, still have breakfast at the Stargazers' Lounge every day. And while they were at the helm at the Atlantic, they hosted more royalty, both of the crowned and the Hollywood variety, since our reconciliation.

Birdie and Leonie, those little darlings, became the apples of my eye. I doted on them, and they on me, and I've watched them flourish as career women. Oh, and I'm a great-aunt several times over! My first great-niece was born in August 1964. Turns out I wasn't the only one with a secret that Christmas season...

We laid our dear Old Man Prestel to rest in late 1968 and renamed the Majestic Theatre auditorium after his irrepressible legacy.

I make the trip to Truro every Valentine's Day—our anniversary— to visit my beloved's grave. To my utter amazement, nobody has ever reported these sightings to the press. I spend uninterrupted hours sitting in contented silence, thinking about Benjamin and knowing that someday soon, I'll be able to tell him all about the adventure that my life has been. He'll take those rings off the golden chain I've worn every day since Valentine's Day 1939, slide them onto our fingers at long last, and we'll dance off towards our next great adventure together.

And now that I'm left reflecting on my life and the choices I've made, I guess there's just one question left to answer: if I had to do it all over again, would I?

I think you know the answer to that.

Melly Calvert

Acknowledgements

I work in the arts, I write about the arts, I live and breathe the arts, and so I know firsthand how much work goes into making the leading lady shine. I couldn't have done it without any of them, so if you'll permit me, I need to thank some very important people.

First and foremost: my mother, Stephanie—Kitty—who has been my champion and my rock. I'm thankful for whatever kind of magic exists in the universe that made me your daughter. I love you to the moon and back. This is for you; this is because of you.

My brother, Mattie, who is bold and daring and hilarious. I truly lucked out getting you for a little brother, even though you did cost me that unicorn from the dream I had when I was four. I love you always.

My dog, Kasey, for being the best writing buddy. I love you and I miss you always.

My best friend, Elizabeth Craig, whose friendship and proofing skills have meant the world to me. Thank you for the looney text conversations and the Tabi nostalgia.

My best friend, Leyna Faulkner. You are my person and I'm so thankful to know you. Thank you for all the fun, the Old Hollywood glamour, and the Robert Mitchum jokes.

Thank you to Nimbus Publishing and Vagrant Press and especially to my editor, Whitney Moran, for taking a chance on a gal with a lifelong dream. Thank you for the enthusiastic support of Melly and Missy, and for the way you've cared for them and for me throughout this process. I'll be forever grateful.

Thank you to my wild family: Nana Bele, Aunt Kim (Laura), Uncle Andrew, Falyn, Aaron, Emily, JP, Josh, Megan, Rhys, Aunt Neica, Ryland, Uncle Devere. And to my father, David—there's no Iron Throne in this book, but I hope you like it just the same.

Ms. Marianne Sears, so much of who I am today is because you believed in me. How I wish you were here to read this. Mrs. Susan Daley, for the ponytail tugs and the encouragement to try creative writing. Dean Jobb, Kelly Toughill, Stephen Kimber, Fred Vallance-Jones, and everyone at the University of King's College School of Journalism for the invaluable guidance. I'm a better writer because I learned from all of you.

The Nova Scotia Archives were a constant source of inspiration, as was Cynthia Henry's book *Remembering The Halifax Capitol Theatre 1930-1974*, and the many Facebook groups dedicated to 'old black and white photos' of Halifax. The first picture I saw of the old Capitol Theatre inspired this story. How I wish I could walk through its doors and watch *It Happened One Night* there.

And finally, as someone who loves old movies and who found inspiration from the many powerful actresses of the era, I can't thank them enough for inspiring me in all aspects of my life. Thank you, Audrey Hepburn, Grace Kelly, Ginger Rogers, Doris Day, Esther Williams, Olivia de Havilland, Joan Fontaine, Bette Davis, Joan Crawford, Shirley MacLaine, Debbie Reynolds, Claudette Cobert, Katharine Hepburn, and the lot.